I often pearls. I would take them out of their case and hold them against me and the desire to clasp them round my neck was irresistible.

They were in my dreams . . . vague, hazy dreams . . . when they crept from their case and put themselves about my neck. Then I thought they crept tighter and tighter round my neck and were trying to strangle me. They had become malicious. There was evil in them.

In the dream I caught the pearls and tried to tear them from my neck. Then the dream changed. 'Toby,' I called. 'Where are you, Toby? Why don't you come when you know I need you?' Then I saw him. He was there. He unclasped the necklace and I was sobbing with relief in his arms . . .

VICTORIA HOLT

The Spring of the Tiger

Collins

FONTANA BOOKS

First published in 1979 by William Collins Sons & Co Ltd
First issued in Fontana Books 1981

© Victoria Holt 1979

Made and printed in Great Britain by
William Collins Sons & Co Ltd, Glasgow

THE
ENGLISH SCENE
*
DENTON SQUARE

Looking back over the sequence of events which brought me to that house of brooding mystery, of sinister undercurrents and disturbing echoes and an awareness of encroaching peril, I pause to marvel at the ingenuity of youth and inexperience, and how, as a girl in that other house, conveniently close to the theatres, it never entered my head to question the unconventional way of life into which I had been born.

I remember waiting at dusk, watching from my window, for the lamplighter to come and light the lamps in the square, and waking in the mornings to the street sounds – the clop-clop of horses' hoofs on the road, the sudden laugh of a servant girl exchanging pleasantries with the milkman as the jugs were filled, the scrubbing of doorsteps and the polishing of brass, all of which had to be done quietly and discreetly so that the gentry could be led to believe – if they ever thought about it – that that which was necessary to their comfort was brought about by magic.

It was imperative in our house in Denton Square that we were especially quiet in the mornings because of my mother. She rarely rose until noon and the reason was that she would not have gone to bed until the early hours of the morning. Her rest was important for she was the centre of the household. Our existence depended upon her, and her moods determined the atmosphere of the house. When she was gay we were very very gay; and when she was morbid or depressed, as she sometimes was, we moved about on tiptoe, talking in whispers, apprehensive, rather like, I said to Meg Marlow, people living on the edge of a volcano waiting for the eruption. I was constantly reading and had just learned of the destruction of Pompeii.

Meg said: 'We have to make allowances. It's her Art.' It was true that when she was not 'resting' her Art took her to the theatre every night and some afternoons. It was those rest periods which I called times of threatened eruption – though it was not anger we feared so much as her moody depression. One blessing was that none of her moods lasted long.

'I'll have you remember who she is.' That was what Meg always said if any of us showed a lessening of our adoration.

My mother was Irene Rushton – at least that was her professional name. She was in fact Irene Ashington, wife of Ralph Ashington, whom she had left when I was two years old.

Meg, my mother's dresser, lady's-maid, part-time cook and devoted slave made me proud and happy when she told me how my mother had walked out. 'She could stand it no more. The miracle is that she brought you with her. That was something, that was. A young child wasn't going to be much use to her career, was it? And she brought you with her!'

It became the catch phrase of my youth. 'She brought you with her.'

'Mind you,' Meg once qualified, 'it might have been better if she hadn't.'

I was puzzled, wondering where I should have been if she had left me behind.

'Some outlandish place,' Meg told me when I pestered her. 'She should never have gone. No life for the likes of her, it wasn't. Hot . . . and not like England at all. Creepy-crawlies everywhere. Spiders! Ugh!'

Meg had a horror of spiders. She had once stayed in the country when my mother was on tour and there had been a spider in her bed. Meg never tired of recounting the horror of that occasion. 'Give me London,' she always finished up with, as though there was a law banning spiders from the Capital.

'So she came home and brought you with her. Of course she was a name before she went away and there were managers who were ready to welcome her back.'

'And she brought me with her!'

'I knew that she never regretted it. She told me once: "I always like coming home and it *feels* like coming home while I've got my Little Siddons to come home to."' My name was in fact Sarah Siddons Ashington, for she had called me after that member of her profession whom she considered its greatest ornament: Sarah Siddons.

When she was in a good mood she called me Little Siddons. Sometimes that gave me a qualm of apprehension for I feared she planned to get me following her to the footlights, a profession for which, I was sure, I had no aptitude.

Meg could tell me little about my mother's life during her marriage, for she was not with her then. Meg had been her dresser before her marriage and immediately resumed her old post when my mother came back to England. There had been a three years' interval.

'I said she should never have gone,' said Meg. 'Marriage, yes . . . but not that sort of marriage. I used to reckon it would be some-one with a mansion in the country and a nice town house and maybe a title to go with it. Now that would have been nice. But then she goes for this Ralph Ashington . . . Good family, mind you. Big place in the country. No town house though . . . only this whatever-it-was in foreign parts. She don't talk about it much, and that's a sign. "And this is Irene Rushton," I said to myself. Well, when you think how it might have turned out . . . I wouldn't have been all that surprised at a Duke . . . and then Mr Ralph Ashington, if you please, planting tea or something in the back of beyond.'

'He's my father.'

'Oh yes, he's your father all right.' She looked at me distaste-fully. 'And not a young man either. A widower. Well, how could she!'

'You saw him, Meg? You saw my father?'

'Twice. Once at the stage door, once in her dressing-room. There was a regular retinue of them. He was the last I would have put my money on. But she made up her mind . . . quick . . . pronto . . . just like that. You know her. "I'm going to," she says. And there she is like a wild horse with the bit between her teeth

. . . running on without looking where she's going.'

'He must have been very attractive because from all those dukes and things she chose him.'

'Never could understand it. Never could to this day. Well, she soon found her mistake, didn't she. "No regrets," she always said. "After all, he gave me Little Siddons."'

I used to get Meg to tell me the story over and over again just to hear the last line.

The other member of our household was Janet, who was Meg's sister. Janet would not have stayed if it had not been for Meg. She was the opposite of her sister – dour, but very efficient. She didn't approve of the household. She had been used to good service, she reminded us, where they kept a butler, footman and a host of maids, besides their own carriage. One day, she maintained, she and Meg were going to live with their sister Ethel who had a nice little place in the country where she kept fowls and sold fresh eggs, vegetables and fruit, and she wanted to run her house as a hostel for travellers. She needed her sisters to help her before she could start.

'Janet would be off like a shot,' said Meg, 'but I could never bring myself to leave my lady and Janet can't bring herself to leave me. So here we are.'

That was our household – just the four of us – Janet, Meg, my mother and myself. There was, of course, Uncle Everard, but he did not exactly live with us. He stayed now and then; and he and my mother loved each other very much.

'They ought to be married,' commented Meg, 'and they would but for *him* and *her*.'

Him was my father, who was still married to my mother, and *her* was Everard's wife, to whom he was still married. These two vague figures stood between us and a regular household of which Janet would have approved, apart from the fact that it would still have been too humble to please her entirely. Meg was less conventional.

'This is Irene Rushton,' she said. 'It's different with theatre folk. You get to understand them . . . living in the theatre.'

My mother did not want me to go away to school. If I did she would have no Little Siddons to come home to. It was necessary, of course, that I should be educated so there was in a way another member of our household. This was Toby Mander, a young graduate just down from Oxford who would have been an actor if he had had any talent. 'One of the multitude,' my mother called him. 'Dear Little Siddons, they are legion. They have a passion for the theatre. They are the Not Quite brigade. They can almost act, but not quite. They can almost write plays, but not quite. With the right sort of talent they might direct or produce, but they haven't got it . . . not quite.' Toby was one of those. He was in love with my mother. 'And that,' commented Meg, 'is a complaint as common as measles. They come too near and get infected, you might say. Not many people have it as strong as your mother.'

'You mean the ability to infect.'

'That's it. I never saw anyone with as much as your mother . . . and I've spent a lifetime in the theatre.'

'It could be said to be endemic to the theatre,' I said, for I had a passion for long words at this stage and was constantly reading the dictionary, discovering new ones and trying them out. 'Like beri-beri in Africa,' I added.

'You and your long words,' sniffed Meg. 'I don't know where you get it from. Not from your mother anyway.'

That was a term of reproach. Anything not inherited from my mother wasn't worth having.

So there was Toby – Tobias Mander – my mother's devoted slave. She had manœuvred one or two walk-on parts for him and he could not show his gratitude enough. One of his ways of doing so was to spend each morning teaching her daughter. Having this love of words I was an apt pupil and I looked forward to our sessions together. We were a pair of conspirators seeking to surprise my mother. We might have known that whatever academic heights I scaled she would not be impressed, for although she was completely poised and greatly sought after at the dinner tables of the élite, she was no scholar. What she really wanted Toby to do was to make me like her. She really was concerned about my welfare and I believe that I was more important to her than anyone – except Everard, of course, and sometimes I thought I was running level with him.

So the days in Denton Square passed pleasantly. It was a cosy world made comfortable by the companionship of Toby Mander and Meg Marlow, the efficiency of Janet, and illuminated by the glittering presence of my mother.

There was the constant excitement of gathering information which I could prise from Meg. The past was like an immense jigsaw puzzle with great gaps in it which were vital to completing the picture.

There was Uncle Everard, a kindly, hazy figure in the background, who was something important in the House, which in due course I learned was Parliament. From the topmost window of the attic we could see the face of Big Ben and we used to look to see if the light was on at the top, which meant that the House was sitting and that Uncle Everard would be busy. He had a small house in Westminster and an estate in the country, I learned. He used to bring me boxes of chocolates tied up with many coloured ribbons. I was allowed to keep the ribbons but the chocolates were usually confiscated as being bad for my teeth.

I must have realized when I was about eight years old that there was a plot afoot to make me like my mother. My teeth, preserved, so my mother said, by a slice of apple to be eaten last thing at night, were encased in a brace because there was a danger of the front ones becoming too prominent. 'We don't want Little Siddons to turn into a rabbit, do we?' said my mother, and for a while I was called Little Rabbit or simply Bunny. She was a great bestower of nicknames. I hated the brace. Then there was my hair. 'Straight as a packet of candles,' grumbled Meg. My mother's hung in rippling curls down her back and she could sit on it. Mine being so different offended my mother and during rest periods Meg would put it into rags before I went to bed. They rarely stayed in place and I would get irritated with them and pull them off so that in the morning I would present a strange spectacle, being half straight and half curly. 'You'll never make a beauty,' mourned Meg, to which I retorted that if it meant suffering the nightly torture of lying on bundles of rags I would have to be plain, thank you.

'It's nothing to thank anyone for,' said Meg ominously.

I was inclined to argue. It was due to Toby. He was a great believer in exercising the mind, and one of our lessons was to take a subject on which we did not agree and argue against what we really believed. One of his theories was that nothing was completely black or white. There were always many sides to every question, so if you disagreed wholeheartedly with something you should try to see points in favour of it.

'Good for the soul,' said Toby.

He used to take me riding in the Row. My mother had said that I must learn to manage a horse, and I was sent to a local riding school where I used to go out on safe old hacks and be put through my paces with a group of young people round about my age until I was considered safe. Then there were the rides with Toby. I enjoyed these very much. Toby was good fun when he stopped being broody about being not quite good enough for the stage. His panegyrics about my mother I accepted because I agreed with them.

The most peacefully happy times of those years were spent in Toby's company.

We read a great deal together and if my understanding of mathematics was nil, I had a good grounding in French, German and English literature.

Toby taught me how to enjoy life. According to him adaptation was the answer. 'If you can't have something, learn to live without it and find something you can have,' he used to say.

I argued that this was a weak attitude and if you wanted something you should go out and get it.

'Others may be involved,' he pointed out. 'You must never ride rough shod over others.'

He was certainly my mentor in those days.

I tried to apply his theories to my life. During resting periods, which were when a play had finished its run and my mother was waiting for something else to turn up, she would be at home a great deal. At first it would be delightful to see more of her, but then I would find that she was not quite the same person as the one who could only be glimpsed for rare moments. The moods set in. Sometimes I would hear her shouting at Meg and Meg shouting back. 'A little more of that and I'll be off.' Meg always stood up to her, but she never took the quarrels seriously. 'Storm warning,' she would say to me with a wink, and then I knew it was best to keep out of the way.

People came to the house with plays for her to read to see if she considered a part suitable for herself. Tom Mellor, the agent, was constantly calling. Sometimes she would be angry because the part wasn't good enough. Bland producers, harassed authors, actors in varying stages of prosperity – they all came to the house. It was a time of turmoil.

Then it would pass and she would be working again. The house would become quiet and empty. That could be depressing.

Toby would take me out then and we would walk along Shaftesbury Avenue, past the theatres until we came to the one at which she was playing. We would both gloat over her name – very large and always at the top. She insisted on that. Irene Rushton in *The Colleen Bawn* by Dion Boucicault.

I felt such a glow of pride to think that Irene Rushton was my mother.

Toby once took me to lunch at the Café Royal and there among the scarlet and gold decor he pointed out famous people. It was one of the memorable occasions of my life up to that time, but shattered by the sudden appearance of my mother squired by a languid gentleman with a most flowery cravat and a monocle. ('Member of the peerage,' Meg told me afterwards when I described him. 'Lord Lummy or something. When I think of what she might have done for herself and she goes and marries that Ralph Ashington!')

Toby went pink and stammered: 'I . . . I thought it would amuse Sarah.'

'Hardly the place to bring . . . a child.'

Then she swept out with people watching, pointing her out. 'That's Irene Rushton.' 'What *the* Irene Rushton?' 'Yes, you know. She's in *The Colleen Bawn*. Wonderful, they say.'

Toby was uncomfortable – the outing spoilt because he had displeased her.

I couldn't see why she should object. Toby had made me so analytical that I had to find the answer. Two unworthy ones kept coming up in my mind. One was that Toby clearly liked me and we had been laughing so much over my first efforts to sample champagne when she came up and she did not like him to be so happy in the company of anyone else – not even her daughter. Another was that perhaps she did not like the idea of my growing up and being old enough to be taken to luncheon at the Café Royal. She was very conscious of her age and had been twenty-six for several years.

This was a new view of her and myself. It seemed I could become an embarrassment to her.

Toby was very subdued and next time he saw her he apologized. It seemed we had all been mistaken. She laughed about the matter.

'So good of you to look after her, Toby,' she said. 'I hope it wasn't too boring for you.'

Toby said emphatically that it was far from boring. It had been the most enjoyable luncheon he had had since . . . since . . . Since she had descended from the heights and sat at his table. Afterwards she said to me: 'So you're stepping out into the world, eh Siddons? Well, mild little Toby is a harmless escort.'

Mild! It sounded disparaging. I should hardly have called him that. And little! He was six feet tall. We used to laugh about his height. 'Hurry up and grow a few more inches,' he used to say. 'I get backache stooping to you.'

I did not realize until they were over what happy days they were. I was to remember Toby's theories very often in the future and to ask myself why it was that one only realized how good things were when they were past. One of the perversities of human nature, I supposed. Or is it that a scene looked back on is often set in a rosy light which heightens only the happy times?

Happy times they undoubtedly were. Everything was fun; my mother's excitedly busy life and the bliss when she did have some time to spare for me; Meg's racy Cockney comments on life in general and my mother in particular; I was even amused by Janet's tight-lipped disapproval of 'things' that went on in the house and her dark prophecies of people's supping sorrow with long spoons, fiddling when Rome was burning and hints of coming to No Good. In Janet's lugubrious manner, No Good seemed to indicate the utmost disaster. And always there was Toby – taken for granted, I fear – my indulgent tutor who did the work purely for love of my mother, and, I realized later, for me, too.

His father was what is known as an industrialist – a man who had made a great fortune and couldn't stop enlarging it.

'Come up from nothing,' said Meg disparagingly.

Of course I defended him. 'All the more credit,' I pointed out. 'You have to be clever to get to something when you've come up from nothing.'

'It's never the same,' said Meg.

Janet had her terse comment. 'Clogs to riches, riches to clogs.'

'She means,' explained Meg, 'that them that comes after him will lose what he's made and be back to clogs.'

'I can't see Toby in clogs,' I said, giggling. 'And as a matter of fact Mr Mander never had them either. He used to sell newspapers at Piccadilly Circus. Toby told me.'

'It's a figure of speech,' said Janet grandly. 'And mark my words it's a true one.'

Toby laughed when I told him. 'No return to clogs for this family,' he said. 'My father will get it all too tied up. He's a financial wizard.'

'You're not one of those, Toby.'

'Oh, I'm not so bad. Hardly a wizard – a sort of lively sprite.'

We laughed a great deal, Toby and I, but we could be very serious over books. He told me about his family. He was the only son – a bit of a disappointment to the Old Man. I consoled him.

'The Wizard would be satisfied with only a more wily wizard than himself,' I assured him.

His father became the Wizard from then on. He was a gruff old man. A rough diamond, said Toby. I called him the Diamond after that.

'He seems to have a genius for accumulating things,' I pointed out. 'Wealth and now nicknames. The Wizard. The Diamond, what next?'

'Work became a mania with him,' commented Toby. 'My mother would have been content with less, but once he had started he had to go on.'

'And so he made his vast fortune. I suppose he's a millionaire.'

'I believe so.'

'You'll be rich one day, Toby.'

'All tied up in Trusts and things for my children and their children and so on for the next thousand years.'

I was greatly amused. I suppose I laughed very easily in those days. I pictured money securely tied up in bags handed out little by little to Toby and his children and his grandchildren. But the idea of Toby's having children was even funnier than the money-bags.

He was a little hurt when I told him this. I had never before seen him so put out.

The Wizard, it seemed, was not such a bad sort. His name was Toby too, but he was always known as Tobias, which I was sure suited him. It was simply that he could not think or talk about much besides money and how to make it multiply while Toby liked to talk about Greek drama and the philosophers and Shakespeare's special genius. The two did not mix well together so Tobias the Wizard and Toby the son did not see as much of each other as would have been desirable in a more compatible relationship though I understood when they met they were polite to each other, respected and liked each other, and the Wizard hid his disappointment while Toby tried to hide his ignorance and lack of interest in the processes of becoming rich.

Sitting in the schoolroom, riding in the park, looking at the show bills of theatreland, talking endlessly, one day was so like another that they slipped by unnoticed.

The Colleen Bawn had come to an end after an exhausting run. The papers had said that Irene Rushton was at her enchanting best.

The last night had been a great success. There had been congratulations, flowers and a special supper party. That was over and it was now rest time.

It went according to pattern and the first days would be wonderful.

On the morning after the party I begged to be allowed to take in her coffee and rolls at noon.

She was sleeping and I put the tray on the table and looked down at her. She was very beautiful. Her hair was brown with chestnut lights in it; she had a small heart-shaped face and her lashes when her eyes were closed lay fanlike on her pale skin. She looked very young, asleep – almost like a child.

I had similar colouring but lacked those delightful contours. My face was, as Meg put it, inclined to be lumpy. My nose was too long and my mouth too big, and there was of course that unmanageable hair. One thing I had inherited were her thick dark eyelashes and brows. In fact mine were thicker than hers, which must have been an asset for she used a pencil to thicken and darken her own.

She had opened her eyes and was laughing at me.

'What are you doing, Little Siddons?'

'Standing and admiring. You look so pretty and so . . . young.'

She was all delight. She loved compliments and never tired of them although she must have had a surfeit. I had chosen the right word when I said she looked young. It occurred to me that her life was a continual battle against the years, and I thought it was a mistake to bring out so much artillery to wage war on an enemy who had hardly yet put in an appearance – and when he did would inevitably be the victor.

'Coffee!' she said. 'Oh, you're an angel.'

'Shall I pour it out?'

'Oh yes, please.' She stretched herself. 'Ah. Luxury! What a night it was! Have you seen the flowers?'

'I can't see the drawing-room for flowers. There are forests of them.'

'Beautiful!'

'Janet says they'll drop on the carpet and Meg is sure they harbour insects.'

'Tell her I hope they're full of spiders, tarantulas who will sidle into her bed at night.'

'So beautiful and so cruel,' I mocked.

'Tom Mellor says that there are at least half a dozen scripts for me to see. It looks as though my rest will be a short one.' She smiled complacently. 'I'd like a good tragic role, I think.'

She talked awhile about roles and her successes. Then she suddenly seemed to notice me for the first time. 'You've put your hair up,' she said. Her face hardened.

'Don't you like it?'

'No, Sarah, I don't.'

She was really put out when she called me Sarah.

I took out the pins which held it and shook it out.

'That's better. You're far too young to put your hair up. Why, it will be five years before that's necessary.'

My hair had definitely depressed her. The happy glow which talking of her successes had given her was gone. She looked anxious, as though she were peering into a future where a daughter with her hair up was proclaiming to the world that Irene Rushton was getting old.

'I shall be nineteen then,' I pointed out, for it was an irritating habit of mine that when a fact occurred to me I had to give voice to it. I should try to grow out of that, Meg had warned me.

It was a foolish thing to have said. She wanted me to stay fourteen for ever. I felt a great tenderness towards her then, for it would have been easy for her to have left me with the shadowy Ralph Ashington so that with the passing of the years I need not have become an embarrassment to her.

She was thoughtful for a moment. Then she said solemnly: 'Is that really so? Nineteen.' She spoke the words as though my reaching that age was a major disaster like the Crimean War or the Indian Mutiny. I tried to think of something to comfort her and sought for some of Toby's homilies or even Meg's or Janet's.

Didn't someone say that experience was one of the rewards of old age or something like that? But I felt such an observation would hardly bring the necessary comfort.

Then she said slowly: 'So it was fourteen years ago . . .' Her eyes took on a dreamy look and I could see that she was back in that day when I had been born. I had pictured it many times, my birth in that strange place where insects abounded and Mr Ralph Ashington presided, and which my mother had been unable to endure so that when I was two years old she had walked out of it with me.

Perhaps it was the fact that I had appeared with my hair pinned up – merely to keep it from falling into my eyes – which had made her feel it was time I knew a little about my origins. Or it may have been that she was in one of the pessimistic moods which made her want to exacerbate her feelings by recalling that time. I was not sure, but she started to talk, and that morning I learned more of my beginnings than I ever had before.

'Fourteen years ago,' she mused. 'So it is fifteen since I first met your father?'

She sipped the coffee thoughtfully and I kept very quiet so as not to divert her thoughts.

'I was barely seventeen,' she went on as though talking to herself. That was an admission which showed she was off her guard. Although my mathematics were not good, I did know that fifteen and seventeen did not make twenty-six, the age she admitted to.

'They were exciting days,' she said. 'I was noticed right from the first. There was not a girl who had more admirers than I did.'

'Of course not,' I said soothingly.

'I was young and frivolous. When I think of the match I could have made . . .'

Lord Lummy, I thought. The Duke of Denton Square, the Earl of Edmonton, the Prince of Putney . . . Yes, I was sure she was right.

'Many of the girls married into the peerage,' she said. 'I wonder I didn't.'

I wondered most what I should have been like with an aristocratic father instead of Mr Ralph Ashington. Different, of course.

'It all happened so quickly,' she was saying. I leaned forward. I didn't want to miss a word. Hadn't I been trying to find out for as long as I could remember!

She was silent, and I prompted gently: 'What was he like . . . my father?'

'Different,' she replied. 'Not a bit like the others. There was a sadness about him . . . a tragic look which began to fascinate me.'

'Did you find out why he looked tragic?'

'His wife had died not long before. He had come to England to try to get over his sadness. Then one night a friend brought him to the theatre. I noticed him in the stalls. His eyes were on me all the time. And the next night he was there . . . and the next too.'

There was nothing very unusual about that. I heard often of these men who went night after night to gaze on the adored one. It was one of the clichés of the Theatre Johnnies, as Meg called them.

'But there was something different about him,' I prompted.

'Oh, very different. He was quite distinguished-looking. His skin was bronzed, and his hair was bleached with the sun. It made him look . . .'

'Outstanding,' I supplied, 'and very attractive.'

She did not seem to have heard that interruption.

'We went to supper.'

'At the Café Royal,' I breathed.

She nodded. 'He talked. He was a good talker when he roused himself and he was eager to talk to me. There was a family estate near Epping Forest, but he was rarely there. He owned a tea plantation in Ceylon and he was in England for only a short stay. He talked a great deal about the place and ... in two weeks he had asked me to marry him.'

'It was very romantic,' I said.

'Romantic! No one thought so. Meg was really spiteful. She didn't approve at all. She had only been my dresser for a year and you would have thought she'd made me ... and owned me. She reproached me bitterly. "All my ladies married into the peerage," she kept saying.' My mother began to laugh and I joined in with her. She went on: 'I said to her: "I'm sorry, Meg, but even if it spoils your record I shall marry whom I wish." Sometimes I think I rushed into it just to spite Meg.'

'I'm sure you didn't. You must have loved him dearly.'

'Sentimental Siddons! But *I* am not in the least sentimental, my child. I rushed into it without thinking clearly. I was fascinated by that hot and steamy land of which he talked so much. I wanted to see it for myself. The colour and the glamour, the turquoise seas, the coral reefs and the waving palms. He had a way with words. Sometimes I think you have inherited that from him. They all said I was throwing myself away. But I went out there. I can remember so clearly ... all the excitement of getting ready, the ship which took us out. Dark nights with stars like gold on midnight blue velvet ... just like that velvet gown of mine. You know the one. I always think of the ship we travelled out in when I wear it. It was all so romantic and exciting and then ... I was there. I remember seeing the house for the first time. I shivered as I entered in spite of the heat of the tropics. It was seven o'clock in the evening when we arrived and the sun had gone ... suddenly. The dark comes quickly ... not like it is here. There's no twilight. It's day one moment and the next ... night. There were lanterns on either side of the door. The house was white and the air seemed full of the hum of insects. It was surrounded by bushes and trees. Everything grows so much faster than at home. There's a sort of steamy smell coming up from the earth. It's like a hot damp blanket.'

'It must have been thrilling,' I whispered.

She was silent for a few moments, then she said vehemently: 'I grew to hate it. I kept thinking about what I had never cared particularly about at home. The rain . . . the gentle rain, not great downpours. I wanted to hear the hansoms going by; I wanted to see the horses pulling the buses, the flower-sellers and the fruit stalls. I wanted the shops and the noise and the traffic . . . even a pea-soup fog would have been welcome. I wanted to come home. I felt caught . . . that was it . . . trapped. Why am I telling you all this, Siddons?'

'I should be told,' I said. 'It's part of my life too. I was born there in that house, in that air like a hot steamy blanket.'

'I made a great mistake,' she went on. 'A terrible mistake. When I knew that I was going to have a child I didn't know what to do. I would have come away before if it hadn't been for that. Three months would have been long enough for me to stay there.'

'I'm sorry. It was my fault.'

She laughed. 'Well, you didn't have much say in the matter. You were a good child, once you'd appeared. Old Sheba had prophesied that I was lucky and you weren't going to give me much trouble.'

'I'm glad I was so considerate.'

'No credit to you, my child.'

'Who was old Sheba?'

'A wicked old woman. I hated her. She ran the household. I would have got rid of her but she was too useful. She crept about quietly . . . They were all so quiet, watching, spying. You'd look up and find her standing there. "Missee call?" she would say. She gave me the creeps. But she was useful. *I* couldn't have managed the place. I'm sure she went through my things looking for . . . I don't know what. Something to discredit me, I was sure. I felt I should go mad if I couldn't get back to the theatre. Ralph was away from the house a good deal. The plantation dominated everything. There was a club in Kandy and some English people, but not the kind to approve of me. Siddons, I felt as if I was going mad. I used to pray every night. You can guess I was pretty desperate to do that! Make something happen, I implored. Something did happen. You!'

'Well, that was something.'

'Open that drawer, Siddons. There's a bunch of keys there. Got them? That's it. The little one there. Here, bring them to me. That one. Open that bottom drawer and you'll see a package wrapped up in tissue paper. Bring it to me.'

This was an exhilarating revelation. I had never known her so talkative about the past. When resting periods began, she always seemed closer to me, and that lasted for a week, sometimes longer, before she began to pine to be back at work and forgot about me. But she was now more revealing than ever before. It was as though seeing me with my hair up made her want to talk.

I brought the wrapped package to her and she opened it slowly. I sat on the bed watching. Underneath the tissue was a picture of her. It was not large but it was beautiful. The colouring was exquisite, and although the miniature stopped at her waist, I could see that she was wearing a sari. One shoulder was bare and over the other fell cascades of lavender-coloured tulle spattered with silver stars. I had seen many pictures of her – she was constantly being photographed – but I had never seen one more beautiful than this.

'Three months after your conception,' she said. 'Can you see the maternal brooding in my eye?'

'No,' I answered.

'It came later. At that stage you were beginning to become a discomfort and an encumbrance. You were a little monster at that time. It seemed like years before you condescended to make your appearance and put me out of my misery.'

'I dare say I was obliged to wait until the appointed time.'

She laughed suddenly. 'When I saw you I thought you must be the ugliest child on earth. Red-faced, wriggling, you were like a little toad.'

'You should have had a seraph,' I said. 'A little angel with golden curls.'

'You improved, though not to seraphic levels. Do you know, I began to grow quite fond of you.'

'It was the miracle of motherhood,' I said. I picked up the picture and looked at it. 'Those pearls become you. You never wear pearls now.'

'Pearls!' she mused. 'Those are the Ashington Pearls.'

'Pearls of great price?' I said lightly.

'You are right.'

'Where are they? I've never seen them.'

'They were not mine. I just wore them. They're part of a family legend. I didn't want them, I assure you. I did for a time and then . . .'

'Tell me more about these pearls.'

'It's a long story. You've no idea of the pride of these Ashingtons. You would think they had descended from royalty. Not Ralph so much . . . the others. I soon became acquainted with the story of the pearls. Before your father and I went out to Ceylon, I spent three weeks at Ashington Grange, the family home near Epping Forest. I can tell you those were not the three most contented weeks of my life. I was crazy to get away from the stifling atmosphere of virtue and family pride and the incessant reminders of my good fortune in becoming an Ashington. It was there that I first heard of the pearls. My elder sister-in-law – the more formidable of the two – told me most solemnly. You would have thought I was taking some religious vow. The pearls are the sacred possession of the Ashingtons. They had come into the family a hundred years before. A Colonel Ashington had served in Ceylon when there was some trouble between the English and the Dutch and they were fighting in Ceylon. Martha Ashington spoke her lines as though she was well rehearsed. So she was. She must have played that scene a hundred times. It was all about the virtues of the British, particularly Colonel Ashington. It was something about the Kings of Kandy being so despotic and so hideously cruel that the Sinhalese yearned to be under the British flag and that was what the valiant Colonel was doing out there . . . putting them under it. Saving the Sinhalese. I didn't listen to that part. I just wanted to know about the pearls.'

'It sounds like a play.'

'It felt like a play when I was trapped in that jungle. A drama though . . . and I yearned for a comedy. I gathered that the valiant soldiers led by the Colonel captured the tyrant of Kandy and they kept him in exile for the rest of his life. His family had ruled for two thousand years. I remember that part. It was like the last line before the curtain of the second act. Now this is where the Colonel comes in. He was very skilled with medicines. They had to be that, for a greater menace than the followers of the wicked King of Kandy were the diseases which could attack those who were strangers to the land. Well, it so happened that one of the mighty nabobs had a son who was attacked by a cobra. The Colonel came along at the precise moment and killed the cobra, but the child was dying, so they thought. By great good fortune one of the herbs in the Colonel's medicine kit saved the child's life. Yes, I really think someone ought to make a play of it. The Ashington Pearls! That would be a good title. Pearls, diamonds, rubies, there is something appealing about them, don't you think?'

I agreed and was all impatience to hear more.

'Mind you,' she went on, 'the story continues on conventional lines. You have guessed the outcome already. Grateful, mighty nabob asks himself what he can give in exchange for his son's life. Nothing could be as valuable to him as that, and the gods will not be very pleased with him if he does not show his gratitude to them for producing the Colonel at the right moment. He grapples with himself. What object does he value most outside his sons and daughters? There are the pearls. So he gave your great-great-great- . . . I am not sure how many greats . . . grandfather the pearls. That's the story and those are the pearls. There were conditions. The pearls were priceless. A fortune in themselves. The Ashingtons, besides being brave soldiers, were sharp businessmen. They tried to have them valued. Each pearl was perfect and of a remarkable size and there is a diamond and emerald clasp which itself is a masterpiece of artistry. The Kandyan nabob made the sort of speech which is considered right for such ceremonies of endowment. The pearls would bring bad luck if they passed into the wrong hands. Only the blood of an eldest son could compare with their worth. The nabob had hesitated to part with them for he feared that might bring him ill fortune . . . but the incomparable pearls were the only object worthy to offer for the life of his son.'

'It's wonderful,' I said enthusiastically.

She smiled at me. 'Dear little Siddons, you are such a child.'

I was ready to accept the fact to please my mother since it put her in the right mood to go on.

'The pearls were mine for a while. They had been worn by your father's first wife and then they came to me . . . but not for keeps. No one *keeps* the pearls. That's one of the rules. I wore them, as you see, while my portrait was painted.' She closed her eyes. 'There was a room where the light was right. It was a dark house, that one. The bushes and trees grew so thick round it. Towards the end I used to dream that they grew up in the night while I slept and shut me in so that I was a prisoner there for ever. You see what effect the place was having on me.'

'But you did escape and you brought me with you. Tell me more about the pearls.'

'As soon as they touched my skin I felt a sort of fascination. I suppose I thought of that Kandyan nobleman and all the people who had worn the necklace before me. The artist who painted me was a pleasant young Englishman. He fell in love with me. He said the pearls were like my skin . . . flawless. His painting of me was perfect but he was never satisfied with the pearls. He said they changed – actually altered in texture – while he tried to paint them. When the picture was finished he took a small boat along the river Mahaweli Ganga and drifted out to sea. The boat came back but he was not in it. Sheba said that the pearls had brought him bad luck. Or I had. I had never thought him very serious when he talked of being in love with me.'

'And you never liked the pearls after that.'

'No, I never did.'

'Where are they now?'

'I suppose Clytie has them. They go to her unless your father marries again and has a son . . . but how can he when I'm alive? There would be no divorce. The Ashingtons would never allow that. So it seems Clytie has a clear run . . . though it's against the rules in a way. She's an Ashington, but if she marries and has a son, they'd go to her son's wife.'

'It's all so interesting to me. Who is Clytie?'

'She is my stepdaughter, the daughter of your father's first wife. I went out there when she was a year old.'

'Tell me more about Clytie. What is she like?'

'She was four years old when I left. I noticed nothing much about her. I rarely saw her. She was left with her nurse all the time. When you came you were in the nursery with her. Sheba looked after you both.'

'Irene Rushton,' I said solemnly, 'do you realize I have just learned I have a sister.'

'A half-sister.'

'I always wanted a sister. Clytie! It's an unusual name.'

'Your father said that when she was born she was like a sunflower.'

'I know. Clytie was a water nymph and Apollo fell in love with her. He turned her into a sunflower so that she would always be turned towards him on his daily journeys across the heavens.'

'What nonsense,' said my mother.

'He must have felt very tender towards her,' I replied softly.

'You're a romantic idiot.'

'At the moment I feel a rather bewildered one. I'm so excited. I have a sister. If only I could see her!'

It was the wrong thing to have said. My mother was clearly wishing she had not told me so much. Her mouth was set rather grimly. She wrapped up the picture and handed me the keys. 'Put it away,' she said. There was a finality about the statement.

The picture was symbolic. She had brought too much out of the hidden places of memory this morning. Secrets were going to be laid away. She would not be so rash again.

I was right. She was not.

Events followed their normal course. Depression set in; moods followed. 'She's like a bear with a sore head,' said Meg. 'Two sore heads,' added Janet, and she added ominously: 'I reckon we'd make a good thing out of that hostelry, Meg.'

Then Tom Mellor came up with a play and it was the right one. Rehearsals began; there were tantrums and the ordeal of learning lines while she changed her personality and became the character she was to play.

'One of these days she'll play a murderess,' said Meg. 'Then we shall all have to look out.'

'You'd see me out of this house like a streak of lightning,' was Janet's comment; and I had the impression that she would not altogether dislike my mother's taking on such a role.

But she played the fascinating siren which suited her beautifully and in a few weeks, after the excitement of the first night and the ordeal of reading the notices next day, for fear some critic should offend her, the days passed as they had so many times before.

We were back to normal and there was not another word about Clytie.

But I did not forget her.

I thought a great deal about my family and longed to know more of them, but there was no one whom I could ask except my mother, and on the occasions when I brought up the matter she showed so clearly that she had no intention of telling me more – and gave such an indication that she was sorry she had betrayed so much – that I realized I had to wait for an opportune moment.

I tried to pump Meg. I was sure she would talk about it if she knew anything. All she could tell me was what I knew already. My mother had astonished everyone by marrying a tea planter and going off to Ceylon from where she had returned three years later with a child, myself.

'Three years was not long enough for people to forget. She was welcomed back with open arms, you might say. She'd matured, they said. Not that she liked the word. Flowered into perfection.

That was better. Well, she's got that . . . whatever you call it . . . that brings them flocking to see her. When she's on stage no one looks at anyone else. Some of the other players like that – I *don't* think! But she's an actress from her toes to her fingertips. She'll act her way through life, that one.'

So all I could get from Meg was the story of triumphs and chances thrown away. I talked of her to Toby, but he knew nothing. He had only seen her for the first time eighteen months ago and fallen under her spell – so much so that he had made himself important to her in the only way he could – teaching her daughter.

I was with him a great deal, as well as during those morning sessions at the work table. He showed me London. Once we sneaked out in the early morning to Covent Garden. It was exciting to see the fruit and the flowers and bustling traders. We went to Kensington Gardens and watched the children – and some grown-ups – sailing their boats on the Round Pond; we went into the Orangery and wandered round the pleached alley; we walked through Kensington Gardens, Hyde Park, Green Park and St James's – grass all the way in the heart of town with only the lovely muted sound of traffic to remind us that we were in the heart of a big city. We walked down Pall Mall where Charles the Second had played the game which gave it its name and paused to pay homage in Whitehall where his father, Charles the First, had lost his head. We sailed along the river to Hampton Court and Windsor.

We played games of our own invention. One of us would hum a bar of music and the other had to guess what it was. We had a quotations game in which a subject was chosen and we had to find a verse or a proverb about it. I liked the animal ones best when one of us would shout 'Ass' and the other would answer: 'The law is an ass.' Or 'Bear' and the answer would be: 'Catch the bear before you sell his skin.' A great deal of it came from poetry, at which Toby excelled; we scored points for correct answers and were not allowed to use the same quotation twice. 'Tiger' brought forth: 'Tiger, tiger burning bright' several times and then Toby came up with one which stuck in my mind and I remembered later.

> 'And their revenge is as the tiger's spring,
> Deadly, and quick and crushing . . .'

'Whose revenge?' I wanted to know, and he quoted the verse from Byron's *Don Juan*.

> 'Alas the love of women! It is known
> To be a lovely and a fearful thing;
> For all of theirs upon that die is thrown,
> And if 'tis lost, life has no more to bring
> To them but mockeries of the past alone,
> And their revenge is as the tiger's spring,
> Deadly, and quick and crushing; yet as real
> Torture is theirs – what they inflict they feel.'

I was impressed and after that we started reading Byron together.

I took it all for granted that lovely summer which was the final chapter to a way of life. I was to look back on it with bittersweet memories in the years to come.

I was a child at heart, whether I put my hair up or not, and it never occurred to me that change was waiting to spring just like a tiger. I thought – if I thought at all – that those summer days would last for ever and we could continue our explorations in the years to come.

The play had a very long run. It was going to be a record everyone said. If it had been a short one I think my mother might have grown uneasy about the time I spent with Toby. She liked her admirers to be always at her call. It was not that Toby adored her any the less. He had just found a way of serving her which was proving to be very pleasant.

Once, greatly daring, Toby took me to the theatre. We did not tell my mother. It was evening and Toby said there was something about a theatre in the evening that there wasn't in the afternoon. I wore one of my mother's dresses. I was as tall as she was. 'You're going to be a lamp post, you are,' Meg had said. 'All skin and bone if you ask me,' added Janet.

'Nonsense,' said Toby, 'you'll be tall and elegant.'

What a comfort Toby was!

The dress was of the simpler kind – one she had worn for an ingénue role – it was blue, which gave my greenish-greyish eyes a hint of blue. I put my hair up – heinous sin – and we set out in a hansom.

What an evening! How we laughed! We gripped hands when my mother appeared on the stage and we were both overcome by emotion at the sight of her.

She was a wonderful actress. I was not surprised that so many people came to see her and that she had been welcomed back with 'open arms'. We saw Everard in the stalls. He had to be careful that he wasn't seen because apparently he was well known on account of his position in the House. He would bring her home and stay, I guessed.

I loved the play. I wept when tears were expected and Toby gave me his handkerchief to wipe my eyes. It was characteristic of me that I had come without my own. As soon as it was over and the actors and actresses were taking their curtain calls, Toby hustled me out.

'I'd love to take you to supper,' he said. 'That would round off the evening, but it would be running it a bit fine.'

I agreed. I imagined getting back to the house to find my mother already there. Her wrath would be great, I knew, for not only was my hair up, but I reckoned I looked quite seventeen years old.

It was exciting coming out with the crowds. We even saw the royal carriage with the Prince of Wales in it.

'With the Princess for once,' commented Toby. 'Not one of the harem.'

I laughed, feeling enormously sophisticated as we set off in the hansom, giggling over the adventure.

Janet saw us coming in. She was noncommittal but I saw the

grim smile of satisfaction about her lips and I knew she was thinking of my mother whom I had begun to realize she did not like very much. She resented Meg's servitude and was always comparing what she called the pollution of London, which she and her sister unnecessarily endured, with the fresh air of the country which, with a little common sense, could be theirs.

I couldn't sleep when I went to bed that night. I lay thinking how exciting life was and how wonderful it was to grow up.

I heard my mother come in. Everard was with her.

I still lay awake thinking of her meeting my father and going to that strange house in Ceylon which I fancied had frightened her a little. I thought of Colonel Ashington and the pearls, and most of all I thought of Clytie. I wondered if I should see her one day. But even then I didn't think of change.

It was a few days after that visit to the theatre when I noticed the woman in the black cloak. I glanced out of my bedroom window and saw her. What called my attention to her was the fact that she seemed to be staring at the house. I couldn't see her face very well because the cloak had a hood and it was drawn forward, hiding a great deal.

I turned away from the window and put some of my clothes away and was thus occupied for about ten minutes. Then I went back to the window again. The woman was still there.

The impulse came to me to go and ask her if she wanted something. Then I realized how naive that would be. She was probably meeting someone or perhaps going somewhere and was too early.

'You're what I'd call a rusher-in,' Meg had told me. 'You don't stop to think. It comes into your head and you say or do it. Then it's said and done and there's no going back.'

Many people passed through Denton Square. It was not exactly a backwater. Then it came to me. Of course she was one of my mother's admirers. That was the solution. Someone gazing in wonder at the house where *she* lived.

As I stood watching I saw Meg hurrying along. She took out

her key, and as she did so the woman crossed the road and spoke to her. Meg nodded and exchanged a few words and then she came in.

I continued to stand at the window after the door had shut on Meg. The woman had turned and crossed the road again. She stood for a little while looking at the house. Then I believe she was aware of me standing behind the lace curtain for her eyes seemed to be fixed on the window.

I didn't know why it was but I felt a sudden shiver run down my spine and a horrible inexplicable fear came to me as I stood there. It was what Janet would have said was like 'someone walking over your grave'.

It seemed a long time – but it could only have been a matter of seconds – before she turned away and began to walk rapidly off. My heart was beating fast as I watched her. I felt there was something strange about her.

So strongly did I feel it, that I went to find Meg at once.

She was in the kitchen and had unwrapped some cosmetics and ribbons she had been out to buy for my mother.

'Look at this,' she said, holding up a pale mauve ribbon. 'The nearest I could get. I don't think it's going to suit her ladyship. I tramped the whole length of Bond Street and couldn't get better.'

'It's lovely, Meg,' I said. 'Who was that woman standing outside?'

'Woman!' Meg was clearly concentrating on ribbon and the difficulty of finding the right colour through the whole length of Bond Street. 'Woman?' she repeated. 'No, I don't think it's going to please her. There's too much red in that mauve. It's the nice bluey shade she wants. What was that?'

'The woman,' I said. 'Who was that woman?'

'Oh her . . . Wanted to know if Irene Rushton lived here. Another of them. They get a thrill just walking down the street where her dainty feet have trod.'

'She looked . . . different.'

'They come in all shapes and sizes, ducky. You'd be surprised at some of the types I've seen hanging round stage doors. I've seen millionaires that look like tramps and penniless young bloods that would pass for the highest in the land. You don't want to take notice of looks.'

'Yes,' I said thoughtfully. 'So it was just another of Irene Rushton's admirers.'

'That's about the ticket,' Meg confirmed.

I couldn't entirely forget the woman. Her image kept coming in and out of my mind. Then I forgot all about her for something quite devastating happened.

I was sitting at the schoolroom table with Toby when he said suddenly: 'I'm leaving England, Sarah.'

It was as though the clock on the mantelpiece had stopped; someone had kicked the jigsaw of my life which I was carefully putting together and in which I had thought Toby did not figure so very largely until that moment. It was like the end of my world.

He smiled almost apologetically.

'Well,' he said, 'it couldn't be expected to go on, could it. I had to *do* something . . . my father's son and all that. Naturally he'd expect me to do something some time. I've been what he calls "marking time" until this was ready.'

'Toby! Going away! You can't. What am I going to do? Who's going to teach me?'

He smiled at me but it was a sad smile. 'You'll have a proper governess or tutor now. It's time you had one. I was only a stand-in, wasn't I? It wasn't serious . . .'

'Not serious! I learned more from you than I ever did from anyone. Oh Toby, you can't go.'

He shook his head. 'Have to. My father's been talking to me very seriously. "Tobias," he said. He always calls me Tobias, you know. I believe when he was a young man he was known as Bias, which is a strange sort of name for him. Bias! Perhaps that's why he prides himself on being so fair-minded. He always sees two sides to everything, you know.' He was rambling on as though to shield me from the shock he knew I must be feeling.

'Where?' I cried.

'To India . . . One of our companies there.'

'*Our* companies. You mean your father's.'

He admitted modestly that he did and then I saw that there were many sides to Toby. As I have said, one of his favourite themes in discussion was that things were never quite as they seemed. I had thought of him as one of my mother's less significant admirers – not quite good enough for the stage, not quite good enough to be allowed to escort her, not quite old enough . . . Mr Not Quite, as she had once called him. I felt angry to have been so blind. Toby who loved literature with a passion, who was the best companion in the world, with whom I could laugh and talk as I could with no one else, he was worth all her other admirers put together – and that included Everard. And all the time he was so important; he, was the son of rich Tobias (Bias in his youth) who had his fingers in scores of financial pies and whose aim in life – only second to making money – was to make Toby such another as himself.

I felt ridiculously naive and taking a long time to grow up.

'He's been waiting for the time,' said Toby. 'Now it's come.'

'Toby,' I said sadly, 'when?'

'In three weeks.'

I threw myself into his arms and clung to him.

'Steady,' he said, patting my back awkwardly as though I were choking. 'Here, steady, Sarah.'

'Don't go,' I begged.

'I've got to, Sarah. I've got to *do* something. I just can't go about like this all my life.'

'Why not?'

'Being my father's son, I couldn't. I've got to be worthy of him.'

'So that you can make a lot of money and tie it up for your sons and grandchildren.'

'There's more to it than that. It's like a game to the old man. It's not a matter of getting richer and richer. Money brings responsibilities. For me this has just been a waiting period . . . a stamping ground.'

I felt I couldn't bear any more. I dared not try to imagine what it would be like when Toby had gone.

The news of his imminent departure was received in various ways. My mother was irritated. Toby had been useful and she hated to lose an admirer. 'Silly old man,' she said. 'Parents should never interfere.' She vented her scorn on Toby. 'I suppose he was *not quite* bold enough to do what he wanted.'

Meg said: 'It was time he went. Frivolling about here . . . no life for a young man. Mind you, I'll be sorry. I quite liked him.'

Janet snorted with satisfaction. 'Did *she* think he was going round doing her bidding for the rest of his life? She's got another think coming.'

But I was the one who was desolate.

He planned all sorts of treats for me during those last weeks, which only made it worse. There was no fun to be found in the Whispering Gallery of St Paul's or among the tombs of the Abbey, or feeding the ducks in St James's Park if you knew it was the last time you would do it together. He took me to the theatre one night – not to my mother's play but to a grand melodrama called *The Silver King*, which sent me into raptures, but these could only last for a few blissful seconds until I remembered that this was the last time I should go to the theatre with Toby.

He, too, was sad. I guessed he was thinking of leaving my mother. We drove back in our hansom, neither of us caring very much whether we were home in time.

Meg let us in conspiratorially.

'They're not back yet. Go on up with you.'

I went to my room and stood at the window watching the hansom carry Toby away.

I could not sleep that night. The moon was nearly full but it threw only a shifting light in my room because there were heavy clouds and a fairly strong wind. I had a deep feeling of sorrow because of Toby.

My mother had not come in. It was half an hour after midnight. She and Everard would have gone on to supper somewhere after the show.

What was the use of lying there trying to sleep? I got up, put on my dressing-gown and went to the window. I caught my breath with a sudden feeling of terror. Standing on the other side of the road was a man. He was in the same spot where I had seen the woman. I could not see his face clearly but I imagined he was middle-aged. Waiting for a glimpse of the goddess? I wondered. He did not look like the sort who would wait at stage doors.

I stood back from the lace curtains which hung across the window and laid a hand on the velvet draperies. He couldn't see me of course because there was no light in the bedroom, but I could see him from the light of the street lamp.

He was waiting for a glimpse of my mother.

I went back to bed but not to sleep. I kept thinking of the future and what it would be like without Toby. My mother would engage a governess, I supposed. She would not consider sending me away to school. There were those occasions – rare though they were – when she wanted her Little Siddons to come home to.

The clatter of hoofs. The hansom was coming down the street. I was at the window. My mother and Everard alighted. They came into the house and the door closed behind them. The hansom moved off. The man was still standing on the other side of the road. I wondered what his feelings were to see my mother go into the house with another man.

I didn't know what it was about those waiting people which filled me with a sense of foreboding, but they did. It was no different, I told myself, from people waiting at the stage door to get a glimpse of her.

I lay in bed still sleepless. My imagination began to plague me. I imagined the man down there was madly in love with her and planned to shoot her or Everard when they emerged from the house. I was in such a state of anxiety that I almost went to Meg for reassurance. I might have done if she hadn't shared a room with Janet. I was sure both of them, with their shrewd Cockney reasoning, would soon throw a douche of common sense on my feverish imaginings.

An hour or so after my mother and Everard had come in I was

still awake. It didn't help at all when I went to the window and saw that the man was there.

What is he doing? I asked myself. I would tell Meg in the morning.

I dozed a bit. It was dawn when I was awakened by the sound of the door being shut as Everard left the house.

I went to the window to watch him go. He walked up the street, tall, very distinguished-looking. Meg had said: 'I reckon he'll be a Prime Minister one day. A pity he's got *her*. Though I don't know whether her ladyship would be a suitable wife for the Prime Minister. It's usually the peerage for actresses, which is a different sort of life if you ask me.'

Then I saw the man emerge from the shadow of the trees. He must have been there all night. I watched him walk slowly away in the opposite direction from that which Everard had taken.

I felt greatly relieved that he had gone, though puzzled as to why he had waited so long. I fell asleep almost immediately.

Meg came in at half past eight demanding to know if I had decided to spend the day in bed.

Sun was streaming though the window. How daylight changed everything. It was like a comforting old nanny shutting away the nasty shadows in drawers – not to be brought out again until darkness fell.

I was on the point of mentioning the man to Meg but I changed my mind.

He was only one of the admirers who took pleasure in looking at the house in which the adored one lived. This was all part of being the daughter of a famous actress.

SCANDAL

*

Toby left two weeks after that. He didn't come to say goodbye. He had reminded me that farewells were upsetting and old friends such as we were didn't need protestations to know that we were friends for ever.

I felt terribly lonely.

Meg tried to comfort me. 'It had to happen. A young man like that can't spend his life playing, you know. It was like a holiday for him . . . a long holiday . . . but there's more serious things in life. It was really playing at being a teacher. There's no excuse now. You'll have to have a real one.'

Janet said: 'I'll not stand for one of them stuck-up governesses, I can tell you. Meals in her own room . . . too high and mighty to eat with us. This is not the establishment for that sort of thing, I can tell you. Little places like this don't have no room for no governesses.'

'The only thing would be school,' put in Meg, 'and young Sarah wouldn't like that and nor would *she*.'

'I tell you the house is not big enough and for two pins I'd be off. I had a long letter from Ethel this morning . . .'

Meg listened to the eulogy on the delights of country life versus that of the town, nodded sagely and was as firmly determined to stay with my mother as she had ever been.

'Oh Meg,' I cried, 'I couldn't bear to lose you too.' Which delighted Meg, of course, although she said grimly: 'Well, you'll have to behave yourself, that's all.'

Janet raised her eyes to the ceiling as though she were in communion with the Above and muttered into the pastry she was making that Some People – which I presume included my mother and me as well as Meg – were beyond understanding.

Then the storm broke.

Everard's wife was going to divorce him. His comings and goings to and from our house had been watched by a detective employed for this purpose. Consequently my mother was to be cited and there was going to be a scandal because of my mother's fame and Everard's position in Parliament.

Everard had always seemed to be a man who would show no emotion, whatever circumstances he found himself in. Toby and I had laughed about it. I said that if he were told his house was on fire he would merely look mildly surprised and say: 'Oh dear, how annoying.' We used to invent dramatic situations for Everard and his response to them. It was very childish, I suppose, but it caused a great deal of merriment. Meg used to listen and a faint smile would twitch her lips. 'You two!' she said. 'Perhaps I'll get some bricks for you to play with.' But she liked to hear us laugh, I know, and she, too, was amused by the imperturbability of Everard. One day she said: 'How such a man ever got himself into this I can't understand.' Then she added darkly: 'Men! There's not much I don't know about them. Never had much to do with them on my own account. But I've done a lot of looking on, you might say . . . and don't they tell you that the looker-on sees the best of the game?'

Well, there was Everard caught up in this terrible situation. Exposure! The political world would know of the liaison with a famous actress and such goings-on (Meg's words) were not what people looked for in their future Prime Minister. 'I'll lay a pound to a penny,' prophesied Janet, not without some satisfaction, 'that this will be the end of him in the House of Commons.'

I wished that Toby were here so that we could discuss it and he could tell me what he thought the outcome would be.

I gathered that there was evidence . . . irrefutable evidence they called it, procured by a detective who had seen Everard enter the house at twelve-thirty and leave at six . . . not once but on several occasions.

My mother reacted dramatically, as was to be expected. She walked about her bedroom – a tragedienne this time.

43

'And what effect will all this have on the play?' she demanded.

'I reckon it will pack 'em in,' said Meg. 'They'll all want to take a look at the scarlet woman.'

But my mother was angry. It wasn't her image, she said. Oh, how she hated that woman who had started all this. Someone had put her up to it. They could depend on that. *She* hadn't the brains to think of it herself.

It was Everard I was really sorry for. I could see what a scandal would mean to him. Not long before Sir Charles Dilke had been in an unsavoury divorce case, to the delight of his enemies and the horror of his friends, and he, too, had been heading for the Prime Minister's stakes. The case had ruined his career.

Everard did not come to Denton Square. That would have been foolish. My mother was fretful, irritable and nervous.

She came home from the theatre alone one night. This was before the story really broke. It had been a miserable evening. Meg was at the theatre and Janet was grumbling all the time with a sort of inner satisfaction and her hints were that this would break up the household. My mother would have to live a more natural life, she hinted. Settle down a bit. Perhaps go back to that husband of hers, which was where she belonged. That would mean of course that Janet herself, with Meg beside her, would reach that haven which was Mecca, Valhalla or the Elysian Fields, whichever one thought of as the ideal state.

My mother went straight to her room, which was on the first floor, and after a while she came up to mine. I had never known her so distraught.

She sat in a chair and looked at me in bed.

She seemed to be assessing me and at length she said: 'This is a mess, Siddons.'

I nodded.

'It's going to be pretty nasty. People can be vicious. It's a good thing you're not away at school. Children can be horrid to each other. You'll be all right, though. It's those of us who are in the public eye who will get the full force of the venom.'

I waited.

'It's going to sound so different from what it really is. I love Everard, you know.'

I believe she did. He was different from the other admirers. He was a steadying influence in her life, which in her more serious moments she knew she needed.

'Of course,' she went on, 'he has always been worried by the situation. It was so important to him to lead a regular and conventional life. He *is* conventional. He hated the way it had to be. But you see we loved each other. I know how different we were – personality and all that – but we were right for each other. Do you understand?'

'Yes, of course I do.'

'There'll be horrible things said. I don't know what it's going to do to either of us. It'll finish his career. How do you think I feel . . . being responsible for that!'

'We're all responsible ourselves for what we do, not other people,' I said, quoting Toby.

She looked at me wistfully. 'Little Siddons,' she mused. 'Not so little now . . . growing up fast. Learning about life. Who told you that? Toby, I suppose.'

I agreed. 'He taught me so much,' I said.

She clenched her fist and seemed angry. 'He should never have gone away. He ought to have had the guts to stand up to his father. He had a certain courage but never quite enough.'

'How can you say that!' I cried indignantly. 'Perhaps it needed more courage to go than to stay. After all, he couldn't go on wasting his time. Besides, he's fond of his father. Nobody should judge other people's actions because they don't know all the circumstances.'

She stared at me and then smiled slowly. 'That's true, dear child, very true. You'll have to remember that in the weeks to come. I wanted to explain to you. We don't talk together half enough, do we?'

That was something I could readily agree with.

'Everard was the only man who really mattered to me,' she said.

I began to think of my father and she knew it.

'That,' she went on, 'was a momentary aberration. What does a girl of seventeen know of love? I admit there have been lovers, but Everard was different. We used to think that when *she* died we'd marry and settle on his country estate with a place in Westminster. I should have made a good parliamentary wife. You're looking sceptical. But it was nice talking about it and Everard believed it would be like that . . . in time. She was there though . . . she was always there. He was tied to her.'

'He married her. He must have loved her at some time.'

'It was more or less an arranged match. Two political families . . . rich landed gentry. You know the sort of thing. He was very young at the time and he didn't know about this streak of madness in the family. It was soon after the honeymoon that it became apparent. The fact is that there were often nurses in the house and at times she had to be put away. Can you imagine a man like Everard . . . set for distinction, certain of parliamentary glory, to be fettered with a wife like that.'

'Poor Everard. I often thought he looked sad.'

'It was his sadness which first attracted me. Strange, that. It was your father's sadness that made me notice him. Perhaps sadness appeals to me. Yes, it does. I wanted to make them laugh and be merry. And then I began to realize how worthwhile Everard was. Clever, different from everyone else. The attraction of contrasts perhaps . . . but it was there . . . a strong iron band that held us together. We love each other so much, Siddons, that even with this hanging over us we can't regret.'

'What will happen?'

'They'll make the most of it. There'll be headlines in the papers. There was the case of Sir Charles Dilke. You don't know about that.'

'I do.'

'Well, you'll know that finished him then. This will finish Everard. He's got enemies in Parliament. Of course he has. A brilliant man always has. There are his political opponents. They're going to start hounding him. And I have my enemies too, you know. They're going to have a field day, these enemies of ours.'

I tried to comfort her, to tell her that it would pass in time.

'No,' she said. 'It will make changes. There is someone behind her . . . forcing her to this. She could never have done it on her own. She's just a shell. That'll make things worse, you can be sure of that.'

I reminded her that it was unlike her to look at the black side. Perhaps it wouldn't happen after all. Perhaps it could be called off. These things were sometimes, weren't they?

I took her back to bed and tucked her in. I gave her hot milk laced with something soporific which Meg knew of, and I left her dozing.

I went back to bed wondering what it would lead to. There was one thing I was certain of. There would be change.

At first it was just a line or two in the papers – rather obscure. The wife of a well-known politician was about to sue for divorce. 'It is whispered that a famous actress is involved.'

Then in a few days it burst on the world. I heard the newsboys shouting in the streets. 'Irene Rushton in divorce case. Well-known politician involved.'

My mother shut herself in her room and went through the papers. Janet was triumphant. 'There! You see what comes of working for an actress!' she implied. Meg was tight-lipped. All her other ladies had married respectably and not one had taken less than a knight. And now this! 'A pretty kettle of fish!' she commented.

Newspaper reporters waylaid my mother. They waited outside the house for her to come home. They invaded the theatre. As Meg had said, it was good for the play. People flocked to the theatre just to take a look at her.

She carried on as though nothing had happened. She was the complete actress and even took a certain satisfaction in the role she was playing. One day she would be the abandoned scarlet woman, the next the injured innocent, at others the brave woman overtaken by circumstance. In a way she enjoyed it. I believed she would have found a certain satisfaction in any role she conjured up for herself.

She talked to me more than she ever had. Whether she thought I was growing up and should know what was happening or whether it was simply that she missed Everard's company and needed someone to confide in, I don't know.

Everard had written to her. He said that when this nightmare was over and he was free they would go away together. They could not marry, of course, because of my father but he was wondering whether something could be arranged with him.

'Poor Everard,' she sighed. 'He is the soul of respectability. Imagine what this means to him. It shows how deeply he loves me to become caught up in a relationship like this. Dear, dear Everard! Perhaps one day it will all come out right. But first we have this terrible ordeal ahead of us. We have to be prepared to have our pasts probed, and maliciously too. Oh Siddons, it is going to be such an ordeal for us all.'

'Mostly for Everard,' I pointed out. 'He will lose his career.'

She nodded grimly. 'He'll have to resign, that's clear. He's been in politics all his life. This will be the end for him.'

I thought: The world is lost for love! And I wondered how he was feeling now. That he loved my mother dearly I had no doubt; but then, with the love-affair kept secret he had been able to pursue his career; he had lived dangerously then, but now the danger had caught up with him.

A gloom had settled on the house. Everything had changed. Only Janet was pleased because she felt that there was a very good chance of Meg's services not being required, and then they could leave at once for Ethel's country paradise.

My mother was playing to packed houses, but when she left the theatre one night several hostile voices were raised against her and she was referred to in no uncertain terms as an immoral woman. She, who had been so accustomed to adulation, was very upset.

She wept when she came home and Meg made a special concoction to send her off to sleep and I fussed around brushing her hair and tying it up with pink ribbons before tucking her into bed.

She could be reconciled playing the various parts required for the moment. There was the woman who had sinned against society, the Mary Magdalen with a heart of gold, the innocent who had been brought into the glare of publicity and was wondering what it was all about, the penitent who would live a life of piety from now on . . . all these she tried. But now the cold facts were too stark to be ignored, and as she faced up to the reality of the situation a deep depression settled upon her.

I was sorry for her because I could see that the spoilt child of nature could not understand why life could be so cruel as to change so completely.

'It will be when the case comes on that the real trouble will start,' prophesied Meg.

Janet raised her eyes to the ceiling. 'There'll be no holding the newspeople. It'll all come out. They'll make a regular bank holiday of it, you see. A nice thing for us all . . . living in a house where *that* was going on.'

'It don't help to go on like that,' retorted Meg. 'Her ladyship will come through all right. You'll see.'

'Perhaps she'll run away,' suggested Janet. 'She did that once before.'

'It might be a good idea,' commented Meg.

The time was passing. We were within a week of the opening of the case. My mother was losing a little of her calmness. She was dreading what might come out in court. I heard Janet and Meg discussing it.

'They'll be raking up everything,' said Janet. 'Her marriage. Why she left him. There'll be some dirty linen washed in public, I shouldn't wonder.'

'Goodness me! What won't come out! These people don't always concern themselves with the truth.'

'Oh, the truth will be good enough for them, I shouldn't

wonder,' said Janet with a grim laugh.

My mother was getting really worried now. She had not been well enough to go to the theatre for a week and the play had closed down. The tension in the house was almost unbearable. We were all trying to steel ourselves for what was to come.

Then the blow fell. I heard the newsboys crying it out and when I bought a paper the big black headlines danced before my eyes. I felt sick. The scene had changed dramatically. What had been a bad dream had turned into a nightmare.

Sir Everard Herringford was dead.

He had shot himself in the study of his Westminster house.

For the first days a certain morbid excitement prevailed. Meg went out and bought all the papers. We went through them before taking them to my mother.

During the first days after Everard's death the matter dominated the front pages with pictures of him, an account of his prospects, which I could not help feeling were made more brilliant in death than they actually were in life. A possibility of becoming Prime Minister had become a certainty; his witty and pungent remarks in debate were quoted. 'All lost for the love of a woman', ran one headline; and when that woman was Irene Rushton there was more ammunition with which to excite the disgust or sympathy of the reader, whichever would be more appealing at the time. In fact Everard was a kind of martyr in one paper: 'caught up in the fever of passion, the husband who had cared for an invalid wife for years and then had fallen deeply in love with one whose charm was known to the world'. On the same day he was the philandering scoundrel who had deceived his colleagues into thinking he was a man of honour.

I think a certain cynicism crept into my nature at that time which I never really lost. I was only fourteen but I was not so inexperienced as to think those colleagues who were now so devastated by the revelations had not been unaware of the relationship between Everard and my mother all along. She was too well known for it to have escaped unnoticed. Moreover he had been so often at the theatre. It was only when his wife decided to sue for a divorce that it became so shocking.

There was a lesson to be learned. In the world's eyes, to sin is mildly regrettable; to have the sin exposed is unforgivable. In other words the sin itself is not to be deplored; it is only bringing it into the open that is so shocking.

Everard had, it seemed, thought the best way for all was to remove himself. My mother wept and said he had done it to save her. I did hear something about some indiscreet letters she had written to him, which he had preserved and which had fallen into the hands of lawyers. It seemed to me, knowing what I did of him, that he would think the noble thing to do was to take his life.

There were pictures of Herringford Manor, Everard's country house in the Midlands. It had been photographed in dark conditions. If it wasn't actually raining at the time it was going to at any moment. But the Manor in which the invalid wife lived had to look gloomy, so that was how they took it – a big, grey stone building – gaunt and sinister. Yet I could imagine it with shrubs in flower on the lawns and the sun shining on grey stone – a very different picture. But it was the House of Tragedy and it had to look the part.

Such stories are, of course, nine days' wonders. People's lives are broken and they have to live with the results, but as far as the interest to the public is concerned that, fortunately, is fleeting.

In a week or so there was no more mention in the papers of what was called the Herringford-Rushton affair. Everard was dead; he could no longer delight and disconcert the Commons with his pungent wit; he would no longer attend the theatre and come home with my mother, advise her on her financial affairs and generally give her the benefit of his wisdom. She was bereft. Thanks to Everard she was not absolutely penniless. He had very wisely invested the little money she had, but it was not enough to live on without the salary she received as an actress – and she was extravagant.

She would have to work very soon, she said; and she was

uneasy as to what her reception would be. She could never endure not being idolized. A hostile audience, I knew, would unnerve her. To see her make her appearance and hear the audience gasp with pleasure before the burst of applause, and to watch the look of happiness on her face, had moved me on those occasions when I had seen her on the stage. I wondered what would happen if that appreciation was not given – or worse still, hostility was shown. I think that was what she feared.

There were long sessions with Tom Mellor. I could see when Janet brought him in that he was not his usual confident self. He did not shout as he had in the past: 'I've got it, Reeny. This is *it*!' Toby and I used to laugh about it and it had become a catch phrase with us. This time Tom was quite serious. He was shut in the drawing-room with my mother for a long time.

It was not a very successful meeting, I gathered after he had gone.

My mother shouted as I went to join her: 'The provinces! Can you see *me* in the provinces! That's what that fool suggests. "Give them a rest, Reeny," he says. "That's what they want . . . a rest." A rest from *me*! Did you ever hear such nonsense.'

For several days she raved against Tom. What sort of agent was he? He was trying to stop her appearing in the West End.

We soothed her – Meg and I – as best we could. This, I realized, was almost as great a blow for Meg as for my mother. When she thought of those ladies she had looked after now sporting their coronets and their strawberry leaves she was appalled to think she had given the best years of her life to an actress whose agent suggested the provinces.

All the same, nothing else was in sight for my mother, and the gloom in Denton Square was as thick as a pea-soup fog.

Then the aunts arrived.

The letter was addressed to my mother, and I took it in with her breakfast tray. The handwriting was firm and large and I was hoping that it was a suggestion for a new play which would be exactly what she wanted.

I sorted out the bills which had come by the same post and went in to my mother.

She was sleeping; she had looked a little older during the last weeks but in sleep she still had the appearance of a child. I put down the tray and kissed her lightly. She opened her eyes and smiled wanly. I packed her round with pillows and set the tray, with the letter propped on it, before her. She seized it immediately.

'Who on earth . . .' She slit the envelope and read, and as she did so a grim smile played about her lips. Suddenly she burst out laughing.

'Here, listen to this:

'"Dear Irene,
We have, of course, heard of the distressing happenings, and although it is so long since we have seen you we do not forget that you are of the family. We should like to call and see you at four o'clock on the twenty-third . . ."'

She grimaced and said: 'Good Heavens, that's today!

'"We are staying at Brown's Hotel for a few days before returning to the Grange and it has occurred to us that, in view of what happened, you may be in need of help and advice. There is the child to think of."'

My mother looked at me and nodded. 'You!' she said. 'The letter is signed Martha Ashington. This is your aunt. The "we" is not royal. There are two of them. Martha and Mabel and Mabel moves in Martha's shadow.'

She turned to the letter. 'There is a PS.

'"We have a proposition to make and shall discuss this when we see you."'

I was excited at the prospect of seeing some of my relatives, but my mother sighed resignedly.

'Just like them,' she said. 'It's rather imperious, don't you think? "We should like to call at four." How do they know that I shall be here? I have a good mind to be out. That would be amusing. Suppose Meg told them: "You would need to make an appointment to see Miss Rushton."'

'But don't you want to hear this proposition?'

'I am sure that anything that came from them wouldn't appeal to me.'

'It must be years since you've seen them. Perhaps they've changed.'

'Not the Misses Ashington of this world. They remain pillars of virtue from nine till ninety.'

'They are at least my father's sisters.'

She looked at me pensively. 'Perhaps I'd better be here. I should plait your hair. It would look tidier that way. What they'll make of you, I don't know.' She was overcome with mirth at the idea and I was pleased to see her laugh as she hadn't for some time.

We spent half the day preparing for them. Janet baked scones and cakes. Meg was glad to dress my mother once more for a part because it was clear that she regarded the coming encounter as a scene from a play. She talked about the two aunts quite a lot that morning and gave impersonations of them: Martha, the domineering one like a man-o'-war going into battle, and Mabel, slightly less formidable but in herself a force to reckon with.

'I spent those weeks in Ashington Grange before we left for Ceylon,' she said, 'and it seemed like years. Oh, very, very proper they were. Everything they did was according to the rules. It was one of God's jokes to give them Ralph as a brother. Ralph was the sort who did everything exactly opposite from the rules laid down by the book. It was rebellion against the influence of his sisters and that grim old Grange.'

I was very eager to see them. I wore a dark blue serge dress with white piqué collar and cuffs and my hair was as tidy as it could be in two staid plaits tied with navy blue ribbon.

Precisely at four o'clock the cab drew up at the door and the two aunts descended. They were dressed in black (like two black crows, my mother said afterwards); they were tall and very up-right. They looked ancient to me but that was probably due to my youth. I think at the time they must have been in their fifties. Martha was two years older than Mabel.

Martha – I picked her out at once – marched (the only term to describe her military approach) to the front door with Mabel very slightly in the rear. Even the knock on the door was like a per-emptory command to open. They were taken to the drawing-room by Meg and I waited for the summons to appear which I knew would come soon. It did.

As I entered it was clear that this was the moment they had been waiting for. I was aware of two pairs of lively dark eyes studying me – that and the jangling jet ornaments they wore. Beads rose and fell over their considerable bosoms and hung from their ears and they both wore large cameo brooches at their throats. Their long black skirts swept the floor.

'So this is the child. Sarah, I believe.'

I met the full stare of those piercing dark brown eyes boldly.

'Yes,' I answered, 'and you are my Aunt Martha, I believe.' I turned to the other one. 'And you are my Aunt Mabel.'

Aunt Martha seemed rather pleased with my ready response and went on: 'It has been a great regret that circumstances have prevented our meeting before.'

'Circumstances' was of course my mother, seated on the sofa looking exquisitely lovely – dressed for the part – in a lavender-coloured chiffon tea gown which she had worn in some play. She kept the clothes she liked and I believed when she put them on assumed the role she had had when wearing them. This one, I remembered, was a beautiful girl of humble origins who had married a man of wealth and had had to face his family. Having seen the play several times I knew what her attitude would be. Charming, incorruptible, whimsical with a slightly roguish atti-tude towards unsympathetic relations.

They ignored her and Martha said to me: 'Well, at this time we thought the hatchet should be buried. We know what has been happening here – ' Mabel's head shook a little in a gesture easily recognizable as disgust and disapproval – 'and we thought it our duty to come and see, at least. We do have a proposition.'

'I am sure my mother and I will be interested to hear it,' I said. 'And it is good of you to come.'

Aunt Martha looked as though she really did possess a halo which was probably invisible to my eyes, having been brought up as I had. 'It was our duty,' she said quietly.

Janet brought in the tea rather ungraciously.

'You do the honours, dear child,' said my mother.

The eyes of the aunts followed me and I felt an urge to show them that although ours was a theatrical household and we had just been involved in a major scandal, we knew how to behave. I, too, was playing a part. It helped in a situation which might prove awkward.

'Cream? Sugar?' I asked – first Aunt Martha, then Aunt Mabel, then my mother.

My mother grimaced at me when I took hers to her.

'You have changed little I can see, Irene,' said Aunt Martha.

'Thank you, Miss Ashington. So have you.'

'We have been very distressed,' put in Mabel. 'We kept the papers away from the servants . . . It's a mercy that the name Ashington was rarely mentioned.'

'One advantage of leading a professional life,' said my mother lightly.

'What we have really come to find out,' said Aunt Martha quickly, 'is how you are *placed*.'

'Placed?' asked my mother.

'I presume you can no longer . . . er . . . follow your profession.'

'But why should you presume that?'

'People must be horrified, and your involvement with this er . . . politician . . .'

'People love to be horrified, Miss Ashington.'

'I am sure that would apply to the very few. You are our brother's wife.' It sounded as though that were a major calamity. 'And Sarah is our niece. We have come to offer her a home. We shall see that she is educated as our brother's daughter should be and she will be brought up in a fitting manner.'

I wanted to cry out my protest. I looked at my mother appealingly.

'My daughter and I have always been together,' she said, 'and we shall remain so . . . until death do us part.'

Not quite the right line for this role, I thought, and wanted to giggle. I thought of her walking out of that dark house in the steamy jungle clutching me in her arms. I could hear Meg's voice: 'It wasn't going to do her career any good, but she brought you with her.'

'What can you offer the child here?' asked Aunt Martha.

'A mother's love,' said my mother affectingly.

'It was a pity you did not think of that before . . . before . . .' began Aunt Mabel but Aunt Martha silenced her with a look.

'You should think about it,' she said. 'This is Ralph's daughter. We have some responsibilities.'

'I should have thought they were his and mine rather than yours.'

'It may be that you are not in a position to carry them out,' said the redoubtable Martha. 'And Ralph himself was inclined to be feckless. And he is so far away. His daughter should be brought up in England in any case. What is happening to her education? She should go to school. Has she a governess? If so, we should like to see her.'

'She has been taught by . . . a tutor.'

'A tutor! A man! Not very suitable for a young girl, but perhaps in a household . . .' That was Mabel who seemed to have a habit of leaving sentences unfinished when she caught Martha's eye.

'We are in the process of engaging a governess,' said my mother with more conviction than truth.

'Governesses are very well in some households but in a situation like this I would recommend school. That is if Sarah remains here.'

'Remains here! But this is her home!'

'Yes, yes, but in the circumstances . . .' Mabel began.

'A governess might well serve the purpose in Ashington Grange,' Martha firmly interrupted. 'A well-ordered household among an orderly society is what a young girl needs.'

'Ours is a well-ordered household,' said my mother.

Aunt Martha sighed. 'There has been a great deal in the papers. I put it to you, Irene, that it is not good for the child to remain here.'

'I shall stay with my mother,' I said.

Both aunts were looking at me. Aunt Martha nodded. 'Commendable,' she said, 'but unwise. We have come to do our duty. I do not know what your financial position is, Irene, but I imagine it is not good. Ralph cannot help you. He is always in financial straits. I believe you are not playing . . . if that is what you call it . . . at the moment, and even an establishment like this can be expensive to run. You have those two women . . . the whole of your staff, I presume. Very small and inadequate, but expensive if the income is not large.'

'I shall be working soon,' said my mother, looking a little depressed, I thought, as she stepped out of the role to reality. She turned to me. 'Sarah, come here, my child.'

I went to her and she took my hand.

'Your aunts are offering you a home in Ashington Grange – a fine old place in the heart of the forest. There you could live as a daughter of your father should.' We were in the play again. I could see that. This was the renunciation scene when the child is handed over to the rich relations for the child's good and the young and beautiful mother makes the big sacrifice of her life. 'There, my darling. It will be better for you. You will have a life of respectability; you will be educated as a member of the Ashington family should be. All you have to do now is say good-bye to me.'

She wanted me to throw my arms about her neck and cry: 'Mother, dearest Mother, I will never leave you.' She was posing there already. The aunts were looking on at me and I was looking across the footlights at the audience. I could almost hear the word: 'Curtain!'

I said in a cool matter-of-fact voice: 'It is kind of you, Aunt Martha and Aunt Mabel, to offer me a home, but I could not leave my mother.'

My mother stirred a little impatiently. The aunts went on drinking their tea.

'You should think about it,' said Aunt Martha. 'We shall be at Brown's Hotel until the end of the week.'

When they had left we talked for a long time.

My mother said: 'I was proud of you, so proud of you. The way you told them to keep their respectability was wonderful.'

'Of course I'd never leave you,' I retorted.

She patted my hand.

'There they were just like two old crows . . .'

'And you were a bird of paradise,' I added, 'and since we are in an aviary what was I? A little peahen perhaps – such modest birds, always following in the wake of a glorious husband. But perhaps that's not appropriate. A wren more likely.'

'They would find a husband for you, I'm sure. Some scion of the gentry, perhaps a pillar of the Church. Oh, you'd hate their way of life, Siddons, and yet . . . and yet . . .' Her frivolity seemed to drop from her for a moment. 'It might be best.'

'What do you mean?'

'I mean that you would have the sort of upbringing your father's daughter should have. You'd be well educated, fit to enter into society and you'd escape from this . . . smear.'

I stared at her. She was really serious. 'I'm thinking of you,' she went on. 'What's best for you.' Suddenly she gripped my hands tightly. 'Tom,' she went on, 'is not very optimistic about the future.'

I felt a coldness in my heart. Was she suggesting that there would be no play for her, that those audiences who had recently been clamouring for her were turning their backs on her?

She said slowly: 'I'd get some parts . . . but they wouldn't be the right sort. You see what happened was all against my . . . my image.'

'Actresses should surely forget about images and act,' I said.

'Ah, words of wisdom,' she replied. She seemed a different person. Yes, those were lines at the side of her mouth. I hadn't noticed them before. Everard's death had done something to her. He had paid his price and she believed she must pay hers.

She went on: 'I'm extravagant perhaps. I have saved very little. I had gifts from Everard now and then and they were carefully invested. It's something. I have to have clothes . . . good clothes. I have to keep up this house. Costs are high and there are Janet and Meg. You see, when one isn't earning . . .'

I was staggered. I had thought little about money before this.

'So you see,' she said slowly, 'one mustn't dismiss the aunts.'

I put my arms about her and hugged her tightly. She seemed to derive some comfort from that. 'As if I would leave you!' I said.

I felt we were very close then.

She went to see Tom the next day and walked back. I think the interview must have been depressing and she wanted to think about the future. She was caught in a downpour of rain and was soaked when she returned. In a few days' time she had the first of those heavy colds which were to become frequent with her. She was in a low state of health because Everard's death had affected her more deeply than we had at first thought.

The aunts called again and this time my mother was in bed and seemed quite ill, so they talked to me alone in the drawing-room and pointed out to me that while they applauded my affection and loyalty to my mother, I was being rather foolish in refusing to live with them.

I thanked them but insisted my place was with my mother.

'We have written to your father and told him what has been happening here,' said Aunt Martha. 'No doubt he will give his opinion and we are sure that he would wish you to come to us.'

'I know so little of my father,' I replied. 'I cannot remember a thing about him.'

'It is all so distressing and disgraceful when it is considered how . . .' began Aunt Mabel.

'When such events occur,' interrupted Aunt Martha, 'it is always best to put them behind us and convince ourselves by our exemplary conduct that we will try to correct the havoc they have caused.'

As I could not in any way hold myself responsible for my mother's desertion of my father and for what happened between her and Everard, I felt mildly resentful; but I was very anxious for what, a few days ago, had seemed quite impossible was now appearing to be faintly probable.

Aunt Martha said: 'We shall be leaving at the end of the week. You can get in touch if you need us at Ashington Grange. Mabel, give her our card.' Mabel handed me one which she took from a bag she carried. 'Moreover,' went on Aunt Martha, 'we shall be coming to London again in a month or two. Perhaps by then you can give us an answer. We shall be at Brown's. But if before that you wish to get into touch with us you can do so at the Grange.'

When they came again the position had not changed very much except that there was talk of my mother's being in a lavish production – one of her old roles. She was naturally elated about this and although nothing could ever be quite the same it looked as though we were passing out of that dreary depression when it had seemed that fate was against us.

I assured the aunts once more that I would never leave my mother. They were very disapproving and demanded to know what was being done about my education. My mother was evasive and Aunt Martha said it was a matter of some concern to them for it was unthinkable that an Ashington should be illiterate. My mother pointed out that I had taught myself to read at the age of four and had had my nose in a book ever since. She believed it would be hard to find a girl of my age who was so well versed in English literature.

'There are other subjects,' murmured Aunt Mabel, and Aunt

Martha agreed with her.

They went, rather disconsolately, I thought.

'I believe they really want to have me with them,' I said.

'They want to mould you into the pattern they consider suitable,' said my mother. 'They want to make you into a little Ashington which means just like themselves. They were always telling Ralph that he should do this and that. It was one of the reasons why he was glad to get away.'

A few weeks later she said to me: 'They're right, you know, about your education. We have neglected it. You're going away to school.'

I was astonished.

'Yes,' she said, 'it's necessary. This is a very good school near York. Ashington girls always went there. It's a sort of tradition in the family.'

'You're making that up.'

'You're to leave in September.'

'But the money. Won't it be expensive?'

'Nest eggs,' she murmured. 'And the new production. It'll be a wild success. I'm back, Siddons. Nothing to worry about now.'

I gradually grew accustomed to the idea of school and when I eventually went I became absorbed by it. Backward as I was in some subjects, I was a long way ahead in others and I had a great desire to learn, which pleased my teachers. At the same time I was always ready for excitement and fun so I was not unpopular with my fellow students. It was a novelty for me to be with people of my own age and I was delighted with my new life. It was a complete escape from the tragic events which lingered on in Denton Square. So absorbed was I in school that I forgot Denton Square for days. I was caught up in the drama of how many marks I should get for my essay and how I should fare in the coming hockey match.

There was one very old mistress who remembered my aunts and was pleased to have another Ashington at the school. 'They were very conscientious hardworking girls and have lived worthwhile lives,' she commented. 'Let us hope and pray, Sarah, that you will be like them.' It was the last thing I had in my mind for the future.

I went home at Christmas. It was not a very happy household. The play had run for a month – a financial disaster for the backers.

Meg told me about it. 'They blamed your mother. They've always got to blame someone. It was a bad play. I could have told them that from the start. Then there was that wicked man . . . calls himself a critic. He said something about the star of the Herringford case not having quite the aplomb or the talent to carry off the innocent of this production. Beast! You see, they're not going to let that be forgotten if they can help it.'

'And how did she take it?'

'Badly. It affected her performance, I reckon. Someone threw an egg at her as she came out of the stage door. Spoilt her velvet wrap. I'll never get that mess off. It's there to stay. I'll have to get rid of the wrap for I never will the egg stain. And it cost a pretty penny, that wrap did.'

'Meg,' I said seriously, 'what's going to happen?'

'That's something I can't tell you no more than you can tell me.'

My mother tried to be bright. Next time she should be more careful in her choice of plays, she promised herself.

I was home for a month. We decorated the drawing-room as we always had. In the past there had been crowds of people coming in and out. A few friends did call over the days of Christmas, Tom Mellor among them, but the relationship had considerably cooled between him and my mother. She blamed him for the failure and he blamed her.

I was glad to escape to school and once more so absorbed into the life did I become that I was content with the occasional letter I received from my mother. I had to write to her weekly, of course. It was a school exercise. I often wondered afterwards what she thought of accounts of the hockey team, tennis, netball and the high marks I had received in English.

By the summer the household had changed a good deal. My mother had aged. I gathered there had been one or two small parts. One had been quite a success, she told me. Janet was more tight-lipped than ever and yet at the same time she betrayed an inner satisfaction. Meg and my mother quarrelled all the time. I was glad when those holidays were over and I could escape to school.

By the next Christmas I knew that something was seriously wrong. My mother had the part of the good fairy in a pantomime.

'Pantomime!' said Janet with a grin of contempt.

Meg said little.

It was a quiet Christmas because my mother had to start work on Boxing Day. She had a cold and was feeling limp. I took her breakfast in as I sometimes did in the old days.

She pretended to be merry but being away so long I was able to see the great change in her. She looked ten years older; there were discontented lines about her mouth. It was while she was playing in the pantomime that the scandal revived in a half-hearted sort of way. Lady Herringford, wife of Everard, had been found dead in a stream on the Herringford estate. It was a shallow stream and Lady Herringford had been found lying face downwards. She had been ill for a long time and there was no suggestion of foul play. 'Her death recalls the tragic Sir Everard who ended his career and life when he was involved in a scandal with an actress . . .'

My mother read the paragraph – not on the front page – and was upset because she was referred to merely as 'an actress'.

'Well, you didn't want your name mentioned,' I soothed her.

She was fierce suddenly. 'Don't you see what it means? They don't mention it because it's no longer important! An actress! As though I were playing in repertory or – or – ' she laughed hysterically – 'pantomime!'

It was a miserable holiday and I was once more glad to return to school, but it took me a week or so to get the memory out of my mind.

Summer came. I had passed my sixteenth birthday and would be seventeen before the year was out. I had not been in the house for more than an hour when I realized that the life I had enjoyed at

Blessington Academy for Young Ladies was at an end.

My mother had changed still more. There were dark shadows under her eyes.

Meg told me first. 'I'm leaving. I was just waiting for you to come home to go. I've had enough. Her tantrums are something I can't put up with no more.'

Janet was there. 'We're leaving for Ethel's place in two weeks,' she said triumphantly. 'She – ' pointing to her sister – 'wanted to give you time to work something out.'

'And my mother?' I asked. 'She doesn't look well.'

'It's her chest. She just gets cold after cold. And she don't take care of them.'

'They come on when she's down in the dumps,' commented Janet.

'Yes,' agreed Meg. 'If only she could get a real chance, I reckon she'd make her comeback.'

She was talking for Janet who was triumphant because of my mother's failure. When we were alone together Meg said to me: 'Her type of actress often has only a limited spell. I know. I've seen it. It's a sort of charm they have. It's being young and pretty in a certain sort of way. They're like butterflies. They fly across the stage and people love them . . . but it don't last. Youth don't last, does it? What's best for that sort is a brilliant marriage. They leave the stage and settle down to be wives and mothers. But with her it went wrong from the start. She should never have married and gone out to Ceylon. That was stepping out of line, you might say, and that's something you have to pay for.'

'And so you're leaving her, Meg,' I said reproachfully.

'There's no help for it. She can't pay us . . . not me nor Janet. The parts will get less and less. She'll soon be grateful for a walk-on.'

'All this because of that affair . . .'

'Oh no, it's not that really. If she'd been a great actress she would have weathered the storm, easy as wink your eye. But she's not a great actress. In any case, what she had wouldn't have out-lasted her youth. It's just that all this has brought on age quicker than it would have come otherwise. I told her at the time that she was a fool to marry where she did . . . but she wouldn't listen. Oh no. She knew all the answers. Well, she got her sums wrong, that's all. I'm going to Ethel's. That'll shut Janet up. Somehow I've had enough of the theatre after all this.'

I talked seriously to my mother. She was in bed. I had insisted she stay there because she looked so wan.

'I don't know what we're going to do,' she said. 'I couldn't afford to go on paying Meg and Janet. We'll have to give up this house.'

'My school fees must have been a terrible burden!' I cried.

She laughed lightly. 'Not to me. It was your aunts who paid for them.'

I stared at her. So those two years when I had acquired an education and had lived my carefree life I owed to them!

I felt a deep sense of obligation and shame.

I said: 'I shan't go back. How can I? We'll have to do something.'

'What?' asked my mother.

What did girls in my position do? If they were alone they became governesses or companions – a far from inviting prospect for the children were usually unmanageable and the elderly ladies disagreeable.

But *I* was not alone. I had a mother to support.

I said: 'The first thing I must do is write to Aunt Martha and Aunt Mabel and tell them that I must leave school. I will explain the position.'

'I can just imagine their satisfaction,' said my mother grimly.

I wrote to them that day.

It was not necessary for the aunts to point out to me the difficult position in which we were placed. I knew it well enough and after a good many hours of discussion in their suite at Brown's Hotel, my mother and I accepted the only solution to our troubles.

'When all is said and done,' said Aunt Martha, 'Irene is Mrs

Ashington and you, Sarah, are our brother's daughter.'

Ashington Grange was the family home and if it were not for the tea plantation my father would be living there. The house, they pointed out to me, was theirs. Their father had seen to that, but had Ralph had a son it would naturally have gone to him. Irene must come to Ashington Grange where she would be well looked after and I should return to school.

My mother at last agreed that she had no alternative. She was suffering from acute depression, I believed. She found it hard to exist without the adulation and admiration which she had always looked for as her due. There would be little of that at Ashington Grange.

She said she would not be able to endure it without me and I could well believe that. The aunts despised her and she disliked them. To have to live on their charity was distasteful to her – but slightly less so than starving in a garret. Also, she said, she had to think of me. The idea of my having to work in some way was more than she could endure. It was not as though there was any kind of work that I could do. Whichever way we looked at it there was only one way out and that was to go to Ashington Grange.

I realized very quickly that I was the reason for the aunts' concern. I think they were excited at the prospect of having a young relative in the house. They were planning for me and Aunt Martha was a passionate planner. I could see that a niece's future could be of greater interest than the church bazaar or the yearly garden party which was held on the lawns of the Grange for the good of the church steeple.

I was firm about not returning to school.

'Absurd!' cried Aunt Martha. 'Ashington girls always remained until they were eighteen.'

'I must be with my mother,' I insisted. 'She is not well.'

'Fiddlesticks! It's a mope, nothing more.'

'She has suffered a great tragedy,' I pointed out.

'Her just reward,' murmured Aunt Mabel, 'after all this . . .'

'You will have to understand,' I replied, 'that if I am coming to live at Ashington Grange my mother will have to be welcomed there too.'

I was amazed to find myself giving orders to these two formidable ladies, but that was how it was and I felt a little tender towards them for wanting me so much that they agreed to my demands.

'It will be necessary then,' said Aunt Martha, 'to engage a governess.'

'I am too old for that,' I protested.

'Your education has been cut short for a . . . whim!' said Aunt Martha. 'A governess there must be. Our sister Margaret was too delicate for school and had a governess . . . in fact many of them. She died.'

'Not of a surfeit of governesses,' I said with a giggle, for I was discovering an uncontrollable desire to tease these aunts, which I realized I should have to suppress.

'You are far too frivolous, Sarah, and this is a serious matter.'

No one knew better than I how serious. However, they gave in. The arrangements were made. We gave up the lease of the Denton Square house and went to Ashington Grange.

FOOTSTEPS IN THE DARK

*

In spite of the circumstances which had brought me to Ashington Grange, I could not help but be thrilled when confronted by it.

At Epleigh station we had left the train and found a coachman eagerly looking out for us. He was taking us to the house in the brougham, he explained, and our baggage would be brought along later by the wagonette.

Epleigh was a village in the heart of the forest – typically English, with a green in front of a Norman church and a few houses scattered round. We came along the road through the forest and suddenly there we were in this delightful oasis, so peaceful on that lovely September afternoon. The cottage gardens were ablaze with starry Michaelmas daisies, bronze chrysanthemums and stately dahlias. In the centre of the green was a pond, beside it was a wooden seat on which sat two men talking. They looked up with interest as the brougham went by. We passed the graveyard with its headstones, some new, some lopsided with age, and then on past a general shop and post office combined. We took a road from the green and soon were before the gates of the Grange. They were wide open and a woman stood at the door of the lodge and curtsied as we drove past. We went along a drive for about a quarter of a mile before we made a turn and were confronted by the house.

It was beautiful – grey stone mellowed by the years. There was an archway in the centre and at the end of the west wing was a tower with battlements and long narrow slits of windows which looked rather definitely out of place with the rest of the house which was clearly of a later period. I learned in due course that the only part left of the Norman fortress which had once stood on this site was the tower. The rest of the house had been built during the reign of Charles I and had miraculously escaped the holocaust of the civil war. Aunt Mabel, who was very proud of the house, told me all this when she realized how interested I was.

At this time I merely had an impression of gracious charm which the Dutch Gable style, so symmetrically designed with its decorations of scrolls, whorls and classical figures, seemed to produce so effortlessly. It was not so much a large house as a beautiful one. Having been built in the early part of the seventeenth century when architects were just beginning to come into their own, it was in the traditional shape with pediment windows, wooden mullions and lead lattices.

I was filled with a sudden pride to bear the same name as such a noble edifice.

We went under the arch and into a courtyard. From there, when we had alighted, we stepped straight into the hall where the aunts were waiting to receive us, looking more formidable in their own setting than they ever had in Denton Square and Brown's Hotel.

'Welcome to your home, Sarah,' said Aunt Martha, taking my hand and giving me a cool peck on the cheek.

'It's a good thing that you are here at last . . .' began Mabel.

They were less cordial to my mother.

I said: 'The house is fascinating.'

Nothing could have pleased them more. Aunt Mabel was faintly pink with pleasure.

'We like it,' she said. 'It's been in the family for over two hundred years.'

'You must be weary from the journey,' added Aunt Martha. 'Jennings can show them to their rooms, Mabel. Will you call her. Your things will be arriving now. Then you can wash and change and we will talk.'

There was a certain triumph in the manner of both aunts. They quite pointedly extended their welcome to me and it was clear that my mother was there on sufferance. I wondered how long a woman who had been petted and pampered as she had would endure that. Fortunately she seemed to be rather dazed at the moment and not to notice it.

Jennings appeared and prepared to conduct us up the wooden staircase with its beautifully carved newel post and banisters.

On the first floor was the long gallery, which was the width of the house and hung with pictures of Ashingtons. I promised myself I would explore that later. My ancestors! It was exciting to come face to face with them after having lived in ignorance of them all my life until now. At one end of the gallery was a balcony, which I guessed was where the minstrels played when they had a ball. I could not imagine my aunts at a ball and the image that conjured up made me smile.

My room was on the next floor. It was spacious with a high ceiling painted with cherubs and decorated with flowers. There was a four-poster bed hung with blue material and matching blue rugs on the floor. There were heavy blue curtains and a window-seat. I gave a cry of pleasure as I went to look out. Below me were well-kept lawns with flower-beds now aglow with autumn flowers. I saw the shrubbery and an enclosed garden where roses still bloomed; I saw the kitchen gardens and away in the distance the trees of the forest. I thought I had never seen such a beautiful view. Ashington! My family home, I thought, and I was filled with an intense excitement until I turned and looked at my mother. She was pale, and a great deal of her charm had been due to her animation; she seemed a different person from Irene Rushton of Denton Square who had been the centre of our lives.

I was being selfish. Of course she was remembering. She and my father had come here soon after their marriage.

'Let us see your room,' I said.

It was on the next floor and much smaller. It contained a single bed with a half-canopy. I thought it charming even though it lacked the grandeur of the one allotted to me. I was angry with the aunts for making the distinction. They should have given me this room and mine to my mother. Perhaps I would suggest the change.

'Thank you,' I said to Jennings, for I felt a great need to be alone with my mother. 'I will find my way back to my room.'

When Jennings left, my mother threw herself into my arms.

'Don't cry,' I said. 'It'll show.'

That was the best preventative. It reminded her of her appearance and she composed her face.

'It's hateful!' she cried. 'They're hateful. Oh, Siddons, I loathe it here. Anything . . . anything would be better.'

'But you agreed we couldn't stay in Denton Square and where else could we go?'

'They hate me,' she said. 'They always did. Right at the beginning I felt it. I hated this house. It gives me the creeps. Do you feel it, Siddons?'

'No,' I said. 'It's no more creepy than other old houses. Any ghosts here would be relations. That's a comforting thought.'

'Not to me. I'd still be an in-law even to them.'

She laughed wanly then. 'It won't last,' she went on. 'It's only a respite. I'll get a part. When Tom knows that I really have gone he'll be after me. That's the way of the world.'

Her eyes sparkled now. Euphoria had set in. She was already seeing Tom arriving at Ashington Grange, contracts bulging his pockets, herself having to be wooed. Her public was clamouring for her. Well, let it clamour. *She* hadn't forgiven it yet.

I left her and when I reached my room I found that some of my baggage had arrived. Jennings asked if she should help me unpack. I declined her help and sent her along to my mother.

Aunt Martha was not a woman to (as she would say) let the grass grow under her feet. The very next day she broached the matter of the governess.

'Really, Aunt Martha,' I cried, 'I am far too old for a governess. I shall be seventeen at the end of November.'

'And only two of those seventeen years spent at school!'

'I had a tutor before.' I smiled, remembering Toby with a rush of sadness. I missed him sorely. 'He was very good,' I added wistfully.

'A tutor is not suitable for a young girl. Our elder sister Margaret had a governess. That was because she was too delicate to go to school. She died when she was eighteen.'

'How very sad to die so young.'

'She was never strong. It was sad, as you say. Don't listen to the servants. They will tell you that she walks the gallery at certain nights looking for her lover. It's the most arrant and romantic nonsense.'

'Had she lost her lover?'

'She was about to marry. Death, of course, separated them. As I was saying, she had a governess. I should prefer you to return to school, but I have been talking this over with Mabel and we think that perhaps while your mother is here you should be too. She will need a certain amount of . . . restraint. You will be the best one to give her that.'

'Restraint! You talk as though she might go raving mad and qualify for a straitjacket.'

'She was always frivolous and the life she has led has not strengthened her character. It was a disastrous marriage from our brother's point of view. But let us not stray from the point. I shall begin my search for the governess immediately. You may rest assured that I shall choose her with the utmost care.'

How I should have liked to return to school but I did realize I should not be happy leaving my mother with the aunts.

It was Mabel who showed me the house. She seemed different when Aunt Martha was not present and even sometimes finished her sentences. The elder sister was certainly the dominating character.

Mabel was delighted with my interest in the house. She showed me the drawing-room, the salon, the dining-room, the winter parlour and all the bedrooms as well as that part behind the screens where there was a commodious kitchen presided over by a cook and numerous underlings. I wondered how I should remember all their names.

They displayed a great curiosity towards me. That was natural enough. I was an Ashington who, at the mature age of seventeen, had just arrived on the scene. I dare say many of them – for only a few were young – remembered the hasty marriage of Ralph Ashington with the London actress which had caused such consternation to his sisters. I wondered how many of them had heard of the scandal. Mabel led me through the wash houses with their coppers of bubbling water and the smell of damp clothes, to the butteries and brewing houses. It was a considerable estate and bigger than it had at first appeared.

What interested me most was the gallery, for it was lined with portraits of the Ashingtons. I noticed that several of the women had been painted in pearls which looked remarkably like those which I had seen about my mother's neck in the picture she had shown me.

'What magnificent-looking pearls,' I said. 'They have a special sort of lustre.'

'The Ashington Pearls,' said Mabel. 'They are part of the family's history.'

She then told me the story of how they had come into the family and it corresponded exactly with what I had heard from my mother.

'They must be kept in the family or there will be an end of it,' she said. 'That's one legend grown up round them. One of our ancestors – this one – ' She pointed to a man in a Regency cravat, frogged coat and fringed waistcoat. It was a full-length portrait. His breeches were striped and the buckles in his shoes very elaborate. 'This one gambled, got into debt and disposed of the pearls to a money-lender. The family had to retrieve them.'

'They belong to the family, I suppose.'

'They must never go out of the family. The wife of the eldest son has them until her eldest son marries. Then his wife has them until her son marries. They are always in the possession of an Ashington.'

'What if there is not a son?'

'It has never happened before this. It is so distressing. There has always been a son until now.'

'What will happen to the pearls now then?'

'Martha believes that something will happen.'

I was puzzled. If my father was going to have a son, who would in time get a wife and provide an owner for the pearls – though a temporary one – many things would have to happen. My mother would either have to return to him or die so that he could take another wife. Even Aunt Martha was not clever enough to arrange that.

'It has turned out to be most unfortunate,' said Mabel.

'Fate has been very disobliging,' I said. 'If I had been a boy how different it would have been.'

'You will have to curb your frivolous way of speaking, Sarah. Martha does not like that at all.'

'I'm sorry, Aunt Mabel,' I said demurely.

I turned to the portrait of my father. He was handsome and there was a jaunty look in his eyes.

'He was too adventurous,' commented Mabel, clasping her hands together and shaking her head at the portrait. 'If he had not been so . . . headstrong, so impulsive . . . if he had considered marriage more seriously, all this might not have happened.'

'What of his first wife?'

'We never saw her. When she died he came back to England and we believed God was giving him another chance. Then he married your mother. He was a gambler. It is one of the family faults. That's why Martha will have none of it in the house. I agree with her. If any of the servants are discovered playing cards they are sent packing.'

'Was my father successful in his gambling?'

'People are always unsuccessful in their gambling, Martha says. Our father was a strictly religious man. He deplored that in Ralph. That is why the Grange is left in trust to us, but of course if Ralph had a son it would go to him. It's a sad thing but the name will die out, of course, unless Ralph has a son. It is most disappointing.

Two daughters! Martha would have been so pleased if you had been a boy . . . and so should I.'

'I am sorry,' I said demurely, 'but there is nothing I can do about it, I'm afraid.'

'Martha said you had inherited your father's lack of seriousness.'

'Martha likes to arrange everything as she wants it,' I said, 'and she wants everyone to adjust to the character she thinks most suitable. Life doesn't work like that, Aunt Mabel, except in a play where the playwright just sends his characters in whatever direction he wants.'

'I shouldn't talk too much about plays if I were you now you have finished with that way of life. Martha will not like it . . . and nor shall I.'

'Oh dear, perhaps we are going to be a nuisance.'

'We must see that you are not.'

I wanted to hear more of the portraits so I let it go at that.

I paused before one who turned out to be the aunts' sister Margaret. She was very different from the aunts and I could not imagine either of them looking in the least as she did – even in their youth. There was a daintiness about her, an air of fragility. She had been painted in an evening dress which looked like blue chiffon; her skin was very fair and her eyes almost amber colour. Her hair was light brown, fine and curly.

'It was painted soon after her engagement,' said Mabel.

'She looks happy and yet . . . as though she is uncertain about something . . . apprehensive. It's a strange picture.'

'Servants are so foolish. They say at night she steps out of the frame and walks along the gallery looking for Edward Sanderton, the man she was going to marry. One girl swore she saw her. All in blue chiffon, she said, and the frame was empty. What nonsense! We told her to pack her bags at once. Nobody has seen Margaret in blue chiffon and the empty picture frame since . . .'

'How long ago did she die?'

'It's twenty-five years.'

'Quite a young ghost. They usually go back a few hundred years.'

'People will have their tales. In my childhood they used to say the tower was haunted. Mysterious lights, chanting voices and a grey-clad nun.'

'And then the blue chiffon ghost became the favourite?'

Mabel shrugged her shoulders. 'You know what servants are. They like to frighten themselves. I know they clean the gallery in pairs and no one wants to go along it after dark. Martha laughs at them and if anyone was going to be haunted it would be Martha.'

'Oh? Why should she be specially selected?'

Aunt Mabel looked at me dubiously for a second or so and I could see that she was telling herself that as a member of the family I should be cognizant of its secrets.

'Well,' she continued, 'it was Martha who first brought Edward Sanderton to the house. She had met him at a country house party and they became excellent friends. In fact . . .'

I stared at her incredulously. The possibility of Martha in love was too much for my imagination.

Mabel looked a little shamefaced. 'He saw Margaret and from that moment he had eyes only for her.'

Poor Martha, I thought. A short-lived romance. No wonder there was a certain asperity in her nature.

'Of course there had been nothing *said* between him and Martha, and in a short time he and Margaret were engaged. They were to be engaged for six months and then marry. Martha and I were to be bridesmaids. There was a great deal of excitement getting the dresses made and everything else done. Margaret was so happy. She had always been delicate, of course, and that was why she had never been to school as we had. She was so pretty. I don't think I ever saw a prettier girl than my sister Margaret.'

'And what happened? Why didn't the marriage take place?'

'There was a cloud over her happiness. I think she could not forget what she had done.'

'What had she done?'

'Taken Edward Sanderton from Martha.'

'But he was never really Martha's, was he?'

'He would have been . . . if Margaret hadn't been there. He liked Martha. They could talk about things. Martha always had very definite views on everything . . . even in those days. Our parents used to say that would never get her a husband. Men don't like women who know too much. They want to be the ones to know. But Edward did like her. He was so interested in her views. But then it all changed because he was head over heels in love with Margaret. Margaret suddenly saw what she had done. You see, Margaret had had other admirers. Martha never had anyone but Edward. Edward was just right for Martha . . . and Margaret had come along and taken him.'

'Tell me what happened to her.'

'She worried. She was afraid she would become Edward's invalid wife. She became ill with worry. She had often been ill but this time she did not get better. She died one week before the day which should have been her wedding-day and it was the tolling of the bells we heard instead of the joyous peal.'

'What a dreadfully sad story!'

'It's from stories like that that the legends start. So, Sarah, if you hear the servants talking I hope you will put a stop to such chatter.' She changed the subject abruptly. 'We shall have to get a picture painted of you, Sarah,' she said. 'Martha was speaking about it last night.'

'My father had a wife before he married my mother,' I said. 'I learned not very long ago that I have a half-sister.'

Mabel's lips tightened at the corners.

'You have seen her?' I asked.

'No,' said Mabel, shutting her lips even more tightly as though in no circumstances should anything escape from them.

'Perhaps you should have a portrait of my sister as well,' I ventured.

'Certainly not,' she said and she looked at me with something like dislike. Then she moved closer to me, seeming almost conspiratorial. 'Perhaps your mother could be persuaded to rejoin her husband.'

'I hardly think so.'

'It is not too late. They are both young enough. That is what Martha said . . .'

I wanted to retort hotly that it was too late. It was fifteen years since they had parted. All that time they had lived separately. One could not expect them to be together just because the Ashington aunts wanted a male heir.

I could not keep my eyes from the picture of Margaret. I thought of the servants' fears and the lovely face growing animated and coming to life as she stepped out of the frame to look for Edward Sanderton whom she had taken from Martha.

'What happened to him?' I asked abruptly.

'Happened to whom?' asked Aunt Mabel.

'To Edward Sanderton.'

'Oh . . . he went away. He shot tigers in India. We never heard of him after that. He sent the family a Christmas card at Christmas for a few years . . . then that stopped.'

As we went out of the gallery I looked over my shoulder. There was an eeriness about the place. I could imagine the legend growing.

My mother and I walked into the forest. It was beautiful for the leaves were turning to bronze and many of them had fallen, making a brown-gold carpet under our feet.

My mother had never greatly admired the beauties of nature but she seemed happier in the forest than anywhere else. I mentioned this and she said: 'It's because I have escaped from the house. I can't see it here . . . and that's something. Oh, Siddons, if you knew how I hate it there.'

'Perhaps we shan't be there for ever.'

'No. Tom will be seeking me out, I know.'

'I suppose you'd be ready to take what he offered even if . . .'

She flinched. 'Oh, it *will* be something good. I wasn't so insignificant that people are going to forget me completely.'

I felt tender towards her. The public had undoubtedly loved her once but the public was fickle. Even I knew that. I knew, too, that the part she was hoping for was never coming.

'I hate those women,' she said. 'Particularly Martha. Frankly, Siddons, she frightens me.'

'She's formidable. But what can she do to hurt you?'

'It's the way she looks at me. I find her watching me when I look up suddenly. It's as though she is plotting something.'

'You're imagining it.'

'I felt like it before . . . when I came here with your father. He used to say, "Martha's a great planner. She decides what's to be done and won't rest until she gets people doing it." I said I knew she didn't approve of our marriage so what was she planning about that. I used to think she was making arrangements to murder me.'

'Irene Rushton,' I cried, 'you are acting again. There is one thing you would always know about Aunt Martha. She would always maintain respectability, and murder is hardly respectable.'

'She gives me the creeps. Oh, how I long to get out of this house. As for you, I believe you are beginning to like it.'

It was true. I loved the antiquity, the knowledge that my ancestors had lived there for two hundred years. I liked the orderly manner in which the house was run and I was glad to be with servants who served me as though they did not question their duty to do so. I was more tired of Janet's favours than I realized. I liked the regularity of meals; I liked morning prayers before breakfast and I admitted to myself – though not to my mother – a grudging admiration for the aunts. I rather enjoyed going to church with them and sitting in the Ashington pew – the two front rows were kept for us as homage to the leading family. I admired the stained-glass windows put in at the time of the Restoration by a jubilant Ashington whose Grange had escaped

Cromwell's vandals and who was rejoicing in a return to the good life. I liked the memorials to various members of the family and the elaborate tombs in the graveyard in that section set aside for the Ashingtons.

It was a feeling of belonging which I understood my mother could not share. She was not of the family as I was. Moreover she was regarded as an intruder and not a welcome one.

I was introduced to the family at the vicarage – the Reverend Peter Cannon and his three rather tall, gaunt-looking daughters all in their thirties, spinsters whom marriage had passed by and who now dedicated themselves to the work of the parish. I liked his surprisingly pretty and vivacious wife, who seemed to regard her daughters with faint astonishment as though wondering how she ever produced offspring so unlike herself. They lunched with us every other Sunday. They were interested in me and had plans for drawing me into certain activities. My mother they treated with great politeness but with a certain reserve as though they were expecting her to act in an odd manner. They sensed at once that she was not their type and they gave no hint that they knew about her connection with Everard, but whether this was due to their excessive good manners or ignorance I did not know.

I was becoming amused by the aunts. Their passion for detail amazed me. I knew that Aunt Martha could not bear anything to be out of place. If she saw that an ornament was not precisely where it should be, she could not rest until she had put it right. Orderliness was the theme of her life. She arranged flowers so that they looked like soldiers on parade. Meals were served at the exact appointed time and to be a minute overdue was to be late. The Grange was kept in meticulous order inside and out and I soon became aware that her greatest concern was that on the death of herself and Mabel it should pass into the right hands.

It was clear that she wanted my mother to go back to my father and produce a son. That was the only thing which would satisfy her. Divorce was out of the question, for she believed in the sanctity of marriage and once a man had married a woman they remained married until death parted them.

I knew what my mother meant when she said she would look up and find Martha's eyes on her speculatively. I had seen a certain glint in Martha's eyes. It was truly as though she were making plans for my mother.

What plans could they be but to get her back to my father? Either that or that she died . . .

A horrible thought! It was my mother's comment that she gave her 'the creeps' that had set that train of thought in motion.

'Well,' I said, answering her, 'we're here so we might as well make the best of it.'

'I believe you want to stay here. When Tom comes I shall have to go to town. Perhaps it would be better if you stayed.'

'You know there's all this talk about a governess . . .'

'Yes. A lot of nonsense.'

'Perhaps not. I don't want to be ignorant. Perhaps if you did get a part I should have to stay here . . .'

'I could get a place in London or stay at an hotel.'

'I would visit you there. Come on the first night . . . !'

'Oh, won't it be wonderful. Perhaps this time next year we shall be looking back on all this as though it was a bad dream.'

We walked together arm in arm crunching the leaves under our feet.

'It's beautiful in the forest,' said my mother. 'What's that strange smell?'

'It's the pines, I think.'

'I like it,' said my mother.

It was wonderful to see her in such good spirits.

When we returned to the house Aunt Mabel met us in the hall. 'We have engaged the governess,' she said.

Her name was Celia Hansen. She had come down for an interview from the Midlands and was to start her duties the following week. There was no point in delay, said Aunt Martha.

Both she and Mabel were enthusiastic about the governess.

That she was a woman of good family was obvious. She had excellent references – one from a titled woman who was, she frankly admitted, a friend, for it was impossible to get one from a past employer simply because there was no past employer. Celia Hansen's story was not an unusual one. She had been brought up to presume she would never be called on to earn a living; her parents had died suddenly and she was alone in the world. When the family debts were settled she had only the smallest of incomes and the house in which she had lived had passed to a cousin. She could have stayed on as a kind of poor relation, but being a woman of spirit, she preferred to be independent of others.

'Very commendable,' said Aunt Martha.

'Showing a strong character,' echoed Aunt Mabel.

They were both pleased with her.

I was full of curiosity to see her and on the following Monday afternoon watched her arrival from my window. The brougham had been sent to the station to fetch her and the wagonette would collect her luggage later.

She alighted from the brougham and stood for a moment looking up at the house. I drew back, not wanting to be caught peeping, but not before I had seen a rather long palish face and smooth brown hair drawn down at the sides of her face to finish in a knob at the back. She was dressed in black – neat and without much concession to fashion.

I knew that very soon the summons would come for me to meet her and it did.

I went to the drawing-room. She was seated on one of the tall-backed chairs – very upright, her gloved hands folded in her lap.

Aunt Martha was smiling quite pleasantly and so was Mabel.

'Ah, Sarah, this is Miss Hansen. Miss Hansen, your pupil.'

She stood up and came towards me. She was of average height. The word average suited her. I thought in that moment that there must be thousands of impoverished gentlewomen all over England, no longer in their first youth, who looked just like Celia Hansen.

She held out her hand and I took it.

'How do you do?' Her voice was low and cultured. I could see why she had made such an impression on the aunts. 'A lady!' as they said approvingly.

'I hope you are going to find me a good pupil and that we shall work well together,' I said.

She smiled – a sort of half smile. It was a lifting of the lips but her eyes did not change. I noticed those eyes then – large, light brown and slightly protruding. There was a fixed look about them. Afterwards it occurred to me that they never expressed anything, but they did bring something unusual to her face which was really the only outstanding thing about her.

'I am sure we shall,' she answered.

'Jennings will show you to your room,' said Aunt Martha, 'and when you have rested . . . do you need to rest?'

Miss Hansen said she did not wish to rest. If she might wash her hands and perhaps change from her travelling clothes . . .

Aunt Martha clearly approved. 'Then,' she said, 'Sarah can come to you in shall we say an hour? And she can show you the room where you will work.'

Jennings was summoned and Miss Hansen followed her out.

'Which is her room?' I asked when the door closed.

'It is on the third floor . . . at the end of the corridor where your mother has her room. It is next to the schoolroom. I really think we have chosen wisely.'

'She is obviously a girl of breeding,' said Mabel. 'There are many like her . . . nowadays. They are brought up to expect a life of comfort and then find they have to earn a living . . .'

Aunt Martha's expression was self-congratulatory. I had noticed that look on her face before when something she had planned had been achieved.

Before going to collect Celia Hansen I went to the schoolroom. A faint smell of polish hung on the air. It looked like a schoolroom. There was a large window at one end and heavy dark red serge curtains at them; there was a big fireplace with a marble mantelpiece on which stood a plain carriage-type clock. There were pictured round the room scenes from the Bible. Moses in the bulrushes, Moses striking the rock, Rachel at the well, Jacob's dream, and Lot's wife looking back and being turned into a pillar of salt. The Old Testament on one side of the room and the New on the other. Cleansing the temple, Jesus at the well. Jesus walking on the water and feeding the five thousand.

There were several cupboards and a long table rather scratched and ink-stained with a bench on one side and a high dignified chair at the head of it, presumably for the teacher. And there were several high-backed chairs about the room. A typical schoolroom, I thought. Here, Margaret had taken her lessons while her sisters were at school. I wondered what *her* governess had been like and whether she had confided in her.

She must have been rapturously happy when Edward Sanderton came to the house, but of course her happiness would be tinged with sadness for she had achieved it at the expense of her sister's. And what a sister! I was sure Martha had been almost as formidable when a young woman as she was now; she would have been something of a terror to a delicate young girl, I was sure.

I pictured Margaret at the table, her beautiful hair falling about her shoulders, telling her governess that she had fallen in love. I could see her face so clearly, sloping shoulders with blue chiffon slipping from them. I thought of the gallery at dusk with shadows falling through the long windows and Margaret stepping from her frame to search for her lover. A rather charming fantasy. I wondered whether she haunted the schoolroom as well as the gallery.

I was standing by the voluminous red curtains when I heard footsteps coming upstairs and along the corridor. I suppose it was because I had been thinking of Margaret that my heart started to hammer against my bodice. It was a strange feeling. The footsteps were slow, laborious, almost as though whoever was making them was finding difficulty in walking. I stared at the door. The handle moved. The door flew open and no one came in. Instinctively I shrank against the curtains. Then I was laughing at myself. Ellen, one of the maids, had entered, and she had walked so slowly because she was carrying a big brown bowl in which chrysanthemums had been arranged. It must have been heavy because it was earthenware.

As she staggered to the table I moved out into the room. She turned with a scream and the bowl fell from her hands. Her face was white, her eyes round with horror.

'Ellen!' I cried. 'What's the matter?'

She continued to stare at me and as she recognized me the colour returned to her face which became scarlet. 'I thought . . .' she stammered. 'Oh, my patience me, I thought you was the ghost, Miss Sarah.'

I laughed but reminded myself that a few moments before I had been shrinking uneasily into the curtains.

'Cook says she might come in here . . . because he first saw her in the schoolroom . . . so Cook says. I dunno, Miss Sarah, but you could have been her. You've got a look of her, Cook says so . . .'

'That's not surprising,' I said. 'If you are referring to Miss Margaret, she was my aunt. Come on, Ellen, we'd better clear this up.'

'There'll be trouble, Miss. Look. I've broke the big brown bowl.'

'I'll tell them it was my fault.'

'Oh, would you, Miss. It *was* you that sort of startled me.'

I laid my hand on her shoulder. She was still trembling.

'I never like coming in here alone,' she confessed. 'And it's a funny afternoon . . . sort of dark so it seems like there's a storm blowing up. I'd rather come here than go to the gallery though . . . but I don't like coming here much either.'

'Run and get an ashpan,' I said. 'And something to mop up the water. Bring a vase and we'll put the flowers in it. I suppose they're to make it look cheerful for the new governess.'

'Mistress said to put them there. The new governess, she says, is a real lady. A lot of them governesses are, Miss. Come down in the world, that's them.'

'That's right. Now get what I told you and in a short time we'll have everything cleared up and ready for this lady.'

She went off cheered because I wasn't a ghost and was going to take the blame for the broken bowl.

As I waited for her I thought how strange it was that the memory of Margaret lingered on after all these years. It was almost as though there was a mystery about her death.

Soon Ellen was back. She cleared up the mess while I arranged the flowers. I set them in the middle of the table.

'There,' I said. 'Doesn't that look more cheerful?'

She looked round the room. I could see that to her it was a haunted room. No amount of flowers could change that.

Celia Hansen was obviously eager to please. Sometimes, so perfectly did she behave, that I thought she must have rehearsed what she said and did. She was determined not to upset the servants and managed to be pleasant without being familiar, which was not always easy. A governess's position in a household could be a very difficult one, she pointed out to me later. One was not one of the servant class; on the other hand, by nature of one's employment one could not expect to be treated as a member of the family. She need not have worried. Aunt Martha had clearly taken to her. *She* had had the idea of employing a governess and *she* had chosen Celia Hansen. Therefore the coming of Celia into the household must be a good thing. There was a great deal to be said for such a philosophy. She could scarcely have applied that judgment to her action in bringing Edward Sanderton into the house. But that was far in the past and Aunt Martha was not one to dwell on failures. Mabel, of course, agreed that Celia was an asset to the household; she solved the problem of my education and was quite self-effacing and grateful – in fact everything that was admirable in the circumstances.

What surprised me most was Celia's friendship with my mother. There was no doubt that they took to each other. Celia proved to be quite knowledgeable about the theatre and told my mother that on one never-to-be-forgotten occasion she had gone to the theatre where my mother was playing.

Celia could describe the play in detail and my mother's part in it. My mother was rapturous. I had not seen her so happy for a long time.

I was the one who perhaps held aloof. I felt mildly resentful about having a governess at my age. Perhaps I remembered those erratic lessons with Toby which, looking back, I realized had been such a joy. Being governessed by Celia Hansen held none of the excitement of those other lessons.

We were a little wary of each other. She must have been over thirty, which seemed to me quite old. Sometimes I thought she looked older – sometimes younger. She was so different from myself. I was impulsive. I had the impression that Celia weighed her words very carefully before she uttered them and that she watched the effect they had on people. I fancied her personality changed a little according to the people she was with. With the aunts she was a model of decorum; she showed just enough gratitude to let them know that she never forgot how glad she was to be in their house, but she never obscured the fact that she had been brought up as they had themselves. Nothing could have delighted Aunt Martha more. I probed the servants to find out what they thought of her. 'A lady . . . oh, a lady,' said Ellen. 'She don't make no nuisance of herself. Cook says some of them governesses give themselves airs. Well, Miss Hansen's got airs in a way . . . but natural ones, if you know what I mean. Oh, they like her all right.'

So she was a success. I wished she would be a little less restrained. I wished she would not come so quietly into the room so that I was not always aware that she was there until I looked up and saw her. Those strange saucer eyes of hers disconcerted me too. There was a certain blankness about them, so that it was impossible to fathom what lay behind them. They never seemed to smile. They matched her manner in a way. Then I learned that she was afraid of me, and after that I felt differently towards her.

We were in the schoolroom reading *Hamlet* together. She had worked out some sort of curriculum, for she was very conscientious. She was to teach me mathematics, French and English grammar and we studied English literature. There was also needlework and what was called Art, which consisted of painting in water-colours – usually a vase of flowers or a bowl of fruit. She was an excellent needlewoman and painted far better than I could. She was strong in mathematics and could quickly solve those problems about trains travelling in opposite directions and how old children were when their aggregate age was so much and one was so many years older than the other and so on. I had always hated such problems as I could never care about the speed of trains nor the ages of non-existent children. But as far as English and French were concerned in any form – particularly literature – I should have been more able to teach her than she was me.

This soon became obvious and it was particularly so when we were studying *Hamlet*. I had always loved it. I knew lines off by heart. Toby and I had discussed it at length.

I found myself getting more and more involved in discussion with Celia and it was clear that she was getting completely out of her depth. Her hands were lying on the table, and I noticed that they were trembling. She hid them in her lap. She seemed to come to a decision.

'I'm not qualified to teach you,' she said. 'I've only had a very ordinary education. I might teach young children . . .' The saucer eyes looked straight into mine unblinkingly but the lips were quivering. She was clearly frightened.

She went on: 'I thought I was fortunate. Everything seemed to be working out so well. Your aunts were so kind to me and I was so proud to meet your mother. But I can see that you consider I am not fit to teach you. You will speak to your aunts and then . . .'

I was silent for a moment. I was so disturbed by the sudden breakdown of that calm façade. This quiet, restrained, poised lady was really a frightened woman who saw a bleak future before her. Those large eyes surveyed me, as expressionless as ever.

'Can you imagine the position I find myself in?' she went on. 'I have been brought up in a house . . . like this one. I never thought my life would change so much. It was all so sudden. When my parents died I had to meet all the debts, which thankfully I did, though it left me penniless. It seemed this was the only thing I could do. I saw the advertisement. I answered it and your aunts were so kind, and so was everyone here. I thought it was a respite, and I could have a few years here and perhaps plan something for the future. But I am not really qualified to teach. I shall have to try to find something else . . . some place where there are children. I should perhaps be good enough for that. It seems that I have come here under false pretences.'

'Wait a minute,' I cried. 'You're taking too much for granted. Who said I was going to tell Aunt Martha that you were not qualified to teach me French and English? *I* didn't. You assumed that. It's true I've always felt I was too old to have a governess . . .'

'I know that and you resent my presence here for that reason.'

'I don't resent you personally. Only the idea that I am a child who must have a governess. I can understand how you feel. In fact it could so easily have happened to me. If the aunts had not come along and brought us here I should probably be in some house trying to earn a living. So I understand how you feel. You are good with figures and far, far better at needlework and sketching. I don't see why you shouldn't teach me these things. As for French, we'll do a bit of that together and I always enjoy discussing literature with anyone. So I don't see why we shouldn't do our lessons quite well together. Cheer up, Miss Hansen. There's no need for you to worry. Stay here until you've decided what you can do. Aunt Martha approves of you and I can tell you that to win the approval of such a lady is a feat of extraordinary magnitude.'

The lips were smiling at me; her eyes seemed to have become more luminous, but their expression did not alter.

From then on we became friends. She was grateful to me for not betraying her and I felt a glow of self-righteousness. I began to like her as one does people for whom one has done a good turn.

So we settled down very comfortably and within a month Celia had become like a member of the family.

Aunt Martha decreed that Celia should have her meals with us for it was absurd for her to have hers on a tray in her room and she could hardly go to the servants' hall. We began to call her by her Christian name and she went to church with us. The Cannon girls persuaded her to join in ecclesiastical activities and she was quite an asset. She embroidered a tray cloth and made a few tea-cosies for the sale of work and was very helpful dispensing tea from the great urn at one penny per cup.

I was aware on occasions of a certain uneasiness in the house and when this occurred to me I used to go to the gallery and look at the picture of Margaret and at those ladies who wore the pearls about their necks.

I wondered what was happening to the Ashington Pearls now. They were in my father's possession, I supposed. They passed to the son of the family and through him to his wife and then to the wife of the eldest son. But what if there was no son? I wanted to ask what was happening to the pearls now. Perhaps Mabel would be the one to tell me.

What was it that was worrying me? Aunt Martha perhaps. There was something purposeful about her as though she were planning something. Then there was my mother. She was still waiting for the day when Tom Mellor would arrive with the play that was going to put her at the top of her profession again. The coming of Celia had had its effect on her. Sometimes I thought that was good, and at others I was not quite so sure. Celia talked a great deal to my mother. They used to have tea in my mother's room. She had a spirit lamp which she had used in the theatre, for she had always liked a cup of tea at odd times. Meg used to complain about it. 'Tea! Tea! In the middle of the night she'll get a craving for a cup of tea.' I remembered that spirit lamp well.

Sometimes I joined them. I had seen my mother quite animated, telling Celia about her various parts and often acting some of them for her benefit. It was good to see her enjoying herself, but afterwards she would descend to depression, which would be the greater for the momentary excitement.

I wondered whether Celia had heard of my mother's involvement with Everard Herringford and the subsequent tragedy.

There was no doubt that she knew a great deal about my mother's theatrical past. I tackled her on this one day when we were walking in the forest.

I began by saying that my mother was delighted that she was so interested in the theatre. I said tentatively: 'Did you hear about her last play?'

'The one which ran for such a short time?'

So she did know.

'It was such a pity,' she said. 'I hate to think of her here . . . wasting all that talent.'

'It was rather difficult for her . . .' I began.

She had walked a little ahead of me. She seemed nervous. Then she turned to me and said: 'I read about it in the papers . . . about the man who killed himself . . . that politician. It was awful for her. I was so sorry for her.'

'So you did know.'

'Very little. It was mentioned in our local paper and having seen her on stage, I remembered. Is it true that whatever happened ruined her career?'

'Yes,' I said, 'it did.'

'How tragic!'

'You must have been very surprised when you came here and found that she was here. Or did you remember the name . . .'

'The name?' she expressed surprise with a movement of her lips. 'Oh . . . Ashington. I don't think I heard that name before. She was always called Irene Rushton, wasn't she? No, I never heard of Ashington so it was a great surprise to find her here. I could not believe it at first.'

'You're good for her,' I said. 'She had so much adulation . . . and to find one of her admirers here is wonderful for her.'

'I like to talk to her of the theatre. It interests me.'

I had been right when I thought Aunt Martha was planning something. I learned what it was from my mother. It was the end of November, quite warm but damp and misty and my mother had one of her colds. They were becoming more and more frequent.

She stayed in bed one day and I went to her room to make tea on the spirit lamp. Celia was at the church discussing the children's Christmas party which would take place on the twentieth of the next month but which entailed weeks of preparation.

My mother was in one of her moods of depression.

'I hate this house more every day,' she said as I handed her her tea.

I sat down beside the bed and sipped my own. There was nothing unusual in that comment. I had heard it a hundred times before.

'Martha's planning something,' she went on. 'I tell you, Siddons, she really does give me the creeps.'

'You have said so before.'

'I remember when I came here with your father. She was always wondering whether I was pregnant. If you had been a boy all would have been well. You would get their wretched pearls and a wife to wear them. They'd be marrying you off already. Then watching to see when the boy was coming along. But your father let them down. He had betrayed the family. Two unsatisfactory marriages and not an Ashington boy from one of them. Martha's a woman with an obsession. Who is going to get those pearls? The way things are going it won't be someone named Ashington. It's like a comedy. But Martha doesn't fit into comedy.' My mother handed me her cup and when I had put it down and returned to her bedside she gripped my hand. 'Something's brewing, Siddons. She has plans.'

'What sort of plans?'

'They concern me. I know it. I see her eyes fixed on me. She's planning to get your father and me together somehow. Either he's got to come home or I've got to go out there. She's got to get us together so that we can do what she discreetly called "our duty". We've got to get a son so that he can inherit the pearls. How is she going to do it?'

'Perhaps my father will come home.' I was excited at the thought. To have been brought here and introduced to a family (although mostly in a portrait gallery) had excited and stimulated me. I longed more than anything to see my father.

'He would never be governed by his sisters. He won't come. He hasn't been back all these years. Why should he come now? I think she will realize she can't get him back and she's now trying to ship me out there. That's her plan. She wants to get rid of me.'

'Would you . . . go?'

'I hated the place. I hated it more than I hate this. At least here I'm not so far from London and Tom knows where to find me.'

I felt sick with pity. Was she still hoping Tom Mellor would come along with that play! She had grown thin . . . unnaturally so, and I knew that the pearly glow of her skin, which had been so appealing when natural, was now acquired painstakingly and fell short of its previous perfection.

'Has she suggested you go?' I asked.

'Hinted. We should be living what she calls a normal married life. Desperately she wants that Ashington boy. She forgets that even if I did meet your father that would do nothing to further her plans. You can take a horse to the water but you can't make it drink.'

'Well, you won't go to Ceylon and he won't come to England, so there is nothing Aunt Martha can do.'

'Sometimes I think when she looks at me she is wondering if there is some way she can make me disappear.'

'Disappear!'

'Off the face of the Earth.'

'You are dramatizing again!'

She looked at me earnestly. 'No, I'm not, Siddons. I'm an encumbrance and Martha doesn't like encumbrances. When they exist she is the sort of woman who will seek a way of getting rid of them.'

'I don't know what you mean.'

'I don't like this house. Sometimes I think I'm being warned. It's eerie. Don't you feel it?'

'It's this talk about ghosts. Margaret in the gallery and all that.'

'It's people's thoughts that can make that feeling. If someone's there plotting something . . .'

'You've acted in too many plays. They get mixed up with real life.'

'The fact remains,' said my mother, 'that if I were out of the way your father could marry again, couldn't he? Perhaps then he'd be lucky and get a son.'

'Don't talk such nonsense. You're not out of the way as you call it. You're here and here you are going to stay. You've got me to look after you, haven't you?'

She smiled at me fondly. 'Dear Siddons,' she said. 'Always a comfort. I can't tell you what a relief it is that you are with me in this strange house of shadows.'

I got up and poured more tea before she grew maudlin, yet at the same time I felt uneasy. There *was* something in the house, something eerie, something warning.

Christmas was approaching and I suggested we decorate the house with holly and ivy. I wondered what a Christmas would be like at the Grange. I did know that two blankets and a goose were presented to each household in the village from the big house and that that was a custom which had gone on for years. I learned that we attended the midnight service on Christmas Eve and another on Christmas morning, that the carol singers called on Christmas Eve and that the vicarage family and the doctor and his wife came to sup with us on the evening of Christmas Day. Dinner was served at midday so that the servants could have the evening to themselves. I supposed that Christmases had gone on like that for years.

Celia and I rode now and then together. The aunts had graciously allowed her to use one of the horses from the stable, which showed how highly they regarded her. I had always enjoyed riding and it was pleasant to have a companion. We were both busy decorating the church for Christmas and our own hall where the children's party was held. The weather turned very cold and the Cannon girls said they were hoping for a white Christmas. Last year there had been skating on the ponds, they told us.

My mother grew even more fretful and talked of other Christmases and she referred bitterly to that one when Tom had persuaded her to take part in pantomime. It had been a great mistake.

The snow held off until Twelfth Night, but the wind was blowing strongly from the east and it was bitterly cold. My mother had always hated wintry weather and she went down with one of her colds. Celia and I persuaded her to stay in bed, which she did readily enough.

The cold left her with a cough which persisted through January. The snow had come and the countryside was blanketed in white. The forest had become an enchanted place, something out of Grimms' fairy tales. I would put on heavy boots and go for long walks. Celia came with me. We liked to stop at an inn called The Foresters and eat a hot pie and drink a mug of cider.

I remember well the day Celia spoke of my mother. She looked very grave as she said: 'I think she is more ill than you realize. She has another cold coming on. It's so soon after the other.'

'She does have these bad colds,' I said.

'She is so unhappy here,' replied Celia quietly.

'She was unhappy in London. Everything went wrong for her after the tragedy. If she could have gone on acting she might have recovered.'

Celia nodded. 'Do you think she should have a doctor?'

'She doesn't want one. I think we should wait awhile. She just has a cold.'

'You would know best,' said Celia.

She was more pensive than usual as we went back to the house.

I thought how good she was, for there was no doubt that she was deeply concerned about my mother. I was grateful to her because I often escaped from my mother knowing that Celia was with her. Escaped seems a strange word, but I have to confess that I was a little weary of my mother's perpetual sighing for the past and her inability to make the best of the present. I found her company more and more depressing and I realized with relief that Celia was able to comfort her better than I could. Celia genuinely admired her and could give her some of that adulation for which she craved. I could then, with a good conscience, go to the library and read for hours; and sometimes I would take a book to the gallery. I loved being there among my ancestors and I would study the painted pearls and make up stories about them. These sessions in the gallery brought me a certain satisfaction. We were a romantic family – most of all my father and my mysterious half-sister whom I had never seen.

It was the last day of January. I remembered the occasion for a long time afterwards. My mother had not improved and on Celia's advice I had suggested we ask the doctor to look at her. Dr Berryman, that friend of the family who, with his wife, often sat at our table, diagnosed a touch of bronchitis and said she should stay in bed. She must get rid of the cough which was becoming persistent.

'Stay in bed until the cough goes,' was his advice. 'And above all keep warm.' He looked at the fire which Ellen had lighted and nodded with approval.

Aunt Martha said: 'Her trouble is that she won't make an effort. Give her the footlights and she'd be dancing for joy and forgetting all about illness.'

There was something in that; but she would have had to recover from bronchitis first.

The next morning a letter arrived from my father, and Aunt Martha solemnly called me to the drawing-room to hear about it.

'It is most disappointing,' she said. 'He will not come home. It would have been most satisfactory if he had. Then there might have been a reconciliation.'

'Oh, Aunt Martha, it is too long. You can't have a reconciliation after fifteen years, just because it would be convenient.'

'I am sure it could have been arranged,' said Aunt Martha, implying that with her all things were possible. 'If only we could get him to come home!'

'It wouldn't make any difference to them if he did,' I said.

Aunt Martha's lips were pressed firmly together. It must be galling for her, I thought, to know exactly what should be done and to be foiled in her attempts. And the fact because it was chiefly about two strings of pearls made me want to laugh at the absurdity to which people's pride would lead them.

'He expresses great pleasure that you are here under our care,' she went on. 'I told him that at least he should come home and see you.'

'He really said he was pleased I was here?'

'Oh yes. He knows you will be properly looked after. He has written to you. In fact I have the letter here.'

I seized it eagerly. I could not wait to read it yet I did not want to do so under Aunt Martha's eyes. The thought occurred to me that she might have steamed open the envelope and read it since it had not been given to me immediately. But I was not sure. Some people regarded honour as a quality that should be adhered to most rigidly; but for people of strong purpose the code could be bent a little to suit their purpose. I was beginning to have strange thoughts about Aunt Martha. My mother's dislike of her, almost amounting to a fear, must have put them into my head.

At last I escaped and took the letter to my room. My hands were trembling as I opened it. It was written in a large rather sprawling hand, not always easy to read.

My dear daughter Sarah,

It is a great pleasure to write to you at last. I doubt that you remember me. I remember you vividly. I was heartbroken when your mother took you away. These things will happen, however, and as she could not settle to the life out here, perhaps she was right to leave it. I have learned from my sisters that you are now with them – your mother also. I am sure you will be happy at Ashington Grange. After all, it is the family home. I plant tea out here. It is a job which demands constant attention. That is why I am tied here. Your aunts want me to return but that is impossible just now. Perhaps one day you will come and pay me a visit. In the meantime I should like to hear from you, Sarah. Write to me and let me know that you have some interest in your father.

Ralph Ashington.

I was excited. I was no longer without a father. I would write to him and we should know each other through our letters. I could ask about my sister.

As I sat there with the letter in my hand there was a knock on the door and Aunt Martha came in. Her sharp eyes studied me intently.

'Well?' she said.

I felt the colour flame into my cheeks. I was not going to show her my father's letter. In any case the suspicion that she had already read it persisted.

'So he has written to you at last,' she said. 'He could have done so before.'

'It's a friendly letter.'

She laughed on a high note of derision. 'One would expect a father to be friendly towards his daughter. He should come home. *I* have told him he should, often.'

'He has the plantation.'

'He should be leading a normal life.'

'Aunt Martha, I'm worried about my mother.'

'I think you should not worry too much. Your mother is a woman who enjoys her ill health.'

'I don't think that is so. You should have seen her when she was working. She was always so high-spirited. The last thing she wanted was to be ill.'

'That's what I imply. There, attention was focused on her. Here she has to try and attract attention so she does it by having everyone dance attendance on her.'

'She coughs a great deal.'

'Fresh air would do her good. It's intolerable that Ralph will not come home.'

With her lips tightly pressed together I thought she looked like one of the strong women of the past. Boadicea riding against the Romans, Elizabeth at Tilbury, the sort of woman who says 'It shall be!' and makes sure it is.

'Perhaps he will one day.'

She shook her head. 'I know him well. I read something in his letters. He does not want to come back. It would be too complicated. He would meet your mother and have to come to some decision. Your father always hated making decisions. He was always a drifter.' She looked angry. 'Everything drifts along until it is too late.'

'Too late for what, Aunt?' I asked.

She did not answer but shook her head impatiently.

'I do believe my mother is more ill than we realize,' I said earnestly. 'I have seen a great change in her.'

Then she said a strange thing which later I saw as an indication of the way in which her mind was working. 'Creaking doors go on creaking for a long time,' she said.

It occurred to me then that she was thinking that if my mother died, my father could remarry and perhaps have a son.

I thrust the thought from my mind as soon as it came. I could not bear to think of my mother . . . dead.

At dinner that evening – the aunts, Celia and myself – we talked of the weather, which showed little sign of improving, and the effect it was having on everything; we talked of the new curate who was coming to help the vicar, the thought of which made Aunt Martha's nose twitch with amusement.

'I dare say the Cannon girls are all agog,' she commented. 'Who knows, one of them might succeed in capturing him. A curate. Not much of a catch. But what can they hope for, poor things?'

'It will be interesting to see the contest,' put in Mabel.

Celia was silent, her eyes cast down. I wondered if she had ever thought of marrying and what her reaction would be if she had the opportunity of doing so.

She spoke frankly about herself now and then. I had heard of the house in the country – a manor house rather like the Grange, the father who had had an accident on the hunting field, I gathered; the mother who had died soon after, the cousin who had inherited the estate and of whom she spoke little, presumably because it was a painful subject. Then there was the governess who had brought her to London to see my mother in one of her plays. She did speak affectionately of the governess, who seemed to have been her greatest friend. One could not probe too deeply, so I had to wait for her to tell me these things.

Aunt Martha said suddenly: 'And how is our invalid?' During the last days she had begun to refer to my mother as 'our invalid'.

'She is a little better,' I replied.

'Not well enough to join us for dinner obviously,' said Mabel.

'Oh no. She is still weak. This bout has taken it out of her considerably.'

'Let a glass of my elderberry wine be sent up with her tray,' said Aunt Martha. 'Who takes the tray?'

'I shall,' said Celia. 'Unless you want to, Sarah?'

'She likes you to take it and chat with her about the theatre while she eats,' I replied.

'The wine was very good this year, Martha,' said Mabel. 'More potent than usual. It makes me feel quite sleepy.'

'It will do our invalid good,' said Aunt Martha.

Celia took the tray to my mother and I went in while she was eating and we all talked together. I had not told her yet that I had heard from my father because I felt it might upset her.

She was soon sleeping so we took the tray away and left her.

In the morning she was not so well. Her cough had worsened

and she had a slight fever. The doctor came and said we must be sure to keep her warm. Let her be propped up with pillows; that would help her breathing; he prescribed some cough mixture which Celia went to collect and during the afternoon she had clearly improved. She dozed a great deal during the afternoon, but the next morning she had weakened considerably and the fever had increased.

Celia was clearly worried and thought we ought not to leave her too long, so we took turns to be with her.

When I was alone with her she suddenly opened her eyes and looked at me in a rather hazy fashion.

'Is that you, Siddons?' she said. 'I'm frightened.'

'It's all right,' I soothed. 'I'm here. There's nothing to be frightened of.'

'There *is* something . . . someone . . . It's in the night. It was there . . . I saw it. It wasn't . . . natural. I opened my eyes . . . It was not quite dark. There was a little moonlight . . . I saw it. It was by the bed. It was watching me . . . a grey-clad figure. Then it moved away . . . faded away. I was cold . . . so cold . . .'

'It was a dream,' I said.

She nodded. 'Yes, a dream. It was like that scene in *The Spectre of the East Wing*. Do you remember, Siddons? I played the lady of the house and the spectre was really someone who was planning to murder me.'

I smoothed her hair back from her brow.

'You were just dreaming of the past,' I said. 'There are no spectres here. I am not far away and Celia is just along the corridor.'

'Celia is a good girl,' she murmured. 'Yes, I'm glad she's near. Siddons, I don't like Martha. I'm afraid of her. I've got a feeling she wants me out of the way.'

'You're getting fanciful again. Celia's going to bring you some nice gruel and one of us will stay and sit with you. All you have to do is rest and keep warm and you'll be well in no time at all.'

She took her gruel and was soon asleep. The doctor came in the morning and I told him about the dream or whatever it was.

'It's a result of her fever,' he said. 'Her temperature's far too high. Keep her warm and with some good nourishment she'll be herself in a week or so. She's had too many of these colds and this is a particularly bad one.'

Celia went to get new medicine for her that afternoon and when she came back she told us that the doctor had said my mother should have a dose last thing at night because it would help her to sleep and what she needed more than anything was restful sleep.

I was very uneasy about her. There was a change in her – a certain wildness in her eyes . . . a fear. She *was* afraid. That hallucination of the grey-clad figure in her room might be something from her imagination, but it was something put there by fear. There had been talk about ghosts as there usually was in ancient houses and this must have lodged itself in her mind and come out in this form. But there was real fear somewhere. When I thought of the gay creature she had once been I was very depressed and anxious.

I could not sleep that night. I wished my room were in her corridor. Celia was there, of course, and had promised to keep an eye on her. That was a comfort. I promised myself that if she did not get any better I would sleep in her room.

So I lay awake. The moonlight was enough to show me the outline of the furniture in my room and being sleepless I began to think about the past and the excitement of the theatrical life, of Toby's taking me to the Café Royal for lunch and meeting my mother there with one of her countless adorers. How different she had looked then from the poor depressed woman in the bed upstairs. Who would have believed anyone could change so much. Change everywhere! Everard, suave, masterful, handsome Everard, dead by his own hand. My mother, the beautiful sought-after actress, a frightened woman dependent upon her husband's relatives. Cruel change! And for me change too. Here I was living in the house of my ancestors, and my father had become a real person through a letter and we were going to write and get to know each other. Perhaps one day I should see him. He would come here or I would go to his tea plantation . . .

A sudden sound from above! Was it? Or had I imagined it? Boards creaked alarmingly in old houses. I sat up in bed listening. Silence. I could hear my own heart beating. Go to sleep, I told myself scornfully. Your imagination is overworking again.

I lay still, listening. A sound, yes, an indefinable sound . . . and up there my mother was sleeping.

I got out of bed and put on my slippers and dressing-gown. I opened my door and listened. Could that really be the sound of stealthy steps?

I looked at the clock by the bedside. I could just make out the time. Half past two. I must have dozed and not realized it.

I closed my door quietly and went swiftly upstairs. I had not brought a candle with me but there was just enough light to show me the way and I knew it well.

I came to the corridor and as I did so I thought I saw the school-room door close. The schoolroom door! I remembered how Ellen had dropped the vase of flowers. The servants were almost as much afraid of the schoolroom as the gallery.

I went quickly to my mother's room and as I opened the door a blast of cold air struck me so forcibly in the face that I gasped. The lattice window was wide open and the wind cut into me like a knife; the fire was completely out and there was a tell-tale trickle of water on the hearth.

My mother was lying on the bed, the bedclothes pulled right back. I went to her. She was icily cold. Then I ran to the window and shut it. I pulled the bedclothes up about my mother. Her skin was deathly cold. She opened her eyes and said: 'Where am I?'

'You're all right now,' I said. 'I'm here.'

Someone was outside the door. It moved slowly and I felt the coldness gripping my body. I was terrified in that split second. My mind was numb and I could not think what horror was about to confront me.

I gasped with relief. Celia was standing there, her feet in slippers, a dressing-gown obviously hastily wrapped about her.

'Sarah!' she cried in astonishment.

'Look!' I cried. 'I found this.'

She shivered and stared at me in disbelief.

'The window wide open,' I said. 'The clothes off the bed. I think even the fire was doused.'

She could only stare blankly at me. Then she said: 'We must do something. Cover her up well. Use that fur rug. We must get her warm quickly. We need hot-water bottles. I'll go down to the kitchen and get them. Make up the fire. Oh, Sarah, we must get her warm . . . quickly.'

She ran to one of the cupboards in the corridor in which blankets were kept. She threw them into my arms and I went back to the bedroom and covered up my mother. I held her in my arms and as the warmth of my body passed to hers she ceased to shiver. Then I went to the fire and tried to stir it up, but it was too dead so I hastily threw on wood and coal and relit it. Celia came back with hot-water bottles and set them in the bed.

Within half an hour the temperature of the room had risen and we took off the fur rug for my mother was then warm. She was murmuring in uneasy sleep.

I tried to hear what she was saying. 'Cold,' I heard. 'It is cold as charity . . . cold as death . . .'

I believed it was a line from one of her plays.

Celia's face was nipped with the cold and I was sure mine was the same.

'I can scarcely feel my hands,' I said.

'Nor I.'

'Do you think she's all right now?'

'She's sleeping quietly.'

'Celia . . . what did it mean?'

'I'm trying to think what it could. Shall I make some tea on the spirit lamp? We need something to warm us up.'

We both knew that neither of us could sleep so it seemed a good idea. She made the tea and we wrapped ourselves in blankets and went into the schoolroom to drink it.

'Celia,' I said, 'someone did that deliberately. Why?'

I did not say Aunt Martha but it was of Aunt Martha that I was thinking. Aunt Martha wanted her out of the way. Had she killed Margaret too, that sister who had taken her lover? I could imagine her reasoning with God. It is better for this useless woman to die so that Ralph can remarry and get an heir. And in the case of Margaret? I will make him a better wife than she will. It is in a righteous cause.

No, it was preposterous. Aunt Martha going to the family pew every Sunday, joining in the responses in her rather deep masculine voice, singing the hymns with gusto. 'Onward, Christian Soldiers'. Yes, that was Aunt Martha fighting a just war for the good of mankind in general and the Ashingtons in particular. She must be mad.

Yes, there was madness in the house this night.

Celia said: 'Thank God you came up when you did. What made you?'

'I couldn't sleep. Some instinct perhaps. Then I thought I heard noises. So I came to look.'

'Thank God,' murmured Celia again softly. 'Had it stayed like that . . . with the window open and that fierce cold wind blowing in . . . that would have been the end of her.'

'It's murder!' I cried. 'It's just as bad as taking a gun and shooting somebody or thrusting a knife into the heart.'

'Murder!' Celia set down her cup and stared at me. 'Sarah, what do you mean?'

'Someone opened the windows . . . someone doused the fire . . . someone uncovered her.'

'Someone . . . yes,' whispered Celia.

'As I came up the stairs I thought I saw the schoolroom door close. Whoever it was must have hidden in here . . . and then . . . slipped away. I should have come here to see. But my first thought was of my mother and when I realized what was happening . . .'

Celia's look was incredulous.

'Sarah, but what . . . why . . . Who would have . . . ?'

I said in what was almost a whisper: 'My aunt . . .'

'Your aunt!' Celia's voice was shrill with disbelief. 'Oh no, Sarah, you can't mean that. Of course it was your mother. She did it herself.'

'But why . . . why . . . ? She was shivering with cold.'

'It's her fever. Imagine her waking. She's burning hot. She would throw off the bedclothes . . . and then open the window and perhaps douse the fire . . .'

'She told me she saw a figure in the room . . . someone who crept in and looked at her. She was frightened, Celia, desperately frightened.'

'She dreamed it. Of course it was one of her fancies. She was half awake and half asleep and in a high fever.'

She was convincing me. Of course Aunt Martha would not have crept into the room and opened the window and then when I arrived have hidden in the schoolroom until she had an opportunity to slip downstairs. But why not? It would be a way to my mother's death which would seem to have come about naturally. No, it was nonsense. I could see that everyone would say it was nonsense. Celia's solution was the logical one.

She went on talking of my mother's illness. She had played many parts; she often imagined herself in those plays. We both knew that. Drama was in her blood and she was liable to act strangely when she was in a fever. It might not have been the first time she had done this.

'I shall sleep in her room in future,' I said.

'One of us should,' replied Celia.

I smiled at her gratefully. 'You're a good friend to us, Celia,' I said.

'I'm grateful to you,' she replied. 'I don't forget that you have helped me through a difficult time. You may be sure I shall do everything to help your mother and you.'

There was, however, nothing she could do. That night my mother's hold on life loosened. She developed pneumonia and as she was already weakening, she had little hope of surviving. Within a few days she was dead. She was laid to rest in that part of the graveyard set aside for the Ashingtons. Her grave was next to Margaret's.

It was a sad house for me without my mother. I reproached myself for having been impatient with her dwelling on the past and deploring the future. Now I remembered only the successful actress whose life had been gay and glamorous.

Change! First one thing happens and then another and in a short time the whole picture is different. There was no one left from my past now. Meg and Janet had sent us a card at Christmas in which they had written that their venture was working out well. 'They're telling us how well they can get on without me,' my mother had said. 'Poor Meg, I'm sure she misses the theatre.'

I doubted I should hear from them again. I was overcome by a strange sense of loneliness. Most of all I missed Toby. But I was young. I would be nineteen in November and a new life was stretching out before me.

Neither of the aunts made any show of mourning for my mother. They did everything they considered right and proper in the circumstances and that finished the matter. Aunt Martha did, I must admit, have the air of a general who has won the first campaign and is preparing for the second. When I was with her I thought how preposterous my suspicions had been and how much more sensible Celia's version of what had happened.

Celia and I rode and walked together. We attended church; we did our lessons and I was beginning to master arithmetic rather for her sake than because I had any interest in it, as I wanted her to think she was useful. But I could not take to needlework even for her. We met John Bonnington, the new curate who, as Aunt Martha rather cruelly said, was eaten alive by the Cannon girls. We decorated the church for Easter and attended the three-hour service on Good Friday; we worked for the fête which was held on Easter Monday and once again Celia proved what a good church worker she was.

As the weeks passed she was becoming more and more a

member of the household. Aunt Martha was constantly talking to her of the past history and glory of the Ashingtons until she was as knowledgeable about the family as any of its members. The idea dawned on me slowly. Celia was pliable; she excelled in those pursuits which pleased Aunt Martha, and she was young enough to have children. Could it really be that Aunt Martha was training her, making her into a possible wife for my father! What a notion! I was being absurdly fanciful.

Then it seemed to me that Celia was becoming more withdrawn. One day she said to me: 'There is really no reason why I should stay here now. I am not educated enough to attempt to educate you. I think I should go.'

'Where would you go to?' I asked.

'I should find other employment.'

'We like you to be here, Celia.'

She smiled, well pleased, and said no more.

Every Sunday she and I used to put flowers on my mother's grave. Celia was as anxious to do this as I was and indeed suggested it.

My father wrote to me again:

You promised to write to me. Please do. I know your mother did not want us to be in touch. But she has gone now and families should be together. It is my hope that I shall see you one day soon. Perhaps I shall come to England or it may be that you will come and visit me here. This is a very beautiful country. It has become home to me. The ancient Sanskrit name for it is Sri Lanka which means the Resplendent Land and resplendent it is. I have a pleasant house on the plantation with a good garden. You know the English will always have gardens wherever they find themselves. Well, perhaps one day I shall show it to you. Write to me please, Sarah.

Ralph Ashington

PS. You should also know your sister Clytie. She is excited at the prospect of meeting you.

I was so pleased with that letter that I answered it immediately, and during the weeks that followed there was a regular correspondence between us.

I learned a great deal about Ceylon. I used to study it on the maps – a pear-shaped island lying off the coast of India. I found the spot where the plantation was situated somewhere between the capital, Colombo, and Kandy. I could picture it from what I gleaned from my father. The hot sun, the heavy rainfall which, my father told me, was three times that of London. 'It's why we're here,' he wrote – 'right in the path of two monsoons. The rain gives us our tea . . . that and the hot sun.'

It was becoming clear in my mind.

Coconuts along the coast [he wrote], rubber on the ridges and on the higher land the most important of all, tea. It's the life blood of the land, Sarah. It has brought work and prosperity and the country needed that after the coffee disaster when leaf disease destroyed the crops and could not be overcome. Of course we have our troubles with tea, but thank God we have been able to overcome them so far. We have other industries too. Our pearl fisheries for one. Some of the most beautiful pearls in the world are found in our waters. I have no doubt you have heard of the Ashington Pearls! Your aunts will have told you of them. They came from Ceylon. We also have emeralds and sapphires and they too are some of the best in the world. But the prosperity of the country hangs on tea . . .

Either my father enjoyed letter-writing or he was delighted to have made contact with his daughter at last. He really made me see the country of which he wrote so enthusiastically. I pictured the coastal plains, the beaches with their palms, the central mass of mountains which culminated in the awe-inspiring Adam's Peak to which in the past pilgrims had travelled to perform religious rites.

It is these mountains which are blessed by the people for they have brought fertility to Ceylon [he wrote]. From the mountains the streams come tumbling down to irrigate the land and the rain gives us the precious water. All our fertility is in the western zone because we are in the path of the rains. The rest of the country – the lowlands of the north and east get the full force of a merciless sun while we are revelling in the teeming rain. Strange, is it not, in such a small country – only two hundred and seventy miles long and one hundred and forty across. You see, smaller than England. But my dear child, all this you can learn from your geography books. What I am trying to do is to get you to come to Ceylon . . .

I learned from him that my sister Clytie was married and the mother of a boy of three. As she was only a year older than I she must have been married when she was very young. My father told me that she had married his manager Seth Blandford and the little boy was called Ralph after his grandfather.

'Do you know,' I said to Celia, 'I'm an aunt. It is astonishing how my family grows about me.'

It was May by now. We were riding through one of the forest paths and it was beautiful. Now and then we came upon clumps of bluebells which seemed to dance in the wind as it ruffled them and changed the sheen of that deep and lovely blue. The trees were ready to burst into leaf and every now and then the cuckoo called as though to remind us that spring was upon us.

'Sarah,' said Celia suddenly. 'I can't stay here any longer. It's wrong. I'm not earning my keep. I tried to tell your aunt only yesterday and she wouldn't listen.'

'Stop worrying. Why should you go?'

She hesitated. Then she said: 'There is a possibility that I am going to inherit some money. Oh, not a great deal, but enough for me to live on in comfort.'

'That's wonderful. And when you do, you will want to go.'

'It seems wrong to have used you. When I needed a home . . .'

'What nonsense. You came to work here. You satisfied us all. Oh Celia, we shall miss you.'

'Your aunt almost forbade me to speak of it. It was almost as though she had plans for me!'

I looked at her quizzically. Did she think what I thought?

'Aunt Martha has plans for everyone,' I said. 'The trouble with her is that she thinks she can manage everything better than anyone else . . . even when it comes to people's own concerns.'

I called her attention to the bluebells and said how I should like to gather them but they never lasted long and they seemed so much more beautiful growing than they ever could in any other way.

She agreed and we rode on in silence for a while. I was wondering what it would be like when she left. Perhaps I should go out to Ceylon to see my father. I could not resist talking of him to Celia. I repeated what he had written in his letters and she listened avidly.

When we returned to the house there was a letter waiting for me and I at once took it to my room to read.

He was delighted, he told me, because I was so interested in the plantation. His sisters wanted me to finish my education before I came out to him. 'They are urging me to come home, which I might well do.' I was excited at the prospect.

It could be arranged [he wrote]. Seth could manage and Clinton Shaw would always help in a crisis. I must have mentioned Clinton Shaw. [He had not.] He owns the plantation neighbouring on mine. It's a small country and the fertile section is in one area, so we have to make the most of the rich land. We help each other in an emergency. Clinton is quite a character. Some people call him the King of Kandy. It is people such as he who really set an industry like this working. He's ruthless, of course. He's got his critics, but he and I have an understanding. I really am thinking of coming home for a while. They tell me out here that I should . . . to see a doctor. But my main purpose would be to meet my daughter. I expect you have changed a lot since you were two!

I was excited. I wanted to talk about this possibility and naturally it was to Celia.

I couldn't find her in the house and I went out down the drive

and through the gates. I paused by the lych-gate and went into the
the graveyard. Celia was kneeling by my mother's grave.

I went to her swiftly and quietly. She looked up at me with
surprise. She had a small pair of scissors in her hand and had
snipped a sprig from the bush she had planted.

'What is that?' I asked.

She turned her expressionless eyes on me and said: 'Don't you
know? You're very ignorant about plants, Sarah. Perhaps that's
something I could have taught you. It's rosemary.'

'Rosemary,' I quoted, ' "that's for remembrance." '

She smiled. 'Trust you to know your poetry better than your
botany.'

She slipped the scissors into her pocket and stood up clutching
the rosemary.

Together we walked to the house.

'You were very fond of my mother,' I said.

'She was important to me,' she answered. 'I shall never forget
her.'

A shock awaited us next morning.

Celia did not appear for breakfast. Breakfast was the one meal
for which there was no set time. One helped oneself from the side-
board from seven-thirty until nine. The aunts usually breakfasted
together at eight o'clock. Celia and I had made a habit of taking
ours half an hour earlier. Celia, I was sure, would not diverge from
this custom unless something unusual happened. I ate some toast,
drank some coffee and went to her room.

Her bed was neatly made and I realized it had not been slept in
and that her case was missing. I opened the cupboard door.
Empty. Then I saw the notes propped up on the table. One was
addressed to me, the other to Aunt Martha.

I slit the envelope.

Dear Sarah [I read],

    I am leaving. I thought it best to do it this way as I know you will all so kindly try to persuade me to stay. I cannot do that. You have all been so good to me when I needed help. I no longer do, so I am leaving. Thank you for your forbearance. When I have a permanent address I will send it to you in case you want to keep in touch.

Affectionately, Celia

I could not believe it. To go like that! But why? I knew that Aunt Martha was insisting that she must stay, but even Aunt Martha could not have made her do so if she didn't want to. Celia was the sort of girl who hated to deny people what they wanted. She would find it hard to say No, so she had chosen this way.

I remembered how she had knelt by my mother's grave. She had really cared about her and in my mother's last days had brought to her that adulation for which she had craved. Of course it was for her sake that she had wanted to stay and now she was dead there was no point in remaining.

Aunt Martha was stunned. I had never seen her so shaken. It was clear now that with the possibility of my father's return she had had plans for Celia.

'And left no address . . .' put in Aunt Mabel.

'We cannot get in touch with her . . . even if we wanted to. And I thought she was such a sensible girl!'

Aunt Martha hated to have her plans frustrated and she was really annoyed with Celia for the first time since she had known her.

I tried to explain. 'It was a job to her, Aunt Martha, a means of earning a living. And when she came into money that was no longer necessary.'

'We treated her like one of the family and were prepared to . . .'

I turned away unable to hide a smile. So she really had planned to marry Celia to my father! Was there no end to her scheming? Then I thought of that night in my mother's room with the windows open and the fire doused.

No, I told myself. Impossible!

It was a strange summer. I missed Celia very much and found myself more and more in the company of the Cannon girls who were indefatigable in their pursuit of good for the church. The curate had not yet been captured, but, said Aunt Martha, his days of freedom were numbered; and how he was going to keep a wife *she* did not know.

I pointed out that it would be his affair and that of the chosen Miss Cannon.

'Young Effie is not so bad,' she said speculatively, and it occurred to me that Effie could well have been selected to take the place which Celia's defection had made vacant. For my father was definitely coming home.

He had written to say that he would come in October. By that time the summer monsoon, which lasted from May to September, would be over and most of the necessary planting would be completed. He might be travelling with his neighbour, Clinton Shaw, who would have business in London with the merchants there, as my father would. At the same time he was to have some sort of examination which the doctor in Kandy had suggested he should. What he wanted most was to see me.

It was good to have this to look forward to and feel excited about. It helped me to get over the loss first of my mother and then of Celia.

I couldn't help being amused by the way in which Effie Cannon was invited to the house, almost as though she were being groomed. She came to dine and we talked about Ceylon and my father's plantation there.

'We were coffee planters at one time,' said Aunt Martha, 'and then we went over to tea. It's a beautiful country, I believe, and it is our duty to develop it. After all, it is one of the jewels in Britain's crown, you know.'

Effie looked suitably impressed but she had no notion of what was in Aunt Martha's mind and when they were beginning to get ready for the harvest festival, she announced her engagement to the curate. Aunt Martha was incensed.

'A stupid girl,' she said. 'How they are going to live on a curate's stipend I do not know.'

'As long as they do, that's all that matters, Aunt,' I said.

'You are being pert, Sarah, and it is not becoming. You always were . . . in your early days. When your father comes home we must entertain a little. There are some pleasant families in Kandy we used to know.' I could see that she was thinking of a wife for my father and it occurred to me that sooner or later I too should be a target for her schemes.

Sometimes I wondered what it would be like to live at the Grange all one's life. Should I become like the aunts, concerned with the trivia of manners and conventions, planning for other people, caring passionately about things like the Ashington Pearls?

I could never do that.

In my heart I believed that when my father went back to Ceylon, I should go with him.

NIGHT IN THE FOREST

❋

My father was sailing on the *Bristol Star*, which was to arrive at Tilbury in the first week of November. I should be nineteen years old that month. He would come straight to the Grange from the docks, travelling by train to the station, and as he could not be sure of the time of arrival he would take the station fly to bring him to the house.

He would be accompanied by Clinton Shaw who was travelling with him. Clinton Shaw had decided to come rather earlier than he had intended in order that they might come together. The doctor had some notion that it would be a good idea.

I was a little disturbed by the repeated mention of the doctor. I spoke of it to Aunt Martha. She said: 'He was never one to think much about his health. People change. And I wonder what this man will be like . . . this Clinton Shaw. I have heard of the Shaw plantation. I always imagined the Shaws were rogues.'

'They must be good friends or they would not be travelling together,' I pointed out.

'I've told Ellen to get two of the rooms ready for them. That large one with the bay windows was your father's when he was here with your mother. I doubt he would like that again. The bridal chamber that was! Give that to Clinton Shaw, I told Ellen. It's one of the best rooms in the place and after all he'll be a guest for a night or two. He won't stay. He'll have business in London. Your father can have either the one next to it or one on the floor above.'

The preparations were made. Both aunts were excited and I guessed that Aunt Martha was determined to get my father married before he returned to Ceylon. She was going through lists of people who lived not too far away and might visit us.

'It is long since we entertained in any style,' she said, 'but there is a time for everything.'

Under the direction of Mrs Lamb, the housekeeper, the maids were set doing an autumnal spring clean; not that Aunt Martha would have allowed an annual cleaning to have been passed over at the appointed time. She had new cushions made and in one case new curtains. 'Something a little more bright and festive,' she commented. 'The Merridews have two daughters,' I heard her say to Aunt Mabel; and she added ominously: 'And one son.'

After my father, my turn would come. I wondered why Mabel had escaped. I supposed that after Edward Sanderton had turned to Margaret, Aunt Martha had determined on a life of single blessedness and decided that she would need a companion. I pictured any possible suitor for Aunt Mabel being shooed away as determinedly as those for others would be beckoned forward.

At last the day of my father's arrival was at hand. There was tension in the atmosphere and I kept flying to the window every time I thought I heard the approach of carriage wheels. It was dark before five o'clock and still he had not come. The lamps were lighted in the hall, as had been the lanterns on either side of the porch. I was continually going from the hall to my room. 'Like a cat on hot bricks,' said Aunt Martha. But she herself was not unmoved and was, I could see reluctantly, caught up in the excitement which pervaded the general atmosphere throughout the house. Appetizing smells came from the kitchen and the elder servants were telling the others what they remembered of Ralph Ashington.

It was half past six when the station fly came up the drive. We were all at the door – myself, Aunts Martha and Mabel; and I knew that several of the servants were looking through some of the windows while others hovered in the hall.

My heart was beating wildly as a man stepped out of the fly. He was very tall and wore a black Homburg hat and a black coat with a short cape attached to it. He did not look towards the house but back to the fly from which he began to help a man. My father! He looked very slight beside the other and I felt a great rush of tenderness towards him.

I ran out and cried: 'I'm Sarah, Father. I'm Sarah.'

I felt weak with emotion. He looked so frail – a shrunken image of the man I knew from the portrait in the gallery.

The other man said in a somewhat authoritative tone: 'Let's get him in, shall we? This damp is no good for him.'

'Ralph!' It was Aunt Martha.

'I'm home,' said my father. 'Yes, I've come home at last. Sarah!' He was looking at me with a kind of rapture.

His companion spoke imperiously. 'I said let us get him inside.'

I felt an irritation with the guest right from the beginning because he had started by telling us what to do. It was not cold. In fact it was rather muggy. Surely it was for *us* to invite *him* inside.

Nevertheless we went in.

My father kept his eyes on me. 'Sarah,' he said. 'Just as I pictured you. Oh, I'm forgetting. This is Mr Clinton Shaw, who kindly agreed to travel with me.'

'Welcome to Ashington Grange, Mr Shaw,' said Aunt Martha. 'We were expecting you.'

He had taken off his hat to expose a thatch of blond hair which was rather startling because the rest of his face seemed to be dark.

'Thank you, Miss Ashington,' he said. 'I'm glad to be here.'

I noticed that my father was breathing with difficulty. 'It must have been a tiresome journey,' I said. 'Are you cold? Do come to the fire.'

'Sarah, I've wanted you to meet Clinton.'

'How do you do?' I said briefly, my eyes still on my father.

'Yes,' he answered. 'I've been waiting to meet you, Miss Sarah.'

I led my father to the fire.

'He has been used to a rather different climate,' said Mr Shaw. 'This takes a bit of getting used to.'

'I am sure that's true,' Aunt Mabel put in. 'We've told Mrs Lamb to have fires lighted in your rooms.'

'Good old Lamb!' said my father. 'Is she still here, then?'

'There's been little change here, Ralph,' Aunt Martha told him. He was smiling at me rather shyly.

'We shall have lots to say to each other, Sarah.'

'I shall look forward to that,' I replied.

'Mr Shaw, would you like to see your room?' asked Aunt Martha.

He said he would and that it was very kind of them to offer him hospitality.

'Naturally we are pleased,' said Aunt Martha. 'Sarah, you take Mr Shaw and Mabel will take Ralph . . . if he needs to be taken. You haven't forgotten the Grange, Ralph?'

'I remember every nook and corner, Martha.'

'They must be hungry,' put in Mabel. 'Are you?'

Mr Shaw spoke for both of them. 'Very,' he said.

'Dinner will be served very soon,' said Aunt Martha.

'If you will follow me, I will take you to your room,' I told him.

I led the way upstairs. Mr Shaw's eyes were on me as we mounted and crossed the gallery.

'Ah,' he said. 'The family!'

He stopped still and looked at me. 'You have a look of them,' he added.

'I suppose that's to be expected since I am one of them.'

He paused before the pictures and I could not, in politeness, hurry on.

'Where have they put you?'

'I am not here. I'm only a recent acquisition, you might say.'

'You mean a recently *recognized* acquisition.'

'Exactly.'

'I know. I'm in your father's confidence. You would stand up well amongst those fine ladies.'

'How kind of you to say so.'

'It's true. I shouldn't say it otherwise. I rarely flatter. Only when it would be foolish not to, of course.'

I looked at him intently. I couldn't help it. It was almost as though he willed me to. His height and the breadth of his shoulders gave him presence. His blond hair and heavy-lidded dark eyes were such a startling contrast that he could not fail to be noticed; he was bronzed, which I supposed was inevitable, living where he did. I noticed his strong white teeth and rather sensual lips. He had annoyed me from the start by giving orders and I had made up my mind to dislike him. I had never seen a man like him before, but then what men had I seen? Those who paid court to my mother? Everard, who always looked like the model of an English gentleman. Toby, who was also one, though of a slightly different mould. Those other admirers. This man had lived abroad a great deal and that had no doubt distinguished him from others. I had been aware of him from the moment he had stepped from the carriage, which was disconcerting. He was the sort of man who demanded attention. My entire interest should have been for my father – but this man kept intruding.

'Ah!' He had paused before a portrait of a female Ashington. 'The famous pearls. Quite a number of ladies are wearing them, I see. You must admit they look very fine.'

'I had no intention of not admitting it,' I said lightly. 'You will want to wash and perhaps change before we dine.' I was reminding him that we had dallied long enough in the gallery.

He bowed his head and we went up the stairs to the next floor. My room was on this one and at the far end of the corridor was that one which had been assigned to him. I took him along to it.

'A very fine house,' he commented.

'It has been in the family for generations.'

'Very commendable.'

'To the house or the family?'

'Both. The house for standing up all those years and the family for keeping its hold on it.'

'Your room is along here.' I opened the door.

'Charming,' he said; and indeed it looked so. The firelight flickered on the furnishings and a lighted oil lamp with a fluted shade stood on the dressing-table.

'We have no gaslight at the Grange,' I told him.

'It would be sacrilege. I am not accustomed to it. In my house it is lamps and candles. We have no gaslight either.'

'Then I have no need to apologize.'

'My dear Sarah, why should you apologize to me!'

I stood back a little and regarded him coldly. I had not expected him to address me by my Christian name.

He understood at once. I could see that he was quick-witted and would rarely be at a loss. He said immediately: 'You must forgive my rough colonial manners. The fact is your father has spoken of you so often and it was always Sarah. You could hardly expect him to give you the quite impressive title of Miss Ashington, could you?'

'Certainly not my father, but with strangers it would be expected.'

'Strangers, yes. But you are not a stranger to me. Let that be the excuse for my forwardness.'

I turned to the door. 'If there is anything you need, there is the bell-pull. Dinner will be served soon.'

'Good. I shall see you then.'

There was a lazy, almost insolent smile on his face as he watched me leave.

I am not going to like him, I told myself as I went to my room. It is a pity my father had to bring him with him. I entered my room and as I turned to shut the door something made me look round. Clinton Shaw was standing at his open door watching me. I shut my door with a bang. I lighted my lamp hastily and looked at my reflection. My face was scarlet.

'No,' I said aloud, 'I do not like him at all.'

I was still thinking of him when I went downstairs.

I remember every detail of that meal; the dining-room with the blue tapestry-covered chairs worked by an Ashington in the Georgian era, those other tapestries older than the house itself hanging on the walls, the gleaming silver which had been with us since Queen Anne, the candles in their sconces – all of which were familiar to me, looked different on that night. Aunt Martha sat at the head of the table with Clinton Shaw on her right. My father was at the other end with me on his right; and as with Aunt Mabel, we only made five, there seemed to be long distances between us.

I thought we should have used the winter parlour as we were such a small party, but Aunt Martha evidently felt this was a somewhat ceremonial occasion.

My father looked better than he had on arrival. There was a little more colour in his face and his eyes were very bright. He was thin, I noticed, but animated. He was clearly feeling deeply the fact that he was in his old home.

He talked a great deal about the past and how the house had not changed at all, and I was aware that his eyes rarely left me. Then he went on to talk of the plantation and Clinton Shaw joined him. They talked of planting, plucking and the trouble they had with pests. Last year it had been nettle grub, the year before that capsid bugs.

'That's how it goes, Miss Ashington,' said Clinton Shaw. 'As in life, so with tea. We have our joys and our tribulations and there seem to be more of the latter than the former.'

I wanted to hear more about the domestic life. I longed to ask questions about my sister, but I felt that was something for when I was alone with my father.

'Have you a good domestic staff?' Aunt Mabel wanted to know.

'That is never difficult,' replied my father. 'There are always those who are eager to earn a living.'

He loved the island, I could see; he knew a great deal about its history and he talked of it glowingly. I fancied he wanted to interest me and make me love it and that he was planning to take me with him when he returned. I listened avidly.

'Poets call it the Pearl on the brow of India,' he said.

'Others have called it the pearl which was dropped into the sea,' added Clinton Shaw. 'You note the emphasis on pearls. That's good business. We have some flourishing pearl fisheries.'

'Clinton is a cynic,' said my father with a smile. 'It is said that

King Solomon once sought the jewels of Sri Lanka – as it was called then – to adorn himself and the Queen of Sheba. There are a thousand legends and superstitions. I could tell you stories of the great dynasties and the early kings . . .'

'We would rather hear about *your* life there, Ralph,' said Aunt Martha firmly.

'The life of one tea planter is very like that of another. Is that not so, Clinton?'

'Quite false,' replied Clinton. 'Your life, my dear fellow, is not in the least like mine. And that, ladies, is something for which you should rejoice.'

'What do you mean by that, Mr Shaw?' asked Aunt Mabel.

'I mean your brother is a model of rectitude and I am scarcely that.'

'You are joking, of course,' said Aunt Martha, making it a statement of fact. I thought that incorrigible man was going to contradict her and then give us an account of the life he led, which I could believe was very disreputable. I guessed he would have a native mistress. Perhaps two. I was sure that he was that sort of man. There was something which told me so in the way he looked at all women . . . at least I hoped it was all women and he had not singled me out. That would have been even more offensive. I was disliking him more and more as the evening wore on. He made me feel uncomfortable as I never had before.

My half-sister was not mentioned; nor was my father's first wife. They must be matters for family ears alone. I meant to ask about my sister as soon as I could.

So we heard instead about the Kings of Ceylon and how the King of Kandy had sought British help against the Dutch, but the British at that time were reluctant to take on new responsibilities. Later it was different.

'England had become the world leader,' said my father. 'Trafalgar had been won and we were becoming an Empire. The revolution had crippled the French. India was the brightest jewel in the Imperial Crown and the East India Company was seeking a base. The Dutch had put up little resistance and had been driven out by the British; the Kandyan kings were violent and cruel and the people of Ceylon welcomed the British, and Ceylon came under the shelter of the Imperial umbrella.'

He turned to me. 'When you see it, Sarah, you will be enchanted. Will she not, Clinton?'

'I hope I shall be there to witness her ecstasy,' he said.

I ignored him and my father went on: 'Picture bamboo-lined streams . . . streams which wind their way through the paddy fields. The mountains are beautiful, Sarah. There is one part which reminds me of our own Lake District. The scenery changes so . . . rather as it does at home. But there it is more dramatic. You go from rice fields to mountains and to forests of wira and palu. They are so tall, those trees. Then up in the north-west where it is dry there is nothing but scrub. The beauty of the country has to be seen to be believed.'

'In fact,' said Clinton Shaw, 'every prospect pleases and only man is vile.'

'Perhaps not all men,' I countered.

'Not all . . . but a great many, I fear.'

We took coffee in the winter parlour and I saw that my father was almost asleep.

Clinton Shaw leaned towards me and whispered: 'I think your father should retire. It has been an exhausting day for him.'

Aunt Martha heard him and rose.

'I do hope you will be comfortable,' she said.

We said good night and went to our rooms.

I knew I should not sleep. I took off my dress and put on a loose dressing-gown, shook out my hair and started to brush it.

I took stock of myself before my mirror. There was only one lamp in my room but I had candles at the dressing-table.

My reflection looked back at me. I wondered what my father had thought of me. And what had Clinton Shaw thought? I realized that ever since I had seen him I had been trying to thrust him out of my mind, but he would keep intruding. He was like that. He would always be pushing forward where he was not wanted. He was too forceful, too forthright. Everard and Toby had been so different. They were so courteous; they made one feel looked after. With this man one felt as though it was necessary to be on the alert all the time and able to defend oneself against that overpowering masculinity.

He was interested in me. He had made that clear. I was sure that had he not been he would have made no effort to pretend he was. I had so often found him looking at me in that bold direct manner and when I showed I was aware of it and resented it, he was quite unperturbed.

Strangely enough, tonight I felt I looked my best. The thick brown hair was as unmanageable now as it had been when Meg had wound strands of it round pieces of rag in the hope of achieving a corkscrew effect by the next morning; but somehow its obstinate straightness suited me on this night. My eyes which were neither quite green, nor grey, nor brown, but a bit of each always seemed colourless to me; now they sparkled and seemed to have borrowed a hint of blue from the dressing-gown I was wearing. My only beauty, which I had inherited from my mother, was my long eyelashes. For the rest I could see I had the Ashington straight nose that was a little too long – Aunt Martha had it in the extreme. There were two types of Ashington mouths – the tight-lipped variety, which the aunts had, and the rather sensual kind which I had inherited from my father. Tonight there was a fresh colour in my cheeks which usually were rather pale. It was to this I no doubt owed my more than usually attractive appearance.

It is excitement because my father is home, I assured myself. But I knew it was something else besides.

That man would not be with us long. He was staying for a few nights and then he was going to London, where he would execute his business and so would my father for a while. I wondered why my father had joined up with such a man. I should have thought he was hardly an ideal companion, but then of course they were close neighbours since their plantations touched.

I was brushing my hair rhythmically when a sound outside

my door startled me. Footsteps. They paused at my door. There was a knock.

I stood up. 'Who's there?' I demanded.

The door opened. 'May I come in?' said Clinton Shaw. 'There is so much I have to say to you.'

I felt the colour rushing into my cheeks. I gripped the hairbrush as though it were a weapon of defence.

'Here! Now!' I cried and my voice sounded shrill. 'In my bedroom!'

He looked round smiling. 'I couldn't think of a spot where we should be less likely to be disturbed.'

'Mr Shaw . . .' I began.

'Please call me Clinton. As I call you Sarah it would be more appropriate. Many of my friends call me Clint. Odd name, isn't it? It is after a place where my family lived and there have been Clintons through the generations. Would you prefer Clint?'

'If I have to make a choice I prefer Mr Shaw.'

'As long as you prefer me in some form that will have to do for the time being.'

'Mr Shaw,' I said, 'I have no doubt that you think you are very witty and irresistible . . .'

'I wonder what put that into your head. I believe it can only have come from your own opinion.'

'I am sure that what you have to say could be said tomorrow and in another place. You are a guest in this house and it is not acceptable that you should come into my bedroom at this time of night . . . uninvited.'

'How delightful it would have been if I had been invited,' he said regretfully.

'I think you are presumptuous and a little insulting. Will you please go or shall I pull the bell-rope?'

'There is so much I have to say to you. It is about your father. I really thought you would wish to know as soon as possible.'

'What about my father?'

'Shall I sit down? It would be more comfortable for us both.'

He did not wait for my reply and looked about him. At first I thought he was going to sit on my bed. Instead of which he advanced into the room and sat in the armchair.

I felt incensed, yet helpless. To order him to leave would be overdramatic yet perhaps I should. To pull the bell-rope and ask for help would be even more so. But here was a man whom I had known for only a few hours coming into my bedroom . . . ! He was looking at me sardonically, reading my thoughts and they seemed to amuse him.

I hated him for putting me into this position. I wondered what Aunt Martha would say if she looked in now. Order him to leave the house, I was sure; and that would be a good thing.

He folded his hands together and regarded the tips of his fingers with an air which I could only call pious and which seemed full of mockery.

Just as I was about to order him to leave he said: 'I know how concerned you are about your father. That is why I wanted to talk to you. He is a very sick man.'

My anger dropped from me. There was only fear for my father.

'You are . . . sure of that?' I stammered.

'I have talked to our doctor. It was he who suggested that he should come home for observation and treatment. I could not allow him to travel alone.'

Now he was putting himself in a different light, but although I knew he spoke the truth about my father I did not trust him.

'That was good of you,' I said grudgingly.

'I intended to come some time on my own affairs. It was only a matter of putting everything forward.'

'What's wrong with him?'

'Lungs mostly. I thought you should know.'

'Thank you for telling me. My aunts will have to know too.'

'I'm not so sure. You see, your father doesn't know exactly what's wrong with him, and somehow I felt I could talk to you more easily. That is why I sought you here in this somewhat unconventional manner. He has told me a great deal about you . . . shown me your letters. He was very proud of them. I'm glad you have come together . . . in time.'

'What can we do?'

'Make him as happy as you can before he dies.'

'You think I . . .'

'You more than anyone.'

'I shall do my best.'

'That's what I wanted to tell you.'

'Thank you.' I stood up, indicating that he should leave, but he did not rise. He merely sat there looking at me as though assessing me, smiling in a way I found disconcerting, even a little alarming.

'Good night,' I said.

He stood up then and came towards me. I was by no means short in stature, being above medium height, but he seemed as though he wanted me to realize how he towered above me.

I stood to one side as though for him to pass. He ignored the hint and said: 'When I go with your father from here to the specialist I want you to come with us. Will you do that? I think it would be helpful.'

'Of course I'll do anything to help my father.'

He put out a hand and laid it on my shoulder. 'Thank you,' he said.

I moved a step backward so that his hand fell. I saw the smile touch his lips.

'Good night, Mr Shaw,' I said again. 'And thank you for helping my father.'

'I'm helping myself too,' he replied. 'My business here is very important to me. We have to see the agents in London every few years . . . or we should do. That's all part of the business. I have another even more important reason for being here.'

He looked at me expectantly as though waiting for me to ask what that was. I did not give him the satisfaction.

He took a step towards me. 'I am looking for a wife,' he said.

I felt the telltale colour rising again. I managed to say lightly: 'Really?'

'Oh yes, there comes a time when a man needs a wife, someone to look after him and keep him steady. That's very important in a life like mine and living where I do there is little selection. It's a recognized custom to come home to find a wife.'

'I'm sure it must be,' I said and turned away. As he did not go I went on: 'I wish you luck in your search.'

'I don't anticipate any difficulty,' he answered.

'Let us hope that the object of your search will share your high opinion of yourself,' I said.

He was smiling at me as I went to the door and held it open. I shut the door on him. Then I turned the key in the lock.

I sat down at my mirror. I had not been so upset since my mother had died. My father very ill . . . perhaps returned home to die, and here was this man whom I could not get out of my mind. He seemed to be threatening me in some way.

I could not understand what happened to me during the next few weeks. I was certainly not in love with Clinton Shaw. At least not in the way I had always thought of love – tender admiration such as Everard had given my mother, doting service which Toby offered, those men at the stage door bringing flowers and sometimes jewellery. No, it was not a bit like that. It was just that he wormed his way into my thoughts. He had taken possession of my mind as he implied clearly he was determined to of my body . . . in time. I had never known anyone like him. When he entered a room the atmosphere changed; it became dominated by him. Attention focused on him; he seemed to be forgiven for what would be unacceptable rudeness in others. It was some power of the personality – an essential male quality – different from that power which my mother had had to attract and which had so tragically deserted her. This was a virile quality, something which people accepted, while resenting it, because they had to. Even the aunts were aware of it. Aunt Martha nodded her head and her lips quivered with suppressed amusement at his outrageous manners, and Aunt Mabel took to wearing frilly collars. Mrs Lamb discovered he liked curry and made efforts to serve it to his taste, for it was a dish we had not indulged in before. The servants vied with each other to do his bidding. Ellen giggled about him

and said: 'That's a man and a half, that one.' A man and a half!
That suited him. He had something extra and it was in his sheer
egoism, his determination to get what he wanted. I was the only
one, it seemed, who made any attempt to hold out against this
overpowering virility. Perhaps that was the reason why he made
a set at me. But no, there was more to it than that.

I was alarmed to see how my father relied on him. It was
Clinton Shaw who made all the decisions and my father meekly
complied. That he was very ill was obvious the first morning
after their arrival. The sharp light of day betrayed his unhealthy
pallor tinged with yellow; the sunken eyes; the fragility of him.

During that first morning Clinton said my father should rest in
his room in order to be ready for his ordeal with the doctors the
next day. I was with my father all the morning and he lay in bed
talking to me.

He told me now that we were alone how much he had wanted
to come and see me and how my mother had been against it.

'She hated life in Ceylon,' he said. 'It is something you either
love or hate. She loved the world of the theatre, glamour, footlights and admiration. Our marriage was doomed from the start.
I was unfortunate in my marriages, Sarah. I hope you will marry
happily.'

'I have never thought of it,' I told him. 'I meet so few people
here.'

'You must come to Ceylon.'

'I want to.'

Then he talked again of the plantation as he had at dinner with a
kind of intensity as though he were trying to impress it on his
memory and make it important to me. He told me that many
people were employed there. It was their livelihood. If anything
happened to the industry, as it had in the case of coffee, that would
be disastrous to many. I urged him to tell me more of my family,
of my sister and whether she knew of me and wanted to meet
me.

'Clytie is an exquisite creature, Sarah. Her beauty is breath-
taking, I think. She is not tall like you. She is small and slight, a

fairy child. Seth Blandford came out to work on the plantation and they fell in love. Now they have this enchanting boy ... my namesake. I wish I had a picture to show you. But you will go out there one day. You will come back with me if ...'

I said firmly: 'I must go back with you.'

'I don't know how long Clinton will be staying here, and I don't know what I should have done without him, Sarah. You do like him, don't you?' He spoke anxiously and gripped my hand.

I hesitated. 'I don't know him. He seems a very forceful character.'

'Forceful indeed. Just the type to manage the plantation. The natives are afraid of him. They think he has some supernatural power, I believe. Oh, he has a way with him. He'll own the whole of Ceylon before he's finished. He's going to be a very rich man, Sarah. He's been so good to me and I was hoping you would like him.'

'I find him somewhat arrogant and his manners could be improved.'

'He's just being natural. So many people look to him as their governor, and of course in Ceylon one can't always maintain the rigid codes of behaviour which are possible in an English country house.'

'Even so ...' I began.

He just patted my hand.

I loved talking to him, to hear about his first wife whom he had clearly loved dearly; she had given him the exquisite Clytie and then departed. Then to England where he was fascinated by the glamorous actress who strangely enough had agreed to marry him. None had been more surprised than himself. It was a marriage doomed to failure and from the ashes of that passion I had arisen.

We took lunch at midday in the winter parlour – soup and the venison we had had hot last evening now served cold with potatoes in their jackets. My father ate sparingly, Clinton Shaw voraciously.

After the meal he announced that my father should rest for the remainder of the day as he was taking him to London on the next. His eyes were on me, reminding me of my promise to accompany them. 'I should enjoy taking a ride through the forest,' he said, continuing to look at me.

Aunt Martha said at once: 'Sarah will go with you. She will enjoy showing you the forest. She has quite a feeling for it, haven't you, Sarah? She likes walking and riding in it.'

'I like the solitude of it,' I replied pointedly.

'We'll share that solitude,' answered Clinton Shaw.

I could hardly refuse to go without making an issue of it. After all, he was a guest.

I went with my father to his room, took off his boots and divested him of his jacket. When he was lying on the bed I said: 'You are very tired.'

He nodded. 'It's good to be with you, Sarah,' he said. 'I knew it would be. I never want to be parted from you again.'

I bent and kissed his forehead. 'You never shall be,' I said fervently and impulsively.

Then I went to my room and changed into my riding habit. I looked rather well in it. It suited my slim – perhaps too slim – figure. I tied my hair back and set the dark grey bowler on my head. Without my hair I could have passed for a boy and, I thought with gratification, quite a handsome one.

I had to admit to myself that I was excited by the prospect before me. Life had been dull so far, I realized. I had been on the scene, yet in the background. Others had taken the principal parts while I had been in the chorus, one of the crowd. Somehow with the coming of Clinton Shaw that had changed. I was becoming a principal and I found that exhilarating.

So at least my emotions were mixed. I was wary, yet I felt reckless. I felt a great desire to do battle with him. Perhaps this was how a general felt when he was going to war and was not quite sure of the enemy's forces but knew only that they were formidable.

He was waiting in the stables and his smile, when he saw me, illuminated his dark face.

'How gracious of you to come. I had a notion that you might default.'

'If I had decided not to come I should have said so,' I retorted. He prepared to help me mount.

'I don't really need help, you know,' I said.

'But I must be gallant and offer it.'

'I am surprised that you should feel that.'

'I thought I had to make a good impression after my conduct last night,' he said as we rode out of the stables. 'To force myself into a young lady's bedroom when I had only met her a few hours before was not what could be called conduct becoming.'

'So you really have learned that. It's a good beginning.'

'You see, from where I come we do not have much dealing with well-brought-up English misses. It makes for a certain crudity. We do have the occasional ladies from Home – wives of fellow planters, etcetera. There is a club in Kandy and another in Colombo so we mix with polite society now and then. We work hard though and there is not often the time to go into town. There is a dearth of *young* English ladies. That is why those of us who are interested in them have to come home to meet them.'

'And you are interested because of your search, of course.'

'I have an idea that it is at an end.'

'You have done well. Why, it was only yesterday that it had begun, I thought.'

'It could have begun much earlier. You see when the ship leaves Colombo it carries with it people returning home. Travelling by ship through tropical waters is very pleasant . . . very conducive to romance.'

'I see. You found your wife on the voyage home.'

'Shall we say I have found the wife I want.'

'And shall I say Congratulations, for I presume you had only to make your selection known and she fell at your feet in a swoon of gratitude.'

'A figure of speech, of course,' he said lightly. 'Grateful she will be. Swoon? No. She is not the swooning type. I am glad. I should have found that excessively boring.'

'Hartshorn is very good, you know. Perhaps I could give you some as a wedding present.'

'I shall want something better than that . . . from you.' I spurred my horse slightly and went forward. I wanted a little respite from him and his innuendoes.

He was soon beside me.

'What do you do in the ancient Grange?'

'Do? What do you mean? I live there.'

'What is life like with the estimable aunts?'

'As it is in such places all over the country, I don't doubt. There are certain estate matters to look after. Aunt Martha is good at that. And there is a manager. Then there are the local good works. We have a church which, like all churches, is in constant need of repair and it is the mission of the village to preserve it.'

'I understand perfectly. I was brought up in a house just like that. I had three brothers and I am the youngest. So you can't tell me much about village life that I don't know.'

'I believe there must be little anyone could tell you which you don't know . . . at least in your own opinion. Therefore it is rather a waste of time telling you anything.'

'There are some subjects on which I am not all knowing and I should, of course, like to be put right on those. Yourself, for instance. Of course I know who you are. I even remember your mother very vaguely. I was out there visiting my uncle on the plantation which later I inherited. I went out finally when I was twenty. There was a certain amount of gossip among the servants when your mother left. I was about twelve then. One is quite aware at twelve.'

'I imagine you were born . . . aware.'

'Not quite, but I quickly achieved awareness. Listening at keyholes, trapping servants into betraying secrets . . .'

'Very unpleasant traits.'

'But what could you expect, eh?'

I did not answer and he went on: 'You can imagine the talk. "I told you so!" That was the theme. They were all saying it from the secretary of the Club to the humblest plucker. Your father had not always been the wisest of men. He was very sad after she left him and he let things slide. You can't afford to do that in tea. He was lucky to have my uncle close at hand and then afterwards, when I inherited, me. Well, it's an old story now. No point in looking back. It's what's to come that concerns us.'

'Tell me about his illness.'

'You have seen for yourself. They can't treat it as it should be treated out there. That's why he's come home. I don't know what the verdict is going to be but it's not going to be good. That much I gathered from the doctor in Ceylon.'

'We must wait and see. It was good of you to concern yourself,' I said grudgingly.

'We're neighbours. Besides . . .' Then he shrugged his shoulders and although I waited he did not pursue the subject.

We rode side by side in silence for a few moments. We had come into the thicket. There was a mist which gave an atmosphere of mystery to the forest. It was like wispy cloud encircling the topmost branches of the trees which now, denuded of their leaves, took on strange fantastic shapes. I think I liked the trees more in winter than summer even. I could weave all sorts of fantasies from their strange shapes.

'This is pleasant,' he said suddenly. 'Do you know when I have sweltered in the heat and the rain has teemed down unceasingly I've dreamed of England. Mostly of the spring though. But now I don't think anything could be as pleasant as riding through the autumn woods.'

'I'm glad to hear that.'

'And there is no one I'd rather ride with than you. Are you glad to hear that too?'

'I'm surprised more than glad.'

'Oh come, Sarah, you are asking for compliments.'

'I meant that I was surprised you should stoop to flattery. You had led me to believe that was quite outside your range.'

'It is. I meant it. I am very glad to find you, Sarah, just as I would have you be.'

We had come to a clearing which I knew well and I broke into a canter. He was quickly beside me. I had the advantage of him because I knew the forest well. I had a great desire to give him the slip. It would be rather amusing for him to be lost in the forest. I turned off on a path. I knew I should come right out into the open soon which would give me an opportunity to gallop.

The forest which had been made by William the Conqueror to provide him with good hunting ground was in parts just as it had been in the days of that monarch; but some places had been cleared over the centuries and little villages had sprung up like oases in the desert. The forest covered about fifty miles in all. 'It is the easiest place to get lost in,' Aunt Martha had warned me when I first came. I knew the part of it near the Grange fairly well but I had been surprised how easy it was on misty days to lose my way. To people unsure of their bearings each tree looks remarkably like another and they could be easily tricked into wandering round in circles.

For him to be lost in the forest would be a first lesson in humility.

I broke into a gallop. We reached the village – a maze of little byways. I turned a corner. Ahead of me was a dense patch of bushy firs tall enough to hide a rider. I slipped into it before he had turned the corner so he wouldn't have seen me. I hid my horse and myself among the trees. I was just in time, for a few seconds later I heard him go thundering by.

I laughed inwardly. 'Come on, Cherrybim,' I said to my horse, 'we've thrown him off.'

Quietly I rode back the way we had come.

It was a short-lived triumph. I might have known he would not be so easily duped. He had quickly discovered my ruse and turned back. Before I could hide myself again he was beside me.

'I always enjoyed a game of hide and seek,' he said.

'I went to look at the firs,' I told him. 'They are particularly green and glistening this year. I think it means a bad winter.'

He made no comment but there was a look about his mouth which told me I should be hard put to it to play tricks on him again.

We rode through the forest for about an hour. Then I remarked that we should turn homeward. It would be dark before five and the mist would mean that it would be even earlier than usual.

We came past the railway station, which was about a mile from the Grange, and I suggested that we take the short cut through the forest.

'It's not dark yet,' he said, 'and won't be for another hour. Let's go a little farther into the forest.'

Feeling rather foolish after having been so easily caught in my attempt to escape from him, which was rather mean since he was a guest and there was no need for me to be ill-mannered just because he was, I agreed.

We had gone a little way when we came to the cottage. It was rather charming, set in the woods there.

'Who lives here?' he asked.

'It's empty just now,' I replied. 'It belongs to the estate. It's too far from the house to use for servants. It was let to some people for the summer. They plan to let it again next summer.'

'It's rather charming. Let's have a look at it.'

It was a pretty little cottage. Virginia creeper grew over the walls and the leaves were now their rich autumn red.

'How quiet it is!' he said. 'Listen!'

We stood together and I felt a sudden excitement. I was enjoying this. I was a little apprehensive. I wanted to know what he would do next.

'Shall we see if it's occupied?' he asked.

'It isn't. I remember Aunt Martha's mentioning it. It's called Parrot Cottage. Someone who lived here long ago had a parrot. He was an old seafaring man and the parrot used to call out strange things which echoed through the woods.'

He was peering through the window. 'Yes, it's empty,' he said. He walked round the house. 'Sarah,' he called, 'there's an open window here. I'm going to get through. Come on.'

Surprising myself I went, though resenting his peremptory command.

'Shall I open the front door for you, my discreet and proper young lady? Then you won't have to climb through.'

'Yes,' I said, 'open the front door.'

'Your wishes shall be respected,' he replied mockingly.

I went round to the front of the cottage and a few moments later was inside. It was very small. There were two rooms downstairs with a sort of small kitchen from which rose a staircase to a room upstairs which ran from one end of the cottage to the other. The roof sloped and there were two small lattice windows at either end.

'I believe the old salt and his parrot were very happy here,' said Clinton Shaw.

I started down the stairs. I had the feeling that I did not want to stay here with him. The cottage was too confined. It seemed to bring us too close together.

'Be careful,' he said, 'those stairs could be dangerous.'

He had caught my arm and my uneasiness increased. I disengaged myself as we reached the lower floor.

'I think the staircase is sound enough,' I said. 'In any case before it is let again I suppose it will be overhauled.'

'Naturally,' he replied. 'I *am* enjoying this. Quite an adventure, isn't it?'

'Adventure? Hardly as stirring as that implies.'

'I find it stirring,' he insisted. 'Imagine all that has happened within these walls. How long has it stood here? Two hundred years, I'll guess. Think of all that could have happened in two hundred years.' He came closer to me. 'Think of all that *will* happen in the years to come.'

'The same applies to every house.'

'I feel something special about this one, do you?'

'No.'

'That's not true. Your eyes tell me. I know what it is. You and I are looking at the house together. Doesn't that seem significant to you?'

'Not in the least. What it means to me is that you and I were riding in the forest, saw an empty cottage and decided to look at it.' I turned to the door.

He laid a hand on my arm. 'One quick look. There's a wood-house just outside. Just a peep . . . then we'll go.'

He unbolted the back door and went to the wood-house. There were logs there, evidently stored by the last occupant and not worthy of being taken away.

'Prudent people,' commented Clinton Shaw. 'Determined to be warm. Snug here though. Protected from the wind by all those trees. But damp . . . decidedly damp.'

I started to laugh. 'You sound like a prospective tenant.'

He laughed with me. 'Do you know I've taken quite a fancy to the place.'

'It's getting darker,' I said. I felt a sudden need to get away. Suddenly the cottage had become sinister. He was standing between me and the door, watching me. I could have almost panicked in those moments.

It was stupid of me for when I stepped towards the door he made no effort to detain me. I walked out into the forest. He bolted the door from the inside and came out by way of the window.

'We leave everything just as we found it,' he commented.

'Shouldn't you shut the window too?'

'The bolt's broken. That's why it was open. Besides, I might want to have another look. You never know.'

'You are taken with the place.'

'I see its possibilities. Yes, I have taken a liking to it.

'The garden's overgrown,' he went on. He was in no hurry to leave. He walked round the cottage. There was about a quarter of an acre of overgrown shrubs at the back before it merged into the forest.

'Foxgloves everywhere,' he said. 'Look!' He stopped and picked a spray of leaves. 'So pretty when the flowers come. Pretty and deadly. Did you know they were called Dead Men's Bells?'

'No. But I did know they contain poison.'

'They are used medicinally and have been of great use to doctors. Odd that they should give life . . . and death. But then, my dear Sarah, you will agree with me that nothing in this life is all bad . . . or all good for that matter. Look at those yews over there. I reckon they have stood there for hundreds of years. Rather beautiful, don't you think? Yet I wonder how many deaths they have been responsible for. Did you know that the leaves and the seeds contain taxine which is about as deadly a poison as you could find anywhere?'

'You seem to have made a study of poisons.'

'In a manner of speaking, yes. When I was very young I had a tutor and it was a passion with him. We did more botany than anything else. I learned that the most beautiful plants were the most deadly. Larkspur, for instance – what a beautiful flower! But the seeds and the foliage can kill. They contain delphine – another deadly poison.'

'Very useful knowledge.'

'Very. In Ceylon, of course, there are different plants . . . equally deadly. Perhaps more so. The old Kandyan kings were experts at mixing the most deadly poisons. They had the variety which could impregnate gloves, boots . . . garments of any sort. A little prick of the skin and that was the end. It's all very interesting, I assure you.'

'But not the kind of knowledge one can put to use in the ordinary way of life, except of course . . .'

We were standing in the garden rather close and I was deeply aware of the stillness all about us. I had a sudden feeling of apprehension. Later I began to think it was a premonition.

I shivered almost imperceptibly, but not quite, for he noticed.

'You're cold,' he said. His voice had changed. It was almost tender and for some reason he moved me in a strange way.

It was as though he were casting some spell over me.

'Come on,' he said. 'We'll go. It'll soon be dark. Do you want to be lost in the forest?'

'It could hardly happen to me,' I said. 'I know my way.'

'It's always a good thing to know your way,' he replied. He put an arm about me and as I moved away from him he laughed.

I quickened my pace and we reached the horses. We mounted and rode back to the house.

The next day the brougham took us to the station and we went by train to Liverpool Street station from where we took a cab to Harley Street.

Clinton Shaw and I sat in the waiting-room for two hours. I thought my father was never coming out. We did not talk much. At least he realized that I did not want that. In fact he seemed to have changed from that brash and arrogant man who had made such a deep impression on me that I could not get him out of my mind.

At length we were summoned to the consulting-room.

My father was not there.

'He is lying in the next room,' said the doctor. 'The examination has been exhausting for him.'

The doctor knew Clinton Shaw for he, it seemed, had arranged this consultation, and it was he who had introduced me as the patient's daughter.

'I have grave news for you, I'm afraid,' said the specialist. 'His lungs are in a bad state. He can't live for more than six weeks . . . two months at the most.'

I caught my breath. Misery overwhelmed me. So I had found my father only to lose him.

Clinton Shaw who was sitting very close to me took my hand and pressed it. For the first time I was grateful to him for being there.

'He is going to need very special treatment which it is impossible for him to have in a private home,' went on the doctor. 'I am therefore having him sent to my own nursing home, where I can keep him under observation. I think you should know that there is small hope of improvement. But we shall do our best and there have been discoveries lately. Who knows . . . But I think you should reconcile yourself, Miss Ashington, that there is very little we can do for him except see that he does not endure great pain and that his last days are as comfortable as we can make them.'

I bowed my head.

'Shall we be able to see him?'

'As often as you wish. The nursing home is not far from here. I assure you it is the best possible place for him and he could not have better attention anywhere than he will get there. He is philosophical. I think he has known for some time that he cannot live long.'

I stood up. Clinton Shaw was beside me. He took my arm and together we went to my father.

It was easier than I had feared and I believe it was something to do with Clinton Shaw's being there. I had to show some courage in front of him. My grief had made me vulnerable and I did not want him to see that.

My father was smiling. He was going to the nursing home, he knew. In fact, I had an idea that he had expected something like this to happen.

'I shall come often,' I said.

'Dear Sarah, that will make me very happy.'

It was not long before the carriage came to take him. We accompanied him and saw him comfortably settled in a pleasant room. Clinton Shaw left us together for a while and we talked as brightly as we could. He was, I think, more intent on cheering me than worried about himself. Clinton Shaw came back with books and papers which he had brought, and then it was time for us to leave.

I was silent during the journey; he sat opposite me, watching me compassionately.

We had the carriage to ourselves and I was glad of it. Just as we came into Epleigh station he leaned forward and touched my hand.

'You were wonderful,' he said.

I felt my lips trembling and turned away.

It is amazing how quickly one accepts a situation and how a

change of routine soon becomes the normal one.

I travelled frequently to London to see my father – almost every other day. Now and then one of the aunts – or both of them – came, and sometimes Clinton Shaw travelled with me. He was not staying at the Grange all the time, although his room was kept for him when he wished to come down. He had taken rooms in a hotel in London where he conducted his business. Sometimes I met him, after I had visited my father, and we travelled back together.

The aunts had been shaken by my father's illness. To Aunt Martha it seemed a personal affront that she should have made such plans for him and been frustrated.

She had dreamed of entertaining lavishly, inviting local families with eligible daughters. Everything went wrong with her plans. My mother had died conveniently and left the way clear; then Celia had acted in a very unpredictable manner and gone away. She had written from a hotel in Southampton to say she was going abroad for a while with a cousin and she would write again when she returned to England giving us an address. Our friendship had been too close for us to lose touch like ships that pass in the night. But Aunt Martha was disappointed in her. My father home at last ... in her power, and since Celia had defected she was determined to find a marriageable girl for him. And what happened! He became ill – so ill that it was clear he could not marry again, much less beget a son whose wife would wear the Ashington Pearls. It sounded rather like The House that Jack Built, and I could have laughed had I been in a laughing mood.

My plans, no less than Aunt Martha's, had gone awry. I had made up my mind as soon as I heard that my father was coming home that I would go back to Ceylon with him when he went. And now it seemed as though he never would go back.

Yet how could one think beyond that terrible doom which was gradually overtaking us.

But for Clinton Shaw I should have been deeply distressed and unhappy, but there was something in my very animosity towards him which made me take an interest in life. I couldn't help it, but when I scored over him in our battles of words I would feel a certain elation. He took my mind off the misery of seeing my father slowly fade away.

Sometimes I travelled up to London alone – although Aunt Martha did not think this was quite right, but the journey by train was not long and the brougham was always waiting when I arrived at Epleigh. She was pleased, however, when Clinton Shaw accompanied me.

'He is a friend of your father's and therefore suitable to escort you,' she said. I wondered what her verdict would be if she really knew what he was like.

Whenever he did appear I managed to look faintly displeased. I would not admit that if he did not join me I felt faintly disappointed. I rather suspect he saw through my deception.

This brings me to that fateful day which was to change my life. It was December. The snow had come early this year. It was going to be a hard winter, everyone said. Mrs Lamb pointed out that there were three times the number of berries on the bushes this year. Nature's way of providing for the birds through a long hard winter.

When I left in my strong boots and sealskin jacket with muff and hat to match, Aunt Mabel was in the hall where a big fire was crackling away.

'I should leave London a little earlier than usual,' she said. 'Martha was saying that she thought you ought not to go till the weather's better.'

'I'll be all right,' I replied quickly. 'He'd be so disappointed if I didn't go. It's not snowing now. The thaw will set in, you see.'

I hurried off. I did not want a tussle with Aunt Martha as to whether I should or should not go.

The weather was better in London, as it always is. The pavements had been swept clear of the snow and the traffic seemed to dispose of that in the roads. There were little heaps of it on the edge of the pavements and that was all.

I saw my father, who seemed slightly better, and my spirits rose. The doctor might be wrong and he had admitted that there might be some discovery which would cure him.

My father was delighted to see me. He had feared the weather might keep me away, but I said – not very truthfully – that it was not so bad in Epleigh.

'The trees provide a barrier to the wind,' he said.

Clinton Shaw came to the nursing home that afternoon.

'I thought I should travel back with you,' he said, 'to make sure you're safe and sound. I'm surprised that your aunts let you come out on a day like this.'

'Aunt Mabel tried to prevent me. I slipped away before Aunt Martha appeared.'

'Wise strategy. It's going to be a wild night. You should be thankful that you have me to look after you.'

'The brougham will be waiting for me at the station.'

'If it can get there.'

'What do you mean?'

'Oh nothing . . . just that it's going to be a rough night.'

Owing to the weather the train was late on leaving and as we puffed out of London the snow was falling fast. Darkness had long descended for it was now nearly seven o'clock. We were going to be very late back. I wondered whether the aunts would be anxious. They would understand about the bad weather, of course, and they would think that I had stayed at the nursing home, which I could have done if it was thought too bad to come back.

'Seems to be quite a blizzard,' said Clinton Shaw. He seemed very little perturbed. In fact, he might have been rather pleased about it.

The train came to a standstill after we had been going for half an hour.

'Evidently a blockage on the line,' said Clinton Shaw. He opened the window intending to look out but the snow immediately came into the carriage so he shut the window quickly and resumed his seat.

'We are going to be very late,' he said. 'What will the aunts think?'

'In the first place Aunt Mabel will say "I told you so". She did say I shouldn't have gone today. Then they will presume that I am spending the night at the nursing home.'

'Being sensible ladies they will accept the inevitable without fuss.'

'I dare say they will.'

'How fortunate that I decided to accompany you.'

'I dare say I could have managed by myself. After all, there is nothing to do but to sit here and wait. When I get to the station the brougham will be waiting for me ... late as I am. So all will be well.'

'Still, you must admit that at times like this a little company is pleasant.'

He was smiling a little secretively. I could almost believe that he had arranged the snow. My thoughts went on in ridiculous imaginings. Witches were said to arouse storms at sea. He was perhaps a sorcerer who could create a snowstorm. Why? What was the point? He certainly looked like a sorcerer.

He was watching me intently. I had an idea that he was trying to read my thoughts. He began to talk about Ceylon and the life there and how exciting it was to be caught in a snowstorm. He would take back memories of it when he went. I asked how long he intended to stay.

'Until my business is accomplished,' he said enigmatically.

'Did you plan to marry here?' I asked.

'Oh yes, I shall take my wife back with me.'

'Is she happy about leaving England?'

'I rather think she is anxious to.'

'Do you think she will settle there happily?'

'Of course. She will be with me.'

'That should make up for anything she has left behind, I am sure.'

'How clearly you see it. I am glad you do.'

'I suppose you see a great deal of her.'

He nodded, smiling.

'Is she in London?'

'Frequently.'

'Perhaps I shall meet her.'

He nodded again. The train gave a jerk. 'We're off,' he said.

It must have been nearly nine o'clock when we came into Epleigh station. It was no longer snowing.

We were the only two who alighted from the train. The porter, Jack Wall, was on the platform. He looked surprised to see us.

'Why, Miss Ashington,' he said. 'They wasn't expecting you.'

'Not expecting me!'

'No. This is the only train running and it'll be the last tonight. I'm just off home. Good thing I live nearby.'

'The brougham . . .'

'Couldn't get here, Miss. The roads are something shocking. The coachman from the Grange walked down to ask about the trains. I told him many of them had been cancelled and he said, "Reckon Miss Ashington will stay at the nursing home." Even a dog wouldn't go out on a day like this, Miss, unless he had to.'

I was aware of Clinton Shaw beside me and I had to admit that I really was glad that he was there.

'What can we do?' I asked.

'We can get to the house,' he said. 'It's not all that far.'

"Tis the only thing, Miss,' said the porter. 'I'm off now. I was just waiting to see the train in. It'll go into a siding now . . . till things get better.'

'Come,' said Clinton Shaw, 'we'll get started.'

We said good night to Jack Wall.

'Be careful of the road,' he warned us. 'It's freezing some places. And mind the drifts.'

Clinton Shaw took my arm.

'We'll take the short cut through the forest,' he said. 'It'll be easier that way. More sheltered from the wind and the path will be less treacherous. Good thing I have my walking stick. It's useful at times like this.'

It was long and sturdy-looking, quite thick, and I could see useful. It had a silver band round the top and he used it a good deal when walking.

The cold air was invigorating and the scene was quite beautiful for there was a half moon which was visible every now and then as the wind sent the snow clouds scurrying across the sky. We went towards the forest and as we reached it the snow started to fall again.

My sealskin coat was a good protection against the wind and my hands were warm in my muff. Clinton Shaw held my arm firmly and we ploughed on.

There was stillness in the forest, in spite of the intermittent gusts of wind. It was eerie in that intense whiteness occasionally lighted by the glow of the moon.

It was a different place from the forest I knew so well – quite unfamiliar. It had been a good idea to seek the shelter of the trees for not only were we protected from the biting wind but we had no drifts to contend with.

Struggling from tree to tree watching with the utmost care where we trod was a slow process. Even so, we seemed to be a long time in coming to the house.

Suddenly Clinton Shaw stood still.

'Where are we?' he asked.

I looked about. I really could not say. It had not occurred to me that I could be lost in that part of the forest which was so near the Grange. I wondered how long we had been walking but I could not get at the watch which was pinned on my bodice. I looked about me helplessly.

'Everything looks so different,' I said. 'We must be quite near the Grange though.'

'Let's go this way,' said Clinton Shaw. 'The trees are thinning a bit.'

I stumbled and he caught me, holding me tightly for a moment.

'I thank God,' he said, 'that I decided to come with you today. What would you have done without me?'

'I should have gone to the house by myself. Or I could have sent Jack Wall to tell them I was there.'

'I am sure you would have been resourceful. Still, I'm glad. Now this should be the Grange through here.'

It was not the Grange, but there was a familiarity about it. There was a path. We took it and before us, its roof covered in snow, was Parrot Cottage.

Clinton Shaw laughed triumphantly. 'At least we know where we are.'

'We're some way from the Grange.'

'I think we should stay here.'

'Stay here!'

'For a rest. To get our bearings. We've been going round in circles. Do you realize that we're farther away from the Grange than when we entered the forest? At least we'll have shelter here. I'll get through the window.'

I knew there was sense in what he was saying and yet it was as though there was a warning in the icy air. If I entered Parrot Cottage something was going to happen. Fate was at my elbow urging me to make a choice.

I admonished myself for my folly. What harm could there be in resting for a while? I was cold and tired . . . more so than I had realized.

He was at the door of the cottage drawing me in. The decision had been made for me. He shut the door with a bang and shook the snow off himself.

'A little warmer in here. What a walk! You all right?' He put a hand to my cheek. 'You're frozen! I tell you what I'm going to do. I'm going to bring in some of those logs from outside and light a fire.'

'Light a fire! We shall only be here until we've rested. We mustn't stay too long. We shall be so late.'

'My dear Sarah,' he said, 'do you realize that there's a blizzard blowing outside? Do you realize that we could not find our way through the forest? We've kept going – but we've had enough. We've found shelter. We'd be mad not to make use of it. If we leave here and go stumbling through the forest we'll be lost. We'd have to rest. We'd get covered with snow and be frozen to death. There's a touching story called *Babes in the Wood*. Remind me to tell you it when we have more time. Now, a fire. Just think how marvellous that would be. There are logs out there. We saw them, didn't we? Who knows, there might be candles. I'm going to look.'

I followed him to the wood-house. The logs were still there.

'Look!' he cried. 'The gods are on our side. That's a lantern. It's got a candle in it.' He took a box of matches from his pocket and we had a light. 'Good! There's a box here. I wonder what's inside. Eureka! Rugs. Several of them. My dear Sarah, this is an adventure. Don't pick them up. You'll make them wet. Let's get a fire lighted and dry ourselves off.'

He carried in the logs and I was surprised how quickly he got a fire going. I was caught up in the excitement. It was wonderful to see the flames leaping in the old grate and I began to feel warmer. Now I realized how exhausting our walk had been and that he was right about the folly of attempting to reach the Grange. We needed a rest.

We sat on the floor by the fire. He was close to me and I noticed how his eyes gleamed in the firelight and that there was a deepened colour in his usually brown skin.

I took off my woollen gloves and held my hands out to the fire. He did the same. I looked at our four hands; his were large, square, capable hands. He was decidedly capable. He knew just how to handle a situation like this.

'When we're drier we'll get the rugs in,' he said. 'I wonder how many there are. Seemed quite a few there.'

'I wonder why they were left behind. They must be damp.'

'Perhaps not. The box seemed quite strong and weatherproof. Ready? Let's go and get them.'

There were four woollen rugs rolled up tightly. We brought them in.

'They're dry,' he said. 'Take off your coat and boots because they must be saturated.'

I obeyed and wrapped myself in one of the rugs. He was right about my boots. They were very wet and, strong as they were, the snow had penetrated.

I took off my stockings for my feet were wet. He had removed his coat and boots and had taken one of the rugs and we sat squatting on the floor.

'Like two Red Indians,' he said. 'This must have been how it felt round the camp fire. Are you hungry?'

'No,' I answered. 'Food's the last thing I'm thinking of. I had tea and fruit-cake at the nursing home before I left as well as a big luncheon.'

'Good. Food is one thing I can't offer. But I do have something.' He reached for the walking stick which was lying on the floor nearby. I watched him with interest as he unscrewed the top. He held it out to me. It was like a small cup. He tipped up the stick and gold-coloured liquid trickled out.

'This will warm you,' he said.

'What is it?'

'Whisky. This stick is hollow. It makes a good container. Very useful in emergencies.'

'Thank you. I don't care for whisky.'

'You need it. It'll warm you. It'll stave off that chill which you will very likely get if you don't take some precaution against it.'

I took the cup and swallowed the draught. It burned my throat. He looked at me steadily. 'There,' he said. 'You feel better.'

I coughed a little. 'It burns,' I said.

'Come along. You must have another. This vessel holds scarcely more than one swallow.'

'Thank you, but I'd rather not.'

'Now, Sarah, this is purely medicinal.' He held out the full cup to me. 'It'll warm you. You must be warmed. What you should have is a hot bath and get into a warm bed. I'm afraid Parrot Cottage cannot offer such amenities. Never mind. This is the next best thing.'

Almost as though mesmerized I took the cup. I did feel the warmth flooding over me. It was good after the cold. I drank the second cup.

He was smiling at me. I watched him drink several cups of the liquid.

'That's better,' he said. 'You feel better, Sarah?'

'I feel a little strange.'

'Of course,' he said soothingly. 'What a night it has been and it is only just beginning.'

'What!' I cried. My voice sounded strange, far away. Something was telling me that now I was warmer I ought to go. I stood up. The room seemed to be slowly circling round. For a moment I thought I was going to fall. Then he was there. He caught me and held me against him. He was laughing at me.

'It's the whisky,' I said.

He gripped me tightly; my head was bent back and his lips were on mine, kissing me as I had never realized people kissed before. I tried to escape but I couldn't. Then I was still and that seemed to please him.

I stammered again: 'It was the whisky.'

'No,' he said, 'it is love.'

It is difficult for me to remember what happened next. It was only later when I began to understand my own nature that I could explain it. Then it seemed as though I had always known this would happen in some way and that I had half wanted it to. I was to live in shame for weeks to come; I refused to look clearly at what had happened and saw only what I wanted to believe.

There was a dreamlike quality about it all. The whisky, which I had never tasted before, had had its effect on me. I felt that I was outside this scene, an onlooker, and the girl who was seduced by a man whom she told herself she heartily disliked could not be myself.

He was full of guile. He knew exactly how to play on my senses. He had chosen the moment with skill and it seemed as though fate was his ally.

When he said it was love I muttered something about the girl he was going to marry. I heard him laugh and somehow that laughter excited me.

'She's here with me,' he said. 'She is Miss Sarah Ashington. I decided she was the one as soon as I set eyes on her.'

I did not know myself. Perhaps I had deliberately refused to.

He had spread the rugs on the floor and rolled one up to make a pillow.

'Even with the fire,' he said, 'it's bitterly cold. Did you know that the warmth from the human body is the most comforting of all warmers on a cold night?'

My sealskin coat was spread on the floor to dry.

'When it's dry I'll cover you over with it,' he said tenderly. 'That and I will keep you warm.'

I kept saying: 'We ought to go now.' My voice still sounded as though it came from a long way off. He lifted me up in his arms and then he put me down on the rugs. I was afraid in a dreamy sort of way, afraid and yet wildly excited. I could feel my heart beating like a drum. He knelt beside me and kissed my brow, my eyes and my throat. I felt his hands on me and then he was beside me, caressing me, whispering to me, and I made the startling discovery that I wanted him to go on. Of course he was a master in the art of making love and it seemed that he knew me better than I knew myself. I thought I was dreaming. I must be dreaming. This could not be happening to me.

'I must go,' I muttered, but I made no attempt to resist him.

'Sarah, my love,' he murmured. 'Didn't you know? It was meant to be.'

I awoke, cold and stiff. I wondered where I was. I was lying on a hard floor, my coat over me. Realization came to me. Nothing could ever be the same again.

I sat up. He was kneeling by the fire, coaxing a blaze.

'What happened?' I cried.

'Bliss!' he said, grinning at me. 'Absolute bliss!'

'We have been here . . . all night.'

'It's eight o'clock.'

'Eight . . . in the morn'ng!'

'It's still snowing. We'll find our way to the Grange though. Daylight will help.'

I covered my face with my hands, remembering vaguely. He came and knelt beside me and drew my hands away from my face. He kissed me.

'You can't tell me you hate me now,' he said.

'I don't know. I can't think what . . .'

'It was all very natural. After all, it had to happen sooner or later. Don't worry. We'll be married just as soon as I can arrange it. I'll take you back with me. You know that was the intention right from the first.'

'Marry *you*!'

'You look surprised. I hope you are not in the habit of sleeping with men casually and then saying goodbye.'

'You . . . you arranged this!'

'Oh yes. I have a contract with the heavenly powers. I want to seduce a girl, so I say: Please put on a snowstorm and provide a cottage in the woods for the occasion.'

'If you had been a gentleman you would not have taken advantage of the situation.'

'Ah, but I am not a gentleman. You know that. I am a cad who has learned to take every advantage which is offered.'

'I think the best thing we can do is to forget it ever happened.'

'That's impossible. You are no longer the virgin Sarah that you were when you came into this cottage last night. Besides, what if there were . . . consequences . . . as there might well be.'

'This is becoming a nightmare.'

'You seemed to find the situation interesting last night.'

'You gave me the whisky to dull my senses.'

'It seemed to revive your senses. You are not the reluctant shrinking young lady you thought yourself to be. You've been awakened, my dear, to the fact that there is something more to life than raising funds for the church roof. I tell you this: You were not meant for single blessedness. You should not blush unseen and waste your sweetness on the desert air.'

'I did not expect such poetic thoughts from you.'

'I know more like that.' He picked me up suddenly and kissed me on the lips – one of those long, startling kisses which made me uneasy.

'Listen, Sarah. I want to marry you. Last night was just a beginning. You were off your guard. You'd lost your serpent's tongue. Last night you were yourself. The cold, the walk through the forest, the whisky . . . they betrayed you. You are meant for love, my darling, and I will be your tutor in that wondrous art. Now here is the plan. We must leave now for the Grange. We will tell them exactly what happened, excluding of course an account of that delicious intimacy which is for us alone. Your aunts are going to be a little distraught. A young girl to spend a night alone in a cottage with a man! I shall imply – without saying so, which would be indelicate and scarcely truthful! – that I was a man of honour. I hadn't my sword with me to put between us as we lay on the rugs but there was a walking stick which had to serve instead. I shall not mention that it contained that nectar of the gods which warmed us both and swept away your inhibitions so that the real Sarah emerged. Have no fear. Leave this to me. In a few days I shall present myself to the aunts and tell them that I want your hand in marriage.'

'Stop it. This is not a joke. I am furiously angry.'

'Now, my dearest, having lost your virginity it will avail you nothing to lose your temper as well. You must make the best of what has happened. You must remember that you did not repulse my advances. If you were the girl you pretend to be you would have run out half naked into the snow. You did nothing of the sort. You allowed yourself to be seduced and I do not think it was entirely distasteful to you. Be yourself, Sarah. It's natural to love and be loved. You and I will be happy together. Come on. Put on your coat and those boots. They are dry now. It's back to the Grange.'

He kicked out the remains of the fire. 'We don't want the place to be burned down, do we,' he said. 'Parrot Cottage! It will always be a favourite spot of mine. As long as I live I shall never forget the night I spent in Parrot Cottage. Are you ready? Let me look at you. Yes, you do look different. You are more lovely than ever. There is a secret knowledge in your eyes. It will take about three weeks, I think. The banns have to be read.'

I did not answer him as he opened the door of the cottage and we went out into the forest.

I felt as though I were still in a dream from which I must soon awaken.

It was nearly midday when we returned to the Grange. Aunt Mabel came into the hall as we entered the house.

'My dear Sarah,' she cried. 'So you stayed the night at the nursing home. It was the wisest thing to do. We guessed, of course.'

For a second or so I hesitated, wondering whether it would save a lot of explanation to let her believe this; then I remembered that we had seen Jack Wall at the station and that he might mention the fact. I could see myself getting tangled up in deceit.

'No,' I said, 'we came last night.'

Clinton took over. 'There was no conveyance and we started to walk. We were lost in the forest but we did find shelter and we waited until we could get back.'

I saw the look of shocked amazement in Aunt Mabel's eyes. Taking shelter all night . . . with a man! I felt the colour coming into my cheeks. Aunt Mabel was merely emphasizing the enormity of the situation. What if she knew exactly what had happened!

Aunt Martha appeared.

'They're here,' said Aunt Mabel unnecessarily. 'They came last night.'

'Came last night . . . Then where . . . ?'

Clinton said: 'How kind you are, Miss Ashington, to be so concerned. The train was very late. There were delays all along the line. We tried to get to the Grange but the blizzard was such that we could not fight against it. We found a place to shelter and were forced to take it until we could get back.'

He had a certain way with women. Even Aunt Martha was not immune to it.

He went on: 'It's all over now. You can rest assured, Miss Ashington, that I did all I could to look after your niece.'

Aunt Martha became practical. 'You need some hot food. There's some oxtail stew in the kitchen. Mabel, go and tell Mrs Lamb to get it ready right away. You'll want to get those things off, I don't doubt. Come down in ten minutes. Then I should think you'd want to rest.'

'It's just what we need,' said Clinton, looking at Aunt Martha with admiration.

I was glad to escape from them. I took off my clothes and put on a warm woollen dress. When I went down to the winter parlour, Clinton was already there. I told myself that I was too upset to want to eat but I soon discovered how hungry I was. Clinton seemed to guess my thoughts and they amused him.

Afterwards we went to our rooms. Hot water had been sent up. I bathed, wrapped myself in a dressing-gown and lay down on my bed.

It was not long before Aunt Martha came in.

The sky was heavy with snow clouds and I was glad that there was little light in the room. I turned my face from the window for fear she should notice something different about me.

She sat down on the armchair.

'This,' she said, 'is most unfortunate. I should like the servants to assume that you came back on the morning train having stayed the night in the nursing home.'

'Jack Wall saw us come in,' I told her.

'Disastrous!' cried Aunt Martha. 'There will be talk.'

'Aunt Martha, we started for home. It was impossible to get here. We were lost in the forest. What else could we have done?'

'People will talk,' she said.

'Let them!' I retorted angrily.

'That's foolish. Everything I plan goes awry. I had thought you might marry and settle here. I have as a matter of fact written to a very dear friend in the North. She has three sons . . . charming young men. They are a very good family although they have recently fallen on hard times. I had hopes that you and one of these young men would find pleasure in each other's company. You could marry and perhaps he could be persuaded to change his name to Ashington. If you had a son . . .'

I felt a little hysterical. 'Oh, Aunt Martha,' I cried. 'Stop it. Stop it! I can't bear it. I'm not going to marry your young man. When I marry I'll marry whom I want to.'

'What is the matter with you, Sarah? You're not yourself. You owe us something, you know. Haven't we taken you in? What would have happened to you if we hadn't? You owe it to us . . . to the family . . . But perhaps this is not the time to talk of these things. In any case there is bound to be gossip. People will be saying you lost your way deliberately. This sort of thing is not good for the reputation of a young girl.'

'Aunt Martha, you took me in, it's true. I thought it was because I am your niece, because I belonged here. I did not know that the bill would be presented and I would be expected to pay for what I have had.'

'This is vulgar, I refuse to discuss it any more.' Aunt Martha rose. 'You seem to have taken leave of your senses. Jack Wall will gossip. The servants will know what time you came in and will tell other servants. You can be sure that before the week's out the entire neighbourhood will know that you spent the night with a man.'

'At least it will put a little spice into their usually flat gossip.'

'It will diminish your chances, I can tell you.'

'Aunt Martha,' I said, raising myself on my arm and looking straight at her, 'I don't care. I simply don't care.'

'I will talk to you later. You are hysterical now, but I think you realize the importance of what has happened.'

She stalked to the door and when she had gone I lay back and tried to laugh at the conventions of the society in which we lived. A young lady was expected to perish in a blizzard rather than seek shelter alone with a man. But in truth I had been out all night. I had been seduced and I had allowed it to happen. My excuse was that he had plied me with whisky to which I was unaccustomed. There was no excuse. My reputation was tarnished.

I kept thinking of what had happened. Vague images which I wanted to forget forced themselves into my memory.

He had changed me. He had brought me face to face with a new aspect of myself. There was a part of me that wanted to be with him, to make love with him even while I hated him; and because of that hatred it was almost unbearably exciting.

I might have known that he would have his way. Part of me admired his persistence while the other part deplored it.

He had a long talk with Aunt Martha, which he told me about after. He told her that he would like to speak with her in private if she would permit it. He had then said to her: 'Sarah is young and innocent and does not realize the importance of what has happened. Dear Miss Ashington, you are a woman of the world and you will understand how deeply I deplore the situation in which we have been placed – through no fault of ours, believe me, Miss Ashington. To have attempted to walk through the forest in that blizzard could have been death to us both. There was no alternative but to take shelter. Oh, I understand your misgivings and, as it happens, I have since my arrival in England fallen deeply in love with your niece and I long to make her my wife. To a lady of your sensible outlook this will seem over-hasty, but, remember, I lived close to your brother. I have read the letters Sarah sent to him. I felt I knew her before I came here. *You* would understand, I know, Miss Ashington.'

She had nodded gravely. They were two worldly people debating how to settle the gossip, to right a wrong which had been thrust upon us.

'"Have I your permission to ask Sarah to marry me?" I asked her,' he went on to tell me. 'Believe me, my darling, permission was most graciously given. She then explained to me that Ashington was a name which had been honoured through the centuries. She seemed to think I might find it so glorious that I would wish to reverse the law of a wife's taking her husband's name. I pretended to consider the idea. What do you think of that?'

'I think you deceive so easily that you must have had plenty of practice in the art.'

'When I want something I go for it. Nothing stands in my way if I can help it.'

'You are quite ruthless.'

'That may be. Now, with Aunt Martha's permission, I shall go down on my knees, dear Sarah, and say: "Will you marry me?"'

'Spare yourself the effort,' I retorted.

He gave me that tender smile and although I knew it to be false, it touched me deeply.

The snow lasted for a week and then the thaw set in. Clinton had gone up to London but the weather was too bad for me to visit my father.

'We want no repetition of that last trip,' said Aunt Martha grimly.

I knew by the furtive looks the servants gave me that they were talking among themselves. The Cannon girls were over-bright and did not refer to it. I wanted to snap my fingers at them all and it occurred to me how bored I should be if I had to spend my life in this restricted atmosphere. I should grow like the aunts in time. But they had never had an adventure such as I had had. How could I be sure of that? Perhaps Aunt Martha and the lover who had wanted to marry her sister . . .

I could picture what was in store. The three eligible gentlemen would be produced. Good family fallen on lean times . . . so lean that one would be ready to marry me and change his name to Ashington so that I could bear a son of that name.

It was so ridiculous, so snobbish and so impossible.

My father was going to die. My dreams of being with him had gone. There was an alternative – an exciting one which made my heart leap at the thought of it.

I missed him. The days seemed long without him – long and

empty. When he had been in the house I had locked my bedroom door for I had half expected him to come storming in. But he did not. I had noticed the teasing look in his eyes. I felt he had discovered secrets in me which were unknown to myself. He had forced me into an intimacy which was revealing not only to him but to me.

I was watching for him to come back . . . waiting for him.

In my heart I knew where I was drifting. Could one marry a man whom one did not love? Was it possible to feel an overpowering physical attraction for a man whose honour one doubted, a man one recognized as one of the buccaneers of life, taking what he wanted and being quite ruthless? I was sure he had been the lover of many women.

As soon as the snow was clear I went to see my father. He had missed me very much and I saw that he had grown weaker. It was more obvious after an absence.

He told me that Clinton had been to see him. He had spoken to him of his feelings for me. 'I am so glad, Sarah. He says he is certain you love him too and that you have given him an indication that you do.'

I sat there fuming inwardly. How dared he!

'My dear Sarah,' went on my father, 'I should die happy if I thought you and Clinton were to marry.'

'Is he the sort of man you would want for a son-in-law?'

'He's strong. He's clever. The Shaw plantation has become the finest in Ceylon since he took over. He has been of great help to me. I have had my difficulties, Sarah, and it has been good to have him as a neighbour. I owe him a great deal. I have often wondered why he did not marry. I fancy the English out there were not to his liking. Women have always found him attractive and he likes them. However, I believe he came to England intending to marry.'

'That seems rather calculated, Father.'

'Oh, it's not like choosing a house or a suit of clothes, you know. He just hoped he would find someone. I had talked so much about you. I even let him read your letters. I remember his saying to me, "I like Sarah. I'm looking forward to meeting her." He was half-way there before he actually saw you. You're very attractive, Sarah, in quite an unusual way. Oh, it would please me very much. I have always felt guilty about you. You were such an amusing child when only a baby. Then your mother took you away and I was denied contact with you. It has been such a pleasure to see you again.'

'You're going to get well,' I said firmly, 'and I shall take you back to Ceylon. I shall be too busy nursing you to think of marrying . . .'

He shook his head. 'We know the facts, Sarah. Let's look them in the face. I shall never go back to Ceylon. You must go though . . . go with Clinton.'

Clinton came to the nursing home. He was going back to the Grange for a day or so, he said. He was lucky to be able to stay with good friends in the country for a respite after strenuous meetings with agents.

'They are as hard as ever, I suppose,' said my father.

'Harder! They are trying to grab all the profit that comes from tea for themselves.'

When we were alone in the railway carriage he came, sat beside me and put an arm about my shoulders.

'I've missed you,' he said. 'Shall we make the announcement when we get to the Grange?'

I did not answer. I could not because he had caught me to him and was giving me those savage kisses which made speech impossible.

'It will be wonderful,' he said at last. 'I promise you, and it will be legal . . . just think of that!'

'I haven't agreed.'

'You're going to . . . tonight.'

'When one marries shouldn't one be in love?'

'It depends on what you mean by love.'

'I should have thought the definition was clear enough.'

163

'Love!' he mused. 'The most alluring project in the world. Love of the body . . . love of the soul . . . Profane and sacred love. My body you know and love, dear Sarah. My soul is a mystery and that is something you will discover gradually. There is little more exciting than a voyage of discovery . . . unless it is love such as we knew . . . you and I together.'

'You took advantage of an unusual situation.'

'That's the way to live, Sarah. Always take advantage of unusual situations. What is it going to be . . . that enthralling life with me, that voyage of discovery . . . or shall you stay here? The Misses Cannon will find you very useful, I am sure, and the church roof will undoubtedly profit. You might even find someone to marry you. You will have to keep it a secret that you spent the most exciting night of your life with your true love in Parrot Cottage.'

'I refuse to listen to such nonsense.'

'And I shall tell Aunt Martha that we are going to be married and I shall go this very evening to see the Reverend Cannon about the banns.'

I did not answer. I withdrew farther from him and sat clasping my hands. I was trembling with excitement. I listened to the motion of the train.

'Going to marry him. Going to marry him. Yes, yes, yes, going to marry him.'

I thought: I am. Yes, I am. It's wrong, I know, but I am going to marry him.

I think Aunt Martha was rather relieved. Aunt Mabel certainly was. In her eyes it was the only proper solution and Aunt Martha was deluding herself that she would be able to persuade him to change his name to Ashington. Before the year was out I would have a son and before the aunts passed away they would see that son with a wife and her portrait could be painted wearing the Ashington Pearls. Then the aunts, mission completed, could say Nunc

Dimittis and depart in peace. They ignored the fact that my father's elder daughter, Clytie, had a son who would come before mine. But his name was not Ashington and Aunt Martha clearly believed she could sweep aside that obstacle.

I wondered about the fabulous heirloom. In the excitement of all that had happened I had not mentioned the pearls to my father. I presumed they were in Ceylon as my mother had been painted there wearing the necklace.

The banns were read and I am sure there was a sigh of relief in the vicarage because the rather unsavoury matter of my night in the forest had come to the most suitable conclusion. Effie Cannon, herself to be a bride before long, was to be my bridesmaid and the doctor was to give me away. It was to be a simple ceremony and I was glad because I was filled with misgivings as the day drew nearer. There were times when I asked myself what I thought I was doing. It was as though my senses and my good sense were fighting a battle together. On the night before my wedding I was really afraid.

What do you know of him? I asked myself. The answer was very little. Then why, *why*?

I only knew that he overwhelmed me, that he aroused passions within me which overcame everything else. That was when he was with me; it was when he was not there that I could not understand myself. Just because of that night in the cottage! Well, it had taught me something and that was that if he went back to Ceylon without me I should be filled with regrets and longings for the rest of my life. Did I want to stay here and become like one of the Cannon girls? Perhaps I was as conventional as my aunts and deep down in my heart I believed that because of what had happened between us I belonged to him in some way and that event must affect the rest of my life. He made me feel that too. It was part of his strategy.

And so I had come as far as this.

My wedding-day arrived. Even as I stood at the altar I seemed to hear a warning voice inside me. 'Wilt thou take this man to be thy wedded husband . . . ?' asked the Reverend Peter Cannon, and I wanted to shout: No. It's a mistake. Let me get out of here and think again.

And yet had it been possible to stop the ceremony I would not have done so.

We were signing the register; we were walking down the aisle, I on his arm. I was aware of the faces in the pews. Everyone in the neighbourhood had come out to see me married. The servants were at the back of the church. I caught sight of Mrs Lamb with Ellen beside her and I could imagine what they were saying. 'Well, 'twas only right and proper after what happened . . .'

Somewhere at the back of my mind was the same thought. Right and proper.

There was a reception at the Grange. He had arranged that. 'You are too good to us,' he had told Aunt Martha. 'Pray leave this to me.'

Aunt Martha protested that it was for the bride's family to provide the reception.

'You are too worldly to be governed by what others have done in the past, I am sure,' was his comment.

She had turned away with that twitching of the lips which indicated pleasure.

So there was champagne and delicious foods which he had had sent down from Fortnum and Mason's. The servants wouldn't like that, I knew. 'So we're not good enough!' I could imagine their saying. 'It has to come from London, does it?'

Soon I would be free of all that.

When the guests had gone he and I walked in the forest. I was quiet and so was he. He had changed; he had become tender and loving. He told me I was never going to regret having married him. So convincing was he that for a time I believed him.

We went back to the Grange. Aunt Martha had given us what she called the bridal suite, which had been occupied by Ashington brides and grooms for two hundred years.

I remembered my mother's telling me about it. 'A great gloomy room,' she said, 'full of ghosts. Brides who had been forced to marry most likely. There was a story of one who jumped out of the window to her death the moment the bridegroom entered the bedroom.'

Clinton shut the door and turned to me. Then he lifted me in his arms and sat me on the bed.

'More to your taste, my love, than the hard floor of Parrot Cottage.'

'And yours, no doubt?'

'Parrot Cottage was a paradise on that night.'

'You are not a stranger to that kind of paradise, I imagine.'

He put his face close to mine and laughed at me. 'Dear Sarah, you will not be a jealous wife, will you?'

'Jealous . . . of you! Of course not.'

'That's good. Jealous women are such a bore.'

'Men too, I suppose.'

He kissed me. 'You mustn't change, Sarah. You must always chastise me with your tongue. You must go on hating and loving me. I can take the mixture all the time.'

He started to undo my dress.

'I will do that,' I said.

'Hurry then or I shall feel bound to assist.'

There was no doubt of my feeling for him. When I lay in his arms he told me he loved me, that I pleased him beyond all women, and if it struck me that it was not quite fitting for a husband to compare his bride with other women on their wedding night, I did not say so. I accepted it. I accepted him. I could forget everything when we were together like this.

I could almost delude myself into believing that I loved him.

The next day we went to see my father. He was delighted that we were married.

'Now,' he said, 'I shan't worry about you any more, Sarah.'

'Were you worried?'

'I can imagine what life was like with your aunts. Not much fun for a young girl. Clinton will take you to Ceylon. How I wish I could be there!'

We drank champagne in his room. I was worried that it might

not be good for him and when I was told by the sister that it could do him no harm, I was saddened because I knew she meant that nothing could harm or do him any good now.

We sat by his bed and talked a great deal; then Clinton and I went back to the Grange.

The next day we went riding in the woods and Clinton wanted to take another look at Parrot Cottage.

We tethered the horses and he went in by way of the window. He opened the door for me to enter. As I stepped inside he picked me up in his arms and swung me round.

'Dear, dear Parrot Cottage,' he said. 'A night to remember, eh Sarah?'

'It certainly had its effect on our lives.'

'You are thinking that if that had not happened here you would never have agreed to marry me. It was like the kiss of the Prince to the Sleeping Beauty. He awakened her to life, remember. A lot of fairy stories are symbolic, you know.'

'I remember you once said you would tell me the story of the Babes in the Wood. Isn't your taste in literature a little infantile?'

'My taste is catholic in all things.' He went to the fire. 'The ashes are still here. Did it occur to you how fortunate we were? Logs in the wood-house, candles, lantern, blankets . . .' He burst out laughing. 'You are looking puzzled, my dearest. Did it occur to you that we were the darlings of the gods that night?'

'It certainly seemed fortuitous.'

'There's a saying that God helps those who help themselves. I suppose that applies to the gods of chance as well.'

'What are you hinting?'

'You have told me I am resourceful. I take my opportunities. I wonder if you realize how resourceful I am, how I *make* my opportunities. It's no use relying on fate, you know. If the mountain won't come to Mahomet, Mahomet goes to the mountain.'

'You like to talk in parables,' I said. 'You couldn't have arranged the snow. That I imagine would be beyond even you.'

He grinned. 'The snow was real enough. What a night that was! The weather had been bad for a while, you remember, and had been growing worse. I liked Parrot Cottage from the moment I saw it. I thought what fun it would be to spend a little time there, the two of us alone.'

I stared at him incredulously.

'I want you to realize what a resourceful husband you have. Do you remember how misty it was when we first saw it. It occurred to me then how easy it could be to lose one's way in the forest. You and I . . . lost, wandering round hand in hand in circles . . . We come to Parrot Cottage. We are tired. We decide to rest there. It is dark and cold outside. Logs in the wood-house and, miracle of miracles, warm rugs. You see how my romantic mind was working.'

'I see it clearly. The logs were there.'

'Yes, they gave me the idea.'

'The rugs, the lantern?'

'Thoughtfully provided by me for the occasion.'

'But how could you know . . .'

'I didn't know. It might have come to nothing. But if ever the occasion should arise the stage was set. That's the first lesson in the road to success. You make your opportunities and when the time comes – *if* the time comes – you are prepared. Mind you, the time may never come. I was taking the long chance. And then the blessed snow . . . the visit to London . . . no brougham at the station. You see, that was luck. That was God helping those who had helped themselves.'

'So you arranged . . . *that*!'

'Come. Congratulate me. I was rather clever, wasn't I?'

'But we lost our way in the forest.'

'*I* did not lose *my* way. Dear Sarah, you see I longed for you. I knew that beneath that fierce antagonism was a passionate young woman, a woman who needed to love and be loved. It was my duty to prove to you who you were . . . to save you before you became like the aunts or the Misses Cannon . . . Oh, very commendable, I agree, but not *you*, Sarah. Oh, definitely not you. You were meant for love and you know it. I made sure when the fates were kind and provided the snow, the delay in the trains, no

brougham . . . well, the least I could do was play my part. I made
sure I knew the way to the cottage. I could have gone there blind-
fold. You see, Sarah, I outwitted you in your own forest. That's
the sort of man I am.'

'You're diabolical!' I said.

'Confess that you like me that way.'

I said nothing. I was thinking of all he had done in taking the
rugs there . . . making sure that he could light a fire. I found I was
laughing with him.

'There's a magic about the forest,' he said. 'The trees take on
the guise of monsters when it grows dark. The old gods are in the
forest. Odin, Thor and the rest. Can you sense them? They are on
the side of adventurers. They come to the aid of those who help
themselves.'

'Then they are undoubtedly on your side.'

'What do you think of me for that little bit of stage management?'

'I repeat that you are diabolical. You played your part well. Not
for one moment did I guess . . .'

'If you had guessed, the play would have been ruined. I'm too
good a player to let that happen.'

'I wonder how good you are. I wonder what you are like when
you cease to act and are simply yourself.'

'That will be a pleasant little conundrum to occupy you through
the years to come.'

'How shall I know when to trust you?'

He took my face in his hands and kissed me. 'Your heart will
tell you,' he said.

I shook myself free impatiently.

'When you are romantic and sentimental I know you are
false.'

'Don't be too sure of that, Sarah. With me you must not be sure
of anything.'

He laughed and turned away. He was going through to the
back door.

'Where are you going?' I asked.

'To get the rugs,' he replied.

'No,' I cried.

But he came back with them. He spread them on the floor and then seized me in his arms.

During the weeks that followed I was constantly with my father. It was clear now that the end was near. I had little time to think of myself or the future. Clinton had said that we could not leave England while my father lived and when he was dead we would leave immediately for Ceylon.

February had come and the crocuses were beginning to make an appearance – mauve, white and gold – with their message that though winter was still with us spring was on the way. Near the pond yellow flowers of the coltsfoot had begun to show alongside the purple butterbur. There were even yellow celandines in sheltered places and green shoots on the elders and the yellow tassels we called lambs' tails on the hazel. The great oaks of the forest still wore their winter look and it would be a few more weeks before the change was visible. I listened to the lapwings mating. It was Celia who had taught me to recognize the songs of birds. It was a melancholy cry ... pee-wit ... peet ... will-o-wit. That was what it sounded like. Theirs was not a very joyous wooing.

Spring has been called the Gateway of the Year. That spring was certainly the gateway of my new life.

My thoughts did not stray for long away from my father. He was going to die soon and my new life would begin in earnest.

Ceylon! That country of which I had heard so much. I had dreamed of going there and had never thought I should go with a husband.

My father died peacefully at the beginning of March, and his body was brought to the Grange that he might be buried among his ancestors.

It was a cold and blustery day but sunny. The funeral would be carried out in the traditional manner, and the mourners would return to the Grange for sherry and ham sandwiches.

It was a moving ceremony and as I looked down on his coffin from my place round the grave I thought of my mother who lay close by and of the sadness of their lives, the incompatibility of their temperaments. Yet I had loved them both. I tried to imagine what it would have been like if they had lived together like a normal married pair.

Life was strange. Theirs had been stormy. What of my own? How would that be?

Clinton was beside me, holding my arm as we walked back to the Grange.

Refreshments were served to the mourners in the hall, and when suddenly I saw Toby I thought I was dreaming. He was standing before me, looking a little older than when I had last seen him in London but definitely Toby. I was overwhelmed with pleasure at the sight of him.

'Toby!' I cried.

He took both my hands in his. 'Sarah . . . you've grown up!'

'It's a long time since we met.'

'Oh, it's good to see you. I went to Denton Square looking for you. No one knew where you'd gone. I went to Tom Mellor. He said your mother had left the stage and gone to her husband's people. I saw the notice of your father's death and came on down at once. I met your aunt and told her I was an old friend, so I was invited back to the house.'

I felt weak with emotion. I wanted to cling to him and cry. He brought it all back so clearly – lunch at the Café Royal . . . a conspiracy between us against my mother whom we had both adored.

'What are you doing in England?'

'I've been here for a month. I shall be going back to Delhi shortly.'

'Do you enjoy it?'

He nodded. 'But it's good to be back in England.'

I thought of Clinton's coming home to look for a wife and I said: 'Toby, are you married?'

'No.'

'You're old enough to be.'

'I was always a little retarded, I fear.'

I smiled. I loved that half apologetic look of his. There was nothing arrogant about Toby. I noticed that particularly, subconsciously I was comparing him with Clinton.

'When are you going back?'

'I intended to stay for about two months. I might extend my stay a bit.'

There was a shine in his dark blue eyes. 'I've thought about you a great deal,' he went on. 'I wondered what was happening. It was a shock to hear that your mother had died.'

'You heard that then?'

'Yes, it came out when I was dining with a friend. They were talking of the stage and someone said Irene Rushton had retired after the Herringford affair and went to the country and died. I was so shocked and kept wondering what had happened to you.'

'I was with my aunts as you see.'

'You . . . here . . . in this ancient setting. Somehow it seems strange to me, Sarah. I put up at the inn last night – the Foresters, do you know it?'

'Yes,' I replied.

'I shall stay there for a while. Now I've found you there'll be lots to talk about.'

'A great deal has happened since we last met, Toby,' I told him. 'A few weeks ago I was married.'

I was unprepared for the stricken look in his face. He stared at me blankly, unbelievingly. It was a reflection of my own feelings. I understood exactly how he was feeling because I felt it too.

'It all happened rather suddenly,' I said quickly. 'My father came home from Ceylon and Clinton Shaw was with him. I'm going back to Ceylon with Clinton soon . . .' What was I saying, babbling on? What had I done? Here was Toby coming home, looking for me, and I was married to Clinton Shaw!

'Well,' said Toby, 'I wish you happiness. When . . . will you be going to Ceylon?'

'Very soon. We did not leave before because of my father. He has been very ill for a long time. We knew he was going to die.'

The look of misery on Toby's face was unnerving me.

'I'd like to see you again . . . before I go,' he said. 'There is so much to hear.'

'Tomorrow,' I replied. 'We'll walk in the forest.'

I knew that Clinton would leave early next morning for London. He was pressing on with arrangements for our departure.

Later that day the family solicitor came to read my father's will. We all assembled in the library – my aunts, Clinton and I.

It was a simple will. There were a few legacies to his manager and some of his workers on the plantation. The two principal beneficiaries were my sister Clytie and myself. The Ashington Pearls would be in Clytie's possession until they were passed on to her son's wife. He had left her his house in Ceylon and certain other assets, but the plantation itself he had left to me.

I looked at the aunts. I saw the colour in Aunt Martha's face which implied suppressed wrath. But what had she expected would happen to the pearls? The tradition was that they should go to the son but if there was no son naturally they would be in the temporary possession of the eldest daughter. *She* had a son and they would be in due course for that son's wife.

I was too overwhelmed by my own inheritance to think very much about Clytie's.

The plantation. Mine

Clinton was watching me closely.

There was a warm glow in his eyes.

Clinton was undoubtedly gratified. He was full of plans. 'We could join up the plantations,' he said, 'and they could be run as one.'

'It seems absurd that I should own a plantation when I know

nothing of such things,' I said.

'My dear, you have a husband who knows a great deal.'

There was no doubt of his satisfaction. I felt bemused because of all this and the overwhelming sorrow of my father's death and because of another remote feeling which I did not want to examine too closely. It was due to Toby's return and the emotions that had aroused in me. When I had seen him I had recaptured the pleasure I used to have when he came to the house, when we did our so-called lessons, when we slipped out on our jaunts. It was a joyous excitement, an intense pleasure.

Why did he have to come back *now*? I asked myself.

I looked ahead to the future yet I was filled with apprehension.

We went into the forest. He was very sober. I had never seen him like that before.

He said: 'Tell me about it, Sarah. Tell me everything.'

So I told him about Everard and what had happened and how my mother had been unable to get the work she wanted, how Meg had at length been persuaded to go to the country and how there was no alternative for us but to come to the Grange.

'She hated it, Toby. It was sad really. I don't think I realized how she must have felt until after. The aunts employed a governess for me. Celia Hansen. She left after my mother died. She came into money and went abroad with a cousin. I haven't seen her since although we became good friends.'

It was so easy to talk to Toby. I told him how my mother had died and of that awful night when we had found her in a high fever with the windows open to the bitter cold. It was a sad end to her glamorous life.

'She was very beautiful,' he said.

'You adored her. But you were different from the others . . . content to adore her from afar and to serve her by taking her nuisance of a daughter off her shoulders.'

'That was one of the greatest pleasures I have ever known,' he said solemnly. 'Remember the fun we had.'

We remembered, recalling little incidents, the jokes and the laughter.

'Happy days,' he said. 'I didn't realize how much they meant until I went away.'

'How is your business, Toby?'

'Not bad at all. I seem to have discovered an aptitude. My father is agreeably surprised.'

'As you were, I suppose.'

'I never thought I'd make a businessman.'

'It must have been an enthralling discovery to find you were so good.'

'Quite good,' he said with a laugh.

'And this is your first trip to England since you went away?'

'It's a long way to come, you know, and there was always so much to do out there.'

'Have you come home . . . as men do . . . to find a wife?'

It was a foolish thing to have said and I realized that as soon as I had spoken. There was a stricken look in his face, and he said suddenly as though taken off his guard: 'Why did you have to be so young, Sarah, when I went away?'

I was silent. Those few words had told me so much. I ought to have known.

We walked on in silence for a while. I smelt the pungent odours of the forest which I believed would remind me of this moment for ever – the damp earth, moss, the pines; among the grass wood anemones were beginning to show themselves. The herald of the swallow, Celia had told me they were called. 'Woodland fairies sleep in the flowers at night. That is why they curl up their petals to make the fairies cosy.' What strange thoughts at such a time!

I said: 'You didn't write to me, Toby.'

'I was never much of a letter-writer. I did write twice though and received no answers.'

'Those letters must have gone to the house in Denton Square.'

He nodded. 'Are you happy?' he asked.

I hesitated and then said: 'Why . . . yes.'

'He looks . . . distinguished,' he said.

'I suppose you could call him that. He owns the plantation next to my father's . . . and that is mine now.'

'What a different life it must have been here from the old days.'

We passed the path which led to Parrot Cottage. I avoided it I didn't want to see it. I was thinking how differently Toby would have behaved in such circumstances. Chivalrous, unselfish, reliable . . . that was Toby.

I said: 'I think we should go back to the house.'

He did not dispute that and we turned back.

'We shall not be very far from each other,' he said, when we came in sight of the Grange. 'I shall be in India. You will be in Ceylon.'

'It looks near . . . on the map.'

'Be happy, Sarah.'

'I shall try to. And you too, Toby.'

He did not come into the Grange. He took my hand and held it as we parted and he just said my name twice. I felt a sudden anger against Fate and I cried out: 'Why did you have to wait so long before coming? It was my mother you loved. I was just the child.'

'It was you,' he answered. 'I learned that. It was you . . . then and always. Goodbye, Sarah.' He kissed my hand lingeringly.

I felt a mad urge to tell him that I was afraid, that I did not love this man whom I had married. It was simply that he overwhelmed me and aroused a certain passion in me which I had found irresistible.

I don't love him, I wanted to cry. It's you, Toby, you. I see it now. Having been his wife I know it more clearly. I want loving kindness, tenderness, not this wild madness which he arouses in me.

Toby seemed to understand. He said: 'We shall not be far from each other. If you needed me at any time . . .'

I went to my room. I shut myself in. And I said to myself: 'Toby, oh Toby, why did you have to come back too late!'

THE
RESPLENDENT LAND
*
THE FAN OF
PEACOCK FEATHERS

I prepared to leave England with feverish intensity. I must accept the life I had chosen. I must learn to love my husband, to merge my sensuous desires with more noble feeling. There was a great deal to admire in Clinton Shaw. My father had been delighted that he was my husband and believed it was the best thing that could have happened to me. There was a power about him, a forcefulness which was the essence of manliness and surely to be admired. I had noticed that he won the admiration of women effortlessly. He was capable. He had a way of looking after one, which should be comforting. He was frank in the extreme and never tried to pretend he was other than he was – except when he was practising some great deception, as when he had lured me to Parrot Cottage.

I must shut my eyes to his faults and dwell on his virtues. The impression that Toby had made on me when he came back into my life had brought home how vulnerable I was. I had fallen straight into Clinton's arms and discovered certain depths in my nature which I would have preferred to be without. I must be honest and add, except when those senses were being gratified. My warm nature would set me open to temptation and I could see that I had given way too readily in Parrot Cottage. Toby had said I was only a child when he left. I think I had remained so too long. I had lived a somewhat artificial life in Denton Square and been surrounded by a spurious sophistication. Then I had been plunged into a life which was in direct contrast – the quiet country life dominated by two middle-aged aunts. I had only begun to grow up when Clinton came and I was still doing so. I became a wife before I was prepared for life. I could see that I must tread warily and should try to begin by falling in love with my husband. I was physically in love with him already but I was wise enough to know that if I was going to make a success of marriage I needed something more than that.

So I flung myself into preparations. I asked questions about the plantation and there was nothing Clinton liked to talk about more. He was pleased to be going back, I knew. He did mourn my father in a way, but Clinton would always be a man who was more concerned with the future than the past.

At last the day for our departure came. We boarded the *Aremethea* at Tilbury and to myself, who had never travelled before, except as a child when I knew nothing about it, everything was of the utmost interest and, as Clinton said, the best thing to help me get over the loss of my father. 'When you suffer a tragedy,' he said, 'the best remedy is a complete change of scene. That's what you are going to get.'

He was known to the captain and officers of the ship and a certain deference was given him, which I was sure he relished. He was considerate to me and initiated me into the mysteries of sea travel as efficiently as he had into the ways of love. There was one thing he greatly enjoyed and that was taking on the role of tutor. When I pointed this out to him he said it was true but only because he had such an interest in the pupil. I was more gentle, I think, because of Toby I felt a little guilty. I had made my vows and must try to carry them out. That was how I saw it. It was amazing to see the effect my changed attitude had on him. He became almost tender; we sparred less and he gave the impression that he was overjoyed because we were married.

There was much to see on the journey. Together we visited the wonders of Pompeii, the souks of Port Said and sailed through the Canal past the lakes and those golden sands where shepherds walked with their sheep, and it was like watching scenes from the Bible passing before our eyes. We sat side by side on the deck and I told myself I would forget Toby and what might have been. It was up to me. As Janet would have said: I had made my bed and I must lie on it.

We spent a day in Mombasa where we bought bright coloured cloth, ornaments and a cow's horn carved in a beautiful pattern. Our long passage was nearing its end.

Very soon now we should be in Ceylon.

We arrived during the morning and as soon as the island was sighted I was on deck with Clinton.

It was a beautiful sight – this green and fertile island rising out of the Indian Ocean.

Clinton pointed out Adam's Peak, the most prominent of the mountains of the interior. It dominated the hills that surrounded it.

'It was a landmark to the old-time navigators,' he said. 'People used to make pilgrimages to it. It has always been greatly revered. The people of Ceylon owe their livelihood to the mountains and they don't forget it. When the monsoon comes – that is in the middle of May and the end of October – the clouds are driven against those mountains and it rains and rains . . . but only on one side of the range. On the other it is arid and a desert. So the population crowded on to this side of the mountains and here we have reaped our rewards from coffee, coconut, cinnamon, rubber and now in the last years the most profitable of all – tea!'

I stared in wonder at the beauty of the scene. Groves of palm trees looked as though they were growing out of the sea, and everywhere was lush and green.

'Soon,' said Clinton, 'we shall see the city.'

I stood entranced as we came nearer and nearer to the island. Clinton gripped my hand.

'At last,' he said, and there was a note of triumph in his voice.

The dock was alive with activity. Men in wide trousers – mostly white and grubby – and with loose jackets made of the same cotton material, were running about seeing to baggage and other matters, shouting and gesticulating. The heat was intense.

Clinton called out something in Sinhalese and he was immediately surrounded. Smiles of welcome lightened their brown faces. He was clearly well known here and of great importance. I listened to the exchanges, overcome by curiosity and a desire to see everything at once.

In a short time we were seated in a kind of cart drawn by horses.

'We are going to the station,' Clinton said. 'That surprises you. Yes, we have a railway from Colombo to Kandy. We shall not go all the way. We're some sixty miles out from Colombo and some twelve from Kandy. Don't worry about baggage. That will be brought to us.'

I climbed into the cart and we went rattling through streets which were so colourful that I was constantly turning from left to right for fear of missing something. Clinton smiled at me. 'Anyone would guess you were a newcomer,' he said.

It was so different from everything I had ever known. The roads were crowded with vehicles of all descriptions – carriages, carts drawn by oxen, and rickshaws pulled by men whose bare dirty feet and thin bodies moved me to pity. The people constantly shouted to each other and the air was full of noise. They ran across the road right in front of the horses and I was afraid many times that someone would be run over, but with much shouting and consummate skill, the drivers of the various conveyances avoided disaster.

One or two called a greeting to Clinton.

'They seem to like you,' I said.

'Not so surprising,' he answered with characteristic cynicism. 'I'm their living.'

I took off my coat. I was far too warmly clad.

'You must be careful to protect your skin,' Clinton told me. 'It's not made for this fierce sun. And don't forget, even when the sun is not shining, too much sun can be dangerous. It's there even though you can't see it.'

I put my coat round my shoulders. At least it was not so hot worn that way.

We reached the railway station where there were crowds similar to those on the dock. I was most conscious of noise and heat.

'We'll soon be at the plantations,' Clinton told me. 'Yours and mine.'

We boarded the train. It lacked the comfort of trains at home, but I was too enthralled by the countryside through which we passed to take much notice of that. Its beauty was breathtaking. During that short journey we passed forests of trees – ebony, satin-wood and, most common of all, the tree of the cashew nut; we passed paddy-fields where the rice – the country's staple food – was growing. I saw sluggish rivers and boats pulling logs and naked children leaping in the water that washed the banks. I caught my breath with wonder when I saw my first elephant. A man was seated on it and the great beast was drawing a load of logs. Then I saw more and more.

Clinton was amused. 'We have more elephants in Ceylon than any other animal,' he told me. 'We make use of them, as you see. They are the best possible workers – strong and full of good sense. Admirable qualities in a helpmeet, as you'll agree. Moreover, they are docile. What more could you ask?'

'It seems strange that they who are so strong should allow themselves to be pressed into service.'

'It is the mastery of man, my dear Sarah. We tame them. Why, when they're wild they can do enormous damage. They would break into plantations and trample down the crops creating havoc. But catch them, train them, and they'll be your good servants.'

'You would enjoy the training, I am sure.'

'It's well worth while, I do assure you.'

I watched the elephants in amazement. It seemed so strange to see those great lumbering creatures, who with one stroke of a massive foot could trample a man to death, being guided to work.

At length we had come to the small station where we were to

alight. Clinton took the bag which I had brought with me, and a similar case of his own, and we stepped out of the train.

There was a great babble of voices. Men were bowing to us. Clinton said: 'Back at last. With my wife.'

The men laughed, which I gathered was a form of welcome, and muttered something which sounded like Mem Sahib.

Clinton held my elbow.

There was a cart similar to the one we had used from the port to the railway station.

There seemed to be a sea of brown faces all around us.

'It's a very short distance,' said Clinton. 'We use the railway a great deal. Thanks to us, it is one of the most prosperous lines in the country.'

Through the greenest of land we drove. A steamy heat was in the air. On either side of the road tree ferns rose, some, I calculated, as high as twenty-five feet; great scarlet rhododendrons grew wild. I noticed plants such as I had never seen before and I learned later that they were endemic to Ceylon. We came out of the road, made dark by the thick foliage which it had been cut through, and I had my first glimpse of the plantation. Green and glistening shrubs covered the hill slopes for what seemed like miles and miles.

Clinton surveyed the scene with satisfaction.

We rode on and there on the hillside I saw a cluster of buildings. My heart sank. Was this my new home? Most of the buildings were one storey high.

'My workmen's homes mostly,' said Clinton, 'and some of the storing houses. Your father's – I mean yours – is only a mile or so away. You'll see my place in a moment. This patch of jungle ahead separates the two plantations. It makes a pleasant prospect too. One would grow a little tired of nothing but tea.'

We had come to what looked like a wood in the middle of the tea slopes; and we took a road through it. After a few moments we came to the house.

It was surrounded by a garden lush with green shrubs, many of them bright with gaily coloured flowers, the like of which I had never seen before. The house was brilliantly white among the greenery and heavy vines climbed over its walls. It was long and two storeys high, L-shaped, with numerous outbuildings.

A young woman ran out, chattering wildly and bowing profusely. She was dressed in a deep blue cotton sari and when she smiled she showed beautiful teeth. She looked at me very curiously.

'This is Leila,' said Clinton to me. 'You'll find her very useful.'

Leila smiled, crossed her hands across her breast and bowed her head.

'First tea, Leila,' said Clinton.

'Yes, master.' The big dark eyes removed themselves from me with great reluctance. 'I bring soon,' she added.

'Thank you,' I said. 'That will be welcome.'

I was feeling very emotional. I was after all being introduced to my new home and my dominating feeling was one of apprehension. It was due to the strangeness of everything, I told myself, and the realization that the past, which included Toby, was indeed behind me. I was now being launched into the unknown.

We went into a hall and our footsteps rang out on the floor of stones arranged in intricate mosaic, the colour of lapis and chalcedony. A light table and two chairs – bamboo, I guessed – were in the hall.

'Welcome home,' said Clinton. He looked at me warily. 'Later I'll show you everything. But first refreshment. We need it. You will taste tea such as you have never tasted before. Fresh from my storing house.'

He had slipped his arm through mine and drawing me close to him kissed me.

'Oh Sarah,' he said, 'this is a dream come true. You here with me. It was what I wanted from the moment I set eyes on you. As soon as we've had that tea I am going to show you round the place. It's bigger than it appears. I've taken a great deal of trouble to furnish it as I wanted it. My uncle built it when it became clear that coffee was a disaster instead of a profitable industry and he decided to venture into tea. It was a gamble then, I can assure you, but labour was cheap and he built the house. I have added to it since. It is not Ashington Grange nor my own family home, but it is suitable for this place and considered quite fine here, I assure you. We'll have some good times here.'

He had led me into a large room with a stone floor and light wood furniture – teak, rattan and some Chinese lacquer – there were chairs, table and a wickerwork settee on which were many brightly coloured cushions.

'The drawing-room,' he said. 'See the folding doors. They open into a room of similar size which is our dining-room. For entertaining we open the doors and we have quite a sizeable room – you could call it a ballroom.'

'Is there much entertaining?'

'Just now and then. There's a club in Kandy and another in Colombo . . . but that's a bit far for us. Now for that tea.'

Two boys had brought it in. Their big dark eyes surveyed me curiously. Clinton introduced me as 'Your mistress'. They bowed solemnly when they had set down the tray. They wore the traditional white shirts and trousers and their feet were bare. The young woman Leila had followed them in.

'All well, master?' she asked.

Clinton nodded. 'I want you to look after your mistress, Leila,' he said.

'Oh yes, yes.' She nodded, smiling as though it would be her greatest delight to do so.

He laid a hand on my arm. 'Leila will see to everything. She will be a sort of liaison officer between you and the others . . . just at first.'

'That's good,' I said.

Leila bowed again and went out.

'She's a good manager,' he said to me, 'and like many of the Sinhalese she delights in having a little responsibility. Her father, Nankeen, is my headman and her brother Ashraf works on your plantation. They're an interesting family. Come and sit down and I'll pour your tea for you.'

When we were seated side by side on the settee he put an arm about me. 'It's all so strange, isn't it?' he said. 'And you are un-certain. It'll be all right. I tell you it will. You'll see.'

He spoke as though he were all-powerful and could mould the future to his desires. I had the feeling that there might be some-thing in that. In fact, since we had arrived in this country I had begun to get a glimpse of the power he held.

He took up his cup and tested the aroma. 'You'll see the tea tasters at work,' he said. 'There's a lot you have to learn about your plantation, Sarah. Now can you detect the aroma this tea gives off? Delicious, don't you think?'

I said it was and indeed it did taste different from every cup of tea I had had before.

When we had finished he wanted to show me the house and I was naturally eager to see it.

On the lower floor besides the hall and the two connecting rooms were spacious kitchens, stone-floored with big white cup-boards. Everything had been freshly cleaned and painted. I saw several servants – boys like those who had brought the tea and two men and two women. They all bowed obsequiously when Clinton presented them to me, and I was sure I would never remember all their names and which was which. They were very curious about me and they were clearly terrified that something might displease Clinton.

He is indeed the Master, I thought, and this is his territory.

There was a laundry-room and a cooling-room where there were boxes of ice which I imagined were very necessary to pre-serve food in this climate.

Beyond the kitchens were the servants' quarters. I was taken into them. They were spotlessly clean and I guessed had been made ready for this inspection which they knew would come.

We went upstairs where there were several bedrooms.

'This is ours,' said Clinton with pride. My eyes went to the bed, which was large and covered with a silken embroidered counter-pane. Mosquito nets hung from the canopy and I noticed that across all the windows was a fine wire-netting. The floor was of dark wood and covered with mats of blue and green to match the embroidery on the counterpane. It did not look as if it had been designed for a bachelor and I wondered when Clinton had given instructions as to how it was to be done, before he went away. On a table was a bronze Buddha about a foot high, seated in the lotus position. The face was lifelike and the eyes seemed to follow me rather sardonically, I thought.

Clinton noticed me looking at it. 'You don't like it.'

'It looks evil in a way.'

'Evil! The Buddha. Certainly not. I hope you don't dislike it too much. It was given to me by a friend. The servants would think it would mean bad luck to the house if I took it away.'

It was rather silly of me to be affected by a bronze figure. I excused myself. I was in a rather emotional state I supposed. I kept thinking of the old days and my outings with Toby and I was beginning to feel homesick already.

At one end of the room were two steps leading to a daïs which was curtained off. Behind this were two hip baths and long mirrors on the three walls. On a table stood a basin and ewer.

'They have obeyed my orders,' he said. 'They have done well. Do you like it, Sarah? I planned it for you.'

'It's beautiful,' I replied, 'but I can't believe you would plan for a woman you had never seen.'

'I knew it was going to be you.'

He put his arm through mine and took me to the other rooms on this floor. There were several bedrooms. All the beds had canopies from which mosquito nets hung and over all the windows was the fine wire-netting.

'We have the occasional guest,' he said. 'Usually when we have a ball – a small one, of course. Mostly planters, their wives and families. The English community. As some of them come from miles away it is sometimes necessary for them to stay the night. Rubber planters, coconut growers, those who produce the rice. Then there are the shippers and those who manage the railways, the civil servants. Ceylon has become a flourishing island since it became a Crown Colony. You have a great deal to learn about the place.'

'I am longing to see my own plantation.'

'Ah yes, you have a great deal to learn. Never fear. I shall be beside you. I'll look after your interests. Seth Blandford is quite a good manager and he is after all your brother-in-law, but . . .'

'Most of all,' I interrupted, 'I want to see my sister.'

'When you are rested, I'll drive you over. It's only a mile or so, and even shorter if you take the cut through the jungle. We call it the wood, but it's jungle really. Lots of this land was, of course, before it was cleared and cultivated. We still can't ride through the wood – the foliage is too thick – but there are paths for walking. I shall drive you over in a kind of dog-cart we have. It's drawn by one horse and it's easy to manage. You'll want to use it yourself eventually, I imagine. You can always ride over but I dare say you'll find the dog-cart easier sometimes.'

As I was longing to meet my sister I declared I was not in the least tired. I changed my travelling clothes for a light oatmeal-coloured silk dress and a flimsy wrap that I might not be too exposed to the sun and put on one of the straw hats I had brought with me.

I saw at once that the dog-cart would be easy to handle and that I should find it a good way of getting about.

We drove through the plantation and in due course came to the house which had been my father's and which was very similar to the one we had just left.

A servant hurried up to take the horse and dog-cart and Clinton leaped down and helped me to descend. My heart was beating wildly at the prospect of at last seeing my half-sister.

I turned to the house. A slight figure was standing in the doorway, a dainty creature, a head shorter than I – but then I was tall – and I thought I had never seen anyone so exquisite.

She was wearing a sari of pale lavender silk with silver thread etched on it. She walked towards me with such grace that I immediately felt awkward. Her black hair was caught back from her brow into a knot and would hang down almost to her knees when loosened, I imagined. She held out her little hands. On her arms tinkled about twenty thin silver bracelets.

When she spoke I was overwhelmed with surprise. 'I'm Clytie,' she said.

For a moment I could find no words. The first that rose to my lips unspoken were: But you can't be my father's daughter. You're not English.

I stammered: 'My . . . my sister. I have so much wanted to meet you.'

She said in a beautiful voice and her English was as perfect as it could be and none would have guessed from that that she was not as English as I: 'How glad I am. It is right that we should know each other. We are sisters . . . though but half. We have lost our dear father. That should bring us close. It has been a house of mourning but that must change now that you have come.'

We regarded each other wonderingly. I must have looked as strange to her as she did to me. But at least she had expected me to be English.

'Clinton,' she said, 'congratulations to you. You have a very attractive wife.'

'Thank you, Clytie. I agree. She was reluctant to take me at first but I persuaded her.'

'We all know of your powers of persuasion,' she answered. 'Please come with me, Sarah, I want to show you my son. Little Ralph is longing to meet you.'

'He is her pride and joy,' Clinton told me.

'He would be anyone's pride and joy . . . if they were lucky enough to have him for a son,' she replied.

Her voice had a lilting quality. She fascinated me completely. There was only one solution. My father's first wife had been Sinhalese. That was why Aunt Martha never mentioned her.

As though I had spoken aloud she drew my attention to a portrait on the wall. It was of a beautiful dainty woman in a blue sari with flowers in her black hair.

'It is my mother,' she said. 'She died when I was very young. I know her only through this picture. There is much we have to say to each other, you and I, Sarah. But first come to see my son.'

We mounted the stairs to a nursery – a room with light draperies, as dainty as Clytie herself.

'Sheba!' she called. 'Sheba! Ralph! Where are you?'

A door was flung open and there was a whoop of delight as a small boy came running towards her. He seized her about the knees and I thought she looked so fragile that he might knock her over.

'Here is my Ralph!' she cried. 'Ralph, what would you say if I told you you had an aunt who has come to see you?'

There was no doubt of his English blood. His hair was dark but not the blue-black kind which is never seen in England; his eyes were dark too but definitely brown. His skin was faintly olive but there was pink colour in his cheeks. He was a beautiful child, sturdy and healthy. I guessed he must be about four years old.

'I never had an aunt before,' he said regarding me with a certain suspicion.

'Well, you have one now,' I told him. I held out my hand and he shook it.

'Have you come from England?' he asked.

I admitted this was so.

'My grandfather went to England and he never came back. He went to Heaven instead.'

'Yes,' I said slowly. 'But I have come and I am glad to find I have a nephew here.'

'Am I a nephew?' He laughed to himself, liking the idea.

Then I was aware that I was being steadily watched. A woman was standing in the doorway. I was not sure of her age but she was by no means young. She was dressed in a green sari and her black hair was drawn back and caught in a large knot at the nape of her neck. Her eyes were large, black and mysterious.

'Here's Sheba,' said Clytie. 'She nursed me and has now turned her attention to Ralph. Sheba, this is my sister. Sheba remembers you, Sarah.'

Sheba's sari rustled as she approached. Her movements were swift, quick and lithe as a cat's.

'Oh yes,' she murmured. 'Remember well. Little Miss Sarah. But you were little – ' she held her hand a foot or two from the floor – 'so little when you went away.'

I wished I could remember her but I couldn't.

'Sheba knows how happy I am that you have come to stay,' said Clytie. She was smiling at me, warmly, lovingly. I thought her enchanting but instinctively I felt I had to be wary of Sheba. Although she was respectful, something in her manner told me that she resented my coming.

'Sheba,' said Clytie, 'they will stay to dinner. Tell them in the kitchen.' Clytie looked at me almost shyly. 'We hoped you would be here today but we can never be sure. We are half prepared. I wanted you to have your first meal in this house. This is where you were born. In this room, wasn't it, Sheba? I was born here too. We are indeed sisters. I hope Clinton won't mind my monopolizing you . . . just at first.'

'My dear Clytie,' said Clinton, 'you know it is my wish always to please you.' He was smiling at her with that appreciation which most men would feel in the presence of someone as beautiful as my half-sister.

Ralph had sidled up to me and had taken my hand.

'You're *my* aunt,' he said and seemed to be overcome with mirth.

'I want to show her the garden,' said Clytie.

'Missee Clytie and her plants!' mumbled Sheba. 'She'd have them growing all over the house I reckon if Master Seth didn't stop it. We'd have the house full of creepy-crawlers.'

She spoke in the rather musical sing-song in which the Sinhalese render the English tongue.

'Clytie is so excited to meet you, Sarah,' said Clinton. 'It is rather a momentous occasion, admittedly. Dear Clytie, we have travelled far. We arrived only today. Sarah has scarcely looked at anything at all. Her great desire was to meet you. Let us eat this meal you have for us and then I am going to take Sarah back. There is tomorrow, you know. You can show her your gardens then and talk yourself hoarse, but we do need an early night and a good rest. One really should after travelling.'

I felt an inclination to oppose him and said: 'I want to see the garden. I long to talk to you.'

She came towards me. She did not walk nor did she run; it was as though she glided. That incredible grace moved me deeply. She caught my hand and smiled up at me.

'Forgive me,' she said in her soft and slightly husky voice. 'Clinton is right. The joy of seeing you overcomes me. It makes me selfish. There is tomorrow. Then we can talk and talk . . .'

'I am not in the least tired,' I protested.

'You are, my dear,' replied Clinton firmly. 'Your excitement hides the fact from you. We'll go straight back after the meal. Clytie knows I am right.'

Sheba seemed to be listening intently. She picked up the boy.

'Is my aunt going to Heaven?' he asked.

There was a strange silence in the room or perhaps I imagined it. I was aware of Clytie's look of startled surprise and that Sheba's dark eyes were fixed on me. It passed almost immediately, but for half a second it was as though a drop of icy water was trickling down my spine.

'Whatever made you say that?' asked Clytie.

'Grandpapa went,' replied Ralph.

Clinton said: 'No, young man. Your aunt has come here to stay.'

Clytie went to her son and ruffled his hair.

'It's past your bedtime,' she said.

'I want to stay and look at Aunt Sarah.'

'You can do that tomorrow.'

'But I want to *now*.'

'Go with Sheba now, darling, and I'll come and tuck you up later on.'

'And sing to me?'

'Yes.'

'And read to me?'

'Perhaps.'

He seemed reconciled.

'Say good night,' coaxed Clytie.

'Good night,' he said. 'I'll talk to Aunt Sarah tomorrow. She's not going to Heaven.'

We descended the stairs. Servants were setting the table in the dining-room, which like ours had folding doors to the drawing-room.

It was not yet dark. Clinton had told me that because of the island's proximity to the equator, the length of the day did not vary more than an hour throughout the year. It would be dark about seven and that was not far off. I saw several oil lamps swinging from the ceiling and there were candles in brass sconces to augment the light of the lamps. They were similar to those which I had noticed in Clinton's house.

Just as dinner was about to be served Seth Blandford joined us. There was no doubt about *his* nationality. His hair was of a reddish tinge and his eyebrows and lashes so light that they were scarcely visible. Apart from that, he was good-looking with excellent features and very pale skin. He was of medium height but looked small beside Clinton.

'Ah, Clinton,' he said. 'Home at last. And you have brought ... Sarah.'

He turned to me and took my hand in a grip which is called sincere and I found uncomfortable because it was so firm that I found it hard not to wince with pain as my wedding-ring cut into my finger.

'It's good to see you,' he said. 'You have a look of your father. What a tragedy. He should never have gone travelling.'

'He insisted,' said Clinton.

'And now he is dead . . . and Sarah is here.'

Clytie was looking at me fondly. 'I am so happy that she has come.'

'Well, shall we have a drink and all get to know each other,' said Seth.

'I should have thought,' retorted Clinton, 'that we all did that – with the exception of Sarah.'

Clytie clapped her hands and two silent-footed servants came running in with glasses on a tray with gin and soda-water. There were limes and some sort of fruit juice.

Clytie poured out the drinks. Then Clinton lifted his glass and said: 'To the homecoming!'

Seth Blandford said quietly: 'The will was a bit of a surprise. One would have thought . . .'

'Old Ralph was always unpredictable,' agreed Clinton. 'He always seemed so conventional and then he did what was least expected.'

'Well, Sarah.' Seth had turned to me. 'What does it feel like to be the owner of a plantation?'

'Bewildering,' I answered. 'Particularly since I know absolutely nothing about it.'

'There!' cried Seth. 'Why?'

'She is his daughter and Clytie had the pearls,' said Clinton.

Clytie put a small fluttering hand on her throat and looked down.

'Temporarily,' retorted Seth with a trace of bitterness.

'I hope you will like what I am going to give you to eat,' Clytie put in quickly. 'We eat a great deal of curry here. It's a native dish. They cook it better than anything else.'

She had managed to change the conversation, which was making me feel uneasy, and she talked about the next day when I should go over to her and see her garden. I must make the further acquaintance of young Ralph who had been so excited at the prospect of my arrival. There was so much we had to talk about. Clothes for one thing. Had I suitable clothes?

'Clinton told me about the climate and I was prepared to a certain extent.'

'There is one thing Clinton knows nothing about and that is women's clothes.'

'He knows how to appreciate them though,' added Seth.

'It is advice Sarah will need and I shall be here to give her that. I will show you where to buy beautiful materials. Six yards will make a sari and there is no sewing to do.'

'My dear Clytie,' I cried, 'can you imagine me in a sari? I'm much too big, I'm afraid.'

'You would look beautiful,' she assured me.

I shook my head. 'Awkward. Unsuited to such a graceful garment. No. I had better keep to my native costume.'

'Well, I will tell you where to buy beautiful silks.'

'That will be exciting.'

It was twelve or so miles into Kandy, I was told, but Manganiya, where we had alighted from the train, was quite close. It was not Kandy or Colombo but the shops there were quite good.

'It will be such a pleasure to have you for a companion,' said Clytie. 'We must have a ball soon, Seth, to welcome Sarah. Everyone will want to meet her.'

It was dark when we went in to dinner.

'We had a scare while you were away,' Seth said as we ate, 'both with tea tortrix and nettle grubs.'

'I'm sure you coped with the trouble,' replied Clinton.

'Oh yes. The crop is as healthy as it ever was.'

'What should we do without you, Seth?'

Seth looked pleased.

I was hungry and the curry tasted good. I listened with deep attention while they discussed the plantation. I kept thinking: This is mine. It's incredible! I could not understand my father's action. Clytie should have had the plantation. I could understand Seth's resentment, which he had already made obvious. Of course Clytie had the pearls in trust for her son's wife . . .

Strangely enough at that moment they were talking of pearls. Seth was saying something about the pearl fisheries in Tambalgam Bay.

'One of your men was caught by a shark. That was the end of him.'

'Who?' cried Clinton.

'Karam.'

'Karam!' repeated Clinton. 'He was one of my best divers. He should have been more careful.'

'Careful! Do you think the man would be anything but careful! The boat was there. The shark charmer was in it. He went down and the thing was lying in wait for him.'

'Karam! A good man. One of the best.'

'I hear there was a good yield last season.'

'That's good news,' said Clinton. 'But Karam!'

'What are these pearl fisheries?' I asked. 'I've never heard of them before.'

Seth looked at Clinton rather slyly, I thought. 'It's not like Clinton to hide his lights under bushels,' he said.

'Hadn't I mentioned them to you?' asked Clinton of me. 'It's a pearl fishery I own up in the north-west. I'll take you there and show it to you. You want to go there when they're collecting the oysters though. That's about the second week in March and the season only lasts from four to six weeks.'

'Pearls!' I said. 'You mean you deal in pearls!'

'It's a side line,' said Clinton.

Seth leaned forward. 'Clinton practically owns Ceylon,' he said. 'He has tea here, pearls in the north-west and rubber in the forests. Half the ships you saw in the harbour at Colombo were carrying Clinton's merchandise.'

'It's necessary to get what we can out of the country,' Clinton explained. 'These products are the livelihood of the people.'

'And the enrichment of those who make it possible,' added Seth.

'They would need to have some reward for their investment and their labour,' Clinton reminded him.

'I'm interested in the pearl fisheries,' I said.

'Trust a woman,' retorted Clinton. 'If you only knew when you put on those fine pearls what it cost to get them, you would pause to think.'

'I must say I never thought of it before.'

'Listen to this, Clytie!' cried Seth. 'And think of it every time you wear your famous pearls.'

'I do,' replied Clytie quietly.

Clinton turned to me and went on: 'The wives and sweethearts of the pearl fishers call the pearls the *lives of men*.'

'Is it so dangerous then?'

'You have just heard that one of my best men was taken by a

shark. Imagine it. The boats leave at midnight so that they can reach the oyster beds at sunrise. Each boat carries some ten divers. They work in pairs and they won't go down unless the shark charmers are in the boat. They chant strange music which is supposed to bring the sharks to such a state of delight that they are unaware of bodies intruding into their waters. Nevertheless every diver carries spikes of ironwood to ward off any shark that refuses to be charmed.'

'I wonder any of the men take on such work.'

'They must work or starve,' said Clytie.

Clinton was watching me intently. 'It's true. There's no alternative. But that is life, don't you agree?'

In that moment I was deeply aware of the strangeness of everything. The heat; the sudden thud of an insect against the netting over the windows; myself in the midst of people whom I really knew little except that they were close to me; the tension which was obvious between Seth and Clinton.

They talked again of the plantation and Clytie told me she would drive the trap over in the morning, pick me up and take me home with her so that we could talk at length and she could show me around.

It must have been about half past nine when we left. Seth and Clytie came out to wave us goodbye.

'Did you enjoy it?' asked Clinton as the dog-cart moved away.

'Very much. I so longed to meet my sister.'

'And what do you think of her?'

'She is charming and beautiful. It was a shock. I was expecting an English girl. You should have warned me.'

Clinton shrugged. 'She takes after her mother. I've heard it said that she is the image of her.'

'I was never told that my father had married a Sinhalese.'

'It happens . . . now and then. Many of the men here have native mistresses. Occasionally there are children. Now and then there is a marriage. Clytie has been educated as an English girl. Your father had an English governess out here for several years. A dragon of a woman, by all accounts. Then Seth came to manage the place and hey presto they are in love and married.'

'Is Seth a good manager?'

'He's not a bad second. He was hoping that the place would go to Clytie of course.'

'A natural enough hope, I suppose.'

'Well, one can never be sure of anything in this life.'

We were silent for the rest of the drive.

In the stables one of the men was waiting to take charge of the dog-cart and putting his arm through mine Clinton led me towards the house. It gleamed white in the darkness. A lantern hung over the door and I was aware of the persistent hum of insects.

We went into the hall.

'Home at last,' said Clinton and he turned to me and kissed me. As he released me I noticed a servant standing watching us.

'Anything wanted, master?'

'No, thank you,' replied Clinton.

We went upstairs into the bedroom. Two lamps were lighted; the mosquito net was in position and I saw the corpses of several insects who had flung themselves against the netting in the hope of getting to the light.

I thought fleetingly of my bedroom at the Grange. Cold winter nights when I hurriedly undressed and leaped into bed to get warm; and the summer when the windows were wide open to the clean fresh air.

'Very different, isn't it?' said Clinton, once more displaying that uncanny ability to read my thoughts. 'Never mind. You'll get used to it. It'll all be second nature in a very short time. And one day I'll take you back for a trip. You'll like that.'

I nodded and he started to undo the buttons of my dress.

'Clinton,' I said, 'is it true that you own a good deal of Ceylon?'

He laughed. 'Seth's exaggeration, my dear. Ceylon is a big country, growing richer under the right sort of management. Some of us know how to extract the most out of the land. I'm just one of many.'

'It seems you own all these things . . . The pearl fisheries, for instance.'

'They fascinated you, didn't they? It's all that talk about the Ashington Pearls which you've been hearing all your life.'

'Most people are fascinated by pearls. So it is true that you actually own pearl fisheries.'

'I have an interest in them . . . as I have in other things. One has to spread one's interests you know. Look at the coffee disaster. We have only just recovered from that. At one time most people believed that if you produced coffee you must make your fortune. And then what happened? The market collapsed. As I've told you, a disease called coffee rust spoilt crops all over the country. Within a few years the trade here was finished. A man of enterprise has to be ready to fall back on alternatives. That's why it is wise to have many irons in the fire.'

'I suppose you are a very clever man.'

'A nice wifely comment.'

'You would always be in a position to take advantage.'

'I like to think so.'

'So now you have . . . what is it? Pearls, rubber, coconuts and tea.'

'Those are the main industries of this country. I was never satisfied with the plantation. It was not big enough. I wanted to extend. Now, of course, although there are two, they will be as one. They are mine . . . both of them.'

'I thought one was mine.'

'My dearest Sarah, what's yours is mine.'

'And yours mine?'

'Of course.'

'So I have a share in the pearl fisheries and the rest?'

He caught me to him, laughing. 'I have plans,' he said. 'Oh, it's good to be back. It'll be so much easier to work the two plantations as one. Seth can remain as manager over there. He's all right for that. But I shall see that the efficiency which was lacking before is now put into operation. I have been making plans for this for a long time.'

'For a long time,' I echoed. 'How did you know the plantation was coming to me?'

'You're your father's daughter.'

'But surely as my sister had a husband who was managing it for my father . . .'

'But not very successfully.'

'Clinton,' I said slowly, 'you *knew* the plantation was coming to me.'

He looked at me steadily. 'What if I did?'

'How?'

'Your father told me. Seth hadn't got quite the right ideas. He couldn't always manage the workers. Your father talked it over with me.'

'You really knew he was going to leave the plantation to me, didn't you?'

'Yes.'

'And the idea was that you should marry me and take it over.'

'Something like that.'

'So that was why . . .'

'Oh come now, Sarah, there's more to it than that. Haven't I shown you how much I enjoy being with you?'

'You enjoy the knowledge that through me you can get your hands on the plantation.'

'I would have had it sooner or later. I would have bought it when the time came. That would not be long the way things are. This was an easy way of doing it.'

I faced him and my eyes were blazing with rage.

'So . . . you deliberately set out to marry me. It was all arranged. You and my father . . .'

'He wanted it, of course. A man doesn't like to see a plantation he has worked for years going downhill because his health is failing and he has to rely on a manager. He knew what it needed to pull it up and he knew I was the one to do it. He knew I'd have it in a few years in any case. You also needed protection. It seemed a good idea for me to marry you and keep it in the family.'

'You are calculating and despicable,' I said.

'Yes,' he replied. 'I know.'

Then he picked me up in his arms and laughed.

'That's right,' he said. 'Protest. Fight. I like it that way.'

I awoke in the early morning. I was lying in the bed with the nets about me. He was there beside me, sleeping.

I felt caught. *I* was in a net, which he had woven with his intrigues.

So he had not really loved me. I was just another woman to him, and I knew there had been many and would probably be many more.

I lay still. Soon the day would come. My first day in an alien land.

Then I thought of Toby and I wondered where he was now. He would have gone back to India. Suppose I were with him. Perhaps I should be lying in a bed rather like this. Mesh at the windows . . . a net over me. But how different that would be.

The room seemed to close in on me and strangely enough out of the mists of my mind I seemed to hear a childish voice saying: 'Is my aunt going to Heaven?'

The words brought back the pricking feeling in my spine which I had felt when the child had said them. There seemed to be a warning in the air.

Later in the morning Clytie drove over in a dog-cart similar to the one we had used on the previous night. She had come, as promised, to take me back with her to the Ashington Plantation. Seth had said that as the place belonged to me now I ought to know something about it.

Clinton was in good spirits. He seemed to be completely un-affected by his revelation and to think that anything he did to offend me could be put right by his love-making. I was deeply hurt and had made up my mind that I was going to learn all I could about the growing of tea and let him see that the plantation for which he had married me, was mine after all.

My spirits rose a little as I drove off with Clytie. She looked slightly incongruous driving a trap, although she was not wearing a sari on this occasion but a light blue silk dress. She had the appearance of a pretty doll who should do nothing but charm everyone with her dainty grace.

'You handle a horse well,' I said.

'Oh . . . the trap. It's easy. I am half English, remember. I was brought up differently from the girls of my mother's country. I look like them, do I not? But I am strong. You will see, Sarah. You must tell me about England. There is so much I want to know. I remember your mother faintly. A soft voice which I liked to listen to. I don't recall what she looked like, but she was very beautiful, I know.'

'Yes, she was beautiful.'

'And when she went away . . . That comes back to me too. The house silent . . . my father's shutting himself away for days. A sort of gloom everywhere. But it was long ago. Sheba told me about it. She said she would never have fitted in and should never have come. But then Sheba loved my mother and did not think our father should have married again. But what a blessing he did, or you would not be here, Sarah.'

We drove the same way as I had gone with Clinton on the previous night.

'When you go back,' said Clytie, 'I will show you the short cut through the woods. I am glad they left that part of the woods . . . jungle really. I believe there is talk of cutting it down too and planting tea. I expect Clinton will want to do that.'

'To whom does it belong?' I asked.

'It's half Shaw, half Ashington.'

'Well,' I said, 'the Ashington part will not be cut down.'

'If Clinton decides . . .'

'It will be a matter for me to decide surely.'

'I see, Sarah, that you are a strong-minded woman.'

We had arrived at the house. Clytie drove the trap into a yard and as we alighted two servants came out to look after the vehicle. I found it a little unnerving the way in which these silent-footed servants appeared from nowhere when they were needed. I felt they must be watching us all the time so as to anticipate our needs; and although this could be very useful I had to admit it gave me an uncomfortable feeling.

It was pleasant to step into the house which was much cooler than it was outside.

Clytie turned to me. 'What first? I'll take you over the house, shall I? It's very similar to your own. Not a bit like the Grange. My father used to tell me about it and I wondered whether I should ever see it. I imagined it guarded by two dragons named Martha and Mabel who would keep me out.'

'Those are the aunts. Martha is a bit formidable. The sort of woman who is going to get her own way at all costs.' A horrible picture came into my mind of going into my mother's bedroom on that bitterly cold night. It was preposterous. I scarcely thought of it now. It was just an aberration which had come to me out of the grief of my mother's death. 'Mabel,' I went on, 'is less fierce. She just goes along with Martha.'

'And you lived with them for a while. It would be different for you, Sarah. You are one of them.'

'They were disapproving of my mother.'

'The beautiful actress. How I wish I could remember her more clearly. Sometimes I lie in bed and try to think back, but all I can remember is Sheba's coming in one morning and saying, "She's gone," and her eyes were glittering as though it was something to rejoice about.'

'Tell me about Sheba. She interests me.'

'Shall I have some cool drinks sent in? There is tea, of course . . . always tea. I dare say we drink even more than you do in England. It's the heat . . .'

Almost as soon as she had spoken a servant appeared and lemonade was promptly served in tall glasses.

When we were alone, Clytie said: 'You were asking about Sheba. She comes from an interesting family. Her brother Nankeen is Clinton's headman. He's clever. Clinton thinks highly of him. Nankeen made an unusual marriage. His wife was Portuguese. The Portuguese did settle here at one time, you know. The professional classes sprang from them and from the Dutch, who were also here. Nankeen is a very handsome man and he attracted this beautiful girl of quite good family. They married. Your Leila is one of the children. Then there is Ashraf, who works on our plantation. Then there is . . . another daughter . . .'

'What does she do?'

Clytie hesitated. 'Oh, Anula is rather unusual . . . She has her own house. She is reckoned to be one of our great beauties. And she is supposed to have what they call Powers.'

'How interesting. I hope I shall meet her.'

'Well, er . . . you might.'

'Is there some mystery about this . . . Anula?'

'Oh, no, no . . . not really. Her family are rather in awe of her. Sheba talks of her as though she is divine. Family pride, that's all. You were asking about Sheba. She came to serve my mother and when I was born she became my nurse. She was a mother to me. She is devoted to me . . . and now to Ralph. I know he is safe with her. In time we shall have a tutor for him . . . an English tutor. Perhaps he'll go away to England to school. Seth wants him to.'

'It must be wonderful to have such a lovely little boy.'

'He is my life. I love him beyond all things.'

'And Seth?'

'Yes, I love Seth too. It is different. Perhaps when you have a child you will understand.'

We had finished our drinks and she stood up. 'Shall I show you the house now?'

I said I should like that and she took me round. It was spacious and very similar to Clinton's.

Ralph was out, she told me. He was having a riding lesson. 'It is necessary to be able to manage a horse out here. Though of course we have the railway which will take us either to Kandy or Colombo, but for getting around locally one often needs a horse. Now let us go into the garden.'

We stepped down. I had noticed that this house, like ours, was raised above the ground. I asked why and Clytie told me that it was a protection against the termites.

'They abound,' she said, 'and they go about in armies of thousands . . . perhaps millions. They would march through a house, eating their way so that in a few hours when they passed on there would be nothing left of it. Just a shell. So we build in this way. These supports you see have been specially treated to keep them off.'

'How awful! To go away and come back to find your house nothing but a shell.'

'It has happened. There are hazards we face out here, Sarah, which you have not dreamed of. You must be careful of the insects. Living here, we have become somewhat immune but you will have to get acclimatized. Beware of the mosquitoes. They are the greatest pest and dangerous too.'

'I seem to have a good deal to beware of.'

There was something English about her garden, and when I pointed it out she said: 'Yes, it was as our father wished it. Here we are able to grow some plants which grow in England.'

It was true. Among the exotic blooms were rhododendrons, geraniums and guelder roses.

'These will remind me of home,' I said.

It was a pleasant hour I spent in the garden with Clytie. The more I saw her the more I was drawn towards her. The fact that she was not entirely of my own race gave her a strangeness which was piquant and attractive.

I think what struck me most as I wandered among the beautiful flowers was the presence of teeming life all around. The air was full of the hum and buzz of insects. Clytie said she did not notice it and I should grow accustomed to it in time. There was an abundance of life and growth due to the heavy rains and the hot sun. There was one moment when I touched the branch of a shrub and recoiled in horror for the branch had become alive. It walked. I stared in shocked horror.

Clytie laughed at me. 'It's a stick insect. It looks just like a piece of branch. That's its disguise.'

'It looks uncanny.'

'You'll get used to it. Everything must seem strange at first but soon you'll be taking everything for granted. I hope I shall see you often, and you have Clinton . . .'

She was looking at me rather anxiously as though inviting confidences.

'Oh yes,' I said, 'Clinton.'

'We were surprised when we heard he was married.'

'Were you? After all, he is not so young.'

'But he never seemed inclined . . .'

'I dare say he came to England to look for a wife,' I said, attempting to speak light-heartedly.

'Well, he found one and it all worked out well. Sarah, Seth's a little anxious . . . about this place.'

'What about it?'

'What will Clinton do?'

'It's not for Clinton to do anything. It's mine. I know nothing about it but I'm determined to learn. I'm going to ask Seth to show me things.'

'I don't think Clinton exactly approves of Seth. Seth always imagines he's critical.'

'Clinton would expect too much from people perhaps.'

She looked at me oddly. 'Yes,' she said slowly, 'perhaps he would. When our father was alive everything went smoothly. Seth had done well. Our father was pleased with him. You must forgive us if naturally we thought . . .'

'You can speak freely with me, Clytie. You and Seth thought the plantation would come to you. That was natural.'

'It would have been better the other way round.'

'What do you mean . . . the other way round?'

'The pearls to you, the plantation to me. But I was the elder and there was tradition. I hate the things. I think they bring bad luck.'

'You have them here, Clytie?'

'Yes. Seth thinks they should be in the bank. They are sometimes. But I have to wear them every now and then. Pearls should be worn, you know. It's as though they sulk if they're not. They lose their lustre. At least that's what I've heard. Our father used to make me wear them. We're going to have a ball to celebrate your arrival. I shall be expected to wear them then.'

'I'd like to see them. I have heard so much about them. Are they really as wonderful as they are made out to be?'

'You shall see for yourself.'

'They are spoken of with such awe. They must be worth a fortune.'

'Oh yes, far more than the plantation. But the plantation would have been better for us. Clinton is sure to take over. That's what Seth is afraid of. Sarah, what if Clinton should want to replace Seth?'

'He couldn't. I shouldn't allow it.'

'I have never known anyone really stand up against him.'

'Well, you don't really know me yet, do you, Clytie?' I felt a sudden lifting of my spirits. He was not going to rule me. He had made a mistake if he thought he had made an easy conquest and through my gullibility he had acquired what he wanted – the Ashington Plantation.

It is mine, Clinton Shaw, I said to myself there in that scented garden. And this is something you will have to learn.

There was a sudden shout of pleasure as Ralph came into the garden. He looked very charming in a suit of Shantung silk, his dark hair shining, his eyes alight with excitement and a faint glow in his cheeks.

'Mama!' he cried. Then he saw me and hung back a little.

'It's your Aunt Sarah,' said Clytie. 'You know her. You met her yesterday.'

He nodded and turned to his mother. 'Mama, I saw a cobra. He came after us. He was going to bite me. I trod on him and then he stood up. He was big . . .' The boy lifted his hands as high as he could. 'He hissed at me.'

Clytie had gone pale with horror.

A Sinhalese came forward, hands folded across his chest, head slightly bowed. 'No, missee,' he said. 'No cobra. No danger to little one.'

'It *was* a cobra,' shouted Ralph his face growing scarlet. 'It was
. . . it *was*!'

'Well, what happened then?' said Clytie, her voice calm. 'Come
and tell Aunt Sarah and me all about it.'

'We were riding in the woods,' cried Ralph. 'We tied up the
horses and walked a bit. Then the cobra came along.'

'And how did you get rid of him?'

'I shot him.'

'With what?'

'My bow and arrow.'

'But you didn't have your bow and arrow with you.'

'I made one.'

Clytie ruffled his hair.

'Ralph has the most marvellous imagination,' she said.

'What's imagination?'

'Romancing.'

'What's romancing?'

'What you do, my cherub.'

'Is it nice?'

'Well, if you don't carry it too far.'

'Is it heavy?'

'What a boy!' said Clytie fondly. 'And you haven't said hello
to Aunt Sarah yet.'

'Hello, Aunt Sarah. Do you like snakes?'

'I shouldn't think so. I have never seen one.'

'Why not?'

'Because there aren't many – only a few little ones – where I
come from.'

'Is that why you came away?'

'Well, not exactly.'

'I'll show you Cobbler. Mama, I'm going to show Aunt Sarah
Cobbler.'

'Where is he?'

'I know. I know.'

He was off. Clytie was laughing as she said to me: 'You'll have to be very much in awe of Cobbler. He's a lifesize toy cobra. A horrible thing. Ralph loves him dearly. He's had him for some months but he's still a favourite. He couldn't say cobra at that time and he called the thing Cobbler. That's how he got his name.'

Ralph had appeared dragging what certainly did look like a deadly snake with him.

'There's Cobbler,' he said. 'Does he frighten you, Aunt Sarah?'

'He is rather frightening.'

It was true. The thing was so lifelike. I examined the yellow glass eyes on either side of his head.

'I can make his tongue come out,' said Ralph. 'You press it here. See. He's going to bite you, Aunt Sarah. Oh he's a bad wicked Cobbler. But I won't let him. I'd kill him with my bow and arrow if he bit you.'

'Well, now you've met Cobbler,' said Clytie. 'Where is he going now, Ralph?'

'I'll put him under the bush. He likes it there.'

We watched him. He was indeed a beautiful child. When he came back his mother took one hand and I the other and we went towards the house.

'Sleepy Sam said hello,' he said.

'You didn't go near him, I hope,' replied his mother. 'Sleepy Sam is an old crocodile. Quite harmless now, I'm sure. There is a sluggish river running through the woods. The banks are marshy. Watch out for the crocodiles when you pass it.'

'What's sluggish?' asked Ralph.

'Just lazy.'

'Like Sleepy Sam?'

'Did you really see him?'

'Yes, he said he was tired and wouldn't bite me.'

Sheba came to take Ralph. She nodded her head at me with a sort of grudging welcome. Ralph ran to her and embraced her round the knees. He started telling her how he had slain a cobra with his bow and arrow.

'It's time for your dinner, you bold bold boy,' she said. 'And then a little rest eh?'

'Oh Sheba, I'm not going to rest. I'm going . . . I'm going . . .'
He looked at us all mischievously. 'I'm going to shoot a cobra.'

'You're going to keep away from the nasty old creatures,
Master Ralphie, or Old Sheba will want to know the reason
why.'

Ralph came and kissed his mother and then, rather shyly, me.
Sheba took him away.

'She resents anyone he takes a fancy to and he's rather fond of
his riding master,' said Clytie. 'She'll complain that he is allowed
to get himself dirty and is led into danger . . . and it is all because
she can't bear anyone to do anything for him. She was like that
with me. Now she has transferred her affection to Ralph. You
know what these nurses are.'

I didn't. Perhaps some day I should tell her about the sort of
upbringing I had had in Denton Square.

Luncheon was brought to us in the dining-room and we ate a
fish called seir which Clytie told me was a form of scomber. 'I
ordered it for you because it was different and you want to try
everything. We do have carp, whiting, mullet and dories – all of
which I think you have in England. You see, being half English I
was always eager to learn all I could about England, so I do know
a little.'

We ate mangoes and tiny sweet bananas, which were delicious.
As we sat talking I said to Clytie: 'You were going to show me
the necklace.'

'So I was. Come upstairs. It's in the safe.'

We went to the bedroom she shared with Seth. Taking a key she
unlocked a door and we stepped into a kind of dressing-room. It
was small and contained a desk and two chairs as well as the safe.
She shut the door after us.

'The servants don't come in here,' she said, 'I dust it myself.
The necklace is kept here in the safe. It is so valuable that the
legends build up round it. It is supposed to be unlucky and it's said
that it would bring bad luck if it fell to anyone outside the family.
I am sure it was to frighten off thieves that that story was put

about. You see when so much money is wrapped up in one thing, some people would risk anything to possess it. The servants wouldn't come in here if I asked them to. It works well.'

'What a fuss about a few pearls!'

'Dear Sarah, they are the Ashington Pearls,' she said. 'One of the finest sets in the world. You will see. Each pearl matches perfectly. Do you know anything about pearls?'

'I know what they look like.'

She laughed. 'Even if you know very little you will see how magnificent these are.'

She went to the safe and began to open it. 'It's easy,' she said, 'when you have the combination.'

The door sprang open. She took out a large case in crocodile leather.

Reverently she laid it on the table. She touched the spring and the lid flew open. There were the Ashington Pearls.

I caught my breath in amazement for they really were magnificent. They were lying on midnight blue velvet . . . two rows of them, one about two feet long the other slightly shorter. There was a lustre about them which glowed with life. Each pearl was of a remarkable size and perfectly rounded and each matched every other pearl. I was fascinated by their pure luminous depth and I felt a great desire to touch them.

'Go on,' said Clytie. 'Pick them up. Look at them closely.'

I put out my hand, but I did not touch them. Somehow I now felt reluctant to.

The clasp was dazzling. It was a combination of emerald and diamonds. I looked closely at what seemed like a coil of rope made of diamonds. I saw then that the gems of the clasp represented a snake reclining among yew leaves. The snake's eye was an emerald and the leaves, like the snake's body, were diamonds.

'Whenever I hear of snakes I think of this,' said Clytie. 'I did this morning when Ralph was telling us his fantastic tale about killing a cobra. It's rather odd, that clasp. Our father once told me that there is a sizeable receptacle inside. Look at the snake's tongue. There is a small hole there. It is told that one of the lords of Kandy, wanting to be rid of his wife, filled the receptacle with some deadly poison, pricked her skin, and the poison from the serpent entered her body and killed her.'

'That's horrible,' I said. 'No wonder you feel there's something repulsive about it.'

'Don't you like it? Don't you think it's beautiful?'

'The pearls are. They are fantastic. But I don't care much for the snake. Of course I know little of pearls, but I have never seen any like this before.'

'Nobody has ever seen pearls like these before. They are unique. That's why it is a great responsibility holding them in trust.'

She picked them up and placed them about my neck. The cold stones of the clasp made me recoil.

'They become you, Sarah,' she said. 'They suit you better than they suit me. They make a different person of you.'

'Let me look,' I said.

Standing on the table was a small mirror in a frame set with pieces of amethyst quartz and turquoise matrix. I took it up and looked at the necklace. It was superb. The pearls seemed to grow warm on my skin and cling to me, as though they were alive, while the clasp was cold digging into my neck. I put up my hand to touch it. I said: 'It's pricking.'

'You've got it round the wrong way,' said Clytie. 'There's no poison in it today,' she added with a laugh.

'Undo it now, Clytie.'

She obeyed.

'Let me see it on you.'

She put it on and faced me.

'It's too heavy for you,' I commented. 'You need something exquisitely dainty.'

'Yes,' she agreed, 'it's too heavy for me.'

She took the necklace off, laid it reverently in its case and put the thing in the safe.

For the rest of the day I could not get it out of my mind. It had come between me and my pleasure in my sister's company.

During the late afternoon Clytie took me back by way of the woods, through those trees – palms as well as ebony and satin-wood.

'We keep the coconuts for our own use,' she said, 'though I think Clinton has some idea of commercializing them. The people on the plantation eat the fruit when it's green and when it's ripe they extract the oil. They make a sort of toddy from the flowers and from the casing they weave mats. Even the empty cups they use as drinking vessels. Nature cannot have provided any growing thing as capable of being put to more uses than the coconut. Why, they even plait the leaves to thatch their huts and use them as platters sometimes.'

The growth was dense in certain places.

'Watch for snakes,' Clytie warned. 'I had quite a shock when Ralph talked of meeting a cobra. He could have done so. We've warned him. That accounts for the bow and arrow nonsense.'

We came to the river with its marshy banks. 'There's old Sleepy Sam, I do believe. Hush! Look. An egret standing there so close to Sam . . . so still.'

I stood for a while watching. I felt very far from home.

'Don't come through the woods yet, unless you're with some-one. As I have said, wait until you get to know it better. You could get lost.'

'And the dark comes quickly here, I know. There's no twilight as there is at home.'

'Twilight must be very comforting,' she said. 'A gentle warning that the night is coming.'

We walked on and soon I saw the white walls of the house through the trees.

Clinton came out. He looked very pleased to see me.

'Have you had a good day?' he asked.

I told him I had enjoyed it very much. 'We are getting to know each other,' I added.

'All very praiseworthy. Come along in and have some refreshment, Clytie.'

'I think I should be getting back before it's dark.'

'I'm going to send someone back with you,' said Clinton.

'That's not necessary.'

'I shall send someone back,' repeated Clinton.

I wanted her to refuse and insist that she would do as she wanted, yet somehow I did not like to think of that frail and dainty creature alone in the dark jungle.

Clinton had his way, of course.

As we approached the house I saw something dart up the wall. I gave a little cry and jumped back.

Clinton laughed aloud. 'Only a harmless little gecko,' he said. 'A lizard, you know. You'll see many of those before you've been here very long.'

Yes, I felt I had come a very long way from home.

During the next two or three weeks I began to grow accustomed to my surroundings. I was no longer startled to wake up and find myself shut in by a mosquito net. I had become used to the knowledge that my marriage had been one of convenience from Clinton's point of view. That he desired me ardently, I must accept; but then he was a man who had desired many women ardently. I was discovering every day that there was a ruthlessness about him that I had only half guessed at in England. I wanted to oppose him, and yet that passion between us, while it lasted, could eliminate all other feelings. Such emotion was, I knew, by its very nature, transient. It was not possible to visualize a comfortable future with Clinton. The dreams which I supposed came to every woman, of raising a family and planning for them with their father, could not fit in with my life with Clinton. I was sure he would want a son; in fact he had mentioned it – a boy who would be made in the image of himself and whom he could bring up to be as ruthless.

As I have said, Clinton was a power in this place. That much was clear, and became clearer every day. All the workers on the plantation went in fear of him. His headman, Nankeen, seemed to regard him as a sort of god. Clinton thought highly of Nankeen.

'He's worth two of Seth Blandford,' he said. 'I can leave him in charge with confidence.' Nankeen lived in a house on the plantation and it was superior to those of other workers. I remembered too, that he was Sheba's brother. He was a sort of overseer – a man of drive and integrity and, so Clinton told me, above all, loyalty.

'A quality, my dear wife,' he added, 'which is to be desired above all others.'

In our drawing-room was a bookcase full of books about Ceylon and many of them on the growing and production of tea. I made up my mind to study them.

Clinton laughed.

'Why are you amused?' I demanded. 'It is natural that I should want to learn. I own a plantation. Have you forgotten that?'

'I believe you want to set up as my rival.'

'It would be a piquant situation.'

'And you, my darling Sarah, do enjoy a piquant situation. I think it would be a good idea to run them jointly. It would save costs.'

'*I* don't think it would be a good idea.'

He smiled ruefully. 'Your father discussed it with me. To tell the truth, Sarah, for a long time Ashingtons has not been as profitable as it should be.'

'Not as profitable as Shaws, you mean?'

'That's exactly what I do mean. I have ideas for Ashingtons.'

'I *might* consider them.'

He picked me up, twirled me round and then held me against him.

'Put me down,' I said. 'You may find that your little ruse to get possession of Ashingtons was not quite so clever as you thought.'

'Dearly beloved wife,' he mocked, 'what are you threatening to do? Make Ashingtons a rival of Shaws? Buy us up in time, I shouldn't be surprised. Let me tell you this: Producing tea profitably is not learned in three weeks by reading books. It's trial and error. It's failure and success. There are more problems in this business than you have ever dreamed of in your philosophy, my love. Look! Why not be a good wife. Be guided by your husband who will love you and cherish you for the rest of your life.'

'I know he will love and cherish my plantation,' I said.

'That plantation does need a good deal of love and cherishing.'

The more he mocked, the more determined I became to oppose him. I had to admit that this gave a fillip to the day's excitement and I looked forward to our encounters. I was gratified to realize that he did too.

I did not see a great deal of him during the day. The plantation covered many acres and he often went off at sunrise and returned at sunset. I was at Ashingtons most days where Clytie always welcomed me and Seth was very pleased that I was taking an interest in the place. If he bore any resentment towards me for inheriting what should clearly have gone to his wife and through her to him, he did not show it. I think he knew of my opposition to Clinton and rejoiced in it.

I would ride with him round the plantation. Sometimes Clytie came with us. She managed to look beautiful in western clothes, but what became her most were her filmy saris which often glittered with gold and silver thread and were made charming with fine embroidery. She had them in all colours – chiefly pastel shades which suited her dark and delicate beauty. Sometimes I would just want to gaze at her in admiration.

From Seth I learned a good deal about the work of the plantation which was carried on in the various seasons. He explained how planting could be done to most advantage at the time of the south-west monsoon although, because of the annual rainfall, this operation could be performed at any time of the year. He pointed out the importance of pruning, which kept the bushes from growing too tall and thus making plucking difficult. I walked with him through the plantation and watched the women at work. They looked at me with curious eyes and I realized that this was not only because I was my father's daughter and owner of the plantation but because I was the wife of Clinton Shaw.

I fancied they were a little uneasy, wondering what the future held in store for them, and I expect many of them believed that Ashingtons would soon be under Clinton's control. There was a slight difference in the demeanour of those workers whom I came to think of as mine and those employed by Clinton. His worked more steadily. They were in awe of him, as I guessed my father's workers had never been of him. And although they were respectful to Seth I could see they had no fear of him.

Clinton was just, I believed, but that inherent ruthlessness was known to all. I gathered that if a man or woman offended against some code of behaviour which he had set up, he or she would be instantly dismissed and it would be no use appealing for mercy. Once a law was made, he had explained to me, it had to be enforced or it became useless.

The fact remained that he had a thriving plantation while Ashingtons limped along and I gathered made too small a profit to plough back much into the business and bring about necessary improvements.

I found Seth interesting because like most people who have a certain knowledge he liked to impart it to someone who was ignorant of the subject. He would talk to me of the trials which beset a tea planter and what had to be looked for. With him I watched the spraying of the crop with a zinc sulphate because, as he told me, there was a deficiency of zinc in the soil and while we watched he told me woeful tales of what happened when red root disease attacked the plants, reducing them to a wet pulp which was not visible until it was too late to save the plants.

How I loved to talk to Clinton of black root disease and charcoal stump rot. He would listen to me with that supercilious smile about his lips and let me run on and then shoot some question at me at which I would betray my ignorance. Then he would kiss me and tell me he adored me and that the budding tea plantress was every bit as fascinating as the girl with whom he had spent that night in Parrot Cottage.

That was the pattern of those first days. Ashingtons seemed to have become more of a home to me than Shaws. Every day I would go over there and I would spend a great deal of time with both Seth and Clytie, for Clytie would not allow me to stay all day out of doors.

'You don't know the climate,' she told me. 'You must not go out in the middle of the day and never without your hat.'

I saw that she was right and I looked forward to my mornings with Seth and then the return to the house when I would be with my sister.

Then there was Ralph, who seemed to have taken quite a fancy to me. He liked to tell me stories of the fantastic adventures he had with snakes and elephants. He had a fantasy elephant called Jumbo because he had heard that there was an elephant who had gone to England to be in a zoo and who was so big that they called him Jumbo. His dark eyes would glow with excitement as he recounted his stories. Clytie and I would take him for walks in the garden and the woods and it was the woods which usually formed the background for his stories. He showed me a tall palm tree on which the letter R had been carved.

'It's my tree,' he said. 'It comes alive when nobody's looking and talks to me. R. That's my name. Ashraf put it on so that the tree wouldn't forget it belonged to me.'

I fancied that Sheba was a little put out by his friendship for me. There was something about Sheba which made me very uneasy. She was always watching me. I supposed that she was a little resentful because I had inherited the plantation which should have gone to her beloved Clytie. Her devotion to my sister matched that she felt for Ralph and was very commendable.

I believed she listened to what Clytie and I said to each other. There was one occasion when I was certain of it.

Clytie said to me after we had taken lunch and were sitting drinking tea which was always served afterwards in place of the coffee we had at home: 'I suppose Clinton talks to you about the plantation?'

'Oh, he is amused by my interest. I believe he thinks I shall tire of it sooner or later.'

'Seth is a little anxious still. He does wonder what is in Clinton's mind.'

'I have told you, Clytie, that I shall be the one to make decisions.'

'Knowing Clinton . . .'

'But you have to know me as well.'

'The fact is, Sarah, Seth loves the plantation. It is his life. When he joined my father and we married it seemed as though . . .'

'I understand. There's no need to feel embarrassed. There shall be no changes at Ashingtons. I promise you that.'

She smiled at me gratefully and it was then that I had one of those strange instincts or whatever they may be that someone else was sharing in this conversation. I turned sharply. The door was slightly ajar. Did I fancy it or did it move very slightly?

'What's the matter?' asked Clytie quickly.

'Oh, nothing.'

I turned back to her and she said: 'I have been thinking a great deal about the ball. Everyone will want to meet you. Your father's daughter and Clinton's wife! It's a double distinction. What shall you wear?'

'I had little opportunity to wear ball gowns at the Grange. I think the aunts were planning some campaign to get me married, but Clinton came . . .'

'And swept you off your feet. Shall we go into Kandy and buy some material for your gown? Leila is a wonderful seamstress. She will make what you want quickly and beautifully.'

'I should enjoy that.'

'Our balls are greatly looked forward to. Ball is perhaps rather a grand name for our little gatherings. We haven't the amenities really, but when the folding doors are back we have a fairly sizeable room. It makes a great excitement.'

We talked of the preparations we should have to make and so half an hour passed pleasantly.

When I rose I remembered that I thought we had been overheard. I noticed that the door was shut. Sheba, I thought. We had been talking of my inheriting the plantation. Poor Shebal She was so devoted to the family that she would certainly be interested in my plans which could affect them. All the same, I couldn't help feeling uneasy when I thought of those bright black eyes watching me . . . wondering about me.

I tried to laugh at myself. I was, in a way, an alien in a strange land. It was only natural that I should be regarded with suspicion and perhaps regard some of them in the same way.

Our trip to Kandy was a pleasant adventure.

We were driven to the station at Manganiya in a sort of brougham by one of the servants and there was a boy of about fourteen who rode all the way on the back steps and clearly felt himself to be of the utmost importance.

There we boarded the train for Kandy.

The city was a delight – quaint and ancient, it had been the last stronghold of the Kings of Ceylon. Situated as it was on the lower step of the great central mass of mountains, it was about sixteen hundred feet above sea level.

I was enthralled by the Temple of the Tooth and the artificial lake. The streets were crowded and I realized for the first time what a mixed people they were. So far those I had seen were mostly Sinhalese; but in the city were men and women of darker hue; they were the Tamils, Clytie told me. There were Moors too, for Arab traders used to come to the island and they had left evidence of their stay behind them. Many of the shops were run by them. There were a few Burghers – people who had descended from the Dutch or Portuguese settlers. They were chiefly engaged in the professions – lawyers, doctors and teachers.

We did not arouse a great deal of attention, for there were several people in European dress, although most of the women wore saris like Clytie.

It was now a cosmopolitan city but it was easy to believe that it had been once the centre of the mountain kingdom of Kandy which had been in control of the entire island.

There were shops of various descriptions. Inside some of these darkish interiors beautiful gems were on display – sapphires, emeralds, rubies and pearls. But it was material we had come to buy, and Clytie took me to a shop where we were greeted by an almost embarrassingly obsequious Arab who brought out bales of exquisite silks for our inspection.

I chose a Bokhara silk, deep blue with a fine tracery of silver which I thought would be becoming.

Our purchases made, we went inside one of the hotels where Clytie ordered tea which we drank with little rock cakes called English Buns because the recipe had been brought out from England. While we were thus engaged, a large woman with greying hair and a skin which had obviously borne the brunt of several tropical years cried out: 'Why, Mrs Blandford! What a pleasant surprise!'

Her voice was eminently audible and as she bore down on us in what seemed like triumph, her bright blue eyes were fixed on me.

'And this must be . . .'

'My sister, Mrs Shaw,' said Clytie. 'Sarah, this is Mrs Glendenning whose husband is in charge of the railway at Kandy.'

'We are all so longing to meet you.' The eyes were frankly curious. 'I am so glad to be the first . . . am I the first?'

'Yes. We have done no entertaining since my sister arrived,' said Clytie. 'She is really settling in. At the ball, of course . . .'

'Ah, the ball! We are so looking forward to it. How do you like Ceylon, Mrs Shaw?'

'I am finding it all very exciting, but as my sister says I have so recently come and it is all so different from home.'

'Home!' sighed Mrs Glendenning. 'How one yearns for home! We go every five years but it is not enough. Mr Glendenning is so absorbed with the railway. As Chief Resident and Locomotive Engineer he has to be here one day, in Colombo the next and then somewhere else. Mishaps are as plentiful here as . . . tea!'

'He must have a very important position,' I said.

'My dear Mrs Shaw, I would be happier if it were less important. You yourself must know what it is to have a busy husband. How is Mr Shaw?'

'He is very well, thank you.'

'We were all certain he would come back with a wife. It was so sad about your father. However, we must not brood, must we. And it all worked out as we expected. They were gambling on it at the Club.'

'Gambling on it?' I asked.

'On you and Clinton. Give them a chance and they'll gamble on anything. It was, after all, the *right* conclusion. Your poor father! He had so much trouble all his life. He will be happy now, looking down and seeing everything so *conveniently* solved. Clinton will have changed, I dare say . . . settled down . . .'

She was a most uncomfortable woman and all the time she was watching me, I imagined she was trying to assess my relationship with Clinton. I was glad when she went on her way.

'The trouble with these people,' said Clytie, 'is that they get so interested in other people's affairs. Life runs to a pattern in the European circle. They entertain, go to the Club, talk constantly of England and occasionally go there. So when someone new arrives . . .'

'And if it's someone like Clinton Shaw's wife . . .' I interrupted.

'Well,' she admitted, 'Clinton has always been one to get himself talked about. He was after all a bachelor for so long and there were mothers with daughters on their hands. They had made up their minds that he would never marry . . . until they heard that your father was going to England and Clinton was with him.'

'I see.'

'You're disturbed. You mustn't be. Just remember that people in communities like this gossip a great deal.'

'Was there much gossip . . . about Clinton?'

'Well, you know how it is.'

'I can guess.'

'That's over now,' said Clytie comfortably and I did not ask her what was over. I felt it was too humiliating to discuss my husband in this way.

We came back in the late afternoon past green paddy-fields which seemed to rise out of the thickly wooded hills, past elephants bathing in the river and working on the banks carrying their great loads, past water buffaloes and bullocks plodding ponderously along pulling carts behind them.

We were met at the station by the brougham.

'You'll be pleased with Leila's efforts,' Clytie told me. 'She is a natural dressmaker and would do very well in Paris or London, I am sure.'

She certainly worked wonders with my Bokhara silk. I was fascinated by her deft fingers as she pinned the fabric on me and regarded her handiwork with admiration shining in her great dark eyes.

'You will be beautiful,' she said.

'*You* are trying to make me so,' I answered.

'I make the gowns for my sister Anula,' she told me in a tone of reverence, as though Anula were the Queen.

I was becoming rather curious about Anula.

'Your sister is very beautiful I suppose,' I said.

'She is the most beautiful woman in Ceylon. *Everyone* thinks so.'

'Then she must be very beautiful indeed.'

'Ah, missee, she has more than beauty. You understand?'

'No,' I answered.

Leila came closer and looked over her shoulder. Then she turned to me and whispered: 'She has powers.'

'What are they?'

'Anula was once great Queen.'

'Long ago?'

'Hundreds of years. She has been born again. One day she will be great Queen again. She can tell what will come. She know much about us all.'

'That might be rather uncomfortable for us,' I said lightly.

I could see that Leila was overwhelmed and considerably in awe of her sister and that she fully believed in those powers she spoke of. I was interested to hear more of this unusual woman but

I realized that I should get little sense out of Leila so I tackled Clytie on the subject.

'They're an unusual family,' Clytie told me. 'Anula is undoubtedly the beauty and the leading light. Nankeen married a Portuguese girl of good family and there are three children: Anula, the eldest, is certainly amazingly good-looking; Leila you know. Ashraf is the youngest. He works for us on the plantation. He will be like his father, handsome, shrewd and clever at his job. A certain legend has grown up round Anula. She believes she was a queen of Ceylon in another incarnation. She certainly has a presence and a look of royalty, no doubt cultivated by her beliefs, but it is definitely there.'

'Is she married?'

'N – no. She probably feels no one is good enough for her. Or she has yet to meet him . . .'

'She would want a prince to fit in with past royalty, I suppose.'

'Oh, these things are very real out here. It is a general belief with many that they have lived before and will do so again. Anula has, as they say, powers. She charms snakes and gets them to do her bidding – so they say – and she is supposed to cure people of their ailments and some . . . so I've heard . . . declare that she doesn't always cure if she wishes it to go the other way . . . Oh, but this is just foolish gossip.'

'I'm interested. Tell me more about this amazing Anula.'

Clytie shrugged her shoulders. 'I know little more than I've told you.' She looked uneasy. Then she said brightly: 'I'm glad you bought the Bokhara. It really will be most becoming.'

I guessed that for some reason she found the subject of Anula somewhat embarrassing.

The day was fixed for the ball.

I had not gone over to Ashingtons that morning. Clytie would be busy and she had refused all my offers of help. I was excited at the prospect of meeting people for I was assured that they were all impatient to meet me. Some would be staying the night at

Ashingtons and some with us. It would be just for one night. Others would ride through the early morning to their various homes.

There was a festive air throughout the house. The servants had lost their silent ways and giggled together. I caught them watching me with curious eyes because, I supposed, all the fuss was in my honour.

Clinton would not drive us over. One of the servants was to take us in the Victoria and he and I would sit under the hood with the driver up in front.

I felt a rising excitement when I put on my dress. It was beautiful, falling off the shoulders in many tucks and cascades of lace and ribbons. I had a small waist, for which I was grateful. It meant that I was able to avoid the tight lacing which would have been insupportable in this climate. My bodice clung tightly to my figure and from my waist my skirt flowed in flounces. I must say it was a triumph.

My unmanageable hair was a problem, so I decided that I would wear it high in the front, pinned very securely to prevent its straying. At least it was thick, but as it was also straight, this indeed was largely responsible for its unmanageability.

The deep blue of the Bokhara silk reflected in my eyes, giving them a touch of blueness and I felt it had been a happy choice.

'Why,' said Clinton, when he saw me, 'you really are a beauty.'

'I'm glad you have come to that conclusion.'

'I merely share your opinion. Isn't it nice to agree for once? Look at yourself. You can't hide your gratification.'

'Leila is a good dressmaker.'

'A clever family. Mind you, your neck's a little bare.'

I looked at my neck and as I did so he came swiftly behind me. He was holding something in his hands. I gave a gasp as I felt my throat encircled. He was fixing about my neck a band of velvet the same colour as my dress.

'What are you doing?' I cried.

'How nervous you are. Did you think I was going to strangle you! I am not tired of my dear wife yet.'

I was staring at my reflection. The ribbon was in place and the front of it glittered brilliantly.

'What is it?' I asked.

'Sapphires. Do you like them?'

'They are beautiful but . . .'

'It's time I gave you a present, don't you think? And what more appropriate!'

'You are giving me these sapphires!'

'Why so surprised? I knew about the dress. I got it out of Leila. I have seen women in these jewelled neckbands and I thought: Just the thing! I'll put a halter about my darling's neck and that'll show the whole world that she is mine.'

'I don't like the sound of a halter. As though I'm a horse . . .'

I went close to the mirror. There were three sapphires – a large one in the centre and two slightly smaller ones on either side.

'They're rather fine,' he said. 'You'll learn something about the stones we find here, I am sure. You'll soon be as knowledgeable about them – including pearls, of course – as you are becoming about tea.'

'Thank you,' I said. 'It was good of you.'

'No more than your due, you know. I want to show you how pleased I am that you are here.'

I was rather moved because he had taken the trouble to give me something that was so fitting. The neckband set with those superb sapphires had changed my appearance. It had added a touch of elegance which I had lacked before.

He caught my hands and kissed them. I withdrew with some embarrassment. A show of tenderness on his part always bewildered me.

'I like them very much,' I said. 'I can see they add something to my ensemble.'

'Let's go. All the men will be envious of me tonight and I shall revel in that, as you know.'

I went out into the hot night with a feeling of happiness. Was our relationship going to change? It had begun from mercenary motives on his part but was he really growing fond of *me*?

We sat close under the hood of the Victoria and as I listened to the clip-clop of horses' hoofs on the road, I lightly touched the sapphires at my throat and I said to myself: We might make it work after all.

Clytie was receiving the guests. The folding door had been flung open and there was a sizeable ballroom decorated with coloured flowers from the garden. Candles flickered in sconces and in the dim light the dresses of the women were softly beautiful. Clytie herself looked like a fairy princess. She was dressed in a sari of pale green – beautiful soft chiffon, and beneath it a glow of silver. Her silky hair was piled high on her head and there was an emerald ornament in it.

My eyes went at once to the pearls. They were magnificent, those two layers of lustrous beauty lying on her olive skin showed to perfection. They glowed and when she turned I caught the flash of green which was the serpent's eye at the back of her shapely neck.

'Clytie,' I whispered, 'you're wearing them!'

'On such occasions it's expected,' she answered. 'Come and stand beside me. Everyone wants to meet you. How lovely you look. Those sapphires . . .'

'Clinton just gave them to me.'

'They're perfect.'

I stood beside her and one by one the people came up to me.

Clytie introduced me gracefully as she did everything, telling me who they were and what they were doing in Ceylon. There were a few rubber planters and coconut dealers but the majority were those who worked in the Civil Service and administration of the island. Some had been in the country for many years; others were new arrivals. Many of them lived in Kandy but some had come from as far as Colombo. This was mainly the English community who, far from home, clung together. There was Sir William Carstairs who was the Judicial Commissioner and one or two others from his department. I noticed the woman I had met in Kandy when Clytie and I had taken tea there, Mrs Glendenning. She greeted me vociferously and told me how enchanted everyone was to welcome me to Ceylon. I must visit the Club in Kandy and indeed become a member.

Her sharp eyes were all over me and came to rest on the sapphires.

'What heavenly stones!' she cried. 'A gift from the fond husband, I'd stake my life.'

'You should not stake your life so rashly, Mrs Glendenning,' I said.

'Don't tell me they are not! But who else would dare? Let me tell you, my dear Mrs Shaw, your husband is a man to reckon with.' She came closer. 'There is no one here who would care to offend him. I wouldn't like to be the one who did that. It would have to be a bold man . . . These men. One law for them, eh, and another for us. That's what they would like. Oh, and your sister is wearing the famous pearls. My husband is most interested in them.'

Clytie overheard that and I saw her touch the pearls nervously.

'Reggie is going to ask you to let him take a close look at them, Mrs Blandford,' went on Mrs Glendenning. 'We have all heard so much about them.'

'There is always a great deal of talk when I wear them,' answered Clytie.

'Such a priceless heirloom,' went on Mrs Glendenning. 'They must be worth all the rest of the jewels in this room put together.'

Clytie had turned away. She had hated the reference to the pearls and I was beginning to dislike Mrs Glendenning. I caught the Judicial Commissioner's eye and smiled. He came over to me and I took a step forward, shutting out Mrs Glendenning.

He was a charming man; he had come out twenty years ago, he told me, and the island was home to him now. He visited the Old Country every five years or so. His family looked forward to it and so did he.

'You see some Sinhalese here tonight,' he said, 'but most of us are English. Many of these Sinhalese work in the government offices. Some come from ancient Kandyan families.'

'The women look so beautiful in their saris,' I said. 'I'm hoping to meet everyone tonight. My sister arranged this gathering for that purpose.'

'I am sure everyone will want to meet you. Oh, here is Reggie Glendenning. He's Chief Resident and Locomotive Engineer and responsible for the railway. The line which runs between Colombo and Kandy is of the utmost importance to us.'

I was introduced to Reggie. A meek little man, I thought him, but he would need to be with such a wife.

He told me at great length about his duties which I found incredibly boring and only half listened to, but when he spoke of the pearls I became more alert.

He had always been fascinated by the Ashington Pearls, he told me. He remembered once calling at Ashingtons and my father's taking them out of their crocodile case to show them to him.

'I had never seen pearls like them,' he said. 'Such lustre. I doubt whether there is a better set in the whole of the world. They were a gift of one of the kings of Kandy to his bride, I heard. They had the reputation of being unlucky because she died in child-birth. Then they came into the hands of the Ashingtons and became known as the Ashington Pearls. I'm going to ask Mrs Blandford to allow me to have another good look at them. I've always been interested in pearls. I should have liked to own a pearl fishery, but engineers don't become pearl fishers, do they?'

I thought: Not if they have overpowering wives who want them to be railway engineers.

'However, I shall ask Mrs Blandford to let me come over and see them in daylight.'

'I am sure she will be delighted to show them to you.'

'She's a beautiful woman,' he said, and I could agree with that.

Clytie came and rescued me. 'We shall be dancing soon and you will be expected to dance with everyone, Sarah,' she said.

When the dancing began Clinton was beside me. 'We shall dance the first dance together,' he said.

'You'll find me inexpert,' I told him. 'There was no dancing at the Grange. Celia Hansen taught me a little, though, when she was with us. The two of us used to dance round the schoolroom.'

'We shall have to help each other. I fancy myself I have about as much grace as an elephant.'

He put his arm round me and attempted to waltz. I was pleased because I had a certain sense of rhythm, which he certainly did not.

'You're happy tonight,' he said. 'Perhaps you like a grand occasion.'

'Do you?'

'I prefer to be with you alone.'

I laughed and he went on: 'Some take their pleasures oddly. You are enjoying ambling round this floor with your poor feet being maltreated by . . .'

'An elephant,' I said.

He held me tightly. 'All these things come to an end. The time will come when you and I will be riding side by side in the Victoria, riding through the scented night to our home . . .'

'I can see that such occasions bring out the sentimentalist in you.'

'It's always there, you know, slumbering beneath that granite-like exterior, waiting to be given the kiss of life . . . like the Sleeping Beauty and her prince.'

'I would hardly have thought you fitted the role of Sleeping Beauty.'

'I'm in the wrong story evidently. This is more like Beauty and the Beast.'

I was laughing aloud. 'We began with the Babes in the Wood.'

'Ah yes, wandering lost in the forest.'

'We could have strayed into Hansel and Gretel. They found the gingerbread house, you remember, and a terrible fate awaited them. You'd have to change roles there and be the witch, I suppose. You were the one who did the luring and for a mercenary purpose. Oh, this is too ridiculous.'

'We are, as they say, "the cynosure of every eye". Do you know they are asking each other: "Would you have believed that Clinton Shaw could be so enamoured of one woman and that woman his wife!"'

'I gather you have a reputation for gallantry of the non-enduring kind.'

'You have been learning a great deal and not only about tea.'

The waltz had come to an end and we went to our chairs.

I danced a spirited polka with Sir William, and Reggie Glendenning was my partner in the lancers. Clinton's partner was an outstandingly beautiful woman, dark haired, wearing a brilliant scarlet sari edged with a gold thread Greek-key pattern. Her sleek black hair was worn high and it was clearly abundant. In it gleamed a ruby ornament. She looked different from the other Sinhalese I had met and I imagined that, as in the case of Clytie, there was European blood there. It set her apart – as it set Clytie apart. This woman was tall – though not as tall as I. She was exceptionally graceful but there was something about her, some quality which was immediately discernible. She was the most striking-looking woman in the room.

She seemed to know Clinton well and I realized that she was one of the few people who had not been presented to me.

I sought the first opportunity to ask Clytie who she was.

'That's Anula, Nankeen's daughter.'

'Oh,' I cried. 'The famous Anula! Oh yes, she is indeed unusual. You didn't tell me you were inviting her.'

'Well, I didn't . . . actually . . .'

'Do you mean she came uninvited!'

Clytie looked uneasy. 'Well, you see, she has been to affairs like this before. She has been brought by someone and . . .'

'Clytie,' I said, 'what are you talking about?'

'Anula is different from the rest of her family. They work for us. Anula never worked for anyone. She has her own house on the edge of the plantation. She has her own carriage . . .'

'She is rich then?'

'Oh, er . . . yes. She came into money. She's a lady of leisure . . .'

'And she doesn't have to be invited. She just comes . . .'

It was all rather strange. I couldn't question Clytie now. I would ask her to tell me tomorrow.

The heat of the ballroom and the exertion of the dance had disturbed my hair and I knew it would be behaving in its usual perverse manner, so I decided to slip upstairs to Clytie's bedroom, which was being used as a cloakroom, and there set it to rights.

I went quietly up the stairs to the room and made for the mirror. Yes, it certainly needed attention. I took out the pins and let it fall about my shoulders. It was in such a state that the only thing to do was start from the beginning.

I was so engrossed in my task that I did not hear the door open suddenly and I looked up and, with a start, realized I was not alone. My heart started to beat ridiculously fast when I saw in the mirror the scarlet-clad woman standing behind me.

It was Anula.

I swung round – my hair half up, half down, which made me feel at a disadvantage beside this svelte and graceful creature.

'I didn't hear you come in,' I said.

'Did you not?' Her voice was low and musical. It suited her.

'I came to fix my hair,' I said as though I had to make some excuse for being here.

'It is dancing . . . and the heat. You are not accustomed to such heat, I know.'

'I suppose I shall get used to it.'

I went on doing my hair while she watched me silently.

'I have been so interested to meet you,' she said.

'I suppose a newcomer to the community is always of interest.'

'And Clinton Shaw's wife . . . of course. May I help? There is one piece here which is not secure. In the polka it would escape, I am sure.'

She had taken my hair in her hands and deftly arranged it. I was aware of her strange exotic perfume. 'There! I think that will stay.'

'Thank you. It hardly ever does stay where I want it to.'

'It is fine hair,' she said, 'and abundant.'

I stood up. She disconcerted me in a strange way. I felt her soft dark eyes were hiding something, that she was trying to probe my mind, to find answers to certain questions.

'I have a little gift for you,' she said. 'I hope you will not take it amiss.'

'A gift? Why, that is very kind.'

'My sister showed me the blue silk of your dress. She cut off a piece for me. So I had something to work with. Ladies here need a fan often. So I have brought you one to match your dress. Please take.'

'Thank you very much. May I look?'

'Please, I want to know if you like it.'

It was wrapped in tissue paper and when I unwrapped it I saw the most beautiful fan made of peacock feathers. That deep blue was my favourite colour.

'It's lovely,' I cried. 'These colours are so beautiful.'

She bowed her head. 'I am so happy that it gives you pleasure.'

'I shall not use it tonight because of the dancing,' I said. 'I will wrap it up and take it home with me. Thank you so much.'

'I wanted to give it to you because you are here with us now and because you are Clinton Shaw's wife.'

'It is most kind of you.'

We did not return to the ballroom together. I left her in the bedroom and went downstairs because I could hear the strains of the waltz cotillion and I had a partner waiting for me.

It must have been half an hour later when, after dancing with me, Sir William Carstairs suggested taking a turn in the garden.

'It's rather pleasant,' he said. 'It's so hot in this room.'

We went out and sat on a bamboo seat among the bushes of rhododendrons which seemed so much taller than any I had seen in England. Sir William told me a little about his work and how he had practised as a barrister in England before he came out to Ceylon. He was a bird-watcher and had seized the opportunity of studying the birds of Ceylon. He told me about the owls and one species in particular which had a cry so uncanny that the natives called it the devil bird.

'Kingfishers and sunbirds, golden orioles and parakeets, they're numerous here in Ceylon,' he was saying, 'but we're particularly rich in wading birds. You must watch for the egrets, spoonbills, storks and herons.'

I assured him that I would, and then I became aware of whispering voices. There must be another seat close by, I gathered, though hidden by the rhododendron bushes.

Someone said rather shrilly and audibly: 'She should never have come tonight. Do you think Clytie Blandford asked her? Of course she never would!' It was Mrs Glendenning who spoke, I realized.

Her companion murmured something and the shrill voice continued: 'Oh yes, I've no doubt she came without an invitation. After all, he forced her to be accepted, and I suppose she feels that even now he's brought his wife here she still has some standing.'

'You'll see the flamingoes on the wet sands,' Sir William was saying more loudly now, and I believed that he was so engrossed in his birds that he had not heard those scraps of conversation.

'I never did approve of the way he flaunted his mistresses,' went on Mrs Glendenning. 'But this one was the chief of all . . . the *maîtresse en titre* as the French used to call it. But we are *not* French, my dear Emma. Of course Clinton Shaw having so much power in this place seems to think he can behave as he likes. Well, now he has brought home a wife we shall expect a return to respectability.'

'Inland,' Sir William was saying, 'you'll find teal and ducks.'

I did not want to stay any more. I stood up and as I caught Sir William's eye I then believed that he had heard that conversation too and, kind man that he was, had been pretending that he hadn't.

Then it occurred to me that everyone here was watching Anula who had been his mistress. She had a house on the plantation, money of her own. Given by Clinton, of course. And when I had been brought here to be introduced as his wife she was here too. He could have stopped her coming but he had not. Instead he had danced with her, welcomed her most likely.

What a fool I had been to think that my marriage was going to work.

We went back to the ballroom. I danced mechanically. I saw Clinton and he was dancing with Anula. I felt sick with rage and misery.

Clytie whispered: 'Are you all right?'

I said: 'Why did you ask that woman?'

It was significant that she knew who I meant. 'I didn't,' she said. 'She came.'

'So you receive people you don't invite.'

'It seemed the best way.'

It was after midnight when we left. How different I felt, sitting in the Victoria with Clinton, from the way I had when we came.

'You're tired,' he said with that tenderness in his voice which no longer moved me to anything but a raging hatred.

I must preserve my anger for when we were alone. Then I would let it burst forth and I would assure him that I was not prepared to be humiliated.

Four people were to stay the night at the house because it was too far for them to go back to their homes. They would leave first thing in the morning. So when we arrived I was occupied in showing them their rooms and it was some time before I was alone with Clinton.

I looked at him steadily and said: 'I want the truth.'

'What's come over you?' he asked.

'That woman, Anula, what is she to you?'

'A very great friend.'

'You mean . . . your mistress?'

'A very special one.'

'She has the glorious title of *maîtresse en titre*. That's how I heard her described tonight.'

'Did you now? That sounds very grand. I am sure she would like that.'

'*I* did not like it.'

'My dear, why should you deprive Anula of a little glory?'

'You call it glory.'

'You called it that.'

'I want to know everything.'

'A glutton for knowledge, that's you. If it's not tea, it is precious stones and now my pre-marital engagements. You are wasting your energies there, my darling. What's done, is done. Anula was my mistress for several years. It was quite a reasonable relationship. She was accepted. There was a time when I thought of marrying her. But I don't greatly care for mixed marriages. There are the children to consider. I knew it must be an English wife for me.'

'With a plantation. I suppose Anula, with all her perfections, could not provide that!'

'You are right. She could not. That is where you scored.'

'I hate you,' I said vehemently. 'You are so . . . coldly calculating.'

'One should be calm when calculating if one is going to reach the right solution.'

'You madden me.'

'I know. I like you maddened.'

'I do not like you in any way.'

'Dear Sarah, don't be jealous. Anula is a handsome creature, I know, but . . .'

'You may go to her whenever you wish and I shall return to England.'

'What! To Aunt Martha. *She* is not such a paragon of virtue, I'll be bound. I might even be the better choice.'

I suddenly wanted to give way to despair. I had been quite happy when we had left for the ball, touched by his gift of the sapphires. But what I had discovered tonight was humiliating beyond endurance. I kept thinking of all the gossip there must be in a community like this. People would be watching me, watching Clinton and Anula. I thought of her coming quietly into the bedroom like a panther and there she had stood watching me.

I pulled off the sapphire-decorated ribbon and threw it on to the dressing-table.

'You might like to give it to Anula,' I said.

'It wouldn't suit her. Rubies are her stones . . . rubies and emeralds.'

'Perhaps one of the lesser minions?'

He laughed and caught me in his arms. 'Dearest Sarah,' he said, 'there is no need for this jealousy. You are here and you are the one. You are my wife. While you delight me why should I want anyone else?'

'That's a sort of ultimatum, is it?'

'That's an idea. A task for you. Make sure you enchant me so much that I cannot look at other women.'

'Please take your hands from me.'

His response was to hold me tighter. I tried to push him off unsuccessfully. That pleased him. He enjoyed showing his superior strength.

'Listen,' I cried. 'I will not endure other people's pity.'

'Pity! They are all envious of you. Didn't you realize that?'

'I was not referring to the discarded mistresses. I overheard a conversation in the gardens. Mrs Glendenning . . .'

'That woman. She's more poisonous than a cobra. I assure you there is no one in her orbit who is not accused of something.'

'Still, I do not like it.'

'You should not have strayed into the garden. Haven't I told you to beware of snakes?' He took my face in his hands and said seriously: 'My dear, dear Sarah. I have known many women. What do you expect? Anula suited me well. She is a strange, mysterious creature. I was often in her house . . .'

'The house you gave her . . .'

'A house I gave her.'

'And the jewels she was wearing?'

'And the jewels she was wearing. You know how generous I am.'

I said: 'Now listen to me. I will not stay here if you expect me to accept your infidelities. It is not that I care . . . personally . . .'

'Don't you, Sarah? I think that is rather immoral of you.'

'Will you be serious? I will not be pitied. I will not be humiliated, and if I discover that you expect me to share you with other women, I shall leave.'

'I could not bear to think of your going back to those wicked aunts.'

'I could go to my plantation. Has that occurred to you?'

'I should come and bring you back wherever you went. You married me, my darling, for better for worse, remember.'

'There must not be too much worse.'

He held me tightly and I was aware of the passion flaring up between us. He changed his mood suddenly. He was no longer flippant.

He said: 'Dearest Sarah, I love you . . . you only. Keep it like that. It can be the most wonderful thing that has ever happened to either of us.'

In such moments of physical accord he could make me believe that.

Our guests left early next morning and when they had gone I went over to Ashingtons to see Clytie. She was waiting for me and was eager to discuss the ball.

'I think it went off successfully,' she said. 'People who stayed the night have already left. They always go early – almost at dawn. I expect yours did too. They were delighted to meet you. You'll be seeing a good deal more of some of them, I expect. You look thoughtful, Sarah.'

When we were settled down drinking lemonade from tall green glasses, she looked at me anxiously and asked if I had really enjoyed it.

'Dear Clytie,' I said, 'you went to such trouble on my behalf. No one could have been a better hostess or taken more trouble to launch me into society.' I looked at her anxious face and suddenly decided to tell her the reason for my misgivings.

'I overheard a conversation in the garden about Clinton and that woman Anula.'

'Oh dear.' She looked concerned. 'How I wish she had not come. In the old days she was not invited, but she came when she wanted to. Clinton used to bring her with him sometimes and no one dared refuse her admittance for fear of offending him . . . and perhaps her. She has a reputation for some sort of sorcery.'

'It was Mrs Glendenning I heard talking.'

'She's a spiteful woman with a malicious tongue.'

'They were talking about being so shocked because Anula was present and I guessed immediately what her relationship with him had been. I tackled him with it last night.'

'Oh Sarah!'

'Don't look so alarmed. Clinton and I understand each other. I made it clear that I would not tolerate his continued relationship with her.'

'I am sure he would not dream of continuing it now.'

Dear Clytie! Her relationship with Seth was a more conventional one, I realized.

She went on: 'It was unfortunate that you should have overheard that woman.'

'I had a meeting with Anula in your bedroom. She brought a gift for me. I left it here last night. I forgot about it when we left. She came into the room while I was doing my hair. She seemed very friendly.'

Clytie frowned.

'Are you worried?' I asked.

Clytie hesitated. 'Anula is a woman of strong passions. She and Clinton used to quarrel violently. She was fiercely jealous. She tried to kill him once. She stabbed him with a knife. He had a wound in his arm. It was hushed up, but I never forgot it. You know, Sheba is her aunt. Sheba told me that Anula is one of the queens of Ceylon reborn. There was a Queen Anula. I read about it. She was the first queen Ceylon ever had. She was insatiable for men and poisoned five of her lovers. She was burned alive by her stepson whom she was planning to poison that she might make her own son heir to the throne.'

'Do they really believe all this?'

'Yes, they do. Sheba says that Anula has special powers. She used them to enslave Clinton. Sheba was one who did not think

Clinton would come back with a wife.'

'I seem to have fallen into a net of intrigue.'

'It's all a lot of nonsense. Anula is just a woman who likes to get her own way and has succeeded quite well so far.'

I stood up. 'I'll show you the gift she brought me. It's very beautiful and she evidently went to some trouble to match my dress.'

We went to the bedroom and there, lying on a table, was my fan wrapped in tissue paper.

I unwrapped it and opened it, spreading the beautiful peacock feathers.

Clytie took one look at it and put her hand to her mouth as she caught her breath.

'She gave you *that*!'

'Yes. Isn't it lovely?'

'Sarah, you mustn't keep it. You mustn't have it in the house. We never use them here. Peacock feathers bring bad luck.'

I stared at her. 'You really believe . . .'

'They make those fans occasionally for visitors. No one here will carry them. It is unlucky. I know it. Peacock feathers mean death.'

Clytie snatched the fan from me. She started to run downstairs with it.

In the garden she applied a match to the feathers. I stood watching them curl into flame.

'Oh Clytie,' I said, 'they were so beautiful . . .'

'She was ill-wishing you,' said Clytie quietly. 'Sarah, you will have to be very careful.'

THE RANSOM

*

At the end of the following week Clinton announced that he had to go to Colombo for several meetings with the shipping agents; after that he had to travel south to Galle and then north to the pearl fisheries. He would be away for about two weeks and as he did not want me to be in the house with only the servants, he suggested that I go to stay with my sister.

Clytie was delighted. She said it would save those journeys back and forth between Shaws and Ashingtons, so I said goodbye to Clinton and she came to collect me with a few clothes and things I should need and we went over in the carriage.

My room at Ashingtons looked over the gardens and to the woods beyond. Clytie had arranged guelder roses in a big bowl to welcome me. She kept telling me how happy she was that I was to stay under the same roof.

I couldn't help wondering whether Clinton was seeing Anula or any other women. I would never be sure of him. Uncertainty was the very essence of our relationship. There was no security, no trusting.

For a short time I would try to forget him. I would have my times with Seth when I would learn more about the plantation; I would have my sessions with Clytie who was fast becoming my dearest friend. It was rather wonderful to have discovered a sister and to find her, though strange in some ways, so completely compatible.

I looked round my room with its creamy curtains of Madras cotton, the inevitable mosquito nets over the bed and the fine wire-netting at the windows and I found it pretty and welcoming. I was determined to enjoy my stay and stop wondering about Clinton and how he might be spending all of his time on his trip.

After coming face to face with Anula and tackling him about his liaison (and receiving such a straight answer), I needed to be separated from him to collect my thoughts. There was one virtue he possessed and that was that he never attempted to lie. He never hedged as most men would have done. 'Yes, she was my mistress.' He said it outright. What I wanted to know was whether she still was and, having seen Anula and knowing Clinton, I believed that it was very possible that they would revert to their earlier relationship with the utmost ease.

At least I had this respite. Perhaps by the time it was over I should have come to some conclusion as to the best way to act.

In the mornings I was with Seth, riding round the plantation, looking with pride on those green slopes of healthy growth which were so important to us. It was a pleasant sight to see the pluckers at work, their baskets slung over their shoulders. They were mostly women and they looked colourful, their head covers falling over their necks to protect them from the sun, and themselves visible only from the waist up, the rest of them being hidden by the plants.

I enjoyed most of my afternoons with Clytie when young Ralph joined us and we would walk in the gardens and in the woods. He liked to stand under the tree with his initial carved on it and talk to it. He was full of vitality and could name quite a number of the plants he found. He never picked them though. 'It hurts them,' he explained. 'They like best to grow in the ground.'

He was a boy to be proud of and Clytie's love for him was obvious in every look she gave him, in every gesture. He was, however, very self-sufficient and impatient of a too great show of care. He seemed older than his four years; he could already read a little; and he liked to be told stories but would get impatient if they lasted too long; he often did not like the endings and supplied his own.

Sheba was constantly hovering over him and I noticed that she was very watchful of me. I understood her interest now that I knew of her relationship to Anula and Anula's to my husband. I wondered whether she had hoped that Clinton would marry

Anula. She had many reasons for resenting me so it was perhaps natural that she did. Also I had inherited the plantation, which I had no doubt she believed should have gone to Clytie and Seth. It was small wonder that she did not want me here. That was the meaning of those sombre glances which came my way. Sometimes, when the lamps were lighted, and I encountered them it sent shivers down my spine.

It was a few days after my arrival when I heard that there was to be a pageant in Manganiya. It was a great concession that it should come there. It had in fact taken place in Kandy and Clytie said she had wondered whether to go there to see it. But it was at night and they would have to take the train. Ralph would have been so excited and would have loved to see it, but she thought that taking him so far was impossible. Therefore it was very good that it was coming near home.

There was a tremendous excitement throughout the plantation. Everyone was going. It was known as the *Esala Perahera* and was conducted by torchlight.

'We should all go,' said Clytie.

Sheba shook her head and said it was too late for the boy; but Clytie overruled her by saying: 'He would never forgive you, Sheba, if he knew you had stopped him. We must go for that reason. One late night won't hurt him.'

So it was agreed.

All through the day and the one before, excitement prevailed throughout the house and plantation. There would be crowds in Manganiya that night. The procession was to take place at eight o'clock soon after dark.

The performers started to arrive in the early morning. We drove out before lunch to see them. Ralph was overcome with excitement. He kept bouncing up and down on the seat of the carriage and calling our attention to the elephants.

'I'm going to ride an elephant,' he declared. 'I've got an elephant. He's all mine. He won't let anyone else ride on his back.'

We smiled at each other over his head and his mother said:

'As you are going to stay up late tonight you must have a rest this afternoon.'

'I don't want to rest this afternoon.'

'If you don't you'll fall fast asleep and you won't see the pageant.'

He considered this. 'I won't,' he said without conviction.

When we returned to the house Sheba took possession of him and carried him off to his room.

Clytie and I drank tea together and I sensed that she was uneasy. I asked her what worried her and she hesitated for a moment, then she said: 'I'm worried about keeping him up. He gets so excited.'

'Oh, it won't hurt him for once,' I assured her. 'Besides, you couldn't disappoint him now.'

She agreed and went on to tell me about various pageants she had seen. Before Ralph had been born she and our father and later Seth had gone into Kandy to see the performances given by the Kandy dancers. They had been most interesting – the same dances which had been performed throughout the centuries usually expressing some legend.

'We must go in and see them some day,' she said. She described the costumes and the dances, but I could see that her thoughts were elsewhere.

On my way to my room I looked in on Ralph. He was sitting up in bed with a woebegone expression on his face.

'What's the matter, Ralph?' I asked. 'Is anything wrong?'

His face puckered and he dissolved into tears. It was the first time I had seen him cry. I went to the bed and put my arms round him.

'Tell me, darling,' I begged. 'What is it?'

'I can't go to sleep,' he sobbed.

'What's that to cry about?'

'I'll go to sleep tonight when the elephants come and the dancers dance. Mama said if I don't sleep now I'll sleep then. And it'll be all over and I won't see it.'

I laughed with relief. 'Nonsense,' I said. 'You won't go to sleep tonight. You'll be too excited. Now dry your eyes and if you lie still and rest you'll keep awake just the same tonight.'

'Will I really?' His mood had changed. His lovely face was transformed by a happy smile. I couldn't help kissing him although I knew he did not like being kissed, but he forgave me on this occasion as I had been the bearer of such relief.

'It's just as good to lie still,' I said. 'Just rest. Don't *think* about having to go to sleep. That'll do. When we go into Manganiya you'll be so wide awake you won't miss a thing.'

'Aunt Sarah, do the elephants dance?'

'Oh, I don't know. We shall have to wait and see, shan't we?'

'My elephant does. He dances betterer than the Kandy elephants.'

I smiled at him and tucked him in. I put my finger to my lips. 'Don't forget,' I whispered. 'Just lie still and don't worry. Resting is just as good.'

He nodded conspiratorially and I tiptoed out.

I looked in five minutes later and he was fast asleep.

We drove in the wagonette brake. There was myself, Clytie, Seth, Sheba and Ralph. The roads were crowded with vehicles of all descriptions – bullock carts, carts drawn by oxen, carriages of various descriptions, horse-riders and rickshaw men. The noise all about us was tremendous as everyone was in a state of great excitement.

Ralph could not keep still. He talked to me a great deal and I could see that there was an extra bond of friendship between us since I had assured him that resting was as good as sleeping.

We left the wagonette at the inn and made our way to the square where we could get a good view of the proceedings. I held Ralph's hand and he skipped along beside me. There was a great press of people. We caught a glimpse of Ashraf in the crowds and Ralph called out to him. Ashraf was a special friend of his. I wondered if Anula was here.

The excitement had already begun. Torches were held high to lighten the scene. Several carts had been decorated with flowers and there were people dressed in colourful costumes. The women's saris were beautiful but most of the men were in the customary white shirts, not tucked in at the waist but hanging down over the white trousers. It was impossible not to be caught up in the excitement.

When the elephants appeared Ralph was dancing with glee. They were magnificently caparisoned. It was as though thousands of jewels adorned them and seated in a cage on their backs, covered by canopies, were the chieftains of the various districts.

The drummers came ahead of the dancers and there in the centre of the square the famous Kandy dancers trod the ancient measures, their hands even more eloquent than their feet. Then the devil dancers performed – grotesque and uncanny, they filled the spectators with fearful wonder; and the absolute silence of the crowd was awe-inspiring.

It was thrilling and different from anything I had ever seen before. It was so foreign and I had not yet become accustomed to the alien music. I was enchanted by the slow graceful movements of the dancers, the colour of the costumes, the scent of flowers and the light from the torches playing on all the faces around me.

Ralph had wriggled his hand out of mine. He was clapping in time to the music. The dancers came close to us. There was a hush throughout the vast crowd. Then there was the singing, a strange chant which moved me in some way. I could not take my eyes from those gyrating bodies.

At length it was over. The dancers moved slowly across the square. The dazzling elephants trundled by. The people began to surge forward.

Suddenly I heard Clytie's voice, shrill with terror: 'Where's Ralph?'

I looked down in astonishment. He was not there.

'He'll be with Sheba,' said Seth.

'Where is Sheba?' cried Clytie.

We looked around. We could not see her.

Clytie was very uneasy and I found myself catching that uneasiness. I told myself that Ralph would certainly be with Sheba. She would have had her eyes on the boy all the time.

It was no use trying to find them in the press of people.

Seth said: 'Let's go to the wagonette. They'll be there, I'm sure.'

Clytie looked around her.

'I didn't see them go, did you?'

'No. I thought he was there with us. We were all so absorbed in the dancing.'

'I thought he was holding your hand.'

'He was. But he let go to clap. He was standing very close to you.'

Clytie bit her lip and did not answer.

I said: 'Seth's right. We should go to the wagonette. Sheba will surely be there with him.'

It took us some time to make our way through the crowd. We reached the inn and went into the yard. Sheba darted out to us from near the wagonette. 'I want to get that boy home,' she said. 'He has been out too long.'

'Now we're here let's all go,' said Seth.

Sheba's next words made me shiver with fear. 'Where's the boy then?'

'Sheba!' cried Clytie, aghast. 'Wasn't he with you?'

'With me! He was standing there with you.'

'Oh God!' murmured Clytie.

And we knew that Ralph was lost.

For a few seconds we were all numb with horror. Then I said: 'We must do something. He's in the crowd somewhere. He must be. He wandered away. He's probably gone after the elephants.'

'What can we *do*?' cried Clytie distractedly. She was shaking from head to foot.

'First we must look everywhere,' said Seth. 'Clytie and Sarah go together. I'll go with Sheba.'

'And if we haven't found him . . .' began Clytie blankly.

'We will,' Seth assured her. 'We must.'

We wandered through the streets. The crowds were dispersing fast now but there were still a number of people about. Eagerly we scanned every corner. We said little. A terrible fear had settled on me. But I told myself that if there had been an accident we should have known. The naughty little boy was hiding somewhere. We found a mahout and asked him if he had seen a small boy. Ralph might well have followed an elephant. The man had seen several small boys but none alone. We enquired of people. Several of them helped in the search. Finally we went back to the wagonette.

A few minutes later Seth and Sheba came back without Ralph.

'Now we must take some action,' said Seth. He was very calm and my good opinion of him grew that night. I was so glad that he was with us. It was possible, he said, that Ralph had been overcome by the excitement, had wandered off and sat down in some corner and fallen asleep. He often did that at home.

We would go back to the house and he would organize search-parties. They would search everywhere and he did not doubt that before long they would find the child.

He put an arm about Clytie.

'My dear,' he said, 'you must go back and wait. It is the only thing. Sarah, you will stay with her, won't you?'

I shall never forget that drive back through the night. I was thinking of the dangers that could befall a child. I thought of the river in the woods, the marshy banks, Sleepy Sam the crocodile, the snakes that lurked in the grass. What would Ralph do when he found he was lost? Being a resourceful child he would try to find us. Perhaps he would try to make his way home.

It did not bear thinking of. But I had Clytie to comfort.

Seth had organized search-parties and they set off. Clytie and I sat together in that room where we had so often cosily drunk our tea and lemonade.

'Where can he be?' Clytie kept saying. 'Oh, why did he stray away from us!'

We sat silently waiting. 'They *must* find him,' I said for the twentieth time. I could think of no way of comforting her.

Slowly the time passed. Midnight . . . One o'clock. Two o'clock.

I thought of a little boy out alone at this hour and I was frightened. I thought of how he had looked lying in his bed that afternoon afraid that if he did not sleep he would sleep that night.

Was he asleep now? It was the most comforting thought. In some safe spot asleep.

Clytie sat still, her fingers plucking at the silk of her sari. At every sound we started up hopefully. It would be the most wonderful thing in the world if we could hear Ralph's voice calling to us.

I thought, if Clinton were here . . .

Yes, if Clinton had been here he would have found the boy by now. What a foolish thought! As if they were not doing everything possible to find him. What more could Clinton have done? There was a power, an invincibility, about Clinton. If only he were here . . .

'What was that?' I started up. I was sure I had heard something. A light footfall . . . Someone at the door. I ran out. Clytie was close behind me. Nothing. But was that a rustle of leaves? Instinctively I knew that someone was near . . . watching.

Then I saw the paper at my feet. I picked it up.

'What is it?' cried Clytie.

'Someone has brought this.'

She snatched it from me and took it to the light. We saw that printed letters had been cut out and stuck on a paper.

We have the boy. He will be safe if you pay ransom. You will hear more. Do exactly as told or he will die.

I thought Clytie was going to faint. I led her to a chair and made her sit down.

I said: 'He's safe then. At least we know that.'

'What does it say? Let me look at it, Sarah. What does it *mean*?'

It was clear what it meant. Ralph had been kidnapped and his kidnappers wanted money before they would release him.

I kept saying to her: 'But he's safe, Clytie. He's safe.'

'Why doesn't Seth come? Oh, why doesn't he come? What are we going to do?'

'Let's be calm,' I begged. 'Let's think what this means. They're demanding a ransom. It means the boy is safe. They have him. They wouldn't harm him. If they did they wouldn't get their ransom, would they?'

'Oh, Sarah, what do you think they're going to do to him?'

'I'm sure he's fast asleep now and knows nothing of the anxiety he's causing.'

'Oh my baby!' she murmured. 'Sarah, you can't guess what he means to me.'

'I can,' I said. 'I know absolutely. But we mustn't despair. We've got to be clever. We've got to get him back.'

'I wish Seth would come.'

It was dawn before Seth came – pale, red-eyed and despairing. When he saw the note he looked stricken. He said we should have to get in touch with the police.

A fearful foreboding had settled on the house. Seth had gone into Kandy to see Sir William Carstairs and get advice. Clytie would not leave the house. She was eagerly awaiting some message from the people who held her son. She was sure it would come soon.

It came soon after noon when the house was quiet during the hottest spell of the day. We did not hear it come. It was lying outside the door with a stone holding it down.

The same method had been used as before – printed letters stuck on to a sheet of paper.

To the boy's mother. Do not call police. If so, boy die. One thing will give you back your boy. Bring Ashington Pearls at seven o'clock and place under tree with R on trunk. When you have done you will have boy. If you do not, he will die. Tell nobody, Mother of boy. This for you alone. Tell and boy dies.

Clytie let the paper fall from her hands. Then she picked it up and read it again.

'The pearls,' she whispered. 'It's the pearls they want . . . Unlucky pearls. Something always happens when I wear them. I hate them. I hate them. When must I go . . .' She snatched up the paper. 'Tonight . . . at seven. Oh God, Sarah. Do you think they'll have him there waiting?'

I was terribly afraid. I said: 'Clytie, we must show this to Seth. We must tell the police. They must try to catch these people.'

'They say don't show it to the police!' she cried in terror.

'Naturally they would.'

'Sarah, they are going to *kill* Ralphie if we tell the police!'

'They wouldn't dare.'

'They say they would.'

'I don't think you should handle this on your own.'

'But they say they will kill him if I don't.'

'These wicked people want the pearls. That's what they're after.'

'They can have them. Do you think two rows of pearls are more important to me than my child's life!'

'No, of course not. But can we trust them?'

She had taken my arm and was looking straight at me. Her poor sad face, her wild eyes, betrayed her anguish.

'I have to trust them, Sarah,' she said. 'I have to do everything to get my boy back.'

'Sir William Carstairs himself would advise . . .'

'If he were brought in they would kill my son.'

'How do we know?'

'How can we risk it? No, no. They shall have the pearls. I would give them this minute. I want my baby back.'

'Try to be calm, Clytie. How can we be sure . . .'

I didn't say it. It would have been too cruel to suggest that she might give them the pearls and even then might not get her son back.

'Sarah, let's go out. Let's go to the tree. Let's see how long it takes to get there.'

I could only humour her. We went out into the heat of the day. I felt dazed with horror and misery. We came to the tree with the letter R carved on it. I thought of the day Ralph had so proudly shown it to me.

'How long it seems till dark,' said Clytie.

I agreed. It seemed a week at least since we had been so excited about going to the pageant and it was only yesterday.

She seemed to read my thoughts.

'This time yesterday he was here with us,' she said. 'There was no warning of danger – oh, if only we hadn't gone. If only I had held his hand all the time. How did it happen, Sarah? How *could* it have happened?'

I suggested we go back to the house. Could she try to rest? Could I make some tea?

She stared at me blankly as though she did not know what I was talking about.

We sat through the afternoon, blinds drawn to keep out the afternoon sun.

Seth was in Kandy. I wondered what they were doing there. We should have told them about this last message. Clytie had promised that if anything came she would send one of the boys with it to Sir William's office without delay. But she refused to do so.

Sheba came and sat with us. She was silent, staring ahead of her. I warmed to her a little. Her devotion to Clytie and her love for the boy were touching.

Sheba said: 'Missee Clytie, he will be back in my arms this night. I know it.'

'You have had a vision?' asked Clytie eagerly.

Sheba nodded, 'I see him in the woods. He is laughing. He is telling me a strange story. This night it will be.'

Then Clytie showed her the note and I knew then how deeply she trusted her.

Sheba said: 'What it say? You tell me, missee.'

Clytie told her.

'Pearls,' she said. 'We have our boy then. They take pearls . . .
then we get boy.'

'Tonight,' said Clytie breathlessly. 'Just as it is dark. Under the
tree with the R on the trunk. He loves that tree, my darling boy.
I'll give them the pearls and then they will give him back to me.'

Sheba clasped her hands together and said: 'He will be back
with us . . . our boy.'

I wished that I could feel as optimistic as they did. Ralph was in
the hands of ruthless men. They were planning to steal a fortune,
for the pearls were priceless. They could not have asked for a
bigger ransom; and they knew that Clytie possessed what they
wanted. Once they had it, how could we be sure they would
return the boy alive?

I thought she and Sheba were not treating the case with enough
caution. Of course Clytie was clearly hysterical with grief and fear
– and so I believed was Sheba. There was one thing they wanted
and that was the return of the child. They would not consider the
possibility that ruthless criminals might be preparing to delude
them, to get the pearls and keep the boy. They could not bear to
face that fact.

If only Clinton were here, I thought again. I fancy he would
have been clear-thinking enough to know what was the best thing
to do. I tried to imagine how he would handle the matter. I was
sure it would not be to take the pearls to the woods and leave them
there. But then the pearls would probably mean a great deal to
Clinton. To Clytie they were nothing but the means of restoring
her son.

How slowly the time passed!   Afternoon dragged on. Six
o'clock. One hour to go.

Clytie sat tense, listening. She was afraid, I believed, that Seth
would return bringing someone from the Judiciary with him. She
wanted us to be alone . . . herself . . . myself and Sheba, so that she
could slip out to the woods.

It was just after six when we found the note. There was a knock
on the door and we rushed out to find no one there but a piece of

paper under a stone.

Mother of boy [it said], let nurse come. You will be watched. You place pearls beneath tree. Nurse walk to right. Follow nurse when pearls put down. You will have boy. If you bring others boy killed.

Clytie went to her bedroom. I followed her. She opened the safe in the dressing-room and took out the case. Her fingers were trembling as she opened it.

'Our last look at the Ashington Pearls, Sarah,' she said, and her voice rose hysterically.

They lay on their midnight blue velvet, exquisite, perfection. The emerald eye of the serpent glittered evilly, I fancied.

She looked at them as though they fascinated her and held her gaze against her will. I thought of all the years they had been in the family and of the women who had worn them. Then I remembered Aunt Martha, who had wanted my father to marry again and have a son who in turn would have a wife to wear these cursed pearls. There was something evil about them which could tempt people to wickedness. Cruel and wicked people were now threatening Ralph because of them.

A legend and a tradition would be handed over to these robbers tonight. Clytie was determined.

She shut the case with a snap. 'What does it matter?' she cried. 'Nothing on earth is worth more than the life of my boy.'

I agreed with her. My only fear was that in acting on this emotional impulse we might not be doing the right thing. I knew, though, that I could not make Clytie agree with this. She could only see a chance to get her son back and she was ready to risk anything to do that. It was the only chance she saw. She did not trust those officials who were trying to work out a solution. While they planned a course of action, Ralph could be killed. A mother's instinct was worth all the clever planning of the judge and his police.

She was impatient when I tried to reason with her. I knew it was useless. She was determined that she and Sheba should go out into the woods and obey those instructions absolutely.

In five minutes it would be dark. Clytie was in a fever of impatience. The hands which held the crocodile case shook pitiably.

'You must stay here, Sarah,' she said. 'They have said no one else. You *must* stay in the house. If you were seen you don't know what they might do.'

Sheba nodded. 'Missee Sarah must stay,' she agreed.

I said nothing. I knew there was nothing I could say. Clytie looked so frail in her pale pink sari, the silver bracelets jingling on her arms, her eyes wide with sleeplessness, her expression taut and tense.

Sheba on the other hand looked calm and confident. She had seen it all in a vision and she knew that they were coming back with the boy.

'He will be out there,' whispered Clytie. 'He will be in the woods. Oh my darling child. I trust he is not frightened.'

'He would never be frightened,' I said. 'To him it will be one of his adventures.'

'Yes,' murmured Clytie. 'Just . . . like that.'

In a few minutes it would be seven o'clock. Darkness came suddenly. I had often marvelled before how the sun was there, brilliant at one moment and suddenly dropped below the horizon and the light disappeared. It was like a shutter falling.

Clytie turned to me. 'Stay here, Sarah. Promise me you'll stay here. Swear it.'

So I swore.

It seemed hours before they came back. I heard them in the garden and I ran down.

Ralph was in his mother's arms and tears were falling down Clytie's cheeks. Sheba was murmuring something that sounded like an incantation.

'Sarah!' Clytie had seen me.

'I heard you. I had to come out.'

'He's here. We've got him. All's well. Sarah . . . Sarah . . . isn't it wonderful!'

Ralph looked from one to the other of us, as I hugged him in relief. 'I've been with my elephant,' he said. 'He's the biggest betterest elephant in the world.'

'We must go in,' said Clytie, her voice trilling with happiness. 'It's past your bedtime.'

Ralph went on: 'There was this wonderful elephant. He had jewels on his back and I sat in a cage and there was an umbrella over me. I was the chief. And I slept in a funny bed . . .'

'Let's go in,' said Sheba. 'Boy can tell us all about it tomorrow.'

So we had recovered the boy for the price of the Ashington Pearls. At least Ralphie was not hurt, which was all that really mattered.

I reminded Clytie that we should now send a message at once to Kandy to tell them that we had the boy, and this was done.

Ralph was clearly tired. He was asleep before he could be undressed. Clytie wouldn't leave him. She sat by his bed and Sheba was with her.

I felt drained of emotion. It had all happened so quickly but I was glad it had been quick. I wondered what more days of such suspense would have done to Clytie.

Sir William Carstairs came back with Seth. They went upstairs and gazed on the boy, who was fast asleep by this time.

Clytie was too bewildered still to take much notice of them. Sheba kept saying that she had known it would happen. Her visions had told her so.

The two men talked to me. I showed them the notes and told them how Clytie had taken the pearls and left them under the tree.

'Good God!' said Seth. 'She has lost the pearls.'

'She considered it well worth while to get the boy back safely.'

Seth nodded. Sir William said: 'She should have allowed us to handle this.'

'She feared for the child's life.'

'I suppose most mothers would have behaved as she did.'

I was sure of it.

I said: 'They won't be able to dispose of the pearls very easily, will they?'

'We have a full description of them,' replied Sir William. 'They will break them up, of course. Every pearl in this necklace is a rarity. We might possibly be able to trace them but it's hardly likely. They have probably been sent out of the country by now. I'm afraid we have to face the fact that they may have been lost for ever.'

Seth said to me: 'You should go to bed, Sarah. This has been a great ordeal for you as well as Clytie.'

I said good night to them and went.

First I looked in at Clytie. She was still sitting by Ralph's bed, although the boy was fast asleep, and would no doubt remain so all through the night.

I went to my own room. I felt light-headed. I had not slept since it happened.

I undressed and crept under the mosquito net. I *was* exhausted yet still I could not sleep. I lay there thinking of the events of the day and night . . . the paper with the letters cut out of printing and stuck on. It was so melodramatic . . . unreal in some way. The manner in which it had come about, the way we had lost Ralph, the recovery of the boy . . . I didn't know how to describe it. Smooth, slick . . . like a play. Not quite real.

My thoughts were going round and round in my head. Something strange about all this. Something sinister.

It then occurred to me that since I had come here and discovered that my marriage had been arranged for me by a scheming husband, life had become vaguely menacing.

There seemed to be a warning in the darkness of the night, in the hum of the insects, in the occasional thump of one against the wire-netting.

There was something here I did not understand. I was caught up in it.

Beware, said the night.

The affair had had such an effect on Clytie that she had been unable to leave her bed for a day or so. I could understand how intense the strain had been. We were only just realizing that, now that the relief had come.

The next morning Ralph behaved as though nothing very extraordinary had happened and that it was the most natural thing in the world to have been kidnapped. He chattered a great deal about the elephants he had ridden and it was all so wildly impossible as to have occurred only in his imagination. But there were one or two comments which provided a clue.

He had slept in a funny bed. He had eaten rice. There was sugar. More sugar than Sheba gave him.

'Who gave you the rice and sugar, Ralph?' I asked.

He hunched his shoulders and laughed at me. '*He* did,' he said. 'A man?'

'There was a cobra,' he went on. 'He had yellow eyes and he came up to me. I got my bow and arrow and shot him dead . . . right through his heart.'

'What man was it?' I asked.

'He made me laugh. "It's a good game," he said. This cobra . . . You know the way a cobra darts, Aunt Sarah? I've got a picture in my book. I'll show you.'

It was such a mixture of fantasy and fact that it was hopeless to try and discover anything.

Clytie said to me: 'Don't ask Ralph questions. Don't let him think anything fearful happened. Don't let him know how frightened we were.'

I promised.

Seth talked to me about it.

'It has been a terrible experience for Clytie,' he said, 'but I'm sure the boy hasn't an inkling of his danger. They were evidently gentle with him.'

'It's strange,' I said. 'It makes me think they must have been people he knew.'

Seth looked grave.

'Clytie wore the pearls at the ball,' he said. 'I just wonder whether someone there . . .'

'It seems dangerous to keep such valuables in a place like this.'

'There's some rule that they have to be worn now and then. They deteriorate if they aren't. They have been worn from time to time.'

'I first heard of this when my mother showed me a picture of herself wearing them.'

'Clytie's mother would have worn them too. So did Clytie sometimes for a special occasion or even when we were alone.' He shrugged his shoulders. 'Well, that is the end of the Ashington Pearls.'

'They may be recovered.'

'Maybe. Clytie's right,' he went on. 'She doesn't want the boy questioned. It's better for him to forget the incident as soon as possible.'

I agreed. For a boy who indulged in such fantasies of the imagination what had happened that night might well seem to him commonplace.

'I'm glad you're here,' continued Seth. 'She has become very fond of you. She always wanted to know you and when you did come she loved you at once. Stay with her for a while, Sarah. This has been more of a shock than we realize. It's not only the boy but the pearls. She'll begin to realize the enormity of what she has done sooner or later. It's going to affect her deeply.'

'But she could never have sold them.'

'No. Your father raised money on them once. They were a sort of security, he said. And I suppose in an emergency if he was prepared to forget legends and prophecies of evil and so on, he could have sold them. I think Clytie could be afraid of some retribution. She is half Sinhalese, remember, and although she has been brought up as an English girl she has heard stories of the old legends from her mother and from Sheba. She could be very upset about all this. It's Clytie I'm worried about now. Ralph is all right. He doesn't realize the significance of what has happened. It's unfortunate that I have to go away almost immediately to Colombo on business. I can't easily avoid it. I hate leaving her but I'd feel better about it if I knew you were here.'

'Well, I am staying until Clinton gets back.'

'I'm so glad. I shall only be away for a couple of nights. It will be a comfort to know that you're here.'

I said again that I should most certainly stay while he was away.

He was right about Clytie. There was a change in her. She was nervous and uneasy. Sheba gave her some concoction which made her sleep and we both promised that we would never leave Ralph alone. I pointed out that now the kidnappers had the pearls there would be no reason for taking the boy. But she refused to listen. One of us must always be on guard in such a way that he would not guess it.

It was only a week since Clinton had gone and he was to stay another week. By that time Clytie would have recovered, I was sure.

Seth went off and I assured him that I would look after Clytie until his return.

The next day when I was in the garden wandering as I loved to among the sweet-scented flowers I heard someone come into the garden. I swung round in alarm. Ever since that terrible night I was on edge, just as Clytie was.

'Clinton!' I cried.

He stood for a few moments grinning at me. Then he seized me in his arms.

'It is good to see you!' he cried. 'I've missed you.'

He had picked me up and I looked down on his face, at that thick thatch of blond hair and the dark eyes which made such a contrast to it; I looked at the sensual lips and already I felt the response rising in me.

'You're back soon,' I said.

He was reproachful. 'Well, you should be pleased about that.'

'Did it go well . . . your business?'

'Perfectly.'

'And so much quicker than you thought it would.'

'The fact is that I was so eager to be with you that I couldn't stay away any longer.'

I laughed disbelievingly. 'You're such a good businessman,' I retorted. 'Don't forget. Half Ceylon belongs to you. You would never neglect business for a whim.'

'A whim! You call my raging desire to be with you a whim!'

'Put me down,' I commanded. 'We may be watched.'

'On condition you go immediately and pack.'

'Something's happened, Clinton. I suppose you haven't heard.'

'What?' he demanded.

I told him of the events of that fateful night. As he listened I saw a smile curve his lips.

'What is there to smile about?' I demanded. 'You find it amusing. It was horrible.'

'What a dilemma,' he said. 'The pearls . . . or the boy.'

'Poor Clytie has been prostrate with worry. I can't leave her, Clinton. I have to stay here. She has nightmares. I seem to be able to comfort her.'

'You can come over and see her tomorrow.'

'I must stay until the end of the week as I arranged to originally.'

'Don't talk nonsense. It's all over, isn't it? The boy's back safely. And I'm home.'

'Yes, but I wasn't expecting you and Seth is away. Clytie needs me. I promised him I'd stay with her. She needs me, Clinton.'

'And don't I? Go on. You're coming back with me.'

'I shall come back at the end of the week.'

'You'll come back now.'

'I have promised to stay until Seth returns and I shall do so. I shall come home on Friday as I originally intended to.'

'My dear Sarah, you're coming home *now*.'

'Can't you understand what a shock this has been to Clytie?'

'Whatever it was is over now.'

'She has lost the Ashington Pearls.'

'She gave them away.'

'For her son. For Heaven's sake, be human.'

He laughed and said: 'I am, Sarah, so human that I want my wife.'

'I shall not leave Clytie yet.'

Suddenly his face hardened. He said: 'Come back before dark. I shall expect you.'

With that he turned and went away.

I was shaken, he had looked so angry suddenly. He alarmed me. He had looked quite murderous.

I went into the house. As I walked across the hall Sheba was behind me.

'Missee Sarah,' she said, 'I worried about Missee Clytie.'

'She's asleep, isn't she?'

'Yes. This has been big shock to her. She love that boy . . . Oh, how she love that boy. Her life, Missee Sarah.'

'I know.'

'Master Seth . . . he good husband. He nice husband . . . very kind. But that boy . . . he her life. You good to her, Missee Sarah. She love you very much. She say me, "Missee Sarah so calm . . . so good for me. What I do without her?" Missee Sarah, stay . . . look after her.'

'I shall certainly stay until her husband comes back,' I said.

Sheba nodded. She seemed very pleased and it occurred to me then that she had witnessed the scene in the garden and that she was afraid I would go home since Clinton had commanded it. She wanted me to stay . . . for Clytie's sake. Yet I wished I could rid myself of the feeling of being watched all the time.

I said nothing to Clytie about Clinton's return. I knew that if I did she would say I must go back to him. I thought of him a great deal. I wanted to be back with him but I was not going to submit to his arrogance. *He* had decided to go; *he* had come back before the appointed time. Well then, he must not expect me to break up my plans because of him.

Clytie seemed better over the next day or so. She still insisted that Ralph be watched over and it was rarely that one of us was not actually in his presence. This had to be manœuvred for it was necessary not to let him suspect that he was being watched over.

I spent a good deal of time with him and I was always alert for the clue which would explain something of what had happened on that night.

Once in his play-room I said: 'Do you remember the lovely elephants with their golden cages and canopies?'

He nodded. 'Mine was the best,' he said.

'You didn't really ride on one.'

'I did. I did. I rode right in the jungle. Mine was the fastest.'

'What happened in the jungle?'

'There was a little house and there was a man.'

'What sort of man?'

'A nice man.'

'Just a man?'

'And a woman. She said, "It's all right. You're going to see your Mama soon."'

My heart was beating fast. 'Where was your Mama then?' I asked.

'You *know*.'

'I don't,' I said. 'Where was she?'

'She was with the others.'

'What others?'

'You and Papa and Sheba and ... my elephant and Cobbler ...'

'What was the man like?'

'He's got yellow eyes.'

'Yellow eyes?'

'They shine. I'll show you, Sarah.' He had picked up the toy cobra, that rather frightening object because it looked so real. Chuckling he pressed the head and the tongue shot out.

'Are you frightened, Aunt Sarah? He'd kill you. It's poison in his tongue. Never mind. I'll shoot him with my bow and arrow.'

The toy swayed for a moment and slowly fell to the ground. Ralph picked it up.

'Yellow eyes,' he said.

'You were telling me about the man,' I reminded him.

'Mama says they're like topaz. That's a stone. It's yellow like Cobbler's eyes.'

I could see it was useless. Clytie was right, and I had promised her not to let him know I was probing. It was clear that he had no notion that anything alarming had happened on that night. He had gone off with some people who had been kind to him and after a while he had come home. It was a simple adventure . . . nothing compared with what happened with his snakes and elephants.

Seth returned and I said that as Clinton was back I thought I should go home. I left in the late afternoon when the heat had subsided.

When I returned the house was very quiet. I expected Clinton would be home by nightfall. I was looking forward to our encounter. I had shown him quite clearly that he could not command me.

I had missed him. Was I fond of him? I did not understand this emotion which took possession of me. It was different from anything I had imagined in those dreams of romance which I suppose come to every young woman. I had been away from him for two weeks and it seemed too long. Had he felt that? Perhaps but it was merely because his business had been completed earlier than he had expected that he had returned home.

When he had left he had had that light of battle in his eyes. I wondered what contracts he had been arranging. They would occupy him completely and then when they were satisfactorily completed he would say, Time for my wife. And snap his fingers and expect her to come running.

'Well, it is not going to be like that, Clinton,' I said aloud.

It seemed long before darkness fell. Silent-footed servants lighted the lamps. I waited and waited. It was nearly midnight and he had not come.

I went to the bedroom. All the time I was listening for his arrival.

I sat at my dressing-table and loosened my hair.

Suddenly I heard a sound outside the door. I started up. There was a gentle tap.

'Come in,' I cried and Leila entered. Her eyes were wide with assumed innocence. She was hiding some secret which she found intensely gratifying.

'What is it, Leila?' I asked.

'I turn down bed for you?'

'It's not necessary.' I turned back to the mirror, watching her reflection in it. She still hovered. I saw the slow smile curve her lips.

'Master not coming home,' she said. 'He did not come all the time you been away.'

'Oh?' I said.

Leila went to the bed and starting plumping up the pillows. She lingered, looking malicious and triumphant in a way.

I wanted to shout to her to go but I was afraid of betraying my disquiet. I didn't want her to know how disturbed and angry her words had made me. My eyes fell on the bronze Buddha which seemed to be watching me superciliously.

'I don't want this thing here, Leila,' I said. 'Would you like it?' She turned from the bed, her eyes wide with horror.

'Oh no, missee. Bad luck.' She smiled rather slyly. 'Master like it very much.'

'I don't believe in bad luck,' I said. 'You can take it and keep it in your room.'

She took it from me, shaking her head. Then she lowered her eyes and gave a sly kind of giggle. 'My sister Anula give it,' she said. 'When she was here . . .' She looked round the room as though when her sister Anula had been here it had been a holy place. Her eyes went to the bed and stayed there.

I wanted to tell her to get out, but I said nothing.

She replaced the Buddha; and I knew then what she was telling me. I knew where he was.

'Good night, Leila,' I said.

She went out taking her secret smile with her.

I stared at myself in the mirror. Colour was in my cheeks and a bitter anger in my heart.

I lay under the mosquito net thinking about him and Anula and the fact that everyone knew of their relationship, which he had not thought necessary to cut off completely even though he had brought home a wife.

A fury seized me. I was agonizingly jealous. I tried to shut out the pictures which would keep coming into my mind.

I did not sleep until it was nearly time to get up. Then I was late rising.

I was determined to give no indication of the emotional stress I was feeling.

All through the next day I was tense and waiting. Every time I heard horses' hoofs I was alert. I rehearsed what I would say to him.

I caught Leila watching me slyly.

'Missee not well?'

'I am very well, thank you, Leila,' I replied coldly.

'Look tired. Not sleep well?'

Almost mocking and would be if she dared. I knew she was thinking of her sister because she always wore a reverent look when she did so.

I felt uneasy, alone in an alien house. I thought of going back to Clytie. That seemed feeble. Besides I did not want her and Seth to know that Clinton had deserted me.

I sent a messenger over to ask how she was and to tell her that owing to my absence there was a great deal I had to attend to here. I should see her very soon.

The messenger came back with a note from Clytie thanking me for all I had done for her and telling me that she was feeling better and had had a long sleep free of nightmares.

I got through the day somehow; but again he did not come.

Another day passed.

It was midnight when he returned. I was lying in the bed we shared when he burst in. I pretended to be asleep.

He prepared himself for bed and then came to the bedside and looked down at me for some moments before he drew back the net.

'Well, Sarah?' he said.

I did not answer, keeping my eyes closed.

'You're not asleep,' he said. 'Stop pretending. You've been lying there in a fever of impatience awaiting my return. Admit it.'

I opened my eyes. 'So it's you.'

'And you are very angry with me.'

'Why should I be?'

'Because I was not here when you deigned to return.'

I sat up. 'What you do is of no importance to me.'

'Don't add lies to your unwifely conduct.'

'It's late,' I said. 'I am rather tired.'

'Don't you want to know what delayed me?'

I got out of bed. 'I think I know already,' I said. 'Why don't you go back there? I am sure you will be more welcome there than you are here.'

'I go where I want,' he retorted. 'Not where I'm told.'

'And,' I replied, 'so do I. I am going to another room.'

He caught me at the door. He put his finger to his lips. 'Servants,' he said. 'They watch. They whisper.'

'Let them.'

'Yes,' he said. 'Let them. But even so you are not going to leave me.'

'I shall go where I wish.'

He caught me and held me fast.

'Don't ever do that again, Sarah. I don't like it.'

'What do you mean?'

'Refuse me.'

'What of you? Where have you been these last two nights?'

'Teaching you a lesson.'

'I don't need to be taught.'

'Let's hope not again.'

'If you think I am a sort of slave and you have only to clap your hands . . . Come here. Go there . . . You have made a mistake.'

His answer was to pick me up and carry me back to the bed. He threw me on it none too gently, and despite myself I felt the old excitement creeping over me. I did not want to run away. I wanted to stay and fight.

It must have been obvious to us both what the outcome would be. He would have his victory but it would not be complete because I would not let him think that he had subdued me by anything but superior physical strength.

WHOM THE GODS WISH
TO DESTROY

*

He was triumphant. There was a complacent air about him. I went round the plantation with him. He suggested it the following morning. I had learned enough to know that there was an orderliness about Shaws which Ashingtons lacked. The workers seemed more alert – but perhaps that was a temporary phase because he was there – but even the plants looked more glistening and a more verdant green.

'I'm going to take you with me next time I go,' he said. 'I want to show you my rubber trees and of course the pearl fisheries.'

'We'll see,' I said, which made him laugh.

He pointed out to me the careful pruning which had taken place.

'There's an art in it. I have the best men. I lured some of them from Ashingtons. That was in your father's day. He used to say to me, "I daren't let you know when I've got a good man. You'll take him from me."'

'I can quite believe that.'

'I've allowed you to spend so much time at Ashingtons so that you could compare the two plantations. I think you know a little now and can possibly see.'

'I think mine is a very fine plantation.'

'I see that a little knowledge is a dangerous thing indeed. There are improvements I'd like to make over there, Sarah.'

'I dare say Seth will make what he considers best.'

'Seth would do what he was told.'

I said nothing. Resentment was rising in me. I knew what he meant. He wanted to give Seth orders. He wanted to combine the plantations. He wanted the biggest and most profitable plantation not only in Ceylon but in the whole of India.

No! I thought. I shall not allow it.

I kept thinking of the previous night and I hated both myself and him.

I was sure he had taken me past Anula's house on purpose. It was a charming place surrounded by flowers. Nankeen was working on the fence.

I said: 'Where is this?'

'It's Nankeen's daughter's place.'

Nankeen looked up and bowed to us.

'Busy, Nankeen?' said Clinton.

'My daughter requested this little repair,' replied Nankeen. 'It is but a small matter.'

'The garden's looking well. My wife is fond of gardens, aren't you, Sarah?'

I murmured something. My resentment was rising rapidly. He was devilish. He was showing me where he had spent those nights when I had waited for him.

'Very nice flowers, Mem Sahib,' said Nankeen. 'Sahib makes pretty garden here.'

Sahib! That was Clinton.

'My wife would like to see the garden.'

I looked at my watch.

'There's plenty of time,' said Clinton with a touch of malice. He had dismounted, and short of turning round and riding back there was nothing I could do but follow.

Nankeen took our horses and tethered them. Then he opened the gate and bowed.

'I tell my daughter,' he said, smiling in a manner which betrayed the fact that he realized there was a certain drama in the situation. He went into the house.

I began: 'I have no intention of paying a polite call on your mistress.'

'To be impolite is hardly what one expects from a lady so shortly out from England.'

Anula was standing in the doorway. Her beauty was breath-taking, I had to admit – that sleek dark hair which shone like satin, those enormous dark eyes. How beautiful were these women and never more so than when they moved. Then their bodies had the grace of a jungle animal which had the effect of making me feel incredibly clumsy. My hair was untidy under my topee which always fell too far over my eyes. I was wearing a muslin blouse and a black riding skirt. I suffered in comparison with this beautiful elegant creature. She had the grace of the Sinhalese and the dignity of her Portuguese ancestors – she had taken the best from both sides. I could really believe she was the reincarnation of that wicked queen.

'It is a great pleasure.' Her eyes were on me, amused by my discomfiture. 'Please come in.'

'Anula longs to show you her house,' said Clinton. 'As for Sarah, she is overcome by curiosity. Sarah loves our houses, don't you, Sarah? They are so different from the ones she has known in England.'

'Come,' said Anula, jingling the bracelets on her arms. 'But first refreshment.'

She clapped her hands. So he provides servants, I thought.

'Anula's speciality,' observed Clinton when drinks were brought. 'She will tell no one how she makes it.'

'It does not intoxicate,' said Anula. 'Not very much.' She smiled at me. 'You are settling in, Leila tells me.'

'Yes,' I answered.

'My wife is amusing herself learning about our ways.'

They laughed together. There was something significant about this.

She was all smiles but I could see that there was an intensity behind those soft looks. She seemed a little uneasy and I wondered whether Clinton was warning her as well as me. It was a ridiculous situation and an intensely humiliating one. Was he implying: 'This is my wife!' to his mistress and 'This is my mistress!' to his wife? Was he telling us both that this was the situation as he wanted it and we must therefore accept it. He was arrogant enough for that

He imagined himself as some feudal lord with absolute rights over everyone.

I would never accept that, I told myself. And yet last night . . .

There was something potent about the drink. Their voices seemed to come from afar. The room tilted slightly. I was aware of myself speaking in a voice which seemed to come from a long way off, yet my answers must have been reasonably intelligible because they did not seem to notice that anything was other than normal.

They stood up so I rose with them. I swayed slightly, but Clinton had taken my arm.

'Very well,' he was saying. 'A quick look and then we must be off.'

So Anula showed me her house. It was small but charming. There were white flimsy draperies at the windows which were covered with the inevitable fine wire-netting. The bedroom was dark for the curtains were drawn across the windows. There was a round bed with draperies falling from a canopy. There was a dressing-table with a three-sided mirror and many ornamental pots, most of them studded with semi-precious stones. My eyes immediately went to the bronze Buddha, of which the one in my room was almost an exact replica. She saw me look at it and picked it up, caressing it with her long white fingers.

'He is important to me,' she said. 'I commune with him. I could not sleep well without him beside me.'

Her eyes were mysterious and inwardly I shivered, feeling suddenly cold in spite of the heat. I could really believe as she stood there with the Buddha in her hands that she was malevolent, that she was indeed possessed of some evil powers and that she was directing them towards me.

She replaced the Buddha and turned to me smiling. Clinton's eyes were on me, maliciously observant. I was picturing them together, and he knew it. It was the purpose of this visit.

A strange fragrance wafted through the house and it was especially noticeable in this room. In a niche in the wall was a stone image. I went to it and studied it.

'My namesake,' said Anula, behind me. 'The first Queen of Ceylon.'

'A very formidable lady,' added Clinton.

'People feared her greatly,' added Anula. 'She had great power.'

'And a very special way with potions,' put in Clinton. 'As you have, Anula. I think the stuff you gave us was a little stronger than usual. Did you find it potent, Sarah?'

'Did it contain gin?' I asked.

'It is my secret,' said Anula, smiling and showing teeth which were quite perfect.

'I heard,' I said, nodding towards the statue in the niche, 'that the lady came to a bad end. Wasn't she burned at the stake?'

'She ceased to be clever,' replied Anula. 'That was her fault. Had she not been foolish she would have gone on.'

'Taking her lovers, giving them poisoned draughts when they ceased to please,' suggested Clinton. 'That must have saved a great deal of trouble.'

'She might have lived for ever,' said Anula, her dark eyes glowing. 'She was on the point of discovering the secret of eternal life.'

I felt I wanted to get out of this closed-in house, away from the implications, the humiliations and the sickly fragrance which filled it.

'What is the scent?' I asked.

'Do you like it?' asked Anula. 'It is basically sandalwood which has been for many years the sacred perfume of the Hindu. Shall I give you some?'

I wanted to say, No, I hate it, but I thought that would betray my feelings, so I murmured a polite thanks.

She opened a drawer and taking out a bottle pressed it into my hands.

'It comes from the white wood of a tree called *Santalum album* – a parasite which attacks the roots of other trees. It takes a hundred-weight of chippings to make thirty ounces of attar of sandalwood. It's about the only wood which white ants don't like. There are legends about it. If you sprinkle yourself with it you wash away any sins you may have committed during the past year.'

'You see why it's popular,' said Clinton lightly. 'So pleasant to be as wicked as you like and then ... Where is the sandalwood? A few drops and now I am a saint because all my sins have been washed away.'

'Comforting,' I retorted, 'if one believes it.'

'You see, Anula,' said Clinton, 'this wife of mine is a sceptic.'

I felt relieved to leave behind the overpowering atmosphere of Anula's house.

Clinton was watching me as we rode away, but I was determined to hide the fact that I was seething with fury and was thinking of some way in which I could take my revenge.

When the idea came to me I could scarcely wait to put it into practice. I rode over to Ashingtons where Clytie greeted me with pleasure. She felt a good deal better.

'I'm sleeping peacefully,' she told me. 'The nightmares seem to have stopped.'

'Now that it's all over you must be wondering what difference it's going to make. In a way you've lost your inheritance.'

'I know. Seth worries a lot.'

'You're all right at the plantation, you know. I should never allow you to be ... ousted.'

She was silent for a while and then she said: 'It is what Seth fears.'

'I have made up my mind what I will do. I am going to set your minds at rest. While I own the plantation you are safe and I am going to make a will leaving it to you on my death.'

'But you are not going to *die*!'

'I don't propose to yet but one never knows, does one? Just imagine if I died now ...'

'I don't want to. It's too horrible.'

'People have to be practical. I'm going into Kandy and to a solicitor. Not Clinton's. I am going to make sure that this is all tied up legally. You would have nothing whatever to worry about then, would you? While I live you are safe and if I die ... then you are still safe.'

'Oh Sarah, I do love you so!'

'Of course you do. I'm your sister.'

'But what does Clinton say?'

'It's no affair of his.'

I could not hide the smile of grim satisfaction. If I were honest this was not only because it would make my sister safe. It was to show Clinton that he could not treat me as his slave.

Clytie made a half-hearted attempt to dissuade me, at least to give myself time to think. I overruled her.

The very next day I went into Kandy, saw the solicitor, drew up the will which was witnessed by two of the solicitor's employees and held by them in safe custody. I brought away a copy with me.

When it was all settled I began to feel uneasy.

Clinton had married me for the plantation. But for that he might have married Anula. Why not? Mixed marriages were frowned on, it was true, by both sides, but once they were a *fait accompli* they were sometimes accepted. There was my father's marriage for one.

I contemplated Clinton's anger if he ever found out. I would not tell him yet. I would save it for one of those moments when I needed some strong weapon with which to strike him. I was sure that moment would come.

When the letter came I was still feeling nervous. Sometimes when I was with Clinton I was deeply conscious of his power. He was so forceful, so very much the master, that I, too, almost accepted him as such. But I could never be entirely sure of my feelings for him. I knew that sometimes I hated him and longed to defeat him. At others ... well, the fact was that he could fill me with an excitement which while it persisted I found irresistible.

When I remembered what I had done I would shiver with fear. The letter then was like a friendly hand stretched out to me, a secret knowledge that if I needed help it was not far away.

We collected our post twice a week from the post office in Manganiya. I always enjoyed riding in to get it. There had been one or two letters from the aunts and nothing more. It was chiefly mail for Clinton which came.

This time there was one for me and the sight of that handwriting, which I knew so well, filled me with delight.

I tore it open there and then and read:

My dear Sarah,

I have for so long wanted to write to you to find out how you were getting on. Everything must have been so strange to you and I know how homesick one can get. I came back here and plunged into work, which was useful. I have thought about you so much. I really don't see why we shouldn't keep in touch and write to each other now and then. What do you feel about that?

I do so want to hear from you that all is well.

Affectionately,

Your old friend and tutor,

Toby.

It was ridiculous to feel so light-hearted, to experience what I can only say amounted to relief.

Toby was not so far off. I looked at the address at the top of the letter. Delhi. We were just an island off the tip of India. Toby, the kindest person I had ever known, was close.

I could see no reason why I shouldn't write to him. What comfort that would be!

Suppose Clinton discovered that I had made a will. He would be very angry. He had planned so cunningly to bring about our marriage because I owned the plantation. Oh yes, he would be angry . . . murderous!

If I wanted to run away I could run to Toby.

I tucked the letter inside my blouse. It was a comfort to feel it against my skin.

As soon as I returned home I wrote a long letter telling Toby about the plantation, about my newly found sister whom I already loved and my delightful nephew Ralph. I did not mention the kidnapping. I thought it was a little too dramatic to start off with.

When the letter had gone I continued to feel happy. That certain blanket of uneasiness which had begun to wrap itself about me had lifted a little.

Two or three weeks after I had answered Toby's letter I had a great surprise. I was in the garden one morning when Leila came hurrying out to tell me that a lady was waiting to see me. I went into the house. I stared in amazement, feeling for the moment that I was dreaming.

Celia Hansen was standing there smiling at me.

'Celia!' I cried. 'Is it really . . . you!'

She came towards me, her arms outstretched, looking faintly apprehensive.

'I should have let you know I was here. I wasn't really sure whether I'd come to the right place. I couldn't go away without finding out. I had to come to see you.'

'Celia, it's a wonderful surprise. How did you get here?'

'You knew I was travelling with my cousin.'

'Yes, you wrote and said you were going to and then I heard no more.'

'I was never much of a letter-writer. I always meant to write. I went away for a while and when I came back I called at the Grange. Your aunts told me you had married and had come out here with your husband. They gave me your new name and address. I said I wanted to write to you. Then my cousin and I set off on our travels again. We came to India and I promised myself that it would be better to see you than write. I lost the address and had to rely on memory. Then my cousin was called home suddenly. I should have gone home with her but I thought I'd stay away a little longer and see if I could find you.'

'I'm so glad you came. You must be tired. How did you get here?'

'I took the P. & O. ship to Colombo. There I caught the train.

I saw the name Clinton Shaw Plantation on bales in the docks and I asked a few questions. Your husband is very well known. There is a hotel near the station in Manganiya. I thought I might stay there for a week or so. Would you mind?'

'Very much,' I retorted. 'We have plenty of room here. It *is* good to see you again, Celia.'

'Oh Sarah, we went through a good deal, didn't we? I often think of your lovely mother.'

'You were one of her most ardent admirers. She loved you for it. It was so good for her to know that there were still some who admired her.'

'It was all so sad, but it's over now. Are you happy, Sarah?'

'It's interesting here,' I answered. 'I inherited a plantation, you know, and I'm learning about tea. You must have some . . . now.'

'Tea would be so refreshing and I should like it especially as it was grown on your plantation.'

'What are we doing standing here! It is such a nice surprise seeing you. I'll have a room made ready for you. You must meet my sister. I am so glad you came.'

Leila was hovering, dark eyes alight with curiosity.

'This is a friend of mine from England,' I said. 'I want a room made ready for her. She is going to stay with us.'

The presence of Celia brought a normality to the house. To have a European woman there somehow detracted from that alien quality, and I felt more at ease.

Celia was delighted with the room which had been made ready for her, although she was apologetic about giving trouble. I had to keep assuring her how glad I was to have her here.

She revelled in the garden and was so interested in everything that it was pleasant to be with her. She and Clytie liked each other. Ralph showed her his elephants and tried to frighten her with his cobra and having succeeded in doing so made her immediately his friend. She was rapidly growing fond of the boy and when she heard how he had been kidnapped, she was horrified. She fully understood Clytie's eagerness to give up the pearls. 'In her place I should have done the same,' she said.

It was a joy to have her to talk to.

Clinton liked her too and actually said it was good for me to have a companion from home. I took her into Kandy and to the Club – of which I was now a member – and introduced her to various people, including the obnoxious Mrs Glendenning. She was warmly welcomed.

Christmas was almost upon us. It seemed incongruous to celebrate it in the heat. I think most of us felt a longing to be home with the cold of winter, the possibility of snow, the carols, the ivy and the holly. We did the best we could. Ralph hung up his stocking and provided some amusement. Clytie decorated a tree and we spent the day at Ashingtons and the next day they all came over to Shaws.

It was a few days later and I remember the evening in detail because it was after that that things began to change.

Celia and I had played with Ralph in the woods and he had proudly shown Celia the tree with his initial carved on it. I could never look at that tree without a shudder and I was sure that Clytie felt the same.

Celia and I had ridden back to Shaws. Clinton came in and we had a drink together. Then we had dinner and afterwards sat in the drawing-room. It was pleasant outside, but the mosquitoes were a pest and Clinton said that Celia would be in peril because they liked fresh blood from England.

We were talking desultorily when the subject of my mother's death came up and Celia clearly became rather uneasy.

At length she said: 'I've always had it on my mind. I don't know whether I did the right thing in keeping quiet. I thought it better at the time . . .'

'In what way, Celia?' I asked.

She looked at Clinton and he said: 'Is it some secret?'

'No, no,' said Celia quickly. 'I am sure Sarah would not want any secrets from you.'

Clinton leaned forward and put a hand over mine. 'Of course not,' he said. 'That's so, eh, Sarah?'

I did not answer. I thought of the great secret and imagined what his wrath would be like if he knew what I had done.

'It's been on my mind ever since it happened,' said Celia.

'Tell us then,' urged Clinton.

She turned her frank gaze on him. 'Do you know what it was like at the Grange? Miss Martha and Miss Mabel . . . I mean.'

'I did meet them,' he told her. 'A pair of dragons. At least one was. The other moved in her shadow.'

'Yes, it was like that. Sometimes I think I imagined it. Your Aunt Martha is a very strong woman, Sarah, a woman determined to have her own way.'

'A not uncommon feminine characteristic,' murmured Clinton.

'She had an obsession,' went on Celia. 'It was to do with the family pearls. She told me about them. You see, there was some plan in her mind. It seems mad . . . it was mad really. That's what I'm getting at. Your father was married to a woman who would never give him a son. They lived apart. Your aunt desperately wanted your father to beget a son and keep the name in the family. It all seemed rather involved. I would hardly believe this. But I know you were aware of it, Sarah. Your Aunt Martha had chosen *me* for your father's next wife while your mother was living. Does that seem mad?'

'I had an idea that it was in her mind,' I said.

'My background was right. I had no money at that time . . . but it wasn't a question of money. She wanted me to be the third Mrs Ashington, to bear a son whose wife would wear the Ashington Pearls before she bore a son whose wife . . . and so on. It all seemed quite crazy and so unlike her. She was so practical generally . . . so down to earth. But there it was. Your father was to come home and marry me. But at that time he had a wife. I know it sounds wild. But I believe she was mad. A strange sort of madness. There are many kinds. This is a reasoning madness . . . the sort that grows out of an obsession.'

'Celia,' I said, 'what are you trying to tell us?'

'I find it hard. It sounds so difficult and quite absurd. You know, Sarah, that my room was on the same floor as your mother's. I heard strange sounds in the night. Your mother was ill. It was only a cold and she was always getting colds. This one had turned to bronchitis. One night I saw your Aunt Martha walking into her room. I thought she was taking a posset or something. I took no notice. Your mother was worse in the morning. Then that night . . . Do you remember that night, Sarah? You came up and you saw it . . . The cold room with that icy wind blowing in. I woke up suddenly and felt that something was wrong. I remember your aunt's going quietly . . . almost stealthily . . . into the room and the next morning your mother was so ill. You went along to your mother's room and found the windows open and the fire out. It must have been like that for an hour or so. We couldn't be sure . . . She may have done it herself. Sometimes I thought she must have. But then I had seen your Aunt Martha going into the room, on that other occasion . . .'

'You mean she murdered my mother!'

'It was murder in a way . . . if she did it. Your mother died of pneumonia but she must have caught her death in that bitter cold. You see I started to work it out. The potion to send her to sleep and then opening all the windows, creeping out and coming back later to shut the windows. If I'm right your aunt was mad. Of course I may have been wrong. That's why I didn't want to mention it. But it was on my mind . . . and has been ever since. I couldn't bear to keep the secret any longer.'

'You said nothing at the time?' said Clinton.

'No, because I wasn't sure. I couldn't believe it. I thought that Sarah's mother had done this herself when she was in a fever and didn't know what she was doing. I tried to tell myself that was it. The more I think of it, the more I believe that Martha was mad . . . she *is* mad.'

I was silent. The story had not taken me by surprise because I had long wondered about Aunt Martha. It was true, I was sure, that she had wanted my mother out of the way, and it had also occurred to me that she had intended to train Celia Hansen as my father's third wife.

Aunt Martha, grim, forceful, a dominating woman, mad! Yes, in a way I could believe that.

We talked for a while and Celia certainly seemed relieved. I supposed that keeping something like that to oneself could have an effect on a sensitive person.

When Clinton and I were alone in our room I asked him what he thought of Celia's account of my mother's death.

He shrugged his shoulders. 'The old girl was capable of anything, I'm sure. She was one of those who would make up her mind what she wanted and go all out to get it.'

'There are people like that,' I said pointedly.

'I believe there are.' He drew me close to him. 'I see I shall have to be watchful of my Sarah. Madness in the family, eh?'

I was to remember that conversation afterwards.

At the end of the week Celia said she should go, but I urged her to stay a little longer.

'Is there any reason why you must go?' I asked.

She shook her head. 'There's nothing to go back to. I wouldn't want to overstay my welcome, that's all.'

'You must know how glad I am to have you. Clinton is overjoyed because he says he feels he can leave us in the house together if he should be called out and have to stay away overnight.'

'If you are sure . . .'

'My dear Celia, you must stay as long as you like.'

'I will stay a little longer then. I must say I was hoping you would invite me to. This place fascinates me and I always enjoyed being with you. Ralph is a darling. What fun it would be to teach him! I would be more qualified to do that than I was when I came to you.'

'That all turned out well,' I said. 'So it's settled. You'll stay.'

After that she said nothing about leaving. When I told Clinton that I had asked her to remain he was all in favour of it.

'It's better for you to have a companion,' he said.

I guessed he was not only thinking of those occasions when he would be away from home. Visions of Anula's seductive bedroom came into my mind.

The days passed quickly. I had another letter from Toby, which he must have written immediately on receipt of mine. He was delighted to hear from me. He told me something about the work he was doing and the community he lived in. He made me see the bungalow which he occupied presided over by a rather rascally Khansamah who cheated him right and left but without whom he would have found it extremely difficult to exist. 'He shops for me and overcharges for everything he buys, but if I tried to do it myself I'd be charged far more. You see, they are all in league against the poor Sahib – particularly if he's on his own without a Mem to take care of him. There is a great deal of entertaining and being entertained. The English community stick together. I dare say you find it very much the same where you are.'

I wrote immediately in reply and told him in a light-hearted way about our Club and the ball which had been given in my honour on my arrival and the busybody Mrs Glendenning. I was sure her type had its representative in his community as well as mine.

It was shortly after writing that letter to Toby that the first of the strange happenings took place. I had decided one day to walk home from Clytie's. It was one of those rare occasions when I was alone and as I came through the woods I was thinking of my mother and wondered if she had ever walked alone in these woods. Jungle, of course, was the right term for them. At one time it must have gone on and on for miles. A great deal of it had been cut down and cultivated to grow tea. If Clinton had his way all this part would be put to use.

I shall not allow it! I thought; and I laughed to myself, thinking of how angry Clinton would be if he knew he would never have the plantation for which he had married me.

People did strange things under stress of emotion. I was guilty of just that. I had been mad with rage when I had gone to the solicitor's office. I would never forget the insult he had heaped on me by staying with that woman. But what angered me most was the fact that I had allowed him to spend the night with me when he returned. I should have fought him with all my strength and although I pretended that I had given way reluctantly, he knew that was not quite true.

How I hated him! How could I have become enmeshed with him? He was not the sort of man I wanted for a husband. I wanted someone gentle, kind, who loved me exclusively. Someone who would comfort and cherish me throughout his life.

It was pleasant to be in touch with Toby.

There was something in the thicket on this day which was different. What was it? I stood listening. Was it Clytie who had said I should grow accustomed to the jungle noises? She was right. I had. Even when I heard something dash through the undergrowth I would not be alarmed. But always one must be watchful for snakes. Yet if one was cautious, it was safe enough. Leila had said she had seen an anaconda in the jungle near the water the other day. They were somewhat rare, but I had actually seen a cobra – a rather frightening sight. It had been curled up sleeping under a tree. I had hurried past. Down by the marshy banks of the river I often saw crocodiles, mostly sleeping and seeming docile enough until they started lashing their tails. Then it was time to get away. I was no longer startled by the odd stick insect, or suddenly coming on a lizard or a chameleon. Geckoes were a commonplace and I had often seen them darting up the walls inside the house.

I was becoming accustomed to this world where living things thrived in the steaming heat as they never could at home.

But that afternoon there was something in the jungle that alerted me. Even before it occurred to me that I was being stalked, I sensed it.

There it was – a sudden breaking of a twig . . . a footfall. It could be a small animal, a hog deer making its cautious way through the undergrowth, aware of danger all about him. Leila's anaconda would make short work of him if he discovered him.

No, I did not think it was an animal.

I could not understand why I felt this sudden fear.

Alone in the heart of the jungle! Yes, but the house was near. I had taken this walk through the woods alone before and thought nothing of it. There again! The cautious step. Now that I had stopped it had stopped too. I went on. There it was again . . . creeping after me.

A strange and unaccountable panic took possession of me. I started to run. The steps were coming after me, crashing through the trees now. An animal. It couldn't be. It would not stop when I did.

I paused. My heart was beating so fast that it was painful.

'Who's there?' I shouted.

There was no answer. Whoever was following had stopped dead when I did.

Now I knew real fear. I started to run again. There it was coming after me.

I ran with all the speed of which I was capable. My relief was intense when I came to the spot where the trees grew thinner. I had reached the edge of the garden. I went in and stood looking back into the jungle waiting for someone to emerge.

No one did.

'Who is it?' I shouted, my voice steady now, from the safety of the garden.

There was no answer. No one appeared. Nothing happened. I went slowly into the house.

It must have been someone following me, hoping to catch me before I reached safety. Who? Why should I have been chased through the woods?

I went up to the bedroom and sat at the mirror studying myself. What a sight! Hair wild, eyes staring, and that puckered look of bewildered fear.

I washed and changed and went downstairs.

Celia was sitting in the drawing-room reading. She looked up and smiled. 'Anything wrong?' she asked.

'I don't know. I had a scare in the woods.'

'A scare. What sort of scare?'

'I thought I was being pursued. It was quite . . . uncanny.'

'Pursued? Who would pursue you?'

'I can't think of anyone. But it was somehow . . . horrific.'

'Was it some animal?'

'You mean stalking me?'

'Perhaps. You know more about jungle life than I do.'

'Celia, it was horrible. It really frightened me.'

'It must have been imagination,' she said.

'No,' I replied. 'It was real enough.'

'Come and sit down. You look quite shaken.'

She began to talk of other things and I knew she was trying to soothe me.

That was the beginning of the strange events.

The next thing happened about two days later. It was the custom to rest in the afternoons during the hottest part of the day. We all took the siesta with the exception of Clinton. Now that Celia was with me I did not go to Clytie's so much or if I did go I would drive over in the dog-cart and it would be just a morning call.

I remember on this morning the heat had been intense. Celia and I had ridden over to Ashingtons together. I was with Clytie and Seth, and Celia had gone into the garden with Ralph. Celia and the boy had become fast friends and I was amused how, in her rather tutorial way, she liked to add to his knowledge. As he was a highly imaginative boy this suited him very well. It was a common sight to see those two, heads close, absorbed in conversation or bent over one of his books which she would read to him.

Seth had been discussing some new method of irrigation. He talked animatedly and it was obvious to me that since I had paid that visit to the solicitor I had taken a great weight off his mind. It was clear that he now had an incentive to work harder and to make the plantation a success. Not that he had not done this before but the fact that he felt secure in his position had clearly had its effect.

When Celia and I returned home we took a light lunch and

retired to our rooms. I did not sleep. I rarely did in the afternoons. Sometimes I read and at others I would find my mind wandering over all that had happened since I had come out here. As I have said, Celia's coming had brought a normality to our existence in some way. Clinton had changed and we did not spar as much as we used to. Celia was there with us and her presence was naturally restraining. Whether he liked that or not, I could not be sure. But he certainly thought it was good to have her there during the day.

It was while I was lying on my bed that I heard a sudden rap on the door.

'Come in!' I cried, expecting to see Celia. If Clinton had returned it was hardly likely that he would knock.

'Who's there?' I shouted again and there was still no response.

I got out of bed and went to the door. There was no one there.

How strange that was! The knock had been so loud. Someone must have been there. One of the servants perhaps. But why should she or he not come in when bidden to do so? And why go away after knocking?

Following my experience in the woods I felt disturbed.

I went along to Celia's room, the door of which was closed as mine had been. I knocked.

'Come in,' she cried.

She was lying on her bed reading.

'You didn't knock on my door?' I asked.

'Knock on your door? Why?'

'There was a knock. I called "come in" and no one came. I got up and looked. No one was there.'

'It must have been Leila coming up with something.'

'Well, why should she knock and go away?'

Celia lifted her shoulders. It was clear that she did not attach much importance to the incident.

'Leila,' I said, 'did you knock at my door this afternoon?'

She had brought me warm water with which to wash before I

changed for the evening meal.

'Knock, missee. Me . . . knock?'

'Yes, during the afternoon. Someone did and when I called "come in", no one came.'

She shook her head. 'I did not.'

'It's very strange. It was so distinct. I was resting on my bed and there was this knock.'

'There is a full moon tonight,' said Leila, her black eyes round with speculation. 'It could be the Spirit of the full moon.'

'Whatever should he knock on my door for?'

'Mayhap he think of you this full moon.'

'Leila, are you sure you didn't bring something and then decide after all not to disturb me?'

Leila shook her head firmly.

'Well, someone did,' I said almost angrily.

'Spirit of the full moon,' said Leila sagely.

I could see that I could get no sense out of her and that I was getting more disturbed than the occasion warranted. It was so irritating to have heard such a decisive knock and then to find all so little interested, except Leila with her absurd suggestions about the Spirit of the Moon. Celia seemed to think that I dreamed it and why make such a fuss about it.

Clinton came in while I was changing. He was in high spirits and kissed me warmly.

'Have you had a good day?' he asked.

'Yes, and you? Clinton, what do they mean when they say the Spirit of the Moon decides to visit you?'

'It means there's madness in the air.'

I felt suddenly frightened. I decided not to mention the rap on my door.

Something strange was going on. There had been another occasion when, walking through the woods, I had fancied myself followed. It was the same cautious stalking. I was really frightened.

I was panting when I reached the clearing. I waited there.

Surely if it were some animal it would come rushing out after me. Nothing came. It could not have been an animal. It was someone who did not want to be seen. Who?

I mentioned it to Clinton and Celia that evening.

'It's jungle nerves,' said Clinton.

'What on earth are they?'

'It's something that obsesses you in the jungle. It has a certain effect on you and you imagine things.'

'This was not imagination. Someone was following me.'

'Hardly likely,' said Clinton.

I caught Celia's eye. She was looking at me anxiously. She was thinking, I guessed, of the rap on my door, which she thought I had imagined.

The next time I'm followed I'll find out who it is, I promised myself.

There was another strange incident a few days later. It was siesta time again and once more I was lying on my bed reading. Suddenly I was aware of a sound and turning I stared at the door. The handle was slowly turning. This time I did not speak. I lay there watching. The door opened very slowly.

I did not know why I should have felt so alarmed but I was deeply conscious of the silence of the house. I waited, expecting someone to come silently into the room. The Spirit of the Moon? A ghostly figure which would point at me and say: 'We are thinking of you.'

Nothing happened . . . only silence.

I leaped out of bed. The corridor was empty.

Something very strange was going on.

I had to find out and I should do so cautiously this time.

I said to Leila when she came in with my hot water: 'You brought up my towels yesterday afternoon, didn't you?'

She looked at me blankly. 'No, missee. I go out all afternoon. To buy cottons for sewing.'

'What time did you go?'

She wrinkled her brow and remembered it was three o'clock. It was half past three when my door had mysteriously opened.

Of course she could have been lying.

Later I told Celia what had happened.

'I heard no one,' she said.

'But someone must have been there to open my door like that. Why?'

'It seems a silly thing to do. Quite pointless.'

'Quite pointless,' I agreed.

'It must have been Leila bringing something and then remembering you were resting.'

'She was out at the time, she says.'

'Are you sure, Sarah, that you didn't leave the door unlatched? Perhaps a sudden breeze . . .'

'I never leave the door open.'

'But perhaps this once you did. It seems the only explanation unless . . .'

'Unless what?'

'Unless you were dozing and dreamed it.'

'Celia, I was awake. I got out of bed and the door *was* open.'

She shrugged her shoulders. 'Well, it's not really important, is it?'

She gave me a searching look and I said: 'It *is* important. Too many strange things have been happening. Twice someone followed me in the woods. It's no use saying I imagined it. It happened. Then the rap on my door.'

'What does it mean?'

I could see that she thought I was making a great deal out of nothing so I let the matter drop. But it was on my mind and I decided I would talk to Clytie. I went over to see her. She was in the garden with Ralph when I arrived.

He ran towards me and threw his arms about my knees – a habit of his and an endearing one. He made visitors feel as though he really was glad to see them.

'I've got a new elephant,' he announced. 'It walks.'

'You wind him up,' said Clytie. 'Ralph is completely devoted to him. He is neglecting all the others on account of him.'

'He's going to take me bathing,' said Ralph. 'We go into the water and it comes right up to me on his back. I am in a gold cage with an umbrella over me. He gets a bit frightened but I tell him it's all right. I won't let him drown. Then we go hunting panthers. Mama, may I have a panther? One that runs so that my elephant can hunt him?'

'We'll see,' replied Clytie. 'It's a matter of first find your panther.'

'Panthers is nice,' commented Ralph, 'but elephants is betterer.'

He ran off to hunt with his elephant and Clytie and I sat down under the shade of one of the palm-trees.

'Is anything wrong?' she asked.

'I don't know yet. Strange things have been happening.' And I told her.

She listened gravely. I was grateful that she did not say it was imagination.

'It looks,' she said at length, 'as if someone is playing tricks.'

'Why should they?'

She pondered this. 'The stalking in the jungle. That could be someone trying to play a joke, an unpleasant one, trying to make you panic. The rapping on the door and opening it . . . that's certainly strange.'

'Next time I shall be off the bed and after whoever it is. Next time I shall make certain who is following me.'

'Be careful, Sarah.'

'What do you mean, Clytie? You speak as though you think I might be in some danger.'

'Whoever is doing these things must have a motive.'

'Some people would say it was imagination.'

'It could be that someone is trying to make you nervous.'

'Who would want to do that?'

'I don't know,' she said, but somehow with a lack of conviction.

'Clytie, you will help me if you can?'

'Of course I will.'

'Then if you know something, tell me.'

'I don't know anything. I can only make a guess. It's embarrassing. I think this may concern . . . No, I'm sure I'm wrong. It's such a wild surmise.'

'Clytie, I am your sister. However wild your surmise, I want to know.'

'People here are different from you, Sarah. They have a different code . . . different ideas . . . I was thinking about Anula. Oh no . . . it's impossible. I shouldn't have said it.'

'You should and I'll say the rest for you. I know that Anula was Clinton's mistress. He has admitted it. She resents my being here. Perhaps she has some notion of driving me away.'

'It was well known,' admitted Clytie. 'They made no secret of it. I think she may have believed he would marry her. He might have done so. Through her mother she is of a noble family and because she was so outstanding right from her childhood her parents gave her an education which the other children did not get. She is the eldest and her mother was alive when she was growing up. She died when Ashraf was born and Leila was very young then. Anula was brought up according to European standards. That is why she is different from the others and would fit more easily into our society. I think it may well be that she resents you and is trying these tricks to alarm you and perhaps drive you away.'

'Surely she couldn't hope to do that by stalking me in the jungle or getting Leila to rap on my door.'

'I told you, didn't I, that it was just an idea that came to me. Anula is a strange creature. Quite a lot of people believe that she really is a reincarnation of the Queen of that name, the first Queen of Ceylon who became so through marrying the King. There are some who refer to Clinton as the King of Kandy. He is so powerful here and is gradually acquiring more and more of the country's profitable industries. A king, you see, of his era. But Anula would become Queen through a marriage with King Clinton and perhaps that was what she hoped for. It would be working out her Karma. She failed once but she was going to succeed this time. That's how her mind would work. Then Clinton returned from England with a bride.'

'Do you really think she would go to great lengths to get rid of me?'

'I really don't know. I'm just trying to find an explanation.'

'I can't imagine that exquisite creature stalking me in the woods.'

'She might have sent Ashraf to do it. Leila could have done the door-rapping. They would obey her absolutely. She has made them believe she has very special powers and they dare not offend her.'

'What shall I do, Clytie?'

'Ignore it. Try not to let it worry you.'

'Clinton and Celia think I have imagined these things. I can see they do.'

'Then don't tell them any more. Keep it to yourself. Be watchful and try to find out who is trying to frighten you.'

It did make some sort of sense. I must remember that I was in a strange land and what would seem wildly absurd at home was not so here. People here thought differently; some might say they were nearer to nature; they held beliefs which seemed strange to us but which were perfectly natural to them. I must not make the mistake of applying the same standards to the people here as I would to those at home.

It might well be that Anula believed she and Clinton were destined for each other. As Clytie had said he was even called the King of Kandy – King in a different sense from the ancient rulers, yet he was the most powerful man here and ruled in a way.

It seemed quite ridiculous, but I was grateful to Clytie for listening and taking me seriously.

Anula was certainly the most likely explanation.

It was like a nightmare slowly creeping up on me. They were such foolish things. I would put something in the place it always occupied and then find it somewhere else. I tried to shrug this off but it was becoming increasingly difficult.

Clinton was aware of it. He said I was a scatterbrain. Leila noticed it; she looked mysterious and I knew she was thinking of the Spirit of the Moon. Celia was getting worried and she, in her turn, was trying not to betray it. As for myself, I was becoming really alarmed. It might well have been my anxiety which made me more liable to do strange things. I could not understand it.

I became nervous when I went into the bedroom. I was always wondering what I would find. When I lay on my bed and tried to rest I would find myself staring at the door, expecting it to open suddenly.

Clinton was away now and then and since Celia was staying in the house I did not go to Clytie. Sometimes I wished I could for I felt the mischief was in this house.

When I was at Ashingtons I felt better. I could talk to Clytie more easily than I could to Celia, but even Clytie was beginning to show a little uneasiness now.

What had happened to me? It was almost as though I was bewitched. Sometimes I would have vague dreams as though I were in a drugged sleep and I would imagine I saw strange figures in my room.

This was beginning to have its effect on me. I was pale. I lost a little weight and there were dark shadows under my eyes.

I tried to conceal this from Clinton. He was the sort of man who thought illness a fault in the sufferers; I knew he would never be patient with an invalid. An invalid! I was not that. I was the victim of some strange . . . spell, some bewitchment which had taken possession of me.

Once in the night when I was sleeping heavily, I heard voices in the room. Clinton was away for the night and I had gone to bed early at Celia's suggestion. Leila had made a warm drink for me which would be soothing, she said. I slept deeply and I was awakened by what I thought was a light touch on my cheek. There was no light in the room. I heard my name spoken. 'Sarah, Sarah, it is the Spirit of the Moon who calls to you . . .'

I forced myself to wake fully. Of course there was no one in the room. It was just a dream.

One day I went to my room and smelt there the faint odour of sandalwood. It sickened me and made me think of Anula. In the drawer was the bottle of scent which she had given me. A drop of it washed away the sins of the year. I could hear Clinton laughing at that.

The bottle must be leaking. There was a dampness round the stopper. I smelt it. Strange perfume, exotic, eastern.

Leila came in. 'I smell sandalwood,' she said. 'It makes something holy in this room.'

'Your sister Anula gave me this bottle.'

Her eyes lighted with respect. 'Then it is specially good. It make of this room holy place.'

'I hardly think that,' I said.

'It is the most important incense, Missee Sarah. When there are festivals people give much money for sticks of sandalwood. That means they earn repentance for their sins.'

'It seems to be associated with sin, this perfume.'

'Oh yes. It is put on the feet of those about to die so that when they go up to Heaven the perfume goes with them.'

'Very interesting. I find it a little sickening, however.'

'Missee Sarah speak against what is sacred.'

Having touched the bottle, the scent seemed to cling to my hands. When I went downstairs Celia noticed it. I told her that Anula had given it to me. She knew about Anula; how much I was not sure, but she made it clear that she did not approve of her. I went on to tell her what Leila had said about the sacred qualities of sandalwood.

'It's a strange perfume,' she said. 'I'm not sure whether I like it or not.'

When I next went to my room I smelt a strong odour of sandalwood there. It seemed to cling to the curtains. I was reminded of Anula's house and I wanted to let a fresh wind blow through the place.

I woke up one morning after a night of deep sleep, feeling heavy-eyed and reluctant to wake up as I sometimes did nowadays.

As I was putting on my stockings I smelt sandalwood and I

realized that it was on my feet! A shiver ran right through my body and the hairs on the back of my neck seemed to be rising. They put sandalwood on the feet of those about to die. Was that what Leila had said?

I think that unnerved me more than anything that had happened so far.

Two days later I was writing to Toby. I had made up my mind that I had to do something. I had refused to face up to it before but I was thinking a great deal about Aunt Martha and I had dreamed of her once or twice, creeping along the corridor to my mother's room. She had murdered my mother. I had suspected it and now I was sure. It was a madness which had crept up on her. One would have thought her to be the sanest person one could meet. Meticulous, conventional, sure of herself and yet capable of an obsession. Hers was all due to those pearls. They had taken possession of her and there was madness in them.

Madness! It was a horrible word and one which I had omitted to use for some time . . . ever since those strange things had begun to happen.

Could it really be that there was some madness in my family? Hadn't Aunt Martha been mad when she crept along the corridor and decided to destroy my mother? She had even selected the bride for my father. Yes, that was madness. I was frightened. I had always been a level-headed person. I did not fly into rages. I had been fairly clear-thinking, reasonably logical, but now I was acting strangely. I was seeing strange things which others did not see. Hallucinations. The figures I had fancied I had seen in my room. What had I seen? I did not know. The light was too dim. It was a presence . . . nothing more. 'Sarah, Sarah, I am the Spirit of the Moon . . .'

The Spirit of the Moon brought madness.

Could I tell Clinton of my fears? No. He would laugh at them. He was my husband but there was little tenderness between us. He desired me with a wild passion which thrived on conflict. I was the same towards him. Was that love? If so, it was not what I had always thought love to be. He would be impatient with weakness because he was so strong. He liked me when I fought him. He wanted no weak or frightened woman. I imagined that Anula would stand up to him, fight him, quarrel with him. She would be his sort of woman.

No, I could not tell Clinton. I had told Clytie a certain amount and she was sympathetic. She believed that Anula hated me and might possibly be trying to get rid of me. I was ready to do battle against Anula if necessary, but I felt inadequate and unsure. Anula could not have come into my room at night. She was far away ... perhaps with Clinton, for all I knew. Tell Celia. I could up to a point but her attitude frightened me. She knew about Aunt Martha and I would often find her watching me with a terrible anxiety in her eyes. Celia was a good friend and she was afraid for me. She had been there when my mother died and she believed that Aunt Martha was mad.

Am I going mad? I asked myself. Is this how madness starts?

Then I remembered those days of my childhood and that there was always one to whom I could take my troubles. He had never failed me; he had always supported me; he had bolstered me up when my courage waned; he had always told me there was something special about me. '*You* can do it, Sarah,' he used to say. 'If anyone can, that's you.'

Toby! I was suddenly weak with emotion because I was already in touch with Toby.

So I wrote to him. I had already told him something. He knew that Celia was with me and he was glad of that. 'She seems a good, steady girl by all accounts,' he wrote. I had not told him about Anula. He would be horrified to think she was still seeing Clinton. It was easier to say nothing about that. But I did want to tell him of the strangeness which had come into my life.

First [I wrote], it began by the certainty that I was being followed in the woods. It's really jungle. You will know well the sort of place. One could get frightened there because of the strange creatures . . . so different from the ones at home. I shall never forget my first glimpse of a cobra and the prickling sensation it sent down my spine. The lizards on the walls . . . so still, and then suddenly darting forward; and the colonies of ants on the march are the most terrifying of all. So perhaps I could get rather imaginative in the jungle. But it has happened twice. I *was* followed. Toby, I am sure I didn't imagine it. There were distinct footsteps. And there was a feeling . . . a definite feeling. It was sinister. Then there was the rap on my door . . . and no one there. And the door opening and the strange drowsiness and the awareness that someone was in my room. Toby, think about this and tell me what you think it means.

There is something else. You will know the scent of sandal-wood. It's a sacred perfume. I had a bottle given to me. I don't like it. One day when I went to my room I found the air full of the smell of it. I went to my bottle. It was half empty. I had not scented my room with it, Toby, yet it was there on the curtains . . . everywhere. I wondered how it had happened. I wanted to find out. I had to, I asked everyone who could have gone into my room. Had they perfumed it? They swore they hadn't. And they looked at me oddly. I knew what they were thinking. I have been acting a bit strange lately. They believed that I had thrown the scent about the room myself. I could see they did. I had talked of the scent to Leila only the day before. She had talked about its being sacred. 'I reckon it was on your mind,' she said. Toby, do *you* believe I would have thrown that stuff all round the room and not known that I had done it? One morning it was on my *feet*. They put it on the feet of those about to *die*. It's a sort of ritual. Someone must have put it on my feet while I slept. That shook me more than anything. It made it more sinister than ever, as though someone is telling me that I am going to die.

I think the hardest thing is to be upset about these things and have to pretend I'm not. Something is happening here, I'm sure of it. That's what I think at one moment. The next I'm asking myself, 'Is there something wrong with *me*? Am I imagining these things?' That's what I ask myself. I have to, Toby, and I want you to reassure me, as you always did.

Now let me tell you what happened. I took this half-empty bottle of sandalwood and I went into the jungle and threw it away . . . right among the tangled undergrowth. I had that strange feeling that someone was watching me. It's a strange feeling, Toby, and one that I have become familiar with lately. I came back to the house. I could still smell the stuff in my room, but I fancied it was fainter. It would gradually subside, I promised myself.

This is one of the most frightening things, Toby. I went to my drawer and opened it and there was the half-empty bottle of sandalwood. I picked it up. It was damp round the top. It was without doubt the bottle of sandalwood which I had thrown away in the jungle. What could I think, Toby? What can I think? I had taken it out and thrown it away . . . and there it was back again. I have tried to reason. I thought of you and what you used to say about facing up to your worries and looking them straight in the face. I think of you a lot, Toby. Well, this could not be the same bottle, I told myself. It was another one. Either that or someone had taken the old bottle and brought it back. Why? I started to question myself then. Had I really thrown the bottle away or meant to and thought I did?

I went out into the jungle to look for the bottle. It was late afternoon. I went straight to the spot where I had thrown it. The growth was thick there. I pushed back the foliage and there where the bottle had been, was a cobra, coiled up, awaiting me.

Imagine my horror. I leaped back and ran as fast as I could back to the house. Clinton had come in. I threw myself at him and screamed that I had seen a cobra in the wood close to the house. They went out, he, his headman Nankeen, with some of the others. I followed them to show them where I had seen it. They had sticks and weapons and things. It was near the edge of the wood, you see, and they were afraid it might get into the garden or into the house

'It was coiled up asleep,' I cried. 'I saw it clearly.' But there was nothing there. They hunted round but there was no trace of the thing. Old Nankeen kept shaking his head and saying: 'No cobra here. No trace cobra.' As though I had imagined it.

I'm sure they all thought I had. Clinton laughed at me and the men were laughing too. 'No cobra, missee,' Nankeen kept saying. I felt foolish. But I *had* seen it, Toby.

Toby, there is something going on here. Write to me and tell me what you think is happening. I have reason to believe that my Aunt Martha was a little strange in the head. Frankly, I'm terrified. This is a cry for help. You are the one in the world who, I feel, can help me most. I knew that when we were in Denton Square and I know it now.

Toby, please, *please* write soon . . .

Having written that letter I must post it right away although it would not go until tomorrow when the post came in, but in spite of this I could not wait to send it on its way.

Celia rode into Manganiya with me and when I said I wanted to go to the post she said: 'Isn't it tomorrow it comes in?'

'Yes,' I replied, 'but I want to get something off today.'

She looked at me oddly and I believe she was thinking this was another example of my strangeness.

So we went into the post office and I myself dropped the letter into the sack.

'It's obviously a very important letter,' said Celia lightly.

'It's to an old friend in India. Toby.'

'Oh yes, I remember.'

I was almost light-hearted as we rode back to the house, such was my faith in Toby.

The greatest shock of all in this most mysterious matter was yet to come. It shattered me so completely that it was impossible to ignore these strange hallucinations any longer.

With Clinton and Celia I had dined at Ashingtons. Clinton and Seth talked a great deal about the plantations and I was always afraid on such occasions that Clinton would discover that I had made sure he should not have Ashingtons. Owing to my state of mind, brought about by recent events, I had felt less bravado and had in fact become, as Janet in the old days would have said, 'afraid of my own shadow'. There were times, however, when my true nature took charge and assured me that there was a logical explanation to all that was happening and all I had to do was catch the one who was playing tricks on me. My natural resilience was such that a few nights' good sleep could restore my normal fighting spirit. Then my fears seemed absurd.

I was in such a mood on this night. Clytie, Celia and I talked of domestic matters, of Ralph and his drollness, of the servants and such things. Then I joined in with the men, which always amused Clinton, and I had to admit that though, when we were alone, he took a delight in exposing my ignorance, he never did so in company. Celia and Clytie were still discussing Ralph. Clytie was very drawn to Celia, I think largely because of the latter's interest in and affection for her son.

At length it was time for us to leave and we drove off in the Victoria. It was always rather thrilling to ride through the night. Although we were on the road the jungle was close and I always listened for the animals which prowled by night. Sometimes one caught the hint of phosphorescent light among the bushes, the glinting of a watching eye, the sudden crash of a body plunging through the undergrowth, and sometimes the sound of scuffles or a cry of terror and rage.

When we arrived at the house Nankeen was waiting for us. A little trouble among the men, he told Clinton ingratiatingly. Would he come and settle it? Gopal's wife had been wicked again. Sahib Shaw would make it right.

Clinton left with Nankeen. Celia went to her room and Leila

appeared to tell me about Gopal's wife, who had never been a good wife to Gopal. 'She is very beautiful. Men like Gopal's wife. My sister Anula say where she be there will be trouble.'

I yawned. I was tired. I wondered how long Clinton would be. 'Soon he come,' said Leila. 'Gopal's wife frightened of Sahib Shaw.'

I went to bed. One of the lamps had been lighted on the dressing-table. It gave enough light to undress by. It seemed that the malevolent eyes of the bronze Buddha watched me. I picked it up and looked closely at it. I'll throw it away I thought; and then laughed at myself. That would be foolish. It was admitting fear. I should just ignore it. What was it but a piece of metal?

I approached the bed and as I did so I recoiled in horror. There curled up on the bed – just as he had been in the undergrowth – was the cobra.

A cobra in the house! I stood staring at it for some seconds. It was a yellowish olive colour and I clearly saw the white crossbands on its back. Thank God it was sleeping! I knew that any movement on my part could arouse it and it would be an angry awakening. It would attack.

I made for the door and ran downstairs calling to everyone.

'Come quickly. Leila . . . somebody . . . There is a cobra in the bedroom.'

Celia was running down the stairs.

'Sarah! What's happened? What's wrong?'

Leila had appeared and one or two of the other servants. Then Clinton was coming through the door. I threw myself at him.

'Clinton,' I said, 'it's there . . . in the bedroom. On the bed . . . coiled up asleep.'

'What!'

'The cobra. It's on the bed.'

Clinton had picked up a walking stick. Three of the men had arrived on the scene. They all started up the stairs.

I followed with Celia. Leila was just behind us.

Clinton flung open the bedroom door and went cautiously into the room – the others a step behind.

There was silence.

I had followed. They were all looking at the bed.

There was nothing there.

I heard the deep sigh behind me and I knew it was Celia. She had taken my arm protectively.

I heard Clinton say: 'We'd better make a thorough search.'

They searched. They went through the house.

There was nothing.

Clinton took me into his arms and said: 'Sarah, what's wrong?'

'I saw it, Clinton. I saw it clearly,' I insisted.

He stroked my hair and said nothing.

'You don't believe me, do you?' I said. 'You think I imagined it.'

Still he said nothing.

'It was there . . . lying on the bed . . . that yellowish colour. I saw it. There was no mistake.'

'Listen, Sarah. It couldn't have been. You'd shut the door behind you when you came out. It couldn't have got out of the room. It would have been impossible. And just suppose it had, it would be in the house somewhere. It's just not here. It's unlikely that a cobra would be sleeping at this time of night. They're night creatures. They hunt for food by night.'

'Yet it was there. It *was* there.'

'Let's forget it.'

'Forget it! How can I forget it!'

'Sarah, what is happening to you?'

'I don't know what's happening to me.'

'You seem to think that someone . . . something is working against you and is trying to . . . Do what? Just tell me.'

'Perhaps someone wants to frighten me away.'

He laughed. 'What nonsense! And are you the sort of person who could be frightened away?'

'I don't seem to be the same person I was when I came here.'

'You mustn't lose that fighting spirit, Sarah.'

Suddenly I wanted to cling to him, to beg him to comfort me. I wanted to say: I'm not going mad, am I? What did you think of Aunt Martha?

Instead I said: 'You don't believe I saw the cobra, do you?'

'You couldn't have, Sarah.'

'Then what happened?'

'It was an optical illusion. Perhaps a trick of the light.'

'I saw it clearly, I tell you.'

'It can easily happen. Something's on your mind and you get this quick impression. You have rather an obsession with cobras, darling.'

'You think something is wrong with me, don't you?'

'I think you have an attack of jungle nerves. You come out here. It's so different from home. You adjust . . . so you think. But you haven't done so completely. Stop worrying. In a few weeks' time you'll be laughing at all this.'

I suppose there was some comfort in this attitude. Perhaps the common-sense snap-out-of-it note was what I needed. Clinton certainly gave me that.

He lifted me in his arms and kissed me.

'We'll forget it,' he said.

'I'll try but they'll all be talking about it.'

'Let them.'

'They'll say I've been selected by the Spirit of the Moon.'

'Much you care what they say.'

He turned out the lamps. The dark night closed in on me.

'I promise you I'll protect you from every cobra in Ceylon,' he said.

Later he announced: 'I'm going to take you away in a week or so's time. I have to go up north to the pearl fisheries. I'm not leaving you behind.'

'I always wanted to see them.'

'I know. The eternal lure. You'll see how they dive for them. The season will be starting soon. I've never seen a cobra up there.'

Oh yes, he did have the power to comfort me.

In the morning my uneasiness returned. I could not convince myself that I had not seen a cobra on the bed. It had been perfectly clear to me. But how could I have seen it if it had been quite impossible for it to be there?

Now the fears began chasing themselves round and round in my head. I was thankful that I had written to Toby. Perhaps it was foolish for I did not see what he could do in Delhi. It was just that I believed he would offer the kind of advice I needed. I wanted him to know what was happening. I wanted to explain my feelings and I wanted his opinion.

Clinton had gone off early. He had said that perhaps in just over a week he might be ready to go to the pearl fisheries. I wondered whether I really wanted to go. It was true that I did want to see how they dived for the pearls and to know something about the industry which was another in Clinton's kingdom. But as my uneasiness grew so did my desire for the truth. Half of me wanted to escape, to get away from this grim shadow which was looming over me and seemed to grow more menacingly near with every incident; on the other hand it was characteristic of me that I wanted to face whatever this was and to discover what it really meant.

If I am going mad, I thought, it would be better for me to know it. I can't go on in this half world of uncertainty.

The next time I saw a cobra I should go to it and touch it and make sure it was real. What a foolish thought. No one would dare to touch a cobra.

Leila brought me warm water with which to wash. She seemed subdued and kept her eyes lowered. She was thinking of last night's incident obviously, but she said nothing which in itself was significant. I wondered what the servants were saying about me. That I had been touched by the Moon Spirit? That I had jungle nerves?

I washed behind the curtain and came back to my bedside to

dress. My bare foot touched something sharp. I stooped and picked it up.

It was a stone – very small like a topaz. I didn't think it was real. It was made of glass, I was pretty sure. It must have come off a button or some ornament. I would ask Leila. I put it in a little pot on my dressing-table while I tried to stop thinking of the cobra and to concentrate instead on my coming trip to the pearl fisheries.

I wondered what clothes I should need. Perhaps Leila could make me something. It would be a pleasant diversion to think of new clothes. Perhaps Clytie, Celia and I would go into Kandy and choose some material.

Then I thought of Celia. If I went to the pearl fisheries she would not want to stay in the house with only the servants. I could not ask her to leave. After all, she had suggested going several times and I had persuaded her to stay. She had become like a member of the family. In any case, I didn't want her to go. I valued her friendship too much. We had fallen back into the relationship which we had enjoyed at the Grange with the utmost ease, which was the way it was with real friends.

I went downstairs. She was in the garden. She looked at me rather sheepishly as she bade me good morning and I knew she was thinking of last night.

I said to her: 'It's no use avoiding the subject, Celia. I know I saw a cobra and nothing will make me think differently.'

'It must have escaped somehow,' she said soothingly. 'What are your plans for today?' she went on quickly.

'I want to go to Ashingtons first. I should like to go into Kandy.' I plunged into the matter which was uppermost in my mind. 'Clinton wants to take me away. He will be going shortly up to the pearl fisheries. He's insisting that I go with him.'

She nodded slowly.

I went on: 'Celia, I have been thinking about you . . .'

Her face broke into smiles. 'Oh, you mustn't worry about me, Sarah, truly you mustn't. I could stay at the hotel. I should be gone by now . . . only I don't want to leave you . . . just yet.'

She put out a hand and it closed over mine. I was moved. I

knew she meant that she would hate to leave me while I was going through this strange period. Her voice trembled slightly.

'I can't tell you what it has meant to me to have you here,' I said. 'You were a comfort to me at the Grange, and now here.'

'I want to stay as long as I can be of any help. I do think it's the best thing possible for you to go away for a while. You'll get your strength back. You'll sleep well at night . . . and then all this will just seem like a temporary sickness. As a matter of fact I have an idea. I wonder if I could stay with Clytie. I could help with Ralph. I do love that little fellow. He's so bright and amusing.'

'I know you have a special feeling for him. I believe old Sheba is quite jealous. Of course, Clytie would love to have you. I'll tell you what. I want to get you and Clytie to come with me to Kandy to buy some materials. Let's go over and see her and you can make your arrangements with her.'

She agreed and later in the morning we rode over.

Clytie was delighted to see us and when she heard that I was going away with Clinton immediately agreed that as Celia would not want to stay in the house without me, she must go to Ashingtons.

'We'll go to Kandy tomorrow,' she said. 'It's too late today. If we went now we should arrive at midday and all the shops would be closed in any case. And it would be too late to go in the afternoon. We'll go early tomorrow morning. Are you feeling all right, Sarah?'

'Why, don't I look well?'

'A little tired, I thought.'

I did not want to tell her about the cobra now. I would do so when we were alone together. Celia changed the subject, sensing my wishes.

I thought what a good friend she was and how I should miss her when she returned to England which she must do in due course.

The following day we went to Kandy and had a pleasant morning selecting some delightful silks in deep red and kingfisher blue. I felt better. I had had a good night's sleep and nothing extra-ordinary happened. I longed to hear from Toby but it was too early yet. I could hardly hope for a reply before I went off with Clinton.

I was trying to face the facts as I assured myself I must. Was it possible, I asked myself, that a woman like Anula could put a spell on someone she wanted to get out of the way? Could she really make me see things which did not exist? I had heard a great deal about the mysticism of India and the same beliefs prevailed here. I had heard of the famous rope trick, though I had never seen it – nor did I know anyone who had – but I had been told that it was an optical illusion, a kind of hypnosis which enabled one man to convince a crowd of people that they were seeing something which was quite impossible. Did Anula possess these special powers? I shivered to contemplate the possibility of this being true. If it were I should be as some creature of hers whom she could govern from a distance. It was an uncanny thought and of course I wouldn't accept it.

Then how . . . There I was back at the beginning, and I had promised myself that I would forget it. I was going to think only of this coming trip with Clinton. Red Bokhara silk would become me. I must fight my way back to that self-sufficient woman I had been before I had been beset by these hallucinations and fears.

We bargained over our silks as was expected, for both Clinton and Clytie had assured me that the shopkeepers despised a buyer who paid the first price asked and considered themselves cheated of a pleasure if haggling did not ensue before a bargain was struck.

Then we went to the Club and drank lemonade slightly laced with gin. It was pleasant and refreshing.

Mrs Glendenning bore down on us and wanted to know what we had been doing in Kandy and why it was that she had not seen us lately. She was delighted to hear of what we had been buying and that Clinton and I were proposing to go on a trip.

'Everyone will say that it is right,' she said, implying that in view of Clinton's reputation it was as well that his wife accompanied him when he was away from home.

I wanted to ask sarcastically what business it was of everyone's but refrained from doing so.

She clearly knew nothing of what I had come to think of as my 'strangeness', which showed that, although I was sure that the servants were aware of it and gossiped in a manner to be expected, their whispers had not, as yet, extended beyond our area.

When she had left, Sir William and Lady Carstairs came into the Club and joined us.

He wanted to know if anything had been heard about that disgraceful business. He was referring to the kidnapping of Ralph.

'It was a terrible affair.' He looked reproachfully at Clytie, who shook her head and murmured: 'It was the only way.'

'The villains. We might have caught them though and retained the pearls.'

'I couldn't risk it,' said Clytie fiercely. 'I had to get my son safely back. I'd do the same again. You must understand that.'

'Perfectly,' said Sir William. 'It is always so. Mothers will never wait for us to act in these cases. But I have every confidence that we shall recover the pearls in due course.'

I wished we had not met him for he had clearly upset Clytie and spoiled our day. However when we rode back with our silks she recovered her good spirits and neither Celia nor I mentioned the pearls. Celia was very good at assessing other people's feelings. She was always the essence of tact.

Having gone early we were back just before lunch. We took a light meal and sat about desultorily during the early afternoon, discussing patterns and new styles.

At four o'clock when the heat of the day was over we went into the garden and Ralph came out to join us.

I found myself wandering off with him alone. He wanted to show me the elephant, he said. He put his hand in mine and chattered away about his animals and I wondered if he ever remembered that night he had spent away from home when he was kidnapped. Clytie said it was a good thing he lived in his dream world so that the event was to him just another of the adventures of his imagination.

He was now saying something about the naughty Cobbler.

'Oh, has he been naughty?' I asked.

'He ran away.'

'Where did he run to?'

'He ran away on his own. He thought he was clever. Then he had a fight with a mongoose and he might have died. But I came along and I was on my elephant and we rescued naughty Cobbler. Come and see him.'

He pulled my hand as we ran across the grass.

He crawled under a bush and came out dragging the toy cobra with him. The reality struck me forcibly and I felt a shudder run down my spine. It was so exactly like the real thing . . . in size, colour . . . everything.

'There!' said Ralph. 'He knows he's been naughty. Aunt Sarah doesn't like you any more, Cobbler. She likes Jumbo better.'

He looked up at me.

'You're very cross with him. Poor Cobbler. He's sorry now. He'll never run away again. You see, he didn't know about the mongoose till I told him. My papa is going to buy me a mongoose. It'll be a good one. It won't hurt Cobbler though. He thinks it will. He's very sulky.'

The thing lay coiled realistically at my feet. Ralph knelt on the grass and put his head right down so that it was almost touching the toy.

'Poor Cobbler.' He looked up at me. 'He's blind a bit, Aunt Sarah. It was fighting with that mongoose. It would have been the end of him if I hadn't come.' Ralph laughed. 'I'm looking at him but he can't see me. He's blinded this side.'

I went and looked down. The cobra had lost one of its eyes. I knelt and saw the dark socket where the eye had been.

'It'll teach you, Cobbler,' said Ralph. 'Why, if you lost the other one you wouldn't see at all.'

I hated the sight of the thing. It reminded me so much of what had happened.

With the perception of children Ralph sensed that I didn't want to touch the cobra. He picked it up and put it carefully under the bush.

The thought hit me suddenly as we were riding home. No. It was too absurd.

As soon as I was in the house I went up to the bedroom and opened the little pot on my dressing-table. The piece of glass was still there – a small piece of yellow stone.

Suppose it was! How had the eye of Ralph's cobra come to be on the floor of my bedroom?

The answer would be, Because the toy cobra had been there.

I held the glass bead in my hand. I must know.

I looked at my watch. It was half past five. I would have to wait until morning to see if the piece of glass fitted into the empty socket.

I was on the point of going to tell Celia what had happened, but something made me hang back. If that piece of glass was indeed the eye of Ralph's cobra it would be interesting to find out how it came to be in my bedroom, but if it turned out to be just a piece of glass they would all think that my excitement about it was another phase of my obsession with cobras.

I must act cautiously, and although my impulse was to dash over to Ashingtons right away that would surely cause comment. Another example of Sarah's odd behaviour, they would say.

I must therefore be patient and wait until tomorrow.

I put the bead back into the little pot. I must be careful that it was not lost and at the very first opportunity I was going to Ashingtons.

I was a little absent-minded that night. On several occasions I found Celia looking at me anxiously. Clinton appeared not to notice. His theory was that the best way to cure me of my oddness was to ignore it.

It was the afternoon of the next day – four o'clock after the heat had subsided a little – that I made up my mind to walk through the woods to Ashingtons. I would go alone so that I should not have to make an excuse for going.

The first thing I had done on rising was to assure myself that the glass bead was there. In view of what happened over the last two weeks I had rather expected it to have disappeared. But no. There it lay. I put it carefully in a tiny silk purse which I kept in my pocket so that I could feel it every now and then to reassure myself.

When I arrived Clytie was in the garden as she usually was at this hour with Ralph, surrounded by his animals, beside her.

Clytie was as glad to see me as ever and went into the house to order tea to be made.

That left me with Ralph.

'Ralph,' I said. 'Come here. I've something to show you.'

He came running, his eyes alight with expectation.

'I think I've found Cobbler's eye,' I told him.

'Where is it, Aunt Sarah? Where is it?'

I took it out of the purse, my heart beating with apprehension for I half expected it to have been spirited away.

It lay in my palm and Ralph peered at it.

'It's a bead,' he said.

'Yes, but it could also be an eye. Poor Cobbler. We must see if it fits. Where is he? In the garden?'

Ralph looked at me reproachfully. 'I wouldn't let him stay out without an eye. Suppose a mongoose came.'

'Where is he then?'

'In my room.' He started running towards the house and I followed.

Sheba was in the hall. 'Where are you running, Master boy?' she asked.

'Sheba! Aunt Sarah's got Cobbler's eye.'

'It might only be a glass bead,' I said

'It's his eye! It *is* his eye!' cried Ralph.

'That nasty snake,' mumbled Sheba. 'Time it was done away with.'

'Come on, Aunt Sarah,' cried Ralph and started up the stairs.

In his room, on a table beside his bed, stood a giraffe with a dormouse lying beneath its long legs. Ralph dived under the bed and emerged with the toy cobra.

'Give it to me,' I said. 'Let's see if it fits.'

My fingers were trembling as I took the glass bead and compared it with that on the other side of the cobra's head. I looked back at the empty socket.

'Look, Ralph!' I cried triumphantly. 'It fits.'

'You've got the shakes, Aunt Sarah.'

'I'm so excited because Cobbler's got his eye back. Now we want some glue.'

Sheba was standing in the doorway.

'Sheba, bring some glue,' cried Ralph. 'Cobbler's got his eye back but it's got to be stuck in.'

'I get,' said Sheba.

Ralph looked at me gravely. 'Sheba doesn't like Cobbler.'

'Why not?'

'She wants to take him away. She says he's too like a real snake. Cobbler *is* a real snake, isn't he, Aunt Sarah?'

'He is to you,' I replied.

'Sheba says I wouldn't know the difference between a live one and Cobbler. I'd know Cobbler anywhere. He's mine.'

Sheba was silently standing behind us.

'Here glue,' she said. As I took it I was aware of her eyes boring into me. She would know about my outburst. Leila would have told her surely. She would be wondering where I had found the glass bead.

I took the glue and stuck in the eye. Ralph watched with absorption.

'Now,' I said, 'you mustn't touch it until it's dry. Roll him up and put him under the bed. Leave him till the morning. Will you do that?'

Ralph considered. 'I might look at him last thing tonight.'

I shook my head gravely. 'The best thing is to forget about him until tomorrow morning. Then his eye will be firmly fixed and he'll be just as he was.'

Clytie came into the bedroom. 'What's all this about?'

I explained: 'Ralph's cobra lost his eye and I picked it up. We have just been fixing it.'

There was a moment of tension I believed – or it might have been my imagination. As for myself I felt elated, vindicated.

'Well, come and have some tea,' said Clytie. 'Did you come all this way just to bring the eye back?'

'I thought it was rather important,' I said and looked at Ralph, who nodded vigorously.

'I hope you said "thank you" to Aunt Sarah,' she said to the boy.

He looked a little surprised. 'Did I, Aunt Sarah? Cobbler will thank you. He wanted to when you stuck it on but he's a bit shy.'

'He probably wants to wait to see whether it stays firmly in before he thanks me,' I said.

'I shall make him thank you for *bringing* it. It'll teach him a lesson. He shouldn't have run away, should he? He went and then he came back. He knew it was naughty.'

Yes, I was beginning to see daylight. He went and came back. Of course he went. He was taken to be put in the bushes and later in my bedroom. That his eye had come off was my first piece of luck.

I was afraid Clytie would ask where I had found it. I didn't want to tell her. I didn't want to talk about it to anyone, not even Clytie, until I had thought more clearly and calmly about it.

In due course Ralph was carried off by Sheba. I warned him once more about touching the eye and he promised not to.

Then I said I would go back home so that I should be there before dark.

Clytie agreed. One must go through the woods in daylight.

I started out and I was soon deep in thought. I assembled the facts. It was Cobbler whom I had seen under the bushes. I must have been watched when I threw the scent away and assuming that I might come to look for it, whoever was trying to persecute me had put Cobbler there. The thing I had seen on my bed was the toy which in the dim light would look like the real thing. Nobody in his right mind would investigate too closely with such a creature so it was the easiest thing in the world to pass off the lifelike toy for the real thing. Someone had put it there and hastily taken it away after I had seen it. But in the process the eye had come off and lay on my bedroom floor.

Oh, what incredible good fortune! Fate was on my side at last. The one who had rapped on my door and opened it was the one who had put the cobra on my bed. The object, of course, was to make me think I was suffering from delusions.

An old proverb flashed into my mind. 'Those whom the gods wish to destroy they first make mad.'

Oh, how I thanked God for Cobbler's eye!

Now I was my old self again. I was gloriously strong and I was going to get to the bottom of this. I was going to find out who had done these things to me and what the motive was behind them.

I stopped short. Here I was in the heart of the woods. And someone was following me.

For a moment I was overcome by a terrible fear. Then my newly found confidence came back to me. I was not going to run away. I had made one discovery, I would make another.

I stood very still and listened. There was silence all around me. The sun was low in the sky. Soon it would drop below the horizon and darkness would descend.

But I was no longer afraid because this afternoon I had learned that my mind was as lucid as it had ever been and that it was not my weakness which was destroying me, but some human being who was attempting to.

I made a decision. The position was changed. *I* would now be the pursuer. I would find out who followed me in the woods. And when I discovered that I would have the answer to everything.

I started walking in the direction from which I had come. Then I paused to listen.

There was no doubt. I *had* turned the tables. Someone was running away from *me*!

Relentlessly I pursued. On and on I went. I was almost back at the edge of the woods before I realized that I had lost the scent.

I stood listening. There was no sound to guide me. I waited for a while and then I started to walk home.

I had not discovered who my enemy was, but this was triumph all the same. I was not mad. I was myself.

They must have noticed the change in me. I had lost a certain hunted look. I was clear-eyed and the fresh colour was coming back into my cheeks.

I realized now how frightened I had been. I suppose there is nothing so alarming as the thought of losing control of one's mind; and that was what I had feared.

I kept thinking of that proverb.

Someone wanted to destroy me!

Who?

When I went to my room in the heat of the day I would consider everything . . . and everyone. No one must be excluded . . . not even Clytie.

What could the motive be? Someone wanted to make it appear that I was mad so that when tragedy happened there would be a reason for it.

'She was mad,' they would say. 'Remember how she has been behaving for a long time.'

My thoughts must go to Anula. Leila could have done all the things which had been happening. Anula had control of Leila as she had of the rest of the family. Nankeen, Ashraf. They would do as Anula bade them. She had come into the open when she had given me the peacock-feather fan. Oh yes, I could see how horrified she must have been when I arrived. She wished me ill.

She wanted to marry Clinton, to live with him as the reigning Queen. I was an obstruction. The devious method made me think first of Anula.

And Clinton? Was it possible that he knew of her plans? What had happened hardly seemed his way. The slow devious methods required to convince a completely sane woman that she was mad was not the sort of thing he would think of. He would make up his mind and want to act promptly. Yet, when he wanted something he was determined to get it. And he would plan in advance. The manner he had set the stage for that night in Parrot Cottage had proved that. He had wanted to marry me because he knew that I was going to inherit the plantation.

Clytie? Nonsense. Not my gentle sister to whom I had felt drawn the moment I saw her. Yet, if I died she would inherit the plantation and it had been after that visit to the solicitor in Kandy that these strange things began to happen.

These were wild thoughts. How could Clytie have put the cobra on my bed? Unless one of the dark-eyed servants who waited on and watched us was a spy in the household working against me.

I was surrounded by intrigue but I was now looking it clearly in the face. It was no use trying to pretend I was not in danger.

I was. All I had to do now was to find out from which direction it was coming.

Nothing had happened since the return of Cobbler's eye and my turn to the offensive in the woods.

Naturally not. My pursuer had been warned.

I must watch constantly. But how relieved I felt.

THE ASHINGTON PEARLS

*

Clinton was looking forward to our trip. He had said he always wanted to show me the pearl fisheries and this was the time to go.

Leila had made up my silks and I was delighted with them.

Clinton was in an affectionate mood when we set out. He was so eager to show me his possessions that he was almost boyish and reminded me a little of Ralph with a new toy which he was adding to his menagerie.

He seemed so delighted to be travelling with me that I could laugh at the suspicions which had been in my mind over the last days. I felt my spirits rising as we boarded the train which would take us part of the way and Clinton pointed out the beauties of the country to me. He grew quite lyrical, which surprised me, and I felt I was discovering a new Clinton. I was happier than I had been for a long time.

We should be away for two or three weeks and when I returned I promised myself I should find a letter from Toby awaiting me. I had written to him before I left explaining about the cobra's eye and I myself had posted the letter. I was eager to know what he would think of all this and what his advice would be.

That I could write to him what I could tell no one near me pointed to the fact that I felt a necessity to keep my counsel and suspect everyone.

The weather was hot and steamy. We were approaching the hottest time of the year before the summer monsoon came to drench the land and provide the tea with that which was essential to its growth.

We passed jungle where the trees grew thick together – evergreens, tree ferns, palms and tufted bamboos. The flowers gave a colourful touch to the landscape – rhododendrons bloomed majestically and orchids of all descriptions flourished there.

We saw the forest of timber – the calamander, satin-wood and ebony. It was an enthralling sight to watch the elephants emerge from the forest pulling their loads or bathing in the rivers as we passed.

When we left the railway we travelled north by road.

Clinton was delighted by my pleasure and I could see that he was really excited about showing me the pearl fisheries – that was the real treat which was to be kept until the last.

He sat back watching me in the carriage which carried us northwards, his arms folded, a smile of complacency on his face.

'Do you know,' he said, 'that some of the most famous pearls in the world come from Ceylon? Of course you did. Didn't the Ashington Pearls come from here?'

'I wonder where they are now?' I said.

He shrugged his shoulders. 'They say there are as good fish in the sea as ever came out. Let us hope that there are as good pearls in oysters as those we already have. I shall enjoy showing you the fisheries, Sarah. I'm glad you came with me. You're looking better than you have for some time.'

'Thank you.'

'Getting over those jungle nerves.'

'I don't think I ever had them.'

'Oh come, you were getting a bit nervous . . . imagining things.'

I flushed slightly. 'Perhaps it wasn't imagination.'

'Oh?'

I looked away across the country.

'Secrets?' he said. He was watching me intently.

I had not meant to speak of it but he had always had an uncanny habit of reading my thoughts.

'Secrets, no. I don't think so. I suppose there are people here who are wishing I had not come.'

'I can tell you of one who is very glad you did.'

'Is that so?'

'He's sitting opposite you at this moment,' he said and leaning forward kissed the tip of my nose.

I said: 'I fancy your mistress, Anula, is not so happy to see me here.'

'Rather naturally she wouldn't be.'

'I hope that relationship is at an end, Clinton,' I said.

'I really do believe you are jealous. I'm gratified.'

'Not jealous. Only curious. She is a very strange woman. She would have all sorts of means of . . .'

He was waiting but I said: 'Oh, it doesn't matter.'

'But it does matter,' he insisted. 'I'm interested. "All sorts of means . . . ?"' he prompted me.

'Well,' I floundered. 'If these people don't like someone . . . if they don't want them here . . . they could attempt to get rid of them.'

'That imagination of yours does run away with you. You are as bad as young Ralph. Anula understands perfectly.'

'That it is all over between you and her?'

'My dear Sarah, you are my beloved wife. It is up to you to see that you share me with no one.'

'You seem to regard yourself as some sort of prize.'

'Don't you? As a matter of fact that's a rhetorical question. I know the answer. Dear Sarah, you have told it to me a hundred times.'

I felt impatient and angry. I thought: He is cynical and arrogant. I could suspect him of anything. I wondered what his reaction would be if he knew I had made over the plantation to Clytie. I could imagine his anger and I found it impossible to meet his eyes.

I suddenly thought of Toby. He would be so concerned for me. He would advise me as he used to in the old days. I was very thankful for his existence and the good fortune which had brought him back into my life.

Clinton was watching me closely.

'You look as if you are harbouring some secret which you find rather pleasant,' he said.

I did not answer and he did not press me to explain. Instead he started to give me some idea of what I was going to see.

'If you understand what it's all about,' he said, 'you'll find it so much more interesting. Nature is wonderful, Sarah. Just imagine. Some foreign substance is formed in the shell of the oyster. It becomes an irritation and the oyster is provided with a sort of secretion with which it can cover the troublesome object so that it becomes encysted, and this happens to be the lustrous substance which we call "pearl". You'll see my divers at work. They are skilled men. They have learned which are the most likely oysters to contain a good pearl. It's strange, but those which are irregular in shape and have been attacked by parasites are the most likely to carry what we are looking for.'

'It sounds absorbing. These men risk their lives, I know. I wonder why they do it.'

'They dive for only a few weeks in the year and earn a good deal of money. I don't think they would want to do anything else. It's not a bad thing to live dangerously now and then. Don't you agree?'

'If the danger meant facing death . . .'

'It would hardly be danger if it did not carry some risk. Wouldn't you rather enjoy a life of adventure than live quietly knowing exactly what every day was going to be like?'

'It might depend on the danger.'

'Ah, my Sarah is growing cautious.'

'Tell me more about the fisheries.'

'You'll see for yourself. I want to show you some of the fine pearls we shall bring up. They are sorted and matched and prepared for sale. I have several places throughout Ceylon where these pearls are made into jewellery combined with emeralds, sapphires and rubies. I shall have something interesting to show you. I might even present you with some beautiful jewellery. How will you like that, Sarah?'

'Thank you,' I said.

'We shall stay near the coast. I have a place there . . . small but adequate for the short time I spend in it.'

'You are constantly revealing your possessions to me.'

'It's a good way of doing it. If I showed you everything at once you would not be nearly so impressed.'

He came and sat beside me and put an arm about me.

'Dear Sarah, I am so looking forward to showing you my pearls.'

He seemed to be laughing to himself as though he were nursing some secret which pleased him.

It had been an extraordinary day. We had arrived at his house in the morning. It was in a beautiful spot on a palm-fringed shore. From this spot the pearl fishers set out to the oyster beds, which were about six miles from the shore.

Surrounding the house was a garden full of flowers and shrubs. There was a drawing-room, a small dining-room and a study. A short staircase led up to the bedroom above. It was a double room and I wondered whom he had brought with him when he visited this place in the past.

There was a dressing-table with candles in brass candlesticks, and the place seemed to be fitted out for a woman to share. I pictured Anula sitting at that dressing-table.

The bed was large and there were the usual draperies – the inevitable mosquito net.

There were several servants who had their own quarters attached to the house and I imagined it was always kept in readiness in case Clinton should decide to visit. I gathered that he was usually here at this time of the year when, as he would put it, the harvest was safely gathered in.

I was enormously interested in everything and he was delighted to show me. He took an immense pleasure in his success. I had noticed this before. It was a boyish quality in him which because it ill fitted that supreme masculine arrogance was in a way appealing.

'Look at this!' he would say, his eyes gleaming. And when he talked of something in which he was interested his enthusiasm was infectious.

The boats and the houses in which they were kept were scattered along the coast, but the palm-trees hid them from view so that they did not spoil the landscape. I learned from Clinton that although the actual fishing lasted for four or six weeks the sorting, valuing and marketing was a full-time job.

'I am going to take you to see the fleet set out,' Clinton told me. 'It's an impressive sight. They leave about midnight so as to reach the oyster beds at sunrise. You had better rest this afternoon.'

I told him I had no need of rest.

'I shall insist. You mustn't be sleepy. I want you to see this.'

'I assure you I shall not be sleepy. I'm so very interested.'

'It's fun, having you with me, Sarah. It's one thing I like about you. You're so interested in everything that goes on.'

'I'm glad there is one thing that pleases you!'

'There are others . . . as you well know. But more of that later.'

It was an interesting day and one I was to remember for a long time.

During it I learned something about pearls and I saw a great many of them being sorted into various categories. Clinton introduced me with a certain pride, which I found gratifying. I think the matter of Cobbler's eye had done me so much good that I was in better health and spirits than I had been for a long time. I saw beautiful pearls with what I learned was called perfect 'skin' and fine 'orient' which meant that they were what would be recognized as the highest quality. In addition to their delicate sheen, their clear translucent colour and their iridescent sheen they must be a complete sphere. Colour, sheen, shape decided the value of the pearl, Clinton pointed out to me, and I could imagine the excitement there must be when the shells were examined for what they would reveal. There were blister pearls, hollow and irregular, and there was another kind afflicted with tiny knobs which was called *coq de perle*; there were baroque pearls, beautiful but irregular in shape; and what everyone hoped for was the perfect sphere, beautiful skin and colour – that would indeed be a pearl of great price.

We dined late and I could see an inner excitement rising in Clinton. He was longing to show me the departure of the fishing fleet.

I wrapped a light coat about me and we went out into the night. It was a beautiful scene, the moon shining on the water, the boats ready to set out.

They were to leave at midnight and by sunrise they would be at the oyster beds. In each boat were ten divers. They would descend naked, Clinton told me. 'It makes movement easier,' he added.

'What of sharks?' I asked.

'That's the risk. But each man will have his ironwood spikes, and there are the two shark charmers. One will go in the boat and the other will stay on the shore. They will sing incantations throughout the operation. None of these men would go without them. They are therefore a necessary part of the operation.'

He explained to me how the divers worked in pairs – one man diving while the other watched the cord on which he was let down. The length of time a man could stay under water was naturally limited even with these skilled men. Fifty seconds was the average time, although some managed eighty; and there had been one man who had distinguished himself by staying under for six minutes. But Clinton did not encourage such competition. Each man must stay according to his ability to do so. These men took enough risks as it was.

We stood on the shore watching the boats slip away. It was a moving sight with the moonlight on the water and the faint rustle of the palms about us.

'You'll bring them luck, I'm sure,' said Clinton. 'Tomorrow we'll have a haul of the finest pearls.'

We walked back to the house.

A servant appeared to see if there was anything we needed.

Clinton dismissed him and we went up the staircase to the bedroom.

Clinton made me sit at the dressing-table.

'Your first night here, Sarah. Do you like it?'

'I found it very interesting,' I replied. 'I wonder where the boats are now.'

'Not very far out to sea. It'll be sunrise before they reach the beds. You shall come down with me when they return.'

He was standing behind me and I watched his reflection in the mirror. He looked secretive and there was a strange light in his eyes.

I turned sharply to look at him. He said: 'I promised you a present, didn't I? You have seen some magnificent pearls today, Sarah. I think you would now be quite a judge. You know something about the skin and the orient of our best pearls, eh?'

He had turned away and opened a cupboard. Inside was a safe. I watched him work the combination and the door opened.

He had taken out a case and as he touched the spring it flew open.

I stared. There were two ropes of pearls which I could see were of the finest quality. Their clasp was of diamonds. It represented a coiled serpent with an emerald eye.

I looked at him in amazement.

'It's . . .'

He took the necklace out of the case and held it before me. Then he swung me round and said: 'Come on, try it on. They say it transforms a woman.'

'It's remarkably like . . .'

He had pushed me into the chair, turned me towards the glass and fastened the necklace about my neck. I was deeply conscious of the touch of the pearls on my skin. I was staring at my reflection. My face had turned very pale.

I said: 'They are a replica . . .'

'A replica!' he cried. 'Do you think I would give my wife anything but the real thing?'

I put my hand up to my throat. I saw my lips move. I heard

myself whisper: 'It can't be. It's impossible.'

'They become you, Sarah. I doubt they ever became any of the Ashington ladies as they become you.'

'I don't understand.'

'Don't you? I should have thought you would have known the family pearls when you saw them.'

'But how . . .'

'I can see that you are making a few simple deductions.'

I swung round to face him. 'It was you then. You . . . who stole them.'

'Oh come, come. It was fair exchange, I promise you.'

'You kidnapped the boy! *You* demanded the pearls as ransom. I might have known.'

'Might you? What sort of opinion do you have of me?'

'Only that which you yourself have given me. I don't want these things. I shall give them back to Clytie.'

'You will do no such thing. They are mine.'

'I thought you had given them to me.'

'You know the Ashington women only have them on lease. They will go to our son whose wife will wear them for a while. You know how it goes . . .'

I wanted to shut out the sight of him. I kept thinking of Clytie's anxious face and how we had sat through that night of anguish and talked and talked, how we had trembled with fear to contemplate what might be happening to Ralph and all the time he – Clinton – was the one. He had planned it all to get the Ashington Pearls. Oh, I was sure they would bring misery to everyone who possessed them.

I gripped them. I wanted to tear them off my neck. I felt as though they were choking me.

'You are a devil,' I said.

He laughed at me. 'And that's why you like me?' he retorted.

'I shall despise you for ever . . . after this.'

'But you will find me irresistible . . . as you always did.'

I tried to undo the clasp.

'It has a special catch,' he told me. 'But I want you to wear them for a while.'

'I shall never wear them,' I said flatly. 'People will know. They will know you for the thief you are.'

'I was going to say,' he went on, 'that I want you to wear them when we are alone. I like to see you in them, Sarah. I always wanted to. Don't you feel they belong to you? Pearls were not meant to be shut away in cases. They were meant to be worn. You will wear them for me, Sarah, when we are alone.'

I was silent, thinking: I will take them back to Clytie. They are hers.

I turned on him suddenly. 'You wanted everything, didn't you?'

'I always want everything,' he answered.

'Life is not like that.'

'Forgive the contradiction but life is just like that. If you want something you go out and get it. It's very likely that you will be successful.'

'You haven't got everything, you know. You married me for the plantation, didn't you?'

'I married you because I had to have you.'

'Because of the plantation.'

'A bonus, my dear Sarah. You are getting angry. You're hating me as you never did before. That's wonderful. I love it when you hate me . . . when you respond to me because you can't resist . . . even hating as you do. I've been looking forward to this moment. I knew exactly how you would behave and I was right. I'm right in every detail. I want you as much as I ever did at first. No, more. Sarah, what times we have together!'

I said: 'I shall not stay here with a thief who is capable of inflicting such anguish on a mother for the sake of a few paltry pearls.'

'Paltry pearls! I wonder the gods of Kandy don't strike you down. Paltry pearls! The necklace of legend, which was given to a long-ago Ashington in payment for a child's life, a necklace which has come down through the ages to be cherished and the very foundation of Ashington tradition.'

'Be silent!' I cried. 'I don't want to hear any more. Take these things off my neck. Put them in their box. I am going to give them back to Clytie.'

'You don't think I acquired them for that, do you? They are yours, Sarah, and you are my wife, and when I say you shall wear them, you shall wear them.'

I faced him. I could feel the pearls on my neck. Their touch affected me strangely. It was almost as though they were living things creeping tighter and tighter round my neck.

If he were capable of doing this he was capable of anything. He could have been the one who was trying to make me believe I was going mad.

But why? He would have his motive. There would always be a strong motive with him.

I said to him: 'You don't always win, you know. You thought the plantation was yours, didn't you?' Then suddenly an idea flashed into my mind. If I were weak-minded he could have taken over the plantation. Was that what he was working for? 'It is not yours, Clinton. It never will be. It is mine and when I die it will go to Clytie.'

I could see he was puzzled.

'Yes,' I went on. 'It's true. I went to a solicitor. I've arranged it. If I were to die or be unable to manage the plantation, it would go to Clytie.'

'You . . . did that!'

'I have a will of my own, you know.'

'You little . . . devil!'

'Ah,' I said, 'I see your opinion of me matches mine of you. But I will tell you this: Everything *I* have done is within the law. I wonder what Sir William Carstairs would say if he knew that you had kidnapped Ralph and bargained for his release. I consider that the lowest form of crime – particularly where a child is concerned.'

He did not seem to hear me. He was clearly deeply shocked by what I had done. I thought he was going to strike me. There was no mistaking the cold fury in his face. He stood watching me for a few seconds. I believe he was finding it hard to control his anger. Then he smiled slowly and I fancied there was a grudging admiration in that smile.

'Time for bed,' he said. 'It has been an exciting day.'

'Take these things off. Undo the clasp.'

'I want you to wear them.'

'I want them off.'

'An ungracious way to receive a gift.'

'These pearls are not yours to give.'

'I won them.'

'Take them off.'

'No.'

'I am going to another room.'

'You are going to stay here. You're going to give that special brand of love and hate which I am beginning to feel I can't do without. You've bewitched me, Sarah. You have just told me how you have deceived me. I should beat you. That's what you need, you know. But here I am just ready to love you because you are my own magnificent Sarah who in her heart wants me, in spite of my sins, as much as I want her in spite of hers.'

'You deceive yourself . . . as you have deceived others.'

'Others maybe . . . never myself. I know you, Sarah. Sensuous, passionate Sarah, who was made for love . . . my love, that is. No one else but me, Sarah . . . ever.'

'Will you please undo this clasp?'

'Let me undo your gown instead.'

'Don't dare touch me.'

'You could not have given me a more enticing invitation.' He had pulled at my bodice and the buttons gave way. I was conscious of his great physical strength. I was no stranger to that. It would not matter now how I resisted him; he would win in the end.

It was what he wanted. My reluctance was his titillation. He was laughing at me, determined to subdue me as he had on other occasions. And he was going to make me wear the necklace.

I fought him . . . desperately, which only seemed to amuse him. 'Shout if you like, Sarah,' he muttered. 'They'll take no notice. They would say it is the master's matter and smile sagely together.'

'How many women have you brought here?'

'I don't keep a record.'

'How many of them have stolen jewels bestowed on them?'

He laughed. 'Those pearls were won, Sarah. I have put them where they belong. You are going to wear them for me.'

'Let me go,' I demanded.

'I'll never let you go.'

'I hate you. I hate everything you stand for. Don't you see that what you did to gain those pearls will make me hate you for ever?'

'I'd rather have your hate than anyone else's love.'

'I mean this, Clinton. I do not want you.'

'Then it will be a new experience for you.'

'This is . . . rape!'

'Piquant situation, I must agree,' he mocked.

I could not hold him off. I was exhausted with the fight; and when I heard his triumphant laugh I hated myself as well as him.

I lay still, sleepless. I thought: Will this night never end? I was lying there beside him and I was still wearing the pearls.

I will leave him, I thought. I cannot stay now.

I thought of Toby. Toby would help me. I would get away. I would take the pearls back to Clytie and I would go to Delhi. Yes, that was the answer. I would ask Toby to help me.

Suddenly I knew that he was awake. His hand curled about mine. I lay still, feigning sleep. I was deeply conscious of the feel of the pearls on my skin.

'Sarah?' he said quietly. 'You're awake, Sarah?'

I did not answer.

He went on: 'I have to tell you something.'

'There's nothing I want to hear from you.'

His hand moved up until it came to the pearls.

'I didn't kidnap the boy, Sarah,' he said.

I was silent.

'You don't believe me, do you?'

'No,' I answered.

'I'll tell you what happened.'

'I don't want to hear the loathsome details.'

'They aren't quite what you think.'

'Spare me.'

'When have I ever spared you?' He leaned towards me and kissed my lips.

'I am very tired,' I said.

'Actually you are wide awake and whether you like it or not I am going to tell you. I've had the pearls for some time. I had them before your father died.'

'What nonsense! I saw them before you stole them. Clytie showed them to me.'

'What Clytie showed you was not the Ashington Pearls.'

'I saw them with my own eyes.'

'What you saw was a replica of the Ashington Pearls.'

I moved impatiently away from him.

'Dear Sarah, you wouldn't know the difference. How could you? They are a work of art . . . that replica. I know. I had them made myself.'

'I suppose you have worked out this explanation because you are afraid of what action I might take.'

That made him laugh. 'When have I ever been afraid of you!'

'You are now. You have betrayed yourself and you are wondering what the outcome will be.'

'Don't you think I would have considered that before I showed you the pearls? Be sensible, Sarah. Listen to me. Some time before your father died, Clytie and Seth came to me in great distress. They were in financial difficulties. Your father did not know about this. He was a very sick man for more than a year before he went to England. He left the management of the plantation entirely to Seth. Seth has his weaknesses – one of which is a compulsion to gamble. He was in dire difficulties. He had borrowed on the prospect of the plantation's coming to him through Clytie. He was in desperate need of money. Neither he nor Clytie wanted your father to know that they had been borrowing money in his name . . . the name of the plantation, that was. Are you listening, Sarah?'

'Yes,' I said faintly.

'The outcome was that they needed a great deal of money if they were going to be saved from disaster. They came to me.'

'Are you telling me that you *bought* the necklace from them?'

'I am telling you exactly what I did. I knew I was going to marry you . . .'

'Before you had seen me!'

'I had heard so much about you. I was in love with you before I saw you. You turned out to be even more desirable than my imaginings. That was just my good fortune.'

'Go on,' I said. 'Tell me the rest.'

'As you guessed, I bought the necklace. Oh, for far less than its value, of course. After all, no one knows what that is. It is beyond price. And with the purchase money I gave a necklace which was – to inexpert eyes – an exact replica of the real thing. I kept the pearls for you, Sarah. I knew it wouldn't be easy to explain so I kept them locked away, but I have noticed lately that the orient has deteriorated a little. It needs the warmth of your skin to bring back its lustre. The famous pearls must not suffer because of Seth's irresponsibility.'

'So . . . according to you it was a replica Clytie showed me.'

'It was.'

'And that was what she gave to the kidnappers.'

'My dear, sweet Sarah! Don't you see what happened? Clytie wore the replica for your welcome ball. It always creates a sensation. I heard Reggie Glendenning talking about it and asking for a closer inspection. He's something of a connoisseur. Clytie was terrified. It's all very well to bring out the false Ashingtons and display them on her neck in candlelight, but good as they are they could not stand up to the daylight scrutiny of an expert.'

'Are you telling me that the kidnapping was arranged?'

'Of course.'

'I don't believe it.'

'Why not? Didn't it all happen rather too easily? Ashraf was an accomplice. Sheba was in it. She'd do anything for Clytie. You can picture what happened. You were all at the festival. Ashraf creeps up and chooses his moment. Ralph went off with him readily and the boy was taken for the night to people he knew. He would suffer little inconvenience from the adventure. The false pearls are supposed to be handed over. It wouldn't surprise me if Clytie still has them.'

I was stunned. Clytie, who seemed so fragile, so feminine, so frank, to have planned the kidnapping, to have feigned that grief which had upset me so!

Clinton knew what I was thinking. 'Clytie is a good and lovely wife,' he said. 'She would stand by Seth no matter what he did. Seth's gambling habits had brought them to this and she did everything she could to save him. At the same time no one must know that she had sold the necklace. In fact I don't think she has the authority to do it. But ever since I saw it my fingers were itching to get hold of it. After all, when a man who works with pearls and knows pearls is brought face to face with what must be the finest specimens in the world he longs to possess them. You understand that, Sarah?'

'I understand your motives perfectly.'

'And you don't despise me now. You only hate me?'

'I shall need to verify all this.'

'Good heavens! Are you suggesting that I add lying to my many sins?'

'I would be prepared for anything from you!'

'Sarah, dearest Sarah, I am so glad you have the necklace now. You are going to wear it when we are alone. I think we had better keep it that way for a while. Then we will think of some way of making it known that I have paid a great price to a fence and it now belongs to you. You are an Ashington. Our son's wife will wear it in due course. The gods are satisfied, I am sure. All you have to do now is produce the son. You have been rather remiss, Sarah. I should have thought you might have done that by now. Never mind, there is time. And I will tell you this: no man could be more content with his marriage than I am with mine. It mustn't change, Sarah. Never let it change.'

I did not answer him. I was thinking of all he had told me, of Clytie's deception, of that dreadful night when we had sat side by side and I had sought in vain to comfort her. And all the time she had been acting a part!

Whom can I ever trust again? I asked myself.

Then I thought of living out my life with Clinton, of bearing children; and I wondered what it would be like when this wild physical passion, which I had to admit existed between us, was finished – for by its very nature it must end. One could not build a future on such a flimsy structure. It was like building a house on shifting sands. One needed the solid rock of friendship, love, trust . . .

Now I was thinking of Toby. There would be a letter waiting for me when I returned.

At last I slept and I dreamed that hands were about my neck strangling me. They were soft hands, lustrous hands; they had begun by caressing me, soothing me and then suddenly they pressed closer and closer. I could not breathe. I started up in terror. My hands went to my throat. I was touching the pearls.

Of course it was the pearls which had made me dream.

What nonsense to have made me wear them as I slept. But I saw his point and it was characteristic of him. He had wanted me to wear the pearls because he had known that I hated to. He had made me wear them while he had taken me against my will. They were a symbol of his power over me . . . a halter that is put about the neck of a slave.

No, I was romancing. He had enjoyed first making me aware of his outrageous villainy and proving to me that even then he was irresistible to me. That had been his object in deluding me into thinking he had kidnapped the boy. Then afterwards, having proved to me that he could arouse me to passion no matter how I despised him, he had told me the truth.

It was a sort of war between us; and war is not the way to build up a happy family life.

How different it would have been if Toby had come back

earlier, before Clinton and my father had arrived. Then we should have carried on that unique relationship which had been ours in Denton Square.

He had come too late. That was the essence of my future.

Clinton was in high spirits. Each evening while we were away I had worn the pearls. He had insisted and I had to confess that they held a certain fascination for me.

Since my dream about them it had seemed to me that they had a certain life of their own. I used to wonder about all the people who had worn them before me. There were those in the gallery at the Grange and even before that the wives of the powerful men of Kandy.

My mother had said they were unlucky. The artist who had painted her in them had killed himself; Clytie had got into difficulties, had sold them and gone to the length of staging a kidnapping of her own son in order to deceive people into thinking they had been stolen.

Pearls which had meant so much to so many people must have a life of their own.

I often studied the intricate clasp which I found difficult to do up and take off which Clinton said was right since it was a safety-catch and should not come undone easily.

The green eye of the serpent flashed with what seemed like malevolence. I examined the little receptacle inside which poison had been placed by one of the owners who wanted to get rid of his wife. I believed it was possible that he could have done it.

If those pearls could speak what tales they would have to tell!

They were regaining their lustre. Clinton said they were becoming sleek and satisfied as though they drew some nourishment from the people who wore them.

'You have the neck for pearls,' he said. 'They obviously like you. Look at the skin of those pearls! Look at the orient! Can you see the difference since you started to wear them? I have pictured you in them so often, Sarah. It gives me great pleasure to see you wearing them.'

He liked to fasten them on my neck himself, to hold them and examine them as I wore them. There was a gleam in his eyes when he did this as though something he had wanted for a long time had come to pass.

I had seen the pearl fishers come back with their prizes; I had watched the opening of the oysters and marvelled at what I saw inside the shells. I had gently touched the layers of mother of pearl; and I had seen those excrescences which were of such beauty and value.

I had watched the sorting of the pearls. I had caught the enthusiasm. And when the season was over we returned to the plantation.

I was very disappointed to learn that there was no letter from Toby awaiting me. There was one from Aunt Martha which I read rather impatiently. All seemed the same as ever at the Grange. Mabel had had two colds during the winter but Aunt Martha was her usual hale and hearty self. I could never think of Aunt Martha without seeing her creeping along the corridor to my mother's bedroom and helping her to her death.

The day after my return I drove the dog-cart over to Ashingtons. Celia was there with Clytie and I knew she would now come back with me.

They were in the garden with Ralph who gave me an exuberant welcome. When I looked at my beautiful, dainty half-sister I simply could not believe that she had been in the plot to kidnap Ralph. I longed to be alone with her so that I could ask her outright whether what Clinton had told me was true.

The opportunity came during the morning. She had gone to her room and I followed her there.

'Clytie,' I said, 'I have to speak to you.'

She looked very startled and I went on quickly: 'Clinton has given me the pearls. He says they are the Ashington Pearls and that he bought them from you.'

She put her hand to the dressing-table as though to steady herself and then sat down.

'It's true then?' I persisted.

She nodded. 'Oh Sarah, I was so worried. You see, we were in such difficulties. We could never have told our father. He wouldn't have understood. Seth . . .'

'Seth had been gambling in the Kandy Club, hadn't he?'

She nodded. 'That and other things. We did not know what to do. He had borrowed on my expectations from the plantation. This sounds horrible but everyone knew how sick our father was. It seemed certain that one day Seth and I would inherit. Oh Sarah, do please try to understand.'

'I do,' I said. 'You were in difficulties and Clinton came along. He gave you a price for the necklace and a replica of the original so that you need not let it be known that you had sold it.'

She nodded. 'It would have worked. Our father's eyesight was failing. He could hardly see at all, you know. He wouldn't have been able to detect it . . . Oh, I know it was wrong. It was not mine to sell really. I was so relieved when it was left to me. I felt that made it better.'

'I can understand all you did, Clytie,' I said. 'I should probably have done the same in your place. Clinton should never have suggested it.'

'It seemed a solution. It was the only solution.'

'And so the necklace which was placed under the tree was the replica.'

She hung her head and said quietly: 'I have it here. It was brought back. I have hidden it away. Sheba helped. She would do anything for me. I had to do it, Sarah. I should have been discovered. Reggie Glendenning would have seen at once. I hated wearing it. I was always terrified when I did. I was afraid someone would detect the fraud. Some of the people here know a great deal about pearls.'

'It was an ingenious plan, Clytie.'

'It was easy really. I knew no harm would come to Ralph. We arranged it so that he went off with Ashraf and he stayed the night with some of Sheba's relations. He had been there before for the night. We made him used to it. He didn't think there was anything unusual about it. He had no idea what we were doing. So you have the necklace now. I guessed Clinton would give it to you. It has worked out as it should really. You have the necklace and the plantation but you have said that in time it shall come to us ... for Ralph. I think that was how it should have been, although as the elder the necklace would come to me. But look at us, Sarah. You are the one who should have the Ashington Pearls. They must look fine on you. It is fate working out. That's how I see it.'

'I shall never be able to wear them in public ... even if I wanted to.'

'They would be recognized, of course. But you will wear them sometimes. I used to slip them on when I was alone. They seemed to weigh me down. It was too big for me, that necklace.'

'I'm glad I know the truth about it at last.'

'Sarah, I'm sorry. Please understand why I did it.'

'Of course I do.'

'And now you have it. It's worth a fortune.'

'Clinton did not give you what it was worth, I know.'

'He gave us enough to pay our debts and something to help us along for the years to come. It was wonderful to have that burden lifted. We are grateful to Clinton, Sarah. And then he gave us this replica which is so good a copy that only experts can tell the difference. It's all there, even the clasp and the miniature poison container in the serpent's mouth.'

'Clytie,' I said, 'you look disturbed. You must compose yourself. We don't want anyone to know that you have been upset.'

She put her arms around me. 'Oh Sarah,' she said. 'I'm so glad you know about this. It's been such a burden to me.'

I kissed her. 'I understand everything,' I assured her. 'Dear Clytie, please don't fret any more. Everything will be all right. You'll see.'

When we rejoined Celia she was with Ralph and I was a little startled to see Cobbler curled up at their feet.

Celia looked from me to Clytie and I wondered whether she guessed that we were emerging from an emotional scene.

As we rode back in the dog-cart, she said to me: 'I shall be sorry to leave here, but I have heard from my cousin. She is not very well and wants me to join her. She has taken a house in the South of France.'

'Oh Celia, must you go?'

'It has been wonderful to see you again, Sarah, and you seem so much better now. There was a time . . . a little while ago . . .'

'Yes, I know.'

'You did seem a little . . . strange . . . distraught . . . as though you were frightened of something.'

I hesitated. The sight of Cobbler lying on the grass had brought back vivid memories. I did not want to talk about them. Coming back to the plantation had brought a strong reminder of all that had happened and the remembrance that someone had been playing tricks on me.

Now that I was back I was going to find out who, and one of the conditions I had imposed on myself was not to take anyone into my confidence about this . . . not even Celia.

I said lightly: 'Oh, I think I was a little run down. The trip to the pearl fisheries has done me good.'

THE SERPENT'S TONGUE

*

I often wore the pearls. They exerted a fascination over me. I would take them out of their case and hold them against me and the desire to clasp them round my neck was irresistible.

They were changing. They glowed with a new life. When I laid them against my skin they seemed to caress me. It was almost as though they wanted to belong to me.

They were in my dreams . . . vague, hazy dreams . . . when they crept from their case and put themselves about my neck. Ridiculous dreams they were, but how real they were in my sleep. Once there was recurrence of that which I had had the first night I wore them. Then I thought they crept tighter and tighter round my neck and were trying to strangle me. This fantasy was clearly the result of all the stories I had heard about this heirloom as well as the drama of the mock-kidnapping and that never-to-be-forgotten night when Clinton had given them to me and let me believe the worst possible of him.

The pearls fascinated me; they repelled me too; and I was unable to resist them. I sometimes thought they were symbolic of my relationship with Clinton.

What I could not understand was that there was no letter from Toby. Mine to him had been a plea for help and it seemed that he ignored it. Perhaps he had moved away from the address to which I had sent it and it had failed to reach him. The thought threw me into panic. I had the dream once more. The pearls were round my neck, caressing my skin, taking something from me which enriched them . . . they crept closer and closer. They were strangling me. They had changed. They had become malicious. There was evil in them. I heard my mother's voice coming to me over the emptiness of space. 'They were cursed, those pearls.

They brought evil to everyone who possessed them.' In the dream I caught the pearls and tried to tear them from my neck, to break them, to scatter them, to lose them forever. Then the dream changed. 'Toby,' I called. 'Where are you, Toby? Why don't you come when you know I need you?' Then I saw him. He was there. He unclasped the necklace and I was sobbing with relief in his arms.

I awoke with reluctance from that dream. I wanted to stay in it ... with Toby.

The pearls were in their case; Toby was far away; and I had heard nothing from him.

It was impossible to keep the pearls hidden. I told Clinton it was unwise for me to wear them.

'No,' he said, 'the people in the house think they are just a gift from a doting husband to his adoring wife. After all, I am in the business and the best of what is going would naturally fall into my hands.'

'I would not want people to know I had the Ashington Pearls. I have to think of Clytie.'

'Clytie has shown you that she can take care of herself. The only precaution you will have to take is not to wear them when you are going into the company of experts.'

I took to wearing them in the evening when Clinton, Celia and I dined alone.

Celia greatly admired them. She liked to try them on. I did not tell her, of course, that they were the Ashington Pearls. She must merely think that Clinton had given me a handsome present. Leila used to stand, with her head on one side, and admire them when she was in the bedroom, putting things away or bringing hot water.

'They are beautiful. My sister Anula has some like them,' she told me. 'My sister has much beautiful jewellery.' She looked sly and secretive, implying no doubt that this beautiful jewellery was a gift from her lover.

Celia was making her preparations to leave. She had booked her passage to Bombay and there she would join the big liner, the

Oranda, which would take her back to England. She was to leave Colombo on the smaller vessel, the *Lankarta*, which would take her to Bombay. I felt a faint quiver of uneasiness at the thought of her going. The house would seem lonely without her and I still had to discover whoever it was who was menacing me. The threat was still there even though I did now feel strong and ready to face it.

It was about a week after I had returned from the pearl fisheries. I planned to go over to Clytie in the late afternoon and return before dark. I set out in the dog-cart and I had not been gone for more than a few minutes when I knew something was wrong.

The cart started to zigzag across the road. I pulled at the reins ... and then suddenly in a split second I saw one of the wheels roll on ahead of me. It is amazing how, at such times of stress, so much can appear to happen in so short a time. It really was as though time had slowed down. I knew I was in great danger. I knew that one of the wheels had come off and that I was going to crash, but for a while it was as though everything stopped. Desperately I tried to think what I must do to save myself. Then the horse reared and I felt myself thrown into the air.

Swiftly darkness descended on me.

I was lying in bed. Clinton was there. So was Celia, Leila and one of the other servants. Clinton was seated on one side of the bed, Celia on the other.

'She's coming round.' That was Clinton. 'Sarah ... Sarah ... can you hear me?'

I opened my eyes. My body felt heavy. I tried to remember. Then in my mind's eye I saw the wheel spinning along the road. I shut my eyes and was immediately lost in a haze of nothingness.

It was two days before I regained consciousness. I gathered then that I had had a very serious accident and I could count myself extremely lucky that I was still alive.

It was a simple matter. The wheel of the cart had come off. I had been thrown in the air and had landed on the road. My ankle was broken; I was bruised and battered and had suffered from severe concussion. Clinton had called in two doctors. I had been gravely shaken. The ankle could be set and would probably give no great trouble. What was more serious was the fact that I had been unconscious for so long.

However, it seemed that there was no really serious damage and after a few days I was able to get up, but of course could not leave my bedroom. My ankle was the great affliction. I could hobble about with the aid of a stick, but I was warned by the doctor that I must take the utmost care not to jar it or put it to the ground if I wanted to return to absolute normality.

Clinton was with me a great deal and so was Celia, who was now most distressed at her imminent departure. I was glad of her company. She read to me and it was pleasant to talk to her. I began to dread her going. She was so calm and reasonable and I had begun to feel very uneasy again.

Clinton told me that he had tried to get to the bottom of the matter and he could not understand why the wheel of the dog-cart had come off. The grooms were supposed to keep everything in order and they swore that they had examined all the carriages only a few days before.

'It's a bit of a mystery,' said Clinton. 'Someone was careless, I don't doubt. I wish I could find out how it happened.'

When the post came in, I looked for a letter from Toby. There was none.

Fear crept into my mind insidiously like a fog. It was only mildly perceptible at first and then it was swirling about me, enveloping me with apprehension. I had not solved the mystery of the first phase of the attack on me which was intended to prove me mad. After having discovered Cobbler's eye, which discovery was followed by my visit to the pearl fisheries, I had been lulled into a feeling of false security. I had temporarily forgotten the important fact that somewhere, close to me, was a ruthless enemy.

I *must* find out who that person was and I was hardly in a state to do so. Why had the wheel of the dog-cart come off when I was taking it out? I did take it out frequently. It was more or less looked upon as my vehicle because I used it more than anyone else. Had that 'accident' been arranged? Was my enemy now cursing the fact that I had escaped what had surely been intended to kill me?

I could not walk in the woods now to try to find out who had made a point of stalking me. But I must find out before the tricks started again. I could not know in what form they would come this time. Would there be more attempts to frighten me? Or would they take on a more sinister aspect? Had it really been an accident in the dog-cart? Or was this all part of the diabolical scheme? If it was so, one thing was certain. Whoever it was would try again.

Clinton had become almost tender towards me. He had been very angry about the faulty wheel and had blamed them in the stables. They greatly feared his wrath and protested their innocence with passion. He was with me a great deal and insisted on carrying me from my chair to my bed each night, although I could manage to get across the room with the aid of my stick.

Clytie brought Ralph over to see me. Leila fussed round me shaking her head and talking – perhaps too volubly – about the carelessness of those in the stable.

I would sit at the mirror and she would do my hair for me. She told me that her sister Anula had taught her how to make a lady look beautiful and had at times allowed her to serve her in this capacity. I asked how Anula was.

'Anula in good spirits, missee. Anula see the future and it is good for her.'

'That pleases her, I dare say.'

'She is very content.'

'Give her my congratulations on this wonderful future.'

'What they, missee?'

'My pleasure in her good fortune.'

'She like that, missee. She speak of you . . . much.'

'About my accident?'

'She say it was meant. It is sign.'

'Sign of what, Leila?'

'I ask.'

Once I fancied I smelt the faint odour of sandalwood in the room and when Celia came in I asked if she noticed it.

She shook her head.

'It's faint, I admit. But it's there . . . as though someone wearing it had been in the room and it had lingered after her.'

'It's a strange scent,' said Celia. 'But I can't smell it now.'

When Leila came in I asked if she could smell it. She shook her head. 'My sister Anula use it. In her house it is smell . . . smell. Sandalwood here, sandalwood everywhere. It remind me of her.'

When I was alone I kept thinking of it. I imagined I could smell it and when I turned to discover where, it was not there. Just an elusive odour that might have been in the memory.

I warned myself. I must not cultivate an obsession about the smell.

During the siesta hour the house was very quiet. Clinton was usually out for he would go out in the mornings and not return until evening. I would find myself lying on my bed listening to the sounds of the house. I would start suddenly when an insect struck the wire-netting. I would find myself lying tense, listening. I knew then that I was becoming very frightened.

When I heard stealthy footsteps outside my room there was nothing I could do but lie there and wait for something to happen. If someone came into my room, threatened me, there was very little I could do about it. I was a prisoner now as I had not been before.

No one came into the room. I could have fancied I heard the footsteps, fancied I smelt the sandalwood.

Lying there I asked myself many questions and the chief of these were: Who had tried to prove me mad? Who wishes me ill? Who tried to kill me in the dog-cart?

Fear had come back into that room and I was helpless now . . . as I had not been before.

If Toby had written to me, if he had let me feel that he was not far off, if he would come here . . . I could talk to him as I could talk to no one else.

Oh yes, I was afraid, particularly at that time when the sun made its rapid drop below the horizon. I had told Leila that I wanted the lamps lighted before daylight ended.

Once she forgot and I sat there in the darkness and was truly afraid. There was no moon. Nothing to lighten the darkness . . . and then suddenly the opening of the door, the second or so of silence before she came in.

'Why, you're all of the jumps, missee,' she said with a deep chuckle.

And even when she lighted the lamps the fear stayed with me. I thought if someone came into this room to do me harm I should be unable to run for help.

Moreover the days were passing and Celia would soon be leaving. I dreaded the day, for then I should be entirely alone. It occurred to me then that my enemy might be waiting for her departure.

Celia was to leave the following day. Everything was packed and ready to go. I felt very depressed because she was going and more than that . . . afraid.

She had been busy packing all day and sometimes I thought she avoided me because the thought of our parting saddened her as much as it did me, and she was one who hated to show emotion. Leila came in to light the lamps.

'My sister Anula ask for you,' she said. 'I tell her you do not like sandalwood. She say she will make a scent you do like.'

'That's kind of her.'

'My sister Anula so clever. She makes many things . . . scent to make ladies loved . . . water to make skin beautiful . . . drink to make sleep. And she see future too.'

'A very accomplished lady indeed.'

I felt better with the lamps lighted.

Leila left me and almost immediately there was a gentle tap at the door. I started, my heart beating wildly.

'Who's there?' I cried rather shrilly.

The door opened and Celia came in. The smile on her face faded as she looked at me.

'Is anything wrong?' she asked anxiously.

'No . . . no. Why?'

'I thought you looked startled.'

'No. Come and sit down, Celia.'

'How are you this evening?' she asked with obvious concern.

'I'm all right, thank you.'

'I think you find it a little depressing to be confined to your room. I'm sorry I'm going. I wished I hadn't booked my passage. This will be our last evening together.'

'I shall miss you, Celia.' I shuddered, thinking what it would be like without her. She had been such a good companion and had cheered me considerably. The thought which kept going round and round in my head was: And I shall be alone.

Sometimes it was late before Clinton came home. I would be alone in this house, apart from the servants who would always seem alien to me, and the house had become like a prison to me because I could not escape from it. How helpless I should be when Celia was gone!

'I shall be thinking of you. You must write to me, Sarah,' she was saying. 'I'll send an address as soon as I have one. I wish I wasn't going. I *hate* leaving you now. But you'll be able to walk properly soon. What does the doctor say?'

'He has been a little cautious so far. But it's getting better, of course. It's so frustrating not to be able to get about.'

'Clytie comes often though, doesn't she?'

'Oh yes.'

'And I dare say she will come more often when I have gone.'

'I suppose so.'

There had been a slight difference in my relationship with Clytie since I had known about the pearls. I could not forget how distraught she had seemed when she had let me believe that Ralph had been kidnapped. Clytie was a good actress. The horrible thought came into my mind. If I died she and Seth would have the plantation.

I kept remembering Clinton's words: 'Clytie would do a good deal for Seth.'

'Now you mustn't be sad on our last night,' said Celia. 'You'll soon be about again and then you'll feel yourself. You are better, you know, than you were before you went away. Then I began to feel very worried about you. My dear Sarah, you have nothing to worry about. You are very lucky really.'

Her eyes had taken on a wistful look and I thought then that hers had been a rather sad and lonely life. She talked little of the past but I had discovered that she had been devoted to her parents. What was her age now? I wondered. She must be in her late thirties. She was one of the millions of women who were devoted to their parents in the prime of their life and then in the end were left lonely.

I believed, to cheer me up, she asked me to let her have a last look at the pearls. I took them out of their case which I kept in the top drawer of my dressing-table.

She held them in her hands and studied them intently.

'Your husband's gift to you,' she said. 'He must love you dearly. That is a comfort to you. How exquisite these pearls are! Each one matches the other perfectly. The clasp is as unusual as the pearls themselves,' she said. 'What a magnificent stone that emerald is. I saw Leila's sister in the gardens this afternoon. I suppose she was visiting Leila. She was wearing a beautiful necklace of what looked like emeralds. I suppose they weren't really, but they were excellent imitations. She is a beautiful creature . . . graceful like some jungle creature. There is a grace about these people, don't you agree?'

I did agree.

'A strange woman, that one. There are all sorts of rumours about her.'

'What sort of rumours?'

'I don't pay much attention. Leila talks about her often, saying how seductive she is. Men are supposed to threaten to commit murder for her! Poor Leila, she is very proud to be related to such a siren.'

'I think they are a very devoted family.'

'I am sure of it. Are you wearing the pearls tonight?'

'I wasn't intending to.'

'Oh come . . . My last night. I love to see you wearing them. They seem to do something to you. Shall I put them on? The clasp is rather difficult to handle, isn't it?'

'Yes, it is rather.'

She clasped them round my neck and stood back to admire them.

'They are so becoming. Of course they need the most magnificent of ball dresses to set them off. When you go to England, which you will do, of course, if only for a holiday, you must give fantastic balls just for the sake of wearing your pearls.'

I sat back in my chair. Every now and then I caught a glimpse of myself in the mirror. My eyes were on the pearls. I was conscious of them, warm, clinging to my flesh.

As we sat talking, Leila knocked. Nankeen was below. He wished to see me. Would I see him?

I asked that he be brought up.

'Shall I leave?' asked Celia.

'No need at all. He has some message from Clinton, I expect.' Nankeen came in, bowing, smiling, obsequious.

'Message from Sahib, Mem Sahib. He detained tonight. See you tomorrow.'

'Thank you, Nankeen,' I said.

When he went out Celia looked at me anxiously.

'He is often detained in business, as you know,' I said.

She nodded and I wondered if she was thinking of Anula's coming to the gardens that afternoon. For what purpose? Had she seen Clinton then?

'I'm glad you're here tonight, Celia,' I said.

'I shall be gone before this time tomorrow.'

'I'm going to miss you very much.'

'Let's dine in your room together tonight, shall we? We'll talk about old times.'

I said that would be very agreeable.

'I shan't expect you to wear your pearls,' she said. 'Let me take them off for you.'

She did so and put them in the case.

Then she left me and came back later. We spent a pleasant evening, except for the fact that I was wondering whether Clinton was with Anula; and I was almost certain that he was. If I asked him, he would tell me the truth. He was unlike most unfaithful husbands in that.

I will not stay here, I thought. If Anula is in truth his mistress, I will not remain as his wife.

If only I could hear from Toby. Perhaps I should write another letter.

I slept deeply that night. I did have occasional dreams. One was that there was someone in the room, a shadowy figure who went to the dressing-table, opened the drawer and took out the pearls.

I was half awake and thought I heard the door close.

It was nothing . . . only a dream.

In the morning the first thing I did was to go to the drawer. The case was there.

Those pearls are becoming an obsession, I warned myself.

It was unwise really to keep the pearls so easily accessible. We should have put them in a safe. That would, of course, call attention to their value and it must not be known what they actually were for Clytie's sake.

I took my breakfast in bed, which was easier since I had broken my ankle, and when I had eaten I thought again of the dream. I got out of bed and with the aid of my stick went to the dressing-table. I took out the case and opened it. I stared in horror. It was empty.

I could not believe it. This was part of my dream. It had not been a dream then. Someone *had* come in and taken the pearls and left the case behind.

I was dumbfounded. I did not know what to do.

I pulled the bell-rope and Leila appeared. I did not want to tell her what had happened. I said: 'Go to Miss Hansen and tell her I must see her at once.'

In a few minutes Celia was there.

I said: 'That will do, thank you, Leila.' And she went out somewhat reluctantly. I wondered if she was listening at the door.

'What on earth has happened?' asked Celia.

'The pearls . . . they're missing.'

'They can't be!'

'They are. I've just opened the case. They're not there.'

Celia looked at me disbelievingly. She went to the drawer, opened the case and stared down at the midnight blue velvet.

'Where . . . ?' she stammered. 'What . . . ?'

'Someone came in last night and stole them.'

'You *saw* someone?'

'Well . . . it was like a dream. I was half asleep. I thought someone came in. Then I thought I'd dreamed it. I have dreamed a lot lately. I dream about the pearls. Celia, what shall I do? I'd better give the alarm.'

'Wait a minute,' she said. 'Let's think what would be best. We've got to be calm about this, Sarah.'

'Those pearls, Celia . . . they're priceless.'

She was thoughtful. She looked at me intently: 'Who would have come in last night?' she asked.

'I don't know.'

'Whoever it was couldn't have done so undetected. The servants would have noticed if the house had been broken into. It must have been someone who could have come in with a key.'

'Clinton?' I whispered.

'Did he come in?'

'I did not see him. I had this dream . . . a sort of half dream.'

'You have had a lot of dreams lately.' She frowned. 'You won't be upset by what I'm going to say, Sarah . . .'

'No, say it.'

'You were acting a little oddly . . . some time ago.'

'I can explain all that. It was someone playing tricks on me. I proved it.'

She was silent for a while, biting her lips thoughtfully. 'Look,' she said at length, 'you have been in an uneasy state. You have recently had a bad accident, which might have proved fatal. You have been dreaming about these pearls.'

'Yes, I know, but . . .'

'People were beginning to notice, Sarah.'

'People?'

'Leila, for instance. The servants. You seemed so nervous, so on edge.'

'I know. Someone was trying to prove I was mad. I learned that.'

'Listen. I may be wrong, but I want to protect you. Do you understand? I hated it when people implied those things about you. I didn't believe it for one moment. I knew there must be some explanation. I don't like Leila's connection with that woman. I don't like it at all, Sarah. We've got to stand against them.'

'What are you trying to say, Celia?'

'I'm saying this: You have been on edge. That wickedness of unnerving you . . . then the accident. You see what I mean. You have these dreams. I have an idea that you may have walked in your sleep.'

'Walked! But I can't walk.'

'You can get round the room with your stick. I know I'm probably wrong, but, Sarah, do let's be sure first. Don't let's give them another chance to say what they have been saying.'

'What do you propose?'

'That we search this room thoroughly. I think it possible that you had this dream about someone taking the pearls. It might have been yourself . . . walking in your sleep. *You* may have taken them from the case and put them somewhere.'

'No, Celia. *No!*'

'I know it sounds ridiculous but do bear with me. I am thinking of you. Please do give it a try. Before you let anyone know that the pearls are missing let me search this room. Now sit in your chair. I will search every corner of this room, every possible hiding place. *Please*, Sarah?'

'Oh Celia, I am so glad you are here. What shall I do when you have gone?'

'You have been good to me. Now do sit down.'

'I'll help to search.'

'No, it's bad for your ankle to move about too much. Leave it to me.'

She went round the room, opening drawers, looking under the bed, opening the cupboard and rummaging through my clothes.

She stood in the centre of the room looking blank and frustrated.

'It's no use, Celia,' I said. 'Someone has taken them.'

'Is there anywhere I haven't looked?' she asked, wrinkling her brows.

Then suddenly she went to the bed and lifted my pillow.

With a cry of triumph she held up the pearls.

I could not believe it. 'So it must have been I who took them!'

'They're on your mind. I think you should speak to Clinton about putting them in a safe place. Never mind now. Don't brood on it. It's the sort of thing anyone might do.'

'Put them in the case, Celia. I don't want to look at them.'

She did so, snapped it shut and put it in the drawer.

'You ought at least to have a little key to lock the drawer,' she said.

'I'll see if I can get one.'

She kissed me lightly on the brow.

'I'll be back later,' she said.

Celia spent the morning with me and we talked of anything but our coming parting which made me very despondent. Her baggage had already gone on ahead of her. It would be awaiting the arrival of the *Lankarta* from Bombay which was to return there that evening.

Clinton came in during the morning. He said he had been held up by trouble in the plantation and had stayed working late in the offices and as he had known he would not be finished by well past midnight he had decided to stay in a room he kept there for the purpose of accommodating him or one of the managers on such occasions.

'It's uncomfortable,' he said. 'I cut myself shaving this morning. They have put the mirror in the wrong place and it was quite dark.'

He indicated quite a deep gash at the side of his mouth.

'Bled like a pig,' he added.

'Not painful, I hope.'

He shook his head. 'But it will take a day or two to heal. I missed you, Sarah. I'll be with you tonight. We'll make it a special occasion, shall we? We shall be alone. What time does Celia leave?'

'The train leaves Manganiya soon after six for Colombo. The carriage is taking her in.'

'Then I'd better say my farewells now in case I don't get back in time.'

He seemed in good spirits and I did not think he had spent the night with Anula.

Celia took lunch with me in my room. Our last meal together.

While we were eating I dropped my fork and Celia came over to pick it up for me. As she rose, she said: 'What have you done to your neck? It looks as if you've scratched it.'

I put my hand up. 'I don't feel anything.'

'It's very slight. I wonder . . . You must have been lying on those pearls. There's quite a sharp edge on the clasp, I noticed.'

'Perhaps it caught me then,' I said.

'I'll put some iodine on it later. Remind me.'

'Oh, that's not necessary.'

'Perhaps not. Still, it's different here from at home. I scratched myself and some venomous insect scenting blood settled on it. It festered and was quite horrible for a time. I'll go and get it in a moment. Just to be on the safe side.'

We talked and I forgot all about the scratch. I thought she had too, but she came back with a small bottle of iodine.

'It may sting a bit,' she said. 'Be prepared.'

She came behind and I certainly felt it. She dabbed the spot with a piece of cotton wool which she had thoughtfully brought with her.

'There,' she said. 'That should heal nicely now. It's hardly noticeable, but you can't be too careful in a place like this.'

She screwed on the bottle cap and slipped it into the pocket of her skirt.

During the day I felt a few twinges from the scratch but thought nothing of it and forgot all about it.

It was a long afternoon, very hot. The rains would soon be with us and we were expecting them any day now. The shrubs needed it and so did we. It would cool the air and rid us of many of the insects which pestered us more at this time of the year than at any other.

I was growing more and more depressed at the thought of Celia's departure. How lonely I was going to feel without her!

It was five o'clock when she came in, dressed for travelling and looking very sad.

'I hate leaving you,' she said. 'When is Clinton coming home?'

'Any time now. But he rather thought you would be gone before he could get back.'

'I know. He's said goodbye. Oh Sarah, I do wish I was staying a little longer . . . until you were able to get about more easily. Well, I see you're dressed ready for Clinton.'

I was wearing my Bokhara blue silk gown for I had dressed early knowing she would come to say goodbye and I wanted to give all my attention to her.

'How's the neck?' she asked.

'All right, thanks. I'd forgotten about it.'

She came round to the back of me, lifted up my hair and looked at the spot.

'I think you'll survive,' she said lightly and added: 'May I have a last look at the pearls? You should wear them with that dress. Come on. I'll do up the clasp for you, shall I?'

I laughed at her. 'I believe you enjoy handling those pearls.'

'Who wouldn't?'

She took them carefully out of the case and put them about my neck.

I was seated before the mirror and I looked from the pearls to her. She was gazing at them almost as though she were looking at a lover.

'How lucky to have a husband who bestows such gifts!' she said.

I did not answer.

Then her deft fingers were fastening the clasp and I gave a little start because she had touched the wounded spot.

'It's that place,' she said. 'Wait a minute. I'm going to move the clasp slightly so that it doesn't rest on it. It's nothing much but you don't want to irritate it.'

'Is it bleeding?' I asked.

'No ... not really. Just a smear. There. You can't feel anything now, can you?'

I shook my head.

'They look magnificent.' She kissed me solemnly on the forehead. 'That's how I want to remember you, wearing those pearls. They look so beautiful on your neck, Sarah.' She paused, listening. 'I believe I hear the carriage at the door. I'd better go.'

'Have you got everything?'

'There's very little hand luggage. The rest, as you know, has gone on ahead. They'll be loaded on board by now. *Au revoir*, Sarah, and I shall never forget what you have done for me.'

I felt very sad. I had relied on her so much. I kept wondering what the house would be like without her.

She went swiftly to the door and stood there for a moment looking at me. There were tears in her eyes.

Then she was gone.

I lay back in my chair listening to the sound of carriage wheels.

Suddenly extraordinary things began to happen to me. I must have sat in my chair for some ten minutes before I was aware of the change which was creeping over me. The pearls lay heavily about my neck. I felt as though they were creeping closer and closer, tighter and tighter. They were suffocating me. That was not all. The room was becoming hazy.

Something very strange was happening.

I tried to stand up. The room swayed. I gripped the chair and hung on to it tightly.

And at that moment Clinton came in.

'Sarah!' he cried and it sounded as though he were whispering. 'What's happened? Sarah . . . *Sarah!*'

He came forward and caught me as I was about to fall. I heard myself say: 'The pearls . . . they're strangling me.'

I was in the chair and he was bending over me.

'Oh my God,' he cried. 'Oh my God *no!*'

The pearls were lying in my lap. He was at the door. I heard his voice: 'Quick! Quick . . . go for the doctor. At once! Do you hear me? Stop for nothing!'

Then he was back with me. He had the pot in which I kept my hairpins in his hand and his lips were on my neck. I was too weak and weary to know what he was doing. I fainted.

When I came round I heard voices. I saw Clinton. He was lying on the floor. He looks so big, I thought irrelevantly. He is bigger than even I thought him. His face was white and he looked strange, unlike himself.

I heard the voice of the doctor. 'Get Mrs Shaw to bed at once.'

Then they were carrying me to bed and I was still only half-conscious.

This is another nightmare, I remember thinking. I shall wake up presently.

Someone was sitting by my bed. It was Clytie. She was holding my hand.

'Sarah,' she murmured when she saw my eyes open. 'It's going to be all right, Sarah. The doctor came in time.'

I opened my eyes wide. It was as though a hammer were beating above them.

'I don't understand what happened.'

'Never mind. Go to sleep now.'

'I want to know . . .' My voice trailed off and I must have dropped off to sleep at once. I was in a strange world. I was at the bottom of the sea and the shark charmer was singing his mournful dirge. There were pearls all over the sea bed. They advanced on me; they covered me and held me fast.

I struggled.

I heard Clytie's voice from a long way off. 'It's all right. It's all right.'

She was beside my bed throughout the night, I believed. It was dawn when I opened my eyes.

'Clytie,' I said, 'are you still there?'

'Yes, Sarah. I'm still here.'

'Where am I . . . and what happened?'

'You're in your bed. You're all right now.'

'What was it all about?'

'You were poisoned. You had a scratch on your neck and the venom entered your body from the clasp of the necklace.'

'The necklace!' I said.

'That cursed necklace,' replied Clytie.

'Poison . . . after all those years.'

'Not after all those years.'

'Who tried to poison me?'

'We don't know.'

'Clinton . . .' I murmured.

'Clinton is in another room. If he hadn't come in when he did . . .'

'What has Clinton to do with this?'

'He has saved your life, the doctor says. He knew the poison. He smelt it and he knew the effect it had. He sucked it out of your wound, Sarah. He couldn't wait for the doctor to come. It would have been too late if he had. It would have entered your blood-stream by then. It's a deadly poison . . . deadly as the cobra's venom. Thank God Clinton came in when he did. He knows a great deal about poisons, even eastern ones, and he recognized the peculiar odour and he also knew what was wrong with you and that he had to act promptly. He followed the primitive custom which is used a lot in the jungle here – sucking out the poison and spitting it out. This is what he did effectively and saved your life.'

Clinton . . . saved my life! And I had thought at one time he wanted to be rid of me, that he and Anula had plotted together. Anula, I thought. She had put the poison in the necklace. Leila would have helped her.

'There's something else, Sarah,' went on Clytie. 'Clinton is very ill . . . very ill indeed.'

'What are you trying to tell me?'

'There was an open wound on his face. He had cut himself. In sucking the poison out some of it entered his body and mingled with his blood.'

'So he has made himself ill in saving me!'

'Yes. There's always a great danger in sucking poison from a wound. It means risking one's life. Only the brave would do it.'

I said: 'I must go to him.'

'Not yet. He is unconscious. The doctor is with him. We have sent for another doctor too.'

'He is very ill then, is he?'

'He is also very strong.'

'Clinton!' I said, and I repeated his name. It was so difficult to believe. Clinton sacrificing himself for me! Clinton dangerously ill because of it . . .

'There is something else,' said Clytie. 'A friend of yours arrived from India to see you. He came in on the *Lankarta* from Bombay last night. He called during the morning but I said you were too ill to see him. He wouldn't go away. He said he would wait. He was so insistent, so anxious about you; he said he had something of the utmost importance to say to you. We told him that there had been an accident and that made him all the more insistent.'

'Did he give a name?'

'Yes. Tobias Mander.'

'Toby!' I cried. 'Oh, I must see him. I must see him at once.'

It was good to see him. He looked different, older, tanned by the sun, but still the same Toby with the kindliness and the humour in his eyes.

'Sarah!' he cried.

He came to me and took my hands. He leaned towards me and I threw my arms about his neck.

'Oh Toby,' I cried. 'I've been so frightened. You didn't answer my letters.'

He took my hands and looked into my eyes. 'Sarah,' he said, 'this is terrible. As soon as I knew everything I sailed for Ceylon. You've been in danger . . . terrible danger. What did you think of what I told you in my letter?'

'Letter, Toby. I've been longing for a letter. You didn't answer mine.'

He looked aghast. 'I've written twice. I've told you of my suspicions.'

'Suspicions? What suspicions?'

'Let me tell you. I met the Bonningtons in Delhi . . . quite by chance in a shop. You know the Bonningtons. He was curate for a while at Epleigh and he married Miss Effie Cannon.'

'Of course.'

'I had only seen them briefly at your father's funeral but we remembered each other. Mrs Bonnington told me that her husband had become a missionary and they were staying only a few days in Delhi on their way somewhere. She said how strange it was for only the day before they had met someone else whom they had known in Epleigh. Celia Hansen, who was travelling with her cousin, had been staying at their hotel, the Shalimar. They had only stayed there one night and had gone on to friends, but it had been very pleasant seeing Celia again.'

'Celia never mentioned that she had met the Bonningtons. That was strange because we talked a good deal about life at the Grange.'

'This is the strange part. I so much wanted to talk to someone about you that I decided to call on Miss Hansen at the Shalimar. I went there. To my amazement I was told that there was no Miss Celia Hansen staying at the hotel, nor had there been at any time. This was bewildering. I said there must be some mistake. I probed a bit. An English lady staying with a cousin, another English lady? At length I gathered that there had been two English ladies staying there. They had left the day before. They were a Miss Jessica and a Miss Cecilia Herringford.'

'Herringford!'

'Once long ago I went to Everard Herringford's country house with my father. I was about thirteen at the time. Everard Herringford entertained now and then and there was some project about which my father needed government help. However we went there for a weekend. I remember there was a daughter, Cecilia. Do you see, Sarah, the woman who came to the Grange as Celia Hansen, the woman who came here, was in fact Cecilia Herringford. I thought it was rather strange at the time that she should have come to you as a governess, but she had gone and that seemed the end of it. Then you wrote to me about the strange things that were happening and you mentioned that Celia Hansen was visiting you. Then I began to get alarmed.

'There is madness in that family through the mother and it occurred to me that there might be a streak of this in the daughter. She had come back to you. Strange things were happening. I wrote to you at once and told you about what I had discovered in Delhi – that your Celia Hansen and Cecilia Herringford were one and the same person.'

'But I never received the letter.'

'Do you think she could have intercepted it? She knew you were writing to me.'

'She didn't know about this encounter in Delhi. She could have had no idea of that.' I shook my head. 'I can't believe this, Toby. Even if she is Everard Herringford's daughter I don't believe she would come here and try to kill me. Why? What had I done?

I believe I know who did this. There is a woman here who is Clinton's mistress. She is skilled in making scents and potions and I am sure, poisons. Her sister works here and she would do all that Anula commanded. But oh Toby, it is good to see you. And you came all the way from India.'

'I had a presentiment that I must. I came back too late once. I wasn't going to do the same again.'

'I'm so glad you came.'

'You should know,' he said, 'that I should come to you from the other side of the world if you needed me.'

I went to Clinton's bedside. He was very ill. He looked so strange, his eyes glassy, his skin a pale yellow colour, his blond hair lifeless. He gave me that smile of reckless bravado which I knew so well and which now made me want to weep.

'Hello, Sarah,' he said. 'This is the end for me. Who would have believed it?'

'Listen,' I cried firmly, 'you're going to throw this off. You're going to get well.'

He shook his head. 'It's got me, Sarah. I know this poison. It's what the old kings used to abolish their enemies. It has a strange odour, only detectable if you're aware of it. It's made from poisonous plants that grow in the jungle. There's not much hope once it's entered your blood. You can linger a day or so on antidotes . . . but it's a killer.'

'You knew this . . . and you deliberately . . .'

'I thought I'd get away with it. I should have done but for this cut. I'd forgotten it. Just a chance, Sarah. If I hadn't nicked myself when shaving . . . But that's life, you know. This is the reckoning. Neat. Fate, that's what it is. If I hadn't been away that night . . . Well, I had had my own way too long. This is Anula's doing. She was determined to be rid of you. Oh, I should never have been any good to you, Sarah. I am not a man for one woman. It would always have been the same and you are not one to endure that. You've too much spirit – look at that will you made. That shook me, I can tell you. It would have passed . . . that fiery passion between us. It's a thing for youth . . . and that's a stuff that'll not endure. He's back, I hear. Good old Toby! Marry him, Sarah. He's the one for you. And you don't belong here. You ought to be back home. I can see it all . . . gracious house, gracious living . . . children . . . and that son whose wife will sport the Ashington Pearls in time. I gave them to you. They're yours, Sarah. You are the Ashington to whom they should belong.'

'It's not like you to give up, Clinton. I should have thought you would have gone on fighting.'

'I'm a man who faces reality. That's how I've got through. In two days' time I'll be dead. They can't get rid of it. They're only slowing down the process, nothing more.'

'Clinton, listen to me. You always wanted a child, didn't you? I think I am going to have one.'

A gratified smile spread across his face. 'Someone to remember me by.'

'I shouldn't need to be reminded even if you weren't there. But you're going to be there.'

'I'm going, Sarah. I want no pretence. I've had a good life. I did what I wanted. I took what I wanted. You'll be happier the way it is. I'm glad he came. All the way from India, I hear. Well, the curtain's going to ring down on this one. Sarah, forgive . . .'

'There's nothing to forgive, Clinton.'

'Don't give me clichés, Sarah. There's everything to forgive. I made you marry me. I wasn't a good and faithful husband. I never should have been. I'm polygamous by nature, a jungle animal. I took what I wanted when I wanted it . . . and life catches up with us sooner or later.'

'But it was a marvellous thing you did for me. If you die you will have died for me.'

There was a shadow of the old grin. 'No nobility intended,' he said. 'I couldn't do without those love-hate battles of ours.'

I sat by his bed and I thought of our life together. I thought, too, of Anula. She would have lost him now.

He lay in his coffin in the room next to the bedroom we had shared. I could not believe that he – the vital, virile lover-enemy was dead. I mourned him bitterly, though I knew that what he had said was true. I could never have found an ideal happiness with him. Indeed, had I ever been truly happy with him?

It was love I needed. I had always needed it, particularly because I had missed it all my life. I wanted tenderness; I wanted a strong foundation on which to build a family life, and I longed for the green fields of home, for a benevolent sun which warmed but did not scorch, for a gentle rain that came unheralded. I wanted fields of buttercups and daisies and yellow celandines. But most of all I wanted a companion on whom I could rely, who would always be there to love and cherish me. I knew exactly what I wanted.

Yet deeply I mourned Clinton.

Tomorrow they would bury him, for burials were quick in this land. This room would be empty, the coffin gone, proud Clinton lost to me for ever.

Darkness had come as I stood beside that coffin, and suddenly the door handle started to turn – silently, cautiously.

The door opened and I felt the hair rise on the back of my head. There was something strange and uncanny about the quietness. I did not know what I expected in that moment. Then I thought: It is Anula come to claim his body.

I stepped back from the coffin. Someone had come into the room. A muffled figure indistinguishable in the gloom.

It went to the side of the coffin. Then the hood was thrown back.

'Celia!' I whispered.

She did not answer but stood for a few seconds looking down on Clinton's dead face.

Then she said quietly: 'So he was the one who died.'

'I thought you were on the boat. How did you get into the house?'

Such a practical detail was of the least importance, I supposed, yet it was the first thing that came to my mind.

'I kept the key of the door. I could not sail. I had to know what happened.'

'What does all this mean, Celia?'

'It means that you didn't die then. But you will now.'

I moved towards the door but she was there before me.

I could see that she carried a revolver and she was pointing it straight at me.

'Celia, have you gone mad!'

'They said I was like my mother. He drove her mad . . . madder than she was at first. He and your mother. That was the end of her.'

'Celia, I know who you are. You are Everard Herringford's daughter.'

'Yes,' she said. 'Your friend found out, didn't he? I read it in the letter he sent you. My father shot himself because of your mother. But she died for it. I saw to that. You are very gullible to believe your prim old Aunt Martha would commit a murder.'

'You deceived me, Celia. You were always so gentle.'

She nodded. 'I am gentle. There are two of us. Celia Hansen, she's a good mild woman, likes people, wants to help them. Cecilia Herringford is different. When her parents died she wanted revenge. They were her life, those two, and she determined that their deaths should be avenged in full. There's a poem you used to like. Do you remember . . .' She began to quote and her voice sounded hollow in that room of death. It was a strange macabre scene.

> 'Alas the love of women! It is known
> To be a lovely and a fearful thing;
> For all of theirs upon that die is thrown,
> And if 'tis lost, life hath no more to bring

To them but mockeries of the past alone,
And their revenge is as the tiger's spring,
Deadly, and quick and crushing . . .'

There was a moment's silence, then she burst out: 'The poet speaks of the love of a woman for a man. The love of a daughter for her parents can be as great. You see, I never had a lover, Sarah, but I know what love is. My parents were my life. I was so proud of my father. He was a very important man. People came from all over the world to consult him. One day he would have been Prime Minister. When my mother was ill I should have been the hostess. He used to talk to me about it. "We'll be at Number Ten Downing Street, you and I, Cecilia," he used to say. Then he became involved with this actress – your mother. I found out about it. I came to look at the house once.'

'I saw you,' I said. 'I wish . . . I wish I'd known. I wish I'd been able to talk to you.'

She shook her head. 'My mother was always strange but this finished her. Then he shot himself and she went completely mad. I looked after her and I knew what had driven her to this extreme. She killed herself . . . and I was alone. I'd lost them both. There was only one thing that could make me want to live. Revenge. Vendetta. I came alive planning it.'

'Oh Celia, I understand your grief. You killed my mother. I am not to blame. I had no part in it.'

'The sins of the fathers are visited on the children,' she said.

'They should not be. I thought you were fond of me. You always behaved as though you were.'

'Part of me was. But I lived for revenge. I could not forget those dreadful days and the scandal and what it did to those two. It was terrible when he killed himself. This is the revolver. I see now that it is what I should use. It makes it more complete.'

'You wanted me to believe I was going mad, didn't you?'

'Yes . . . mad as she was. It's a terrible thing to lose your mind and know it. I think that's worse than anything. I wanted you to suffer as she had. It was too easy, that other. Your mother died too easily. But then I had thought that she must die . . . and that would be enough. So I came with my false name and my story of needing work. And when it was over and I went away there was an emptiness in my life. I thought of you. I had only taken one life and both my father and mother had died. I wanted a life for a life. But it is a greater tragedy sometimes to lose one's mind than one's life. I know. I've seen it. So I decided you should be mad.'

'So you played tricks on me. The taps, the sandalwood scent . . .'

'Yes, to throw suspicion on your husband's mistress.'

'And the cobra.'

'Yes, the toy cobra.'

'And finally you decided to kill me.'

'Yes, I began to see it had to be a life for a life. You survived the accident in the dog-cart and I thought of the pearls. I was fascinated by those pearls and I wanted you to think in your last moments that it was your husband's mistress who had done this. You see, your mother was my father's mistress. It worked out to a kind of pattern. That was what I wanted . . .'

'Celia, you are cruel . . .'

'Yes, but I loved them. They were my life. There was nothing . . . nothing at all when they had gone. They were taken from me by a wicked woman. I shall be at peace when I have taken my revenge. If I let you live you will marry Toby Mander now. I took the letters he wrote to you. It was a shock to know he had discovered who I was. I knew he was coming from Bombay on the *Lankarta*. He had said so in his letter. I had to be quick. I should have done it more subtly if I had had more time.'

'Put that revolver away, Celia.'

She shook her head. 'There are two bullets here. One for you, one for me.'

'It's crazy,' I cried.

'I am crazy,' she answered.

She lifted the revolver. It was pointing straight at me. Her lips were moving. 'Oh my father, my mother . . .' I heard her murmur. 'This is the end. I am coming to you. They will put me away if I lived, as they used to put you away, Mother. But you will be avenged.'

That moment will be imprinted on my memory for ever. The shadowy figure of the mad woman and the dead body of Clinton lying in his coffin between us.

It was almost as though Clinton lived in that moment. I seemed to hear his voice calling to me: 'Live. Live. You owe it to me to live. I don't want to have died in vain.'

I threw myself on to the floor as the bullet shot over my head. I heard Celia murmur: 'Dead. This is the end. Now, my dearests, I am coming to you.'

I was lying there numb as the second shot rang out.

POSTSCRIPT

*

It all happened so long ago and looking back it seems like something out of another life. I could almost believe it had never happened if I had not my tall son as living evidence.

I called him Clinton and he is exactly like his father; he will be such another, I know – strong, ruthless, determined to have his way, egotistical, assured of material success and capable of the utmost heroism. I love him dearly and I know his father would be proud of him.

He was six months old when I married Toby.

I have been a very lucky woman. I have experienced two marriages and each gave me a great deal. I have now reached a serenity of love and understanding which I know is the most desirable state in life, but looking back I should not have wanted to miss that turbulent period of searing passion which taught me so much about myself.

But Toby is the man with whom I was destined to share my life. Together we have raised a family – two boys and two girls – and I am as happy as anyone can hope to be.

I sent a manager out from England to run the Shaw plantation and it flourishes. I have made over Ashingtons entirely to Clytie and Seth. About once every three years Toby and I go out to visit them. It is a strange and haunting experience for me to walk through those woods and recall the terrors I suffered in that house. The servants, I know, will not go singly into the room where Clinton's coffin had stood and Celia killed herself. They will remember always.

Anula married a wealthy Sinhalese businessman whom I guessed she had previously refused on account of Clinton. Leila told me, 'She very rich lady now.'

The aunts both died and left me the Grange. Toby put the charge of the Indian side of the family business into the hands of one of the managers and he is in London most of the time. We have a town house but the children love the Grange and we are often there.

My portrait hangs in the gallery now, complete with pearls. The clasp has been thoroughly cleaned and it was shown to me that the body of the serpent and the stems of the leaves were hollow and that this provided a good storing place for the poison.

I wear the necklace now and then for Toby's position in the financial world means that we entertain frequently both in London and at the Grange. I think the aunts would be pleased at the way things have turned out, apart from the fact that there will be no one named Ashington to wear the pearls.

One day it will be the wife of Clinton's son whose portrait hangs in the gallery.

I tell myself that he would like that.

Fontana Paperbacks

Fontana is a leading paperback publisher of fiction and non-fiction, with authors ranging from Alistair MacLean, Agatha Christie and Desmond Bagley to Solzhenitsyn and Pasternak, from Gerald Durrell and Joy Adamson to the famous Modern Masters series.

In addition to a wide-ranging collection of internationally popular writers of fiction, Fontana also has an outstanding reputation for history, natural history, military history, psychology, psychiatry, politics, economics, religion and the social sciences.

All Fontana books are available at your bookshop or newsagent; or can be ordered direct. Just fill in the form and list the titles you want.

FONTANA BOOKS, Cash Sales Department, G.P.O. Box 29, Douglas, Isle of Man, British Isles. Please send purchase price, plus 8p per book. Customers outside the U.K. send purchase price, plus 10p per book. Cheque, postal or money order. No currency.

NAME (Block letters) _____

ADDRESS _____

_____

_____